THE GREENWAY

CONSPIRACY

THE GREENWAY CONSPIRACY

A SYMPHONY OF TIME NOVEL

Book 1

G T DONNELLAN

ga

GALLAN AMRAL

Published in Ireland

in 2013 by Gallan & Amral Enterprises Ltd

www.gallanamral.com

First published in paperback 2013

Copyright © G T Donnellan 2013

All rights reserved.

G T Donnellan has asserted her right under the Copyright, Designs and Patents Act 1988 to be identified as the author of this work.

A CIP catalogue for this book is available from the British Library.

ISBN 978-0-9927252-0-4 (paperback)

ISBN 987-0-9927252-1-1 (e-book)

All characters in this publication are fictitious and any resemblance to real persons, living or dead, is purely coincidental.

for Martin

my inspiration always

Acknowledgements

Tullie's story has been incarcerated in my mind for many years, and it is thanks to so many people that it is now free to roam the world.

 First and foremost, a heartfelt thanks to my husband, Martin for his loving encouragement and support every single day. It is unlikely The Greenway Conspiracy would have seen the light of day without him.

Secondly, I owe a huge debt of gratitude to my family for their love, encouragement and support. To Fionnuala for the wonderful cover design, and the magic of life; and to Will, Siobhán, Liam and Niamh for the specialness they bring to my life. To Brendan and Klara for their patience, gentleness, encouragement and love which makes the world such a lovely, warm, safe place to be. To my sister, Myra, for being there for me; my brothers: Frank, Michael and Vincent, and their families. And to my sister, Carmel: I wish you could be here to read this.

Thank you also to Tanya Dickson, my dear friend, who shared her own writing journey with me, encouraging and supporting me every step of the way to reach this pot of gold at the end of the rainbow. Tullie says Hi!

Thank you to all my readers and booksellers for getting behind this series. I am eternally grateful.

Table of Contents

PART 1

PART 2

EPILOGUE: RANDELL KANE DEAD ON GREENWAY

ABOUT THE AUTHOR

PART 1

CHAPTER 1

Tullie grimaced. She hated being interrupted but forced herself to smile politely.

"How can I help?" she asked, pushing back from her crowded workbench, and he visibly relaxed.

"I've . . . a . . .," he began, running his fingers through his blonde hair, intensely annoyed with himself.

"I'm stuck," he finished in a rush, and began pacing jaggedly back and forth before her.

"But...but...," he tried again, then stopped suddenly and gestured her to follow him, striding off without waiting for her answer.

Tullie glared at his departing back, but there was no one to witness the scene. What was so important that couldn't be scheduled like everything else? Despite herself she was intrigued. Jed was acting so out of character. Whatever it was must be incredibly important, and difficult, to have him in such a flap.

"What's up, Jed?" she asked in her quiet voice, following him into his inner sanctum.

Walking behind his desk, he reached into the top right-hand drawer and the back wall silently slid away to reveal a benched work area. Small crates lay where they had been unceremoniously tossed against the left wall, their contents spread across every possible work space. He smiled widely at her unladylike whistle.

"Tullie," he stated, coming around to take her arm

and lead her forward, "this is top, top secret."

"Dangerously top, top secret," he added in a rush, grabbing her arm tightly as he looked deeply into her large green eyes, "way beyond anything I've had you work on before for me."

"Men have died for these," he said, emphasising every word, his eyes demanding understanding. His eye contact was intense, and the seriousness of the situation penetrated her brain slowly and she began to pull back.

"I'm between a rock and a hard place," he explained a little, holding onto her deftly. "I wouldn't involve you, or anyone else, believe me, if I could avoid it."

"What is all this?" she asked shakily, pushing away his hand and stepping behind the desk. "What are they?" His hidden workspace was at her toes, his treasures strewn before her. Blood relics, she guessed, and her face darkened in anger.

"Come closer and see for yourself," he pleaded, placing his palm in the small of her back and inching her forward slowly. He watched her every move closely, looking for that 'hook' moment she was so famous for. If anyone could crack this puzzle Tullie could. But could he keep her safe? Would she keep his secret? But it was the end that mattered; the end he had been running towards for ten years now, and it was within his grasp at last! He could feel their ghosts surround him. He would see them right. But he needed to know what he was protecting; what they died for. Knowledge is power, he affirmed: he would not lose again!

The makeshift benches were littered with normal-looking rock fragments big and small. Hints of colour squinted at her from their entombment; he hadn't tried to brush away the dust, just align pieces with similar edges, an amateur's work, she realised.

"Your work?" she asked to confirm, glancing briefly in his direction and he nodded.

"Who else has worked on these, Jed?" she asked, one hand hovering tentatively above a set of pieces, he saw, elatedly.

"Nobody, Tullie," he answered truthfully, "maybe nobody ever," and she glanced keenly at him. Again he had surprised her. His tone was reverential, even bordering on awe and wonder. Tendrils of concern worked at the edges of her mind but she pushed them back. There was too much of the unusual here to pass up; she loved a good puzzle more than anything.

"Why do you want them worked?" she asked lazily, turning her full attention on him now.

"I can't tell you that, Tullie," he replied, holding her gaze.

"What resources do I have to work with?"

He gestured to the room.

"Just what's here?" she asked, incredulously, and he nodded.

"No lexicons?"

"None exist that I know of," he replied calmly.

"Databases?" but he shook his head.

"And timeframe, Jed?"

"As long as it takes," he countered.

"What about my other work?"

"It can wait," he shrugged indifferently. This was his top priority but he was playing it cool with her. Silently, she began to work through all the angles, step by step, blocking out his presence.

"I cannot guarantee success, Jed," she said quietly, leaning back a little from him.

He kept quiet. No need to spook her now but he couldn't countenance failure. The word simply didn't exist in his vocabulary.

"I need time," she added, deep in thought, and he understood her perfectly.

"The door opens from the inside," he said, and she nodded.

"Only I have the code from the outside," he added from the door. "You'll be safe here."

*****

Standing back, Tullie observed the fragments before her, mentally sorting them into workable grids. Alone, she ran her hands over the pieces, feeling for their energy. Working with the patterns she realised that she might be dealing with more than one tablet or seal. Her body told her it was time to quit for the day, she had spent enough overtime already, but her curiosity overrode her fatigue and grabbing a quick drink from Jed's stash she returned to the benches refreshed and excited. Discounting his arrangement entirely, she spread out the fragments, grouping them differently, placing similar chunks apart rather than together, and allowing her intuition to override her logic. It was a painstaking job. Her eyes burned from the bright lights he had brought in and the cool air dried her exposed skin. Bit by bit the individual groups grew and with each placement she felt she was getting closer to the truth. Finally, all that was left unaccounted for of Jed's work was a small bunch of smithereens. Ignoring these for the moment she turned to the sorted groups excitedly.

Starting with the smallest group she was able to reconstruct it without too much trouble. The pieces fitted together perfectly and, although incomplete, it gave her hope that she had indeed stumbled across several artefacts rather than just one. By the third reconstruction she was surprised to observe that all the compiled objects were of similar size and shape. The fragments hadn't hinted at this at all. This was a real breakthrough! The fourth grouping brought her down to earth; it proved impossible to form into any cohesive pattern at all so she abandoned it and moved onto the next one; it was likely she had mixed up pieces but was confident she could work it all out now. The next two were straightforward; they were nearly complete. Elatedly she ran her fingers over their surface as if reading braille and she could feel the graceful curves of ancient letters or symbols; she was sure of this now. Another amazing breakthrough! Jed would be so excited. The seventh pile was small; just two pieces was all she had isolated, and these didn't really form any cohesiveness either. The eighth was small too but she had enough pieces to fill in the rim of the object, just the inner core was missing. That looked to be just one piece, she mused, from the smooth inner rim. It was also a little larger than the others; the alpha piece, she named it, smiling. This one, she felt, would help uncover what was on the others.

By the time she had worked through the unplaced fragments a few times daylight was beginning to stream through the windows in the outer office. She was exhausted but elated. Reaching for her phone to call Jed she realised that although it was light it was still too early to call him and instead she turned it on her latest discoveries and clicked happily. Hugging her phone she moved to the outer office propping Jed's door ajar, and logged on to the server. She would not sleep now anyway, she decided, so she might as well begin to identify possible lexicons or databases that would assist in identifying the patterns before Jed arrived. Contrary to what he had said, she was sure some existed that would help.

*****

Tullie looked up as Jed entered the Lab.

"Hey, brought you your favourite brew," he said, coming over to join her, noticing she was still wearing her clothes from yesterday.

"An all-nighter?" he asked, and she nodded, stretching her tired shoulders and pointing to his inner room. Following her in, Jed whistled softly as he leaned over first one bench, then another, holding his coffee cup away from his body. Several almost-completed seals lay before him, not just one! No wonder he couldn't get the pieces to make sense!

"I'm just this close to concluding your project," she said excitedly, holding up her thumb and index finger, "this close! Am I good, or what! From what I can make out, we're only short a few small pieces for each one, apart from these two; just fragments really but they connect at main junctions. Whoever has these pieces can solve the puzzle and you know I want it to be me! Any chance there were more where you found these?"

He shook his head and watched her slim figure as she collected her mocha from her desk. Her curly red hair had escaped its confinement and bounced lazily around her pale face as she turned to face him, shaking her head to release the build up of tension.

"Mmm, that tastes good," she purred, licking the cream from around her tiny mouth, as she turned to look at the unplaced rubble distractedly, "I needed that!"

6

"You really shouldn't pull all-nighters," he replied half-heartedly, moving away from the work benches and coming to join her at her desk. She grinned conspiratorially back at him, looking beautiful and fresh although she hadn't slept all night. How does she do it, he wondered, as he reached an arm around her waist and she snuggled into his side, slugging on her coffee as if it was her life-line.

"I do like my overtime," she giggled. "Bit too much for you, then?" and she laughed outright. "Well, you know I've got my long weekend ahead on the Mountain. I think I might take off now, if you don't mind? I was keen to get a good start for you before I left but never in my wildest dreams did I expect so much to come together so quickly!" she said excitedly. "I miss the Mountain, Jed! You understand what I mean. Silence as far as the eye can see! That should clear my head! While I'm there I'll call in on mum and see if she has any unassigned fragments I can have a look at."

His gentle sigh belied the elation that was coursing through his veins. She had enough for him to go on. A long weekend wouldn't make any difference now to his plans. He doubted she'd find anything extra on her travels but it was no harm to let her try – up to a point.

"Tullie," he cautioned, "you can't tell your mum about this. You can't tell anyone. Understand?"

"I won't," she promised, "your secret's safe with me, Jed."

Turning to go, she laughed, the sound tinkling around the lab bringing much needed life to the old place.

"Take care of my babies," she smiled, "then on Monday we start on possible translations. I'm sure the patterns point to some obscure lexicons so while I was waiting for you I downloaded a handful from the server

7

ready for go! I've never used them in real life application so we might have a challenge on our hands. But, that's the fun of it all!"

"And the colours?" he asked, walking slowly around the benches again.

"Not sure yet how they feature," she called back truthfully, "or even if they do. But, in all these kind of things, nothing is put there by accident. I'll have another go at compiling the rest when I get back."

"Go on, girl. Go! It's your birthday. Go have some fun," he laughed, following her to the door. "Your grandad will be very excited to see you. It's how long now since you've been back? Five years? Four? Might be time to bury the hatchet, Tullie."

"You're a fine one to talk," she shot back at him.

Throwing him an enigmatic look, she grabbed her laptop, and with a peck on the cheek she was gone and he returned to survey her work. Damn, she's good, he thought excitedly, as he reached for his phone. He was back on track!

*****

The warm air pushed against her as she sped down the country lanes and she threw back her head and laughed exuberantly. It was great to be away so early on a Friday. She was very pleased with what she'd got done. She could feel the ancient world of the message unravel in the deep recesses of her mind. She was wired! She always felt this rush when she was close to a successful compilation, and even happier that she was seeing Jed out of a situation. Responding to her slightest movements, Salvie upped the ante and she leaned into the wind. She was in her element on this bike and she sent a prayer of thanks to her grandad for the umpteenth time. She hadn't heard from him in a while now, sadness at not being back for so long creeping up on her. She missed their times together deeply though but she had a feeling she was only hurting herself. He wasn't going to change any day now! As if sensing her mood, Salvie slowed down a little and soon the trees on either side were swishing smoothly by, the sun splintering through the leaves dappling the ground in front of her. She loved this time of year and the freedom of the big outdoors; something she sorely missed in the enclosed lab. But she belonged in both worlds, she knew, one the Jekyll to the other Hyde.

Shifting in her seat she adjusted the gears and forked off to the right for Matheson. Three hours to here. Not bad, she thought. Slowing down further she slid her visor up and let her eyes travel over the fields of yellow as far as the eye could see. Dipping down to the crossroads she felt completely enveloped in a yellow green world. Running Salvie down the gears, she stopped for a breather. There wasn't a sound to be heard. Not a cricket, not a bird, not a weevil moved in the growing heat. The whole world seemed to be holding its breadth. She stretched, letting the silence into her core. It was good to be home! But again, with the freedom came the odd memories that broke in upon her musings when she least expected them; memories for which she had no explanation, and impulsively she swung left, away towards her real home, the Mountain.

As she travelled in-country, the ground began to rise and before too long she had left the corn fields far behind her. The windy roads demanded all of her attention as she wound left and right around hairpin bends as she climbed on the old road and she felt her misgivings evaporate. At the crossing ahead she swerved right, careering into the gravel car park at the rear of Rosa's, dust billowing behind her. She stopped in the shade and her mind began to wander again, and she allowed the memories to come: they seemed at home here. Then, with a bang the back door swung open and there stood Big Bob expectantly. Removing her helmet, her red hair fell in riotous curls around her shoulders. Parking Salvie in the shade, in his old spot, she made her way across to BB.

"Hey girl," he said, and he reached out enveloping her in his huge arms, "you're a day early! Didn't expect you 'til tomorrow. Breakfast or lunch then?" he asked.

"What do you think," she replied, smiling back, "breakfast! Lots and lots of glorious breakfast, please!"

Ravenous, she sat in her usual place and plates of waffles, bacon and syrup disappeared without trace into her slight frame.

"Hey, slow down," said Big Bob, smiling happily, "when did you last eat anyway?"

"Day before yesterday," was the muffled reply.

"Ah, so you pulled another all-nighter," he grinned. "I don't know how you do it! Youngsters today!"

She threw him a mock punch and they laughed together. He was really glad to see her.

"You been up to the old place yet?" he asked casually, settling himself across from her.

Drinking deeply, she sighed with contentment and held out her mug for another refill.

"On my way shortly, if Silvie can carry me," she grinned, patting a small tummy bulge.

"Hey," she continued, "how's the place doing? Anjie still hanging about?"

BB nodded at her loaded question.

"But he's not there now," he said, "he's off doing something or other. You'll have the place to yourself. He'll be back later."

He looked at her closely, noting the tiredness beneath her eyes.

"Hang on," he said patting her shoulder, and giving her a conspiratorial wink. "A package was delivered for you yesterday. I reckon you'd be by so I held onto it for you. I'm supposed to give it to you tomorrow. Can't think what it might be!"

Without saying any more he left, returning a few minutes later to hand her a small package. She reached out excitedly and took it from him.

"No," he said sternly as she began to rip at the covers, "not 'til tomorrow!"

She threw him a mischievous look as she headed for the back door. He watched her bag the package in Salvie's pannier and roar out of the car park heading for Traveller's Mountain, a slip of a thing in black leathers on top of a powerful black steed. Reaching into his pocket he dialled Anjie's number.

"Where are you, man?" he asked, worriedly. "Any news?"

Tullie worked Salvie's gears as she rode thoughtfully up the road, heading for Traveller's Mountain, and home. The summer foliage threatened to swamp her path but she could clearly see where Anjie's truck battled it back with every journey. Apart from his tracks there was none other to be seen, she was pleased to see. She had the place to herself. The gate was closed but not locked and wriggling in her seat she walked Salvie through, the gate clanging shut behind her. Looping her helmet on the handlebars, she rode bareheaded up the track towards the house. The smell and colours of summer assailed her from every side. This place was in her very blood, she realised. She'd missed it, as she did him. Around the last sweep, the house came into view, a low lying log cabin that expanded at odd angles taking up the space it needed from the surrounding wilderness. She wheeled round the back and parked Salvie in the shade. Reaching for the package she walked to the back door and let herself in.

The place looked almost exactly as it had the last time she was here. Nothing had changed a whit apart from the books, she decided critically. There was even less space now, she was sure of it. Where did he get them all, she mused, as she wandered around the place taking in the aroma of home and noticing the little things: the mouse on the left hand side of the computer, the dusty paper bending out of the top of the printer; the open book by the bed; five mugs hanging in the kitchen. There wasn't a speck of dust to be seen even on the old coffee pot. She wondered idly when he'd turn up. After all, he had promised.

Still cradling the package she made her way onto the back porch and relaxed into the battered rocker. The view of Traveller's Mountain was breathtaking. It rose from the very porch where she was sitting, stretching up and back from the house, inviting her to get up and climb which she did without thinking. Bees buzzed past her busy in their labours and butterflies wafted about, riding the breeze that always cooled in summer. She remembered the last time they had come this way together. He had a puzzle for her to solve, as always. She shook her head sadly. That was another lifetime!

Finding a groove to sit in, she looked the package over carefully, feeling its contents. She couldn't decide what was in it so, tentatively, she started to pick at the tape that held it. Two old objects emerged; a rectangular brown wooden box, rich with design, and a small envelope yellow with age. She sniffed the box but couldn't make out the wood it was made from. It smelled faintly of roses. She knew she should leave them until tomorrow but she wasn't one to put off until tomorrow what could be done today. Selecting the box, she ran her fingers over the surface until she found what she was looking for. Clever, she thought, and pressed. It opened without a struggle to reveal two objects snuggling against the velvet lining. The ring looked small and insignificant, white gold with inlaid amethysts that wound diagonally around both the inside and outside. It was beautiful and appealed immediately to her minimalist appreciation. Holding it up she found it caught the light in amazing ways, rich with colour. She loved it! Without thinking, she slid it onto her ring finger on her left hand. It fitted perfectly although it had seemed so small. She felt a trickle of energy up her arm and wondered if the previous owner was trying to tell her something. She smiled. It felt good and she knew about those feelings. She trusted them instinctively and she had always been right. She was meant to have this ring, she knew. Waving her hand in the light of the mountain she felt she had come home; she was where she was meant to be. Thank you, grandad, she smiled and hugged her hand to her chest.

The other object in the box, a magnificent torque necklace, she would wear less, if at all, she thought sadly. It too was made of white gold with the same inlay of amethysts in matching design along the sides. The centre piece was designed like a delicate daisy and inlaid with several small irregular stones, with a large circular amethyst centre piece, stirring yet another memory she couldn't place. She held it in the palm of her left hand, where it curled to fit, necklace touching ring, and marvelled at its lightness. It beckoned to her, willing her to put it on but she was happy with the ring only.

13

She had never been able to wear anything around her neck; the very thought of it made her breath shallow as if her throat was constricted. But this beautiful thing felt different. Its lightness made her feel like she could ride the wind! She lifted it up to her throat but felt the same tightness instantly. She moved it away and the feeling left abruptly. Pity, she sighed. She had hoped this beautiful object would feel differently. Someday, maybe, she sighed again, still hopeful as she slid it back into the box. A deep longing gripped her heart and looking up suddenly she felt as if the mountain itself had been holding its breath! She shook herself, feeling a coolness that wasn't there previously. A shadow flitted across her face and drops of rain began to fall randomly around her. Shoving the yellowed envelope and the box back into the padded package she made her way quickly back to the porch. Where did that cloud come from, she wondered, and then noticed the dark clouds gathering off to the west, peeking from behind the mountain. She had been so engrossed in her gifts that she hadn't read the signs! All had gone quiet. There was a storm coming.

Settling back into the battered rocker, snug in the shelter of the porch, she withdrew the yellowed envelope again, prodding it gingerly. It had an unusual seal she noticed, maybe something grandad had picked up in his many travels. She yearned to open it, to delve its secrets but she had made a decision to leave that until tomorrow. Reluctantly she slipped it into her bag with the necklace and sat there happily, running the ring around and around her finger as the rain began to fall in earnest. The lack of sleep and BB's huge breakfast began to catch up with her. Where was he, she thought, as sleep took her deep into its embrace?

Memories merged into dreams as she dozed. It was always the same. Someone was calling her, searching for her. The voice was plaintive, a woman's voice, the panic clearly evident. Tullie hid behind the rocks as the voice

14

came closer, the voice whispering now, urgently. Then the rustling started from the other side; the sound of a mob crashing towards her and the voice became silent. She stood up to get a better view, to reach out to the woman, to tell her she was here; she was safe. She knew the woman! She knew her! A crouched figure beckoned from the high grass then the pain started in her shoulder and she began to fall.

Waking with a start, Tullie walked through the darkening house but there was still no sign of him or Anjie. She shrugged. They'd be close by. Where one was the other would follow. Eating simply from the well stocked fridge, she went to bed early and was asleep in minutes. Much later, Anjie smiled grimly as he stood outside her lit window. The reinforcements would be here tomorrow but tonight he'd keep safe again. Damn Jake, he swore! Where the hell was he this time! This was their biggest threat yet and he'd gone AWOL! Pushing all thoughts of what tomorrow might bring, he settled to watch.

CHAPTER 2

It was dark and eerily quiet when Tullie awoke. Lying peacefully in her old bed she revelled in the comforts and smells of home. If she had her way she'd set up her own lab right here on the mountain. That way she'd have the best of both worlds at her fingertips. Her mind wandered back to the items she had put together for Jed. Some of the symbols or letters made sense to her in a subliminal way but she couldn't quantify what it was. She felt drawn to these pieces. But then, she felt drawn to every piece of work, she smiled in the darkness. Reaching for her phone to check the time, she brought up the pictures she'd taken just before Jed arrived. She knew it was against policy to take any picture in the lab ever; never mind in his secret space! She should call or text him and let him know but she had no signal here on the mountain. Then, shrugging, in the dim light from the phone she made the first connection. These three were names: three different names, she knew intuitively. But whose names, or what, she mused. Lying there she moved the screen up and down noticing the missing parts as well as noticing the completeness of what she had too. Excitement mounting, she knew she wouldn't sleep any more so she dragged on an old sweater over her pyjamas and went to power up her laptop.

Dawn was breaking as she took her coffee and laptop out onto the back porch. It caressed Traveller's Mountain with skeletal fingers of pink, peach and soft yellow, and she sat back and soaked up the scene. The air was cool this morning and she hopped inside for some slippers. The birds were in flux when she returned, and she looked about curiously to see what had disturbed them. How she loved this time of day! Nature prostrated all

16

its beauty for man to see and feel but so often it goes unnoticed. I'm guilty too, she grimaced, too busy most of the time. The rocker creaked as she fitted herself into its shape and she let the world wash over her for a while watching the mountain come awake. It took her a while to register Anjie and BB's lumbering forms coming down towards her. They were moving slowly, stopping to look here and there as if they had lost something. As they came closer, they saw her on the porch and waved.

"Coffee?" she called, waving back, moving towards the kitchen expecting them to follow but they stopped by the porch. Bringing them their coffees, she noticed their unsmiling faces for the first time and uneasiness gripped her.

"What's happened?" she asked, in a rush. "What's up?"

Anjie continued to look back up the mountain so BB looked sideways at her and patted the porch edge. She sat down gracefully, looking at him worriedly.

"It's grandad?" she asked shakily.

He nodded. Anjie looked at her for the first time.

"Can't find him," he muttered. "He went hiking, we reckon, after he had lunch with BB on Thursday. I found his stuff on Bear's Ledge yesterday. Found his knife down over the side. Been up on the mountain since. Found nothing except some darn big paw prints up on the ledge."

"See for yourself," he said, handing her his phone.

The paw prints were enormous, even Tullie had not come across specimens like these before.

"We found no blood, Tullie. No indication of any fight or danger of any sort," said BB, putting a comforting hand on her arm. "That's what's so strange, Jake disappearing like that. Must be a reasonable explanation but damned if I can make it out," he said, and scratched his balding head in frustration.

"Jake'll be alright," added Anjie, "I've seen him do stranger things. But not without special reason this weekend though!"

"But if he's been gone since Thursday he'd have had to find shelter from the storm last night," blurted Tullie, turning over all their shelter spots in her mind.

"Tried them all," Anjie said loudly, interrupting her reverie, looking angrily out over the mountain as if it was all its fault.

Tullie stood to face him, her face expressionless, waiting for more. She respected Anjie, and if he was worried she had reason to be alarmed.

"Two storms," he stated evenly, turning to face her directly. "There was an unusual storm on Thursday afternoon as well; lasted only a few hours too."

"Tullie," BB said standing to face her too, "I'm afraid we haven't told you everything."

She looked from one to the other, expectantly.

"You see," he continued, "Jake sent us this early yesterday," and they both thumbed their phones urgently.

As Tullie raised her mug to her mouth, they stopped, following her movements closely.

"I think you'd better see this," continued Anjie, holding his phone for her to see.

Stunned, she looked from the phone to Anjie and BB

and back. They said nothing but regarded her evenly. The picture was grainy but not so grainy that the ring on the man's finger couldn't be seen clearly. It glowed in the gentle morning light. The exact match of the one Tullie now wore.

"Time to get off this mountain until we know more," Anjie noted softly, his body taut with alertness. BB nodded.

Grabbing his phone, she paced along the porch away from them, her eyes darting back and forth from finger to phone. Dully, she registered that it was Anjie calling the shots again! Uncertain, she fingered her ring gently making no attempt to remove it. There had to be a link here she knew; so did they.

"Tullie," called Anjie authoritatively, but she ignored him.

"Tullie," echoed BB, moving to stand with her at the end of the porch.

"BB, where did this ring come from?" she asked calmly, holding up her left hand in front of his face. "Why are you both running scared from two rings? What is going on here?"

Getting no response from BB, she shrugged and moved across to Anjie.

"What am I supposed to make of this? Tell me, what's going on! And," now her green eyes flashed angrily, "when did we get wireless coverage on the mountain?"

"And who the hell is the guy wearing the same ring as me?" she yelled at them both.

BB and Anjie exchanged the briefest of glances but Tullie read them perfectly.

"You think I'm in danger, don't you," she asked incredulously, "or is this some lousy party trick, like before?"

"No trick, Tullie," said BB quietly while Anjie went back to scanning the mountain warily.

"Until we get to the bottom of this, we need to get you off the mountain. Go to Jane's. She's expecting you anyway. Or spend some time with Jenny. Jake will answer all your questions when he gets back, I promise," he said, and hugged her warmly.

Anjie was waiting beside Salvie as she carried her laptop from the house. Ignoring him, she set the throttle high and spun out of the yard. In her side mirrors she could see him talking on his phone then the drive curved and he was gone. Clucking in annoyance, she sped past the two camouflaged sentries at the gate. Nothing had changed at all! She should never have come back!

CHAPTER 3

Her mind whirled with questions as she gunned Salvie down the mountain. Speed helped soothe her nerves: she had to concentrate on the winding roads and let go of what had just happened. Despite their concern, she felt no threat from the man who wore the ring. She felt no anxiety for Jake either. He was alright wherever he was, she was sure. She knew what else she needed; she needed work and she knew exactly where to go. The streets were still empty as Tullie drove through the outskirts of Matheson. Old Dan would let her in at the museum and she could spend the ninety minutes going through her lexicons until her mum turned up for work. That would be a welcome distraction. Maybe by then Jake would have turned up. The cool air pushed against her as she gained speed and she was glad she'd worn her leathers. Rush hour hadn't kicked in yet and the lights were flashing. She opened the throttle a little more and eased forward, keen to get off the road for once. The bike that hit her, a Suzuki Bandit, the twin of her own, appeared out of nowhere, slamming recklessly through the lights and straight into her. She felt the impact whack her front wheel and she was shot backwards out of her seat spinning in midair before her head hit the ground with a dull thud and the world went black.

The noise from the crash was deafening. The two joy-riders struggled to get up but Tullie lay limp and unmoving. Sirens sounded from nearby and within seconds two police cars were approaching from opposite ends hoping to cut off the offenders. They were too late; the tragedy was spread out before them on the road.

*****

"911. How can I help you?"

"We need an ambulance immediately. Three down. Joy-ride gone bad. Crossing of High and Laurel," reeled off Johnson as he squatted down beside the still, young woman, looking for a pulse.

"Sir! She's alive," he called back to his boss who was standing beside the other two young men, boys really, he cursed inwardly.

Satisfied that they were not seriously hurt, he left the team to it and shuffled towards where Johnson was covering Tullie with an emergency blanket. Within minutes two ambulances screeched around the corner, sirens blaring and lights flashing. By now a small crowd had gathered on their way to work. The police had the area cordoned off, keeping the crowds back and making room around the three. Tullie lay unconscious, her blanket reflecting the flashing lights. Her vitals were strong but she had taken a big hit, the medic reported, and she needed treatment urgently but she should make it. The other two barely needed a check-up at the hospital! Within minutes, both ambulances were off again heading as fast as they could to Matheson General. Behind them the police cars began to peel away in different directions leaving a team on the ground to find out as much information as possible from the gawking crowd.

"Right," said Detective Meryck. "Let's do this thing properly and put these scumbags away 'til they start shaving, at least!"

Nodding assent, the police spread out and approached the crowd.

"Johnson!" called Meryck. "Find out where we can find a coffee and debrief. I've had a long night already! I need something to keep me going."

*****

An hour later, the Task Force poured into Starbucks for breakfast.

"So, nobody saw nothing then?" asked Meryck, surveying the empty faces sucking on their lattes.

They all nodded dully. It was always the same. Accidents drew crowds, even one this early. They weren't there to help, just voyeurists catching a cheap thrill on the back of someone else's misery. A waste of time asking, their body language said.

"Anyone know who the victim is?" he asked. "Any ID?" The shuffle of frustration was his only reply.

"Anyone find anything useful then?" he asked into the noise.

Joining the group, young Johnson heaved a red, leather bag, and some keys, onto the table.

"Just these, Sir," he said. "I think they belong to the victim."

Meryck raised an eyebrow.

"Well, Sir," answered Johnson, "I don't think the other two would bring their laptop on a . . ."

He was interrupted by the waitress who brought his coffee and when she didn't leave immediately, they all turned to look at her expectantly.

"They're Tullie's, Tullie Bell's" she said, her voice trembling, "Where did you get them? Have they anything to do with the accident?"

"I gave her that bag exactly a year ago for her birthday," she explained to Johnson, nervously. "Is she ok? What's happened to her? I'm meeting her later," she asked, still holding onto his coffee.

"Looks like we have a name!" called our Meryck. "Go back, write up your reports. Johnson and I will take it from here."

It took only ten minutes to get Tullie to the hospital. The medics had staunched the flow of blood from her head wound and secured her fractured leg for the journey. She remained unconscious but breathing freely. Her blood pressure was normal. Without delay she was rushed into theatre. The rounds of tests and checks began. Somewhere deep down Tullie registered the chill of the operating theatre as they cut away her torn and bloody clothes, then a sharp jab in the back of her hand and blackness claimed her once more.

*****

Tullie's mum was cleaning up in the kitchen when the phone rang.

"Hi Jenny," she said. "Tullie's not home yet. I'm just heading out to work. How can I help you?"

Within seconds, her heart pounding loudly in her chest, she was in her car charging down the road to Matheson General.

Jenny was waiting for her at the door.

"She's in surgery, Mrs Bell," she said, taking Tullie's mother by the hand and drawing her into the Waiting Area.

"What on earth happened?" asked Mrs Bell. "She called me a couple of hours ago from Traveller's Mountain saying she'd meet me at work. That's all I know. She's never called me from there before. Felt something wasn't right."

"Mrs Bell, I presume? I'm Ron Meryck, the detective in charge of your daughter's incident. I hear she's going to be ok," he said overhearing the conversation between the two women and stepping up to introduce himself.

It was a lie, of course. He had no idea how she was doing but it helped to offer hope. It helped the family, and it helped him do his job. Christ! What a life, he thought.

Mrs Bell burst into tears. She was frightened for her daughter. It was terrible not knowing how she was. She was so grateful for any news. She wanted desperately to get her home and away from everybody. But she was relieved, so overwhelmingly relieved, that she was ok.

"When can I see her?" she asked between sobs.

"She's still in theatre," replied Meryck, eying her thoughtfully.

Mrs Bell wasn't listening. She was looking down the corridor at a trolley that was being pushed towards them. She knew, just knew, it was her Tullie. She charged in that direction, hotly pursued by Jenny and Meryck. It was her Tullie, her gorgeous Tullie who had never been sick a day in her life, lying white and still under the blue hospital blankets, tubes and wires peeking out from under the clothes, and a thick bandage encircling her fragile skull, tendrils of red hair peeking out underneath, a bulky IV bandaged to the back of her right hand, and a huge cast encasing her left leg from knee to toe.

"Is she ok?" she cried as she ran forward. "I'm her mum."

"Tullie, Tullie can you hear me?" she called gently reaching out to grab her hand.

"She's going to be just fine. She's a tough one," the taller one said ready to intercept Mrs Bell. "Just give us a few minutes and we'll have her set up in her room and you can stay with her as long as you want then."

Mrs Bell nodded as she mopped ineffectively at her tears and slowly followed her daughter down the corridor. Jenny reached over to hug her and together they entered the room after Tullie, Meryck following at a slower pace, missing nothing. Behind him came the doctor, his white coat flapping, his eyes down, going through the paperwork on his clipboard.

"Mrs Bell, I presume?" asked Doctor Carney. "May I have a word please?"

"Doctor" asked Mrs Bell, turning from the bed and shaking his hand slowly, "Is she ok? Will my daughter be ok?"

"Mrs Bell, I'd like to chat to you in private, if I may?" asked Carney, nodding, and at the same time indicating his office further down the hall. "Your daughter came round briefly after surgery. We have every hope that she'll make a full recovery but we're keeping her sedated for the moment. But I need some details for her records."

"Of course," replied Tullie's mum, breathing a sigh of relief. "How can I help?"

Dr Carney help up his hand and motioned for her to follow. Jenny went to sit by Tullie's side, and gently took her hand in hers. It felt so cold, so lifeless. Jenny shuddered despite herself. She felt so helpless.

*****

Meryck observed all that was going on. He missed nothing. He didn't like hospitals. He never had. And he stayed away from them as much as he could. Young Johnson could manage this. He stepped down the corridor and gestured to him. The young detective was drinking a cup of cold coffee a little further down as he chatted up the Receptionist. Meryck nodded for him to stand outside Tullie's hospital room. He wanted to know everything that happened, when it happened. He had that peculiar feeling in the pit of his stomach that said 'trouble' since he first saw her lying on the damp ground. He didn't like it but he had learned never to dismiss his instincts. It probably is just a random joy ride hit and run case, he mused, but something about this very usual scenario held his attention in a way he again wished it didn't. Taking his phone out of his trousers pocket he pretended to be checking his texts as he slowly walked towards Dr Carney's office. Immersed in his texting, he appeared not to notice the two people sitting inside, deep in conversation that seemed to be of a distressing nature. Well, that's to be expected, he thought to himself, but no matter how hard he tried to dismiss his feelings, that peculiar feeling in his gut only intensified. Carney appeared to be asking Mrs Bell about her daughter's medical records. Meryck could lip read perfectly but swore quietly under his breath as he couldn't see Mrs Bell's response. He could tell by her demeanour though that she was shocked.

"Mrs Bell," Dr Carney was saying, "we have an unusual reading on your daughter's blood type. Is this a surprise to you?"

"Well, yes," replied Mrs Bell, sitting upright, "it is. What do you mean, unusual?"

Dr Carney didn't answer.

"Can you tell me your blood type, Mrs Bell please? Purely for the records, of course."

"I'm O RH positive," replied Mrs Bell.

"I see," replied Carney thoughtfully, writing everything down. "What type of work do you do, Mrs Bell?"

"I'm the archivist at the museum," replied Mrs Bell, looking more puzzled by the minute.

"Did you do military service?" he asked.

"No," replied Tullie's mum, "but my father was a Marine and I have a brother who was in the Air Force".

"What about your husband, Ma'am? Is he in the services? Any stints abroad, that kind of thing?" continued Carney.

"No Sir," she replied, smiling rather ruefully. "My husband has always chased pink gold."

"Pink gold?" he queried, his eyebrows reaching for his hairline. He didn't have the time or inclination for puzzles right now.

"Yeah, pink gold. Shrimps, you know. He's a shrimper. Fishes out of Skyway mostly, aboard a 40 foot fibreglass," she replied simply.

"Any foreign ancestry?" he continued.

She shook her head.

"What's all this about anyway?" she asked.

Carney pulled at the neck of his shirt with his thin, white fingers, dislodging his tie a little, giving him more the look of a naughty schoolboy than the experienced doctor he was. He flipped page after page on his charts without giving her an answer, without even looking up. The vertical furrows between his eyebrows deepened and he chewed on the edge of his bottom lip unconsciously.

"Dr Carney, what is going on here please? Is there something you're not telling me?" she asked again, fear gripping her stomach.

Carney looked up instantly at this interruption, his grey eyes fresh and alert despite his night's work, and waved a hand dismissively in front of his face.

"Just a glitch on your daughter's vitals, Mrs Bell. We cannot seem to identify her blood type. Probably one of the newer ones we haven't on file. We're checking with the International Blood Bank."

Leaving Mrs Bell open-mouthed, he motioned for her to rise and join him at Tullie's bedside.

"We'll run the screen again, Mrs Bell. And we'll outsource to another lab just to be sure. Do you have any other children?"

"No, just Tullie," she replied in a daze.

Neither noticed the lurking Meryck as they made their way down the corridor continuing the discussion as they went.

"And your husband's name?" asked Carney.

"Bill Boyd," she replied. "My ex-husband," she added sadly.

"And his blood group is..?" continued Carney.

"B, B negative, I believe," she contributed without giving it much thought.

"And you never had any problems with Tullie's blood results before?" he asked searchingly.

"Well, no," she replied firmly. "You see, Tullie has never had a sick day in her life!"

"And her full name is Tullie Bell or Tullie Boyd?" he asked quietly.

"Thula Megan Bell," replied Tullie's Mum in a whisper,

"but we've always called her Tullie."

Dr Carney stopped and turned fully to Mrs Bell, his hand on Tullie's door, Johnson just two feet away, his face in the local paper.

"Mrs Bell," he asked, "is Bill Boyd Tullie's natural father?"

Tullie's Mum stood rooted to the spot, sweat beads forming on her forehead.

"Mrs Bell," he prompted none-too-gently, "it's imperative you tell me the truth! Is Bill Boyd Tullie's natural father?"

So, it was going to come out then, one way or another, this secret they had kept hidden all those years. But not today, she decided! Lifting her tear rimmed eyes to him, she answered truthfully while keeping the lie hidden.

"Bill Boyd is the only man I've ever had sex with. We, well, you know, had sex before we got married. Not something to be let known back then. But we've always called Tullie, Tullie Bell. That way she can reconcile our wedding anniversary with her birthday. Not that young people give a fig about those things these days," she smiled wanly.

Carney sighed. Just another secret child out of wedlock then! He opened the door and she followed him in.

*****

Meryck joined Johnson and they conversed in low voices for a short time. Johnson settled in for the long haul. Meryck placed a call as he left the hospital.

"Yep," he said, "you heard me correctly. A full birth

certificate for one Thula Megan Bell."

"Mark it urgent," he growled, lighting up his first cigarette of the day, the tip glowing brightly as he puffed deeply.

Coughing, he sat gratefully into the car leaving the door open so his wife wouldn't smell the cigarette smoke later. He really should give them up. But he inhaled deeply and felt the calmness descend. There was a smell of rain in the air; he could smell it despite the smoke. It was unusual weather for this time of year; late June, overcast and heavy, and storms. What it needed was a good storm right now to clear the air, Meryck thought. He loved a good storm. He might even give shrimping a try too when he met up with Mr Boyd. Wonder how a storm affected that, he mused. He grinned. This job definitely had its perks. He let his head rest back and continued to gaze lazily around the hospital car park which was nearly deserted in the early morning. He was on cigarette three when the ringing started in the car.

"That was quick" he said to no one in particular as he reached for his mobile.

"Hello, Meryck here," he answered.

But there was no reply and the ringing kept going. It took him a few seconds to realise it wasn't his phone but another with the exact same ring tone somewhere in the car. Turning around to the back seat he switched on the interior light. There was Tullie's bag sprawled across the back seat, the ringing coming from inside. He reached over and grabbed the bag, searching inside quickly for the phone. But he was too late. Whoever it was had rung off. It didn't take him long to find out who was calling. Jed. Now who might he be? It was worth following up especially since there were sixteen missed calls and the same amount of texts. The boyfriend, perhaps? Who else could be so persistent this early on a Saturday morning?

While he wanted nothing better than to sit there and smoke a few more lazy cigarettes he knew he should get back in there and find out more about this Jed guy, where he lived and all that. He suddenly realised that he hadn't asked where Tullie lived. Things had moved too fast. No, it was he who was distracted! He was getting old! And he still hated joy-riders! Johnson would have the information but best to cover it again just in case. Taking one long, last puff, he headed back to the hospital entrance, carefully extinguishing the butt in his little hot box; his name for it. He was very careful not to leave any evidence behind him ever, not even a cigarette end. He'd empty his hot box back at the station. Too many jobs in the field, he reckoned. But it never killed anyone to be careful, in fact, just the opposite. He could take the incoming call anywhere. After all Tullie wasn't in intensive care and he'd be in the corridor.

As he neared the door he could hear a female voice talking on her phone. It was Jenny. He nodded to her genially and ambled by reaching for his own phone in response. It was a trick he used regularly, in fact, so much so, it was second nature now. He took the pretend text, standing to answer it just a few feet away from Jenny. From what he could hear she was talking on the phone to someone about Tullie's accident. When she began to cry he felt it was time to move on, and then he heard the name Jed. She was talking to Jed. So he changed his mind and hung around waiting for her to end the call.

CHAPTER 4

Jed settled to the last of the paperwork happily while in the background the footage from the week sped through from the security cameras. The flashes on the screen were unusual and caught his attention. Coming out from behind his desk he thumbed through the last few sections until he got a better view. 5.30am Friday. It was Tullie, two hours before he got there with the coffees. She had taken the pictures on her phone, the flashes blinding him as he watched. He re-ran it again and again just to be sure but there was no mistaking it. She had taken pictures, one for each set. Damn! In seconds all his hard worked plans began to swiftly unravel. Damn the girl, he raged, as he beat the desk again and again! Damn! Damn! Damn!

He found his hands were shaking as he dialled her number but there was no reply so he left a brief message for her to call him back. Then looking at his watch he grimaced. She'd be fast asleep, and there was no signal on the Mountain. He'd catch her tomorrow morning. Taking up his phone again he dialled another number. He needed help shifting this stuff, and quick.

By morning they were labelled, crated, and loaded into his truck and once more he tried to call Tullie but got no answer. Swearing, he thumped the wheel in frustration! He'd got to get those pictures! Steadying himself he entered his destination into the GPS, choosing the fastest route to his destination. Matheson was not too far out of his way to Tinakilly, he thought, and he decided to make a detour and speak to her in person and destroy the pictures one way or another. Careful of his precious cargo he manoeuvred slowly out into the early morning traffic tweaking the route to include the additional stop. Then an hour out of Matheson he got the call.

"Ah, Jenny," he said, putting her on speaker mode "what's up?"

He liked Jenny for a number of reasons, not the least of which she was a friend of Tullie's. She was naive and sweet and trusting which made her easy to manipulate. An invitation here and an invitation there to society events was all it took: he needed her on his arm and she played the game of 'who's who' brilliantly and he plied her with praise for every bit of gossip she provided. He worked her effortlessly and she loved him for it unaware of the secrets she revealed to him. Knowledge is power, he repeated his mantra; but somewhere in his lonely heart she was shining a light for him to follow.

"It's Tullie," she sobbed. "She's been in an accident."

It took several minutes for Jed to find out the whole truth. Jenny needed comforting and while his mind raced and his heart beat anxiously he pulled over to give her his full attention. Pulling at his collar he rolled down the window and let the fresh air blow over his tired body as he talked. They couldn't have got to her so soon!

"No, no! It's not your fault," he said over and over again. "It's just an accident, Jenny. It can happen to anybody. And she's going to be alright, isn't she?"

Gradually the sobs faded away and he told her he'd be there in a short while and take care of everything. After he hung up he stepped out of his truck and checked his cargo. He had nothing to eat or drink in the vehicle and he was both hungry and thirsty but he didn't believe in having food in the truck. He was fastidious in keeping his personal space pristine. He was also fanatical about keeping his space impersonal. The truck could belong

34

to anyone. There was no trinket or embellishment
of any kind to link him to it. It was even registered to
the business that owned the business but he made
damn sure no one used it but him. Looking around the
deserted countryside he had one more check to do.
Sitting back into the driver's seat he reached under the
steering wheel and pushed the concealed button. The
central panel slipped speedily back silently and he ran
his eyes over the weapons, checking and checking again.
He felt better when he had done this. He knew he was
becoming more obsessed with checks these days; no
one knew about the extra surveillance at work. It was
his personal gear that adorned his personal space and
he alone who checked it. Tullie wouldn't know he knew
about the pictures. And she hadn't told him either. But
she probably would soon, he reasoned, when she'd
finished the job. But that might be too late! It's just as
well she doesn't know how much her entire world will
change with her success, he sighed; with so many looking
for the seals, and one on her doorstep who would kill
for them – and has already, he reckoned grimly. Pay back
can't come soon enough; he ground his teeth in fury.

*****

It was some time before Jenny even saw him waiting
for her but it was worth the wait. Meryck deduced that
Jed was desperate to get in touch with Tullie; he was on
his way to the hospital now. So, he'd get to meet him in
person without having to travel to wherever he lived. He
just had to stay put. That suited him just fine.

"How is she doing?" he asked Jenny, holding the door
open for her.

"She's still the same," she whispered back,
still mopping her eyes with a now-soaked paper
handkerchief.

Silently, he handed her some new ones. He always

35

carried paper handkerchiefs. They came in handy in his line of work. With a wobbly smile, she took them, and moved ahead of him into the hospital proper. It was very quiet inside. You could hear a whisper from ten feet away. Eerie place, hospitals, he mused darkly, people sick and dying and not a sound to be heard. He followed her, head down. It was quite a shock to have the silence so abruptly and loudly broken by his own phone. He answered quickly, cupping the mouthpiece.

"Yes?"

"Mr Meryck, Sir," said the voice on the other end. "This is Sally in records. You wanted the full birth certificate details for one Thula Megan Bell?"

"Yes," he said again.

"Well, Sir, I have a problem. I can't find any mention at all of a person of that name been born in Matheson."

"Extend the search country-wide," he ordered, slowing down behind Jenny.

"I have done that already Sir. I can find no record of any Thula Megan Bell. I'm running an international search now. That'll take a few more hours to complete but I thought I should let you know what I've come up with so far," she replied.

"Is there any other alias you'd like me to search?"

He thought for a moment.

"Do a search for Thula Megan Boyd, eighteen to twenty-five years bracket" he answered quietly. At this stage Jenny had continued ahead and was out of hearing range.

"Include Tullie instead of Thula too – just a local search on the Tullie ones. Check adoption agencies and hospitals too. She's been to university, I believe. Don't know which one but see what comes up. Bound to be a paper trail out there somewhere."

"And, Sally," he said, "thanks."

"You're welcome, Sir," she replied brightly, and hung up.

He caught up to Jenny again outside Tullie's door. Johnson was making a hard job of the crossword and was trying to enlist Jenny's help. Good strategy, he thought. He'll make a fine detective some day. He went and stood beside them.

"What clue are you trying to solve?" he asked.

"Three down Sir," replied Johnson, colour creeping up his neckline.

He was doing the Quick Crossword and was stuck at "Container for dirty washing (4, 6)".

"Definitely a bit of a basket case, Johnson, eh?" laughed Meryck, winking at Jenny.

"But it doesn't fit, Sir," replied Johnson glumly, which drew a laugh from Jenny.

"Course it doesn't," she giggled pointing to an adjoining clue, "that answers wrong!"

He left them to it and wandered to Tullie's door. Mrs Bell was sitting by the bed, holding her daughter's hand like she would never let it go. He knocked softly. Startled, her head jerked around sharply but she beckoned him in.

The smell of hospital stuff hit him as he entered. He had extra sensitive smell and he knew the room was pleasant but he experienced it more intimately than he would have wished. He could see the drip disgorging its contents slowly into her veins and he quickly averted his eyes. He could feel himself begin to sweat.

"How is she doing?" he whispered, drawing up a spare chair and focussing his attention on Mrs Bell.

"Just the same," she replied. "The medical staff told me she came round a bit after surgery which is a good sign. The scans were clear. Just the nasty head wound, some deep grazing and bruising on her left arm, and the fracture on her left fibula," she nodded to the ghostly white cast. There was a slight pause as if she was still taking all this in, that it was a nightmare she'd awaken from soon.

"She's been asleep the whole time. I want to wait 'til she wakes up just to make sure she's ok," she whispered, rubbing Tullie's hand gently.

"I understand," replied Meryck, not unkindly. "I'd do the same myself."

"Have you informed the family?" he asked gently.

"No, I haven't yet," she said worriedly. "It's just me and Bill - my ex. He's on the water. The shrimping; it's a night thing ," she explained. "I'll catch him later on when they make port."

Meryck nodded, pretending he didn't know already. It was time for a few details to go in the book. He drew out his notebook and asked Mrs Bell if she'd give him a few details. Ten minutes later he left the room with all that he needed to bounce off Jed as he rushed to see Tullie. He was not at all what he expected!

Jed paused calmly in the corridor, adjusting his Gucci sunglasses on his blonde head. His muscular body was encased in a dark suit which was set off with a white shirt and yellow tie, loosely tied, Meryck saw. A bright yellow tie, for Christ's sake, thought Meryck! He was forty if he was a day. Not exactly boyfriend material, he grunted. Holding strong manicured hands before him, Jed said, "Sorry. Excuse me, please," in a deep sonorous voice and made to pass Meryck.

"Just a moment, Sir," ground out Meryck, flashing his badge, "who are you exactly? And what's the hurry?"

Jed paused again instantly and introduced himself, filing away Meryck's name for future reference.

"I'm Jed Bell, Tullie's boss," he replied amicably, and offered his hand to Meryck.

Shaking his hand firmly, Meryck noticed the worry on his face.

"How's she doing?" he asked.

"So-so," replied Meryck.

"They're only letting family in, for now," he smiled apologetically as Jed turned to Tullie's door.

"Then that's ok, detective" returned Jed, easily, "I'm her uncle."

"Nice man," said Meryck to Jenny. "You know him well?"

Five minutes later he had all the details on both of them, too. Johnson watched in admiration. Jenny never even knew she was being grilled thoroughly. That man had style! Meryck moved to leave, turned to Johnson and nodded.

"We're off now, Jenny," said Johnson. "Can we offer you a lift home?"

"No, thank you," said Jenny, her eyes wistful as she took in the scene in the room, "I'll hang on a little longer." Jed was hugging Mrs Bell who was sobbing uncontrollably into his shoulder. Meryck had the distinct feeling she wished it was her in his arms! As he started to walk away he nodded to Johnson, and asked,

"Fancy a waffle?"

CHAPTER 5

Dr Carney left Tullie's room with more answers than questions and went straight to the lab. He wanted very badly for someone to tell him they'd screwed up. The lab was almost empty at this time of the morning which was something to be grateful for anyway, he reckoned crossly.

"Ryan, tell me you've got that damn machine working properly. I can't prescribe accurately until you do!" he said imperiously fending off questions.

"Well, that's just the thing, Dr Carney," replied Ryan, scratching his head with the tip of a pencil, "it is working properly!" handing him a new sheaf of results. "I've run them five times just to be sure against the IBB but none of the thirty two match..." and he shrugged.

The results were exactly the same. Blood Type UNKOWN. The letters jumped out at him, and he swore.

"Does the administrator know?" he asked Ryan quietly.

"She's right behind you," nodded Ryan, as the doors swished closed. "I just requested a Maintenance Order and she wanted to know why."

"Tom, what's going on?" asked the administrator manoeuvring herself in front of Carney to look directly in his face, and nodded to the next office which was empty. Walking inside, aware of Ryan's curious gaze following their every step, she closed the door while he drew the blinds.

"Now what have we got that is so serious?" she

41

asked.

"Results UNKNOWN, Dr Crawthorne," he answered baldly, handing her the results copies. "Checked six times now. Even went to the IBB. The victim is early twenties, female; the result of a joy rider's hit."

He was talking too fast in his nervousness, he knew. He ran his fingers through his hair. Get a grip, he told himself sternly, moving around the room agitatedly. She read the paperwork carefully, taking in every detail several times over. Finally, satisfied, she looked up at him.

"Well, let's not get our knickers in a twist just yet. It's probably nothing," she shrugged. "Get a new sample and we'll run it again here, and at Mercers. They've got the new Langereis and Junior profiles from Japan last month. When I heard we had a possible technical problem," she said, stressing the word 'technical', "I checked who was on the early morning shift at Mercers. It's Matt. He'll keep it quiet until we know for sure what we're dealing with."

She paused, weighing up Carney closely. He stopped pacing and turned to face her. Making her decision quickly, she reached for her bag and withdrew an aging envelope.

"Have a look at this," she said gravely.

Carney withdrew the contents and looked at her in surprise.

"But these are over twenty years old! What relevance have they?" he blustered, thrusting them back at her in annoyance.

"Those are what we should be considering," he added, pointing to the papers she still held.

"Twenty-five years old, to be precise," she corrected. "Now read them," she instructed, unmoved by his outburst.

Silence filled the room and now it was her turn to pace. Carney began chewing at his bottom lip, never a good sign. He'd be a disaster at poker, she decided. But he's a bloody good doctor. The best she'd worked with in a long time. He deserved to have a thumbs-up on what they might be stumbling into. But there was only so much she could share.

He looked up at her, eyebrows arched deep into his hairline, and whistled silently.

"You kept a copy?" he mouthed, afraid even to say the words out loud!

She nodded. They scanned them together again hoping they were mistaken but in every detail both lab reports were in agreement apart from gender, age and time. They knew the drill. But they wanted to be sure. She was only a child really.

Tugging the papers from his shaky hands, she returned them to her handbag.

"These do not exist. We do not know anything about these! Agreed?" she whispered into his ear.

He nodded, running his long fingers through his dark hair, again.

"Now, you draw the new samples yourself from this girl and we'll take it from there," she instructed. "You personally supervise Ryan here. Put it on video. I'll take the samples to Matt and do the same. Nobody leaves here 'til we get to the bottom of this."

"Who else knows about these?" she asked, holding up Tullie's results as she made for the door.

He thought for a quick moment.

"Just Ryan. There's nobody else in the lab," he answered. "And Mrs Bell, but she probably hasn't made much sense of it. I told her we couldn't make out her daughter's blood type and that we're running the tests again."

"I'll give Ryan the 'double-check, to-be-sure routine'," she said as she headed for the door. "The 'keep it to ourselves so we don't get egg on our face when it comes out we've cocked it up' story. You fob Mrs Bell off; whatever it takes, short of downright lying. I can't support you there. Right! Let's get this done!" And she was gone.

*****

Rosa's was practically empty when they got there but it was worth the drive. He had found it by chance when he got here five years ago and had been a regular ever since; at least as often as he could. He ordered double waffles with bacon and syrup washed down with coke: Johnson had a burger with fries on the side. He preferred coffee. They sat at the deserted bar and ate at their leisure, neither saying a thing, each ruminating over the events of the morning that brought them here. Big Bob served them, grinning and helpful.

"Bad crash in town earlier," said Meryck to him nonchalantly as he poured them refills.

"Yeah?" asked BB, pausing in his pouring to look at the cop closely. He recognised him as a regular. "What happened?"

"Bike crash near the museum," mumbled Johnson, his mouth full.

"Bloody bikers!" spat BB, "They come in here all the time. Nice people but they think they own the road."

44

Meryck nodded. He knew all about that. He could feel his anger rising.

"Two bloody drunken, joy-riders," he told BB gruffly. "They went straight through the lights. Took out a young girl on her Suzuki! They're all right of course, just bruises and scratches. She's up in Matheson General still out cold!"

BB went very still.

"When this happen?" he asked quietly.

"About two hours ago," said Johnson, pushing his mug forward for a refill.

"You know how she's doing?" he asked, looking to Johnson now. "Tullie Bell from Traveller's Mountain has a Suzuki," and he nodded up the road. "Known her since she was a toddler."

" Yeah, that's her name," said Johnson. "Out of danger we believe but she got one hell of a knock! We've just come from the hospital. Her friend Jenny's up there. And Jed," he added.

"Hmmm. Jenny's a nice girl," he commented, "worked for me a while back. She and Tullie been friends since high school. Hear she's at Starbucks now. Now uni material, if you get my drift."

"That a fact?" joins in Meryck. "You know the families well then? All locals?"

"Sure, I know them well! Been in and out of here since they arrived," informed Bob. "Jenny Mallin, well, the Mallin's turned up about ten years ago. Money, lots of money there. Some brains too but not as much as Tullie's family. Boyd's been here as long as I can remember. Tullie's real bright. Must have taken it from mum's side of the family as dad's not bothered about

45

that sort of thing too much though. Have a place, I've heard, over near Tinakilly. His family's into fishing. Pity about the divorce. Had them pinned as lifers. Believe they were schoolyard sweethearts. Now that's real nice."

Smiling, Bob ambled off to serve a new customer, another biker, looking for a hot breakfast and a place to unwind before taking to the open road again.

Meryck grabbed his coffee and motioned for Johnson to join him at a far booth well away from prying ears. He noticed BB hadn't mentioned Jed at all and stored away that information for later.

"Right," he said, once they were seated and Johnson had waved off another refill from Bob, "what have we got?"

These sharing sessions were crucial. Meryck had hand-picked Johnson for his attention to detail in any situation. He was not disappointed. But it seemed that all was just routine stuff, a joy ride gone bad. They had the culprits: Tullie was going to be ok, so why did he feel like the sky was about to fall in. He shook his head. One thing he could see clearly though was that Johnson was taken with Jenny.

"Done?" he asked.

Johnson nodded and waved goodbye to BB who was on his phone.

As they pulled up in front of the station, Meryck turned to Johnson;

So," he said, thinking his way forward, "chase up the legals then: school records, birth certs, social security, university records, marriage cert, divorce docs, the works. I want to know what this family eats for breakfast!"

Johnson nodded.

"Right away, Sir," he said.

"And Johnson," he called after him, "find out where Tinakilly is."

CHAPTER 6

Galvanised into action, Carney grabbed his kit and made his way doggedly to Tullie's room. Double-gloved he prepared to take an extra round of blood samples for testing. Jenny and Jed decided this was a good time to leave and Mrs Bell didn't dissuade them. It was great that they came but it was great that they were leaving too. She stepped outside and waved them off, genuinely thankful for their support on this terrible morning. The corridor was deserted. Back inside the room Carney was busy drawing blood from Tullie's arm. Glancing around once more, she furtively slipped her mobile from her pocket and dialled.

"We have a problem. Tullie's been in an accident and there's a problem with her blood work," she whispered. "Where the hell is Jake? I've been trying to call him all morning!"

"I know" said BB calmly. "Where are you? We're on our way."

"I'm at the hospital," she said, giving the location and further details about Tullie's injuries, putting the phone away as Carney came out of the room.

"How is she doing?" she asked quietly. "When will you have the results?" she continued, nodding to the vials.

"We'll know in a few hours," he replied. "We're outsourcing to Mercers immediately and Ryan will double-check here again."

"Don't you worry," he continued, smiling at her now. "It'll be ok. I'm sure it's just a technical glitch."

"Now, why don't you go home and have a rest," he suggested. "Tullie will be out all day. She's sleeping peacefully. The rest will do her good. If you'd like to come back at teatime, she should be awake by then."

"Thank you, doctor," she said gratefully. "I'm glad she's in good hands. I think I might take you up on that offer. I need to call in at work anyway. I'll just get my things."

Carney turned on his heel and headed down the corridor towards the lab. As Mrs Bell watched he was met at the nurse's station by a blonde, gawky guy. Ah Ryan, she presumed. Moving into the room, she asked,

"Did you get that? They're outsourcing to Mercers."

"Got it! Now, get going. Meet you in an hour," and the phone went dead.

*****

Back in her office, Dr Myra Crawthorne examined the old results again for some time. Pouring herself a coffee, she ruminated on that night twenty-four years, ten months and two days ago exactly when she was in Ryan's shoes while she waited for the samples. Found unconscious floating in Bear's Lake by some night poachers he was lucky to be alive. He'd taken quite a beating. Some fight maybe, she thought. His eyes though, they were funny. When she saw the colour that they had entered on the records she thought someone had made a mistake. Purple, they said. Now, who had eyes like that? Bound to be contacts, she dismissed. That was, until she did the blood work. She couldn't work out type. She redid the test twice, three times, four times but still that same result; UNKNOWN. When Dr Osterwalder came for the results because she was so slow in handing them over, she was terrified. Terrified she's be sacked. Terrified she's handled some foreign blood! She was too scared to tell him so she just shakily handed him the result sheets.

"What's all this," he'd asked, angry as hell that she hadn't done her job correctly.

Bloody woman, he was probably thinking, she mused, smiling a little now. He never did like women lab technicians. Bloody man's job, he'd say out loud in his 'Sue me! See if I care!' old general's voice. And he got away with it because he was such a great doctor. And his bark was worse than his bite anyway. It was he who had secretly blood screened her for five years to make sure she was not infected. But not infected by what? She'd never found out. She'd spent a huge chunk of her life looking to see if her eyes were changing colour and nobody gave her any answers. Then she had let it go after he died and there was no more screening; no more questions. And definitely no more answers. And not a whisper, ever, of their guest anywhere in the media.

She remembered clearly when they'd come for him. The hospital annex where he was being treated was cleared apart from essential personnel; herself and Ostenwalder, the only two aware of the unfolding drama. Most lights were turned off but she could remember the dark shadows, and what light there was reflecting off metal. He walked out of the room! She'd always remembered that. A near-death victim only an hour before! For nights, she'd awaken in a sweat, heart pounding, from the memory of it all. His purple eyes glinted in her direction, boring through her, and then he was gone. Noiselessly. Disappeared into thin air. Then there was the commander. She shivered now, just as she did back then.

He motioned Ostenwalder and herself into the vacated room. He didn't bother to turn back on the light. His voice seemed to come from the very darkness itself.

"Matter of national security," he said coldly. "This will never be spoken about again. Are we clear on that?"

"This never happened!"

Without waiting for an answer he was gone. Seconds seemed like hours, and then Ostenwalder reached over and turned on the light. Every single thing had been removed from the room! It was completely stripped! They were standing in an empty shell, the smell of bleach choking them. She hadn't recognised the smell before. She had thought it was the smell of her own fear at first, she smiled ruefully. Then Ostenwalder took charge. They showered, she remembered, together, fully clothed. He never let her out of his sight. Then they showered naked, one after the other, and dressed in hospital scrubs. He bagged their clothes and as they left the washroom a hand reached out and disappeared with the bundle. Ostenwalder ushered her into his office where he proceeded to draw blood from her right arm; she always remembered clearly which arm. Then he indicated that she do the same for him. He put the samples into a bag, went to the door and another disembodied arm reached in and took it.

Lost in reverie it took several knocks for her to answer the door. She put down her cold cup and opened the door for Carney.

"Two vials, as you requested," he informed her a little too loudly.

She motioned him in and shut the door firmly after him.

"Ryan nearly finished setting up?" she asked.

He nodded.

"Then let's get going," she said. " And remember, this is just a technical glitch until it isn't," she added, eyes fixing on his double gloves and giving him back one test vial. The other she slipped into a small padded envelope.

"Go! Get it done!" she motioned him to the door. "I've got to use the bathroom first."

Carney sighed and made his way down the empty hallway, deep in thought, clutching the red liquid as if it were hell on earth.

Myra made for her private bathroom and silently flicked opened the window.

She waved.

In answer, a figure detached itself from the tree line, raised his hand in acknowledgement and quickly and silently held out cupped hands for the package. Dropping it safely, she shut the window and flushed the loo, running the water briefly before opening the door.

In the corridor, the two agents approached the nurse's station and flashed their ID's briefly.

"We're here for Tullie Bell," the tall one delivered in a clipped tone, gesturing behind him to the medical team that followed. "Matter of national security. Where is your administrator's office?"

Myra wasn't surprised when the men were ushered in by a scared-looking orderly. She had been expecting them, just not so soon. She fervently hoped that Matt had gotten away; he was their best ticket out of this new mess.

"Let me guess," she said coldly, holding up her hand to forestall their usual pitch, "matter of national security, and all that! Been there before, gentlemen."

"Then you know the drill," the shorter one said quietly. "Get him in here."

"She's only a child," she began, but reached for the phone nonetheless.

They waited in silence.

Then the door burst open and a distraught Carney strode inside.

"Tullie's been moved," he burst out, and fell silent as he spotted Myra's guests.

"Ah, Dr Carney, I presume," said the taller agent, not moving a muscle.

"This is a matter of national security," added the other, stepping forward. "You'll have to come with me," and he gestured towards the door.

Rushing forward, Myra grabbed Carney's arm, and led the way. The calm of the corridor did nothing to assuage their inner turmoil; the removal order was proceeding smoothly. Carney pulled back towards the lab but was forestalled by the barrel of a gun against his side.

"There's no need for that," intervened Myra, allowing Carney time to catch a glance at a stunned Ryan as he signed an official-looking document. Official Secrets, no doubt, he reckoned.

"We'll co-operate fully," and she nudged Carney viciously.

"Let's do what they say, Tom," she said quietly, and shrugged, but her eyes conveyed the message he already knew, "What chance do we have?"

CHAPTER 7

Tullie was in a wonderful place. She felt so peaceful, her body didn't hurt anymore. The sand beneath her feet tickled her toes and the calm ocean beckoned. She dropped her flowing robe on the beach and made her way into the water. It lapped her naked body silkily as she made her way further and further in. The intricate markings on her left arm shone in the moonlight, swirling down to her fingers and up over her shoulder. They made her feel strong; invincible. She lay back in the water and looked up at the twin moons chasing each other across the sky as they did every night. Was it her imagination or were they closer together than she remembered?

She wasn't concerned when the whispering began. She had expected it. On the shore, he stepped forward, hearing it too, ready to protect her, as always. Gesturing for him to stay, she stood up in the water. On cue, the water coalesced around her, hands reaching out to touch her reverently. She heard each thought. But she was searching for one mind tonight. Sighing, they receded until just one figure remained. She was unaware of her presence so she reached out and touched her. Her dream shattered and she was jolted back into her body rudely.

She was in a moving vehicle, restricted in some way. She could feel her body intensely. It had experienced damage but was healing nicely. Her dream tickled away at the edge of her consciousness as she lay very still trying to figure out where she was. The markings were real! She could feel them moving minutely on her arm and she felt comforted. She could also feel the presence of people in close proximity to her. She could sense fear. She was guarded, but for good or ill? Tullie moved in her sleep and someone instantly reached out and added more sedative to her drip. She quieted down immediately into empty slumber, her dream bond broken to be replaced with another.

On Greenway Island, the seagulls circled wildly, screeching and wheeling, but no one bothered to investigate. Deep in its bowels Man-x moved silently along the corridors, his purple eyes scanning the darkness as if it were day. He was a long-forgotten treasure now. He had posed no threat nor offered any new scientific discovery. He was just an oddity. But one they still couldn't explain so they kept him hidden, and they explored his DNA tirelessly. And twenty years later they were no closer to finding out who he was or where he had come from. He was human, was all they could say, but unlike any other human. And exceptions were always seen as dangerous, the nail that had to be hammered down. And hammered they had, time and again but he offered no resistance. It was not part of his mission to do so. His mission was simply to kill.

He could sense her presence suddenly after all this time. He didn't seek answers as to why now, he just accepted it was time. He had been sent for this. When it was over he'd die. He felt nothing about either situation. All emotion had been bred out. He was just an automaton.

Tullie could feel him too. She felt his cold menace close around her neck and she struggled to breathe. The ring burned her finger, tracing patterns up her wrist and beyond. She could feel its strength. And she could feel someone else too. But she didn't know who he was; didn't know whether he was friend or foe. She struggled against her bands and felt them snap. She could hear a voice calling and she felt another jab and slipped away into dreamless sleep.

"I told you to keep her sedated," he shouted at Carney.

"Pull one more stunt like that and you'll regret it!" he continued threateningly.

Carney crouched back in the ambulance sweat pouring from his body. There was nowhere to move, no way of doing anything to get them out of the crisis they were in. Myra's eyes followed his every move. She had been taped up in the second seat at the side, nearest the door, leaving Carney free to administer to Tullie. Anjie watched vigilantly from the bottom of the gurney, crouching down on the wheel rim, his eyes never wandering away from them both, his gun held loosely now. The driver pushed hard, siren wailing until they cleared the outskirts, then a weird calm descended. The girl was rambling, going from periods of serene calm to thrashing frenzy. Carney knew it was his job for now to keep her sedated and he had already given her a shot through her IV but it hadn't seemed to work. He was worried about the second dose but she seemed ok. He wished he had more monitoring equipment but the ambulance was sparsely furnished. He leaned over to check Tullie's irises and felt a little better. He looked over at Myra and nodded reassuringly. They travelled forward at breakneck speed in suspended time wondering, not for the first time, what they had got themselves into.

*****

Meryck was rudely awakened by his phone ringing under his pillow. He always kept his phone under his pillow so it wouldn't wake his wife, even after she'd moved to the next room years ago. He was disorientated it was so bright!

"'Lo," he said groggily.

"This better be good, Johnson," he added grumpily

56

looking at the clock. He'd only been in bed less than an hour! He'd just put one investigation to bed last night when this Tullie one came up on the way home. He was desperate for some decent sleep.

"Sir," said Johnson. "Sorry Sir, but you'll want to take this. Tullie's gone. And Carney is missing too."

Meryck was already dressing.

"Where are you, Johnson?" he asked.

"Downstairs, Sir. Thought you might like a lift," he said.

The hospital was incredibly normal for what had just happened there. Tullie had been moved. In fact, her room looked as if it had never been occupied. It was completely empty. Meryck had to check his notes to make sure he'd got the right room. A matter of national security they had been told but Johnson had not been able to verify this. A thorough job, he decided grimly. The smell of bleach sickened him. Looking a bit grey around the gills he moved down the corridor to an open window.

"Sir," said Johnson approaching, "Dr Myra Crawthorne, the administrator, is missing too. No sign of a struggle."

"Anybody see anything?" asked Meryck.

"Nope," replied Johnson, bouncing back and forward on his toes. "They're taking this national security stuff pretty seriously."

"How did you find out then?" asked Meryck.

"Anonymous text," replied Johnson.

"Hmm," said Meryck, "don't suppose you have any lead on that number yet either?"

"Not so far, Sir," replied Johnson.

"I wonder why they took them? And them only? Why not do the Official Secrets stuff on them too like they did with the lab guy?" Meryck thought out loud. "Any word from Mrs Bell?"

"There's a car on the way to her house now. Never turned up for work," replied Johnson. "We can't seem to raise her on the phone either."

"Good job, Johnson," he said, patting him on the shoulder. "Bloody mess, eh? Find out if they took anything else, will you?"

"I can tell you that now, Sir," he called back as he moved away to consult with a waiting police officer. "All records of Tullie Bell are gone. Not a scrap of evidence remains. It's as if she's vanished into thin air."

Meryck grunted. He'd suspected as much.

"Sir," said Johnson, hurrying towards him now, "there's a problem at the Bells! When the police got there they found the fire brigade putting out the fire. It'll be another few hours before we know if there are any bodies in there. The place is gutted. Possibly arson."

"Shit!" growled Meryck. "I knew she was trouble the moment I clapped eyes on her!"

A shout interrupted his tirade. Another police officer hurried towards Johnson, holding discs aloft.

"Sir," he said, "we pulled the surveillance. Bit dark but we found some footage worth looking at," and he indicated the lab.

"At last, something concrete!" growled Meryck, fingering the cigarette packet in his coat pocket longingly.

The footage was dire. They were crammed into the small back office in the lab, Meryck, Johnson, the officer with the discs and two others. More eyes, more information, he'd said and Johnson had rounded up two more to join them. They were looking at the footage from the cameras at the rear of the building. An ambulance came into view followed by a laundry van.

"Are these cameras normally so bad?" grumbled Meryck.

"Sir, I've already informed Rogers we're sending this his way the minute we're finished with it here, and to put a Top Priority on it! If anyone can do something with this, he can," whispered Johnson.

Despite the fact that it was early morning it was really hard to see anything in detail. They made out four figures entering the hospital through the main doors and then ten minutes later, a nurse and an orderly appeared with a gurney which they loaded onto the ambulance. They were joined by Crawthorne and Carney who signed off on the paperwork and joined Tullie in the back: then the siren was sounded and they set off northwards. On another camera they saw two men exit from the rear with a laundry cage which they placed in the back of a Laundry van and pull away northwards too.

"Ten minutes," whistled Johnson as they saw the vehicles pull away again, "and they knew where the bloody cameras were too! Maybe Rogers can at least tell us whether they were male or female! Great starting point! Turning out to be one helluva day!"

Absent mindedly, he continued to look at the screen, his mind racing with possibilities. These were professionals; he had no doubt about that. He knew the modus operandi like the back of his hand. But what ops crew? That was the million dollar question! Drawing his phone out of his pocket he rose to leave the room.

59

"Stop the tape!" shouted Johnson, excitement filling his voice. He'd spotted something.

"No! Not there! Back it up a bit!"

Meryck turned cancelling the call. They watched the bike leave the car park screeching round the corner to take the west exit. It should be possible to get a licence plate ID from that angle.

"Get that to the lab straight away!" Meryck instructed, turning to Johnson. "I want that ID asap!"

"I want to know who he is yesterday!"

CHAPTER 8

It was Thursday and Jake was still mulling over Tullie's birthday present. Each year, since the day they found her, had been the same. When was the right time to let her have the jewellery? When was the right time to tell her? No matter how long he searched or where he'd looked he had found no information on them at all; not a single whiff that might bring him closer to her real identity. He'd decided not to ask Jane's help. She would be real mad at him for keeping these from her all these years. But how to do break the news to Tullie? He knew this was the year but he felt such a failure for not manning up and doing it earlier, and for not having anything to offer by way of explanation. He knew he had to find a way. He was getting no younger and his battle wounds, those on the inside as well as on the outside, bothered him more and more. Anjie knew. He carried the same scars. But his had caught up with him finally. He didn't have the luxury of waiting another year.

He took the jewellery pieces from their hiding place behind the bookcase in his study and carrying them reverently to the table, he slowly opened the case. The two items lay snuggled in its cosy interior and he reached in gently and held them across the palm of his hand so the sun could fall across them, the way it had the day he first found them tucked into her little bundle of clothes as he followed his daughter down the mountain with their precious bundle. Lifting them to his nose he swore he could still smell the scent of baby off them. They felt so light in his big hands, the very way she felt too, he remembered, all those years ago. Getting up from the table he left the pieces to one side and took up the case to look at it carefully. A good choice, he thought, for such cargo as these. But he needed an extra element for her; she loved puzzles and he wanted this to be a challenge for her to solve. He walked around from kitchen to study and back, pulling at his thin beard, until his eyes fell on the rose oils. That would do the trick, he thought. He took the box outside to the porch and sprinkled it liberally with the oil leaving it to dry in the morning sun. Relieved he had finally made the decision and acted on it he made another choice. He looked at his watch. Eleven, it read. Time to have a shower and shave, he decided; the box should be dry by then and he'd head down to BB's, have some lunch and leave the present there for her as if it came by post.

At first, BB didn't recognise the new Jake that marched purposefully into the diner.

"Hey man, cool ponytail!" said BB loudly, coming out from behind the counter and slapping Jake on the shoulder, "and face like a baby's bottom to boot!"

"'Twas time," drawled Jake, running a large hand over his bare jaw line, "I was turning into a mountain troll with that growth!"

They laughed together, old companions of many years, and sat down together to eat. As usual the conversation wound its way around to Tullie.

"I have run out of options, BB. This is the year," said Jake directly, twirling his drink anxiously.

BB nodded but said nothing, reading the signs accurately, and they drank in companionable silence for several minutes. A man had to make up his own mind.

"How you going to do it?" he asked, his curiosity finally winning out. They'd been through this many, many times before: Jake, Anjie and him.

Jake withdrew the box from the bag he was carrying and the faint smell of rose filled the air. It was perfect! Looking around to make sure no one was watching he sprung open the top and they both looked at the priceless objects within.

"She'll love these, whatever," said BB, feeling the troubles of the world on his shoulders. He loved Tullie. He didn't want her hurt, but hurt she would be, and confused, he knew, and angry. But you cannot run away from whom you are forever, he sighed. The past has very long fingers.

"It has to be now?" he asked, knowingly.

Rummaging in his bag again, Jake nodded twice. He had made up his mind; he wouldn't change it again. As BB watched, he withdrew a small faded envelope and a new large padded package. Without further explanation he put the box and the faded envelope into the package, sealed it and handed it to BB.

BB saw that Tullie's name was on the outside.

"Oh no," he said, waving his hands in front of Jake, "no man, this is your baby! All yours! And Jane's!"

"I'm not asking you to explain anything to her," Jake stated. "Just let her have the package on her way through here Saturday, as if it arrived by post, and I'll take it from there. You know how much she likes having a puzzle to solve."

"And BB," he asserted, "Jane doesn't know anything about these."

"Nor the other," he finished so quietly BB had to strain to hear.

His eyes on stalks at this new piece of information, BB looked at his oldest and most trusted friend in the whole world and knew he couldn't deny his request. Without a word he took the package from Jake and went to put it in the safe. When he got back, Jake was gone.

Reaching home, Jake strode purposefully up the mountain. Today he needed its solace more than ever and the lake drew his melancholy gaze, its deep velvet reflecting the bountiful heather and building clouds. A storm is coming, he thought wryly as he sucked on the unlit butt of his cigar, settling himself into his favourite lookout spot effortlessly. To the left a kestrel was hovering above its hapless prey. He sat intrigued, fixed on the moment, waiting with bated breath for the swoop. He didn't have to wait long. This time the bird went away hungry though. Something had disturbed the prey. Reaching for his binoculars he trained them on the area. At first he could see nothing; then he spotted a low movement in the wild furze. Following it eagerly he saw it was heading directly for his position. He calmed his breathing and stilled his body. Still it came. Still he couldn't see what it was.

Jake held his breath. Whatever it was had stopped feet away. He felt a tickle of apprehension in the pit of his stomach and then it was gone. Slowly he let the binoculars slip from his hands and reached in his belt for his knife. As the seconds ticked by, beads of sweat began to gather on his brow and make their way down his face unheeded. Then Jake watched in awe as the giant dog moved into vision, head bowed in submission, tail curled beneath him. Standing as tall as a pony, his mottled brown body bulged with muscles. Time stood still! Then inch by inch the massive head rose to observe him closely, and it was then Jake saw his eyes. They were the colour of deep amethyst, serene and intelligent. Instinctively he rose, backing away from the creature slowly, the knife held out in front of him, to put as much distance as he could between them. But he had moved too far away to the right and the ground vanished from beneath his feet, and he fell backwards down the mountain with a startled oath.

CHAPTER 9

Disheartened, Guidrius moved along the open road towards Traveller's Mountain. He was tired, bone tired. And weary beyond belief. The last and final search had been a dead-end too. There was no place else to go! He began to think about what he'd do if he'd never find her and the thinking wasn't pleasant. Grim alternatives pushed through his consciousness; not one brought any hope or joy. He had to find her! The moment he realised he had lost her was imprinted on his memory like a burning fire that no water could quench. They had come through hell to get here, escaping narrowly with their lives. She was so small, and all would have been ok if she hadn't cried, but all babies cry. The sound had reached Man-X and he had followed them through at the last second and he had fought to protect her. Their battle took them down the mountain away from where he had hidden her. As if she knew what was at stake she became quiet, so quiet.

Programmed to kill, standing nearly seven feet high, Man-x was awesome in battle with lightening fast reflexes and an arsenal of weapons. Trained to protect, and his equal in height and strength, Guidrius was fast and deadly but it was a battle of uncertain outcome. These Halfers didn't give up, bred to kill like beasts, but beasts with extras. They knew nothing of defeat or victory, love or hate, justice or injustice, just orders to be accomplished. Guidrius was constrained by his loyalty and love; he couldn't leave her alone in this world but he had to get rid of Man-x or they would never be safe. The only way was to outwit these things; they were more action than strategy and here Guidrius had the upper hand. Man-x came at him straight; he stood between him and his target so represented a hostile that had to be taken out. Flames of cold fire and compressed energy sparkled between them as they clashed but stealthily Guidrius led him further and further away from her, taking blow after blow in the process, egging him on, drawing him to the edge of the cliff.

Finally, they joined together in close fatal combat on the edge, rocks breaking and crumbling beneath their feet and spinning lazily into the depths below. There was no sophistication left in the fight now; they each had the other's measure and time was running out. The veins on Guidrius's arms stood out like silver and purple vines, twirling and twisting as he strained to avoid the deadly hands of Man-x who was pressing forward, ever forward with no concern for his own mortality; he was bred for this moment only. They were nearly there, he saw. Just one last lunge and they would both go over. Coldly, patiently, Man-x drove forward, all thoughts subservient to the prime order to kill his enemy. Guidrius felt Man-x rip his side open as he grabbed for him and together, protector and killer, they tipped off the mountain side and after a few weightless seconds plunged into the cold water below.

It was a calculated move and it worked. Man-x's enhanced circuitry blew instantly, and as he sank beneath the waters, he resumed human form. Gasping for breath in the coloured water, Guidrius watched him slip away and breathed a huge sigh of relief. It had worked. But it had taken its toll; he was bleeding out, his sticky blood squirming around him like oil in water. He watched, fascinated, for some moments willing the healing to start but it was slow in coming and he could feel himself slip away. In desperation he looked around for a current that would take him back to her, and pointing his feet in the direction of the nearest shore, he lay back and let the mild current take him in as he faded into unconsciousness.

He didn't know how long he lay there and when he tried to rise he felt weak, very weak. Looking up at the cliff above him he offered an invocation of protection for the cosseted baby and dragged himself across the shingle to lie exhausted in the protection of the grasses. He needed more time. In the growing darkness he looked out from his slight vantage point above the lake and searched for Man-x but he was nowhere to be seen. Resting his head on his arm, he exposed the scarred flesh of his side to the elements and slept as healing drew its cloak across his battered and bruised body and night descended.

It was well past midday when the heat of the sun roused him. He stretched gingerly and patted his body carefully. He was ok. It took him seconds to spy out the best route back up the mountain; he was nearer than he expected, and with his energy renewed he made quick work of climbing back up to her. But when he got there, she was gone! Frantically he searched around the area in ever widening circles, panic mounting higher with each completed turn. On the deserted mountain there was not one single piece of evidence to suggest what direction she had been taken or by whom. In frustration and pain, he reached back his head and howled transmuting into his primeval form, a massive dog standing as high as a pony, hair sleek and mottled in colour, ears laid back and eyes the colour of amethysts. His massive paws grabbed the ground in huge chunks as he howled again and again in deep despair but it didn't bring her back or point out where he should travel to find her. So right there he made a pact with himself: he'd hold this form until he found her or stay like this forever. Nose down, he rooted for her scent and he found it, a faint shimmer on the breeze and he bounded in delight. He had a start! But his start had not found her, he sighed deeply. He had travelled as far as man can go; widening his search with each passing year until he had been everywhere and anywhere but with no sign of her, and now twenty-five years later he was back, his head hanging down to his paws in dejection. There was nowhere else to go. He had lost her forever. And there was now no way back. He had failed her. He had failed all of them. He whimpered, letting himself go at last, tears dripping from his eyes, spattering the ground as he limped onwards and upwards.

And then, unbelievably, back right where it started, when he had totally given up, when his tears had drained him dry, he got the scent again; faint, very faint on the breeze, close to where he had lost her. Within seconds his entire world shrunk to encompass the small area. His heart beat rapidly in his breast and his tired body hugged the ground as he approached. He was so engrossed in his search that he hadn't noticed the rabbit until it thumped and fled and the kestrel overhead called out in frustration at missing its meal. He swore to himself quietly. He had been clumsy. He had been distracted. But who wouldn't, in his position, he allowed himself. He sent out a greeting but was surprised when it bounced back unanswered. He crawled forward, inch by inch, slowly and stealthily until he was directly in front of her position, then he stopped and tested the air. He sensed anxiety and caution, but he was so overwhelmed that he had found her he didn't stop to think what he might look like to her now, battered and worn and scruffy; he didn't stop to change back! Slowly, with head bowed, he rose to greet her and found himself looking at Jake who was looking back at him, mouth open in astonishment. He started to speak and reach out in greeting but it was his huge paw that reached for the man and his voice came out as a growl. He watched in amazement as the man stepped away from him and fell off the mountain.

Without hesitation, Guidrius leapt after him.

CHAPTER 10

The crash of thunder woke Jake from his slumber and he couldn't remember at first where he was. His head throbbed painfully and he felt like he'd run a couple of marathons back to back! The rain beat relentlessly against the window as he felt his way around the dark room. Gingerly he made his way to the kitchen and it took every bit of energy he possessed to brew some fresh coffee but it was worth the effort. Gulping eagerly, he opened the back porch door. The rain fell in sheets, bearing in from the west, shrouding the mountain from view. He had built his porch for the very shelter it now provided, and he never lost his love of standing there dry and unharmed while the storm raged only feet away from him. Storms energised him, proffering an insight at power beyond his personal capabilities. He could feel his energy returning as the coffee hit home. But something bothered him, niggled away incessantly at the back of his mind. Shaking his head, he stepped outside to his rocking chair and stopped dead in his tracks. Further down the porch sat Guidrius examining his hands in detail. He had needed all the time the man slept to reform into human shape. The memory was faint but the experience of ages helped to bring about the transformation. He felt - weak – in comparison to the massive dog.

Something about this man bothered Jake but he couldn't put his finger on it. How long he stood there staring he couldn't remember later. The man said nothing either just stared back from the shelter of the porch. Then drawing his hand across his eyes, Jake reached out and pulled the rocker forwards and turning it around he sat and faced Guidrius. Again, they regarded each other for what seemed like an eternity, each trying to probe the depths of the other without words. Jake felt that tickle of apprehension again.

Guidrius knew it wasn't working. He would have to talk this thing through. He had so many questions and this man was the first link he had found to her. But it was the man who spoke first.

"That's a bad storm," he nodded to the mountain. "I'm glad you made it down here to safety. You're welcome to stay for the duration."

Guidrius started to speak but no words emerged. It had been a long time, too long, he mused wryly. Clearing his throat he tried again.

"Thank you," he said, without moving. His voice came out gruffly and he coughed again.

"Are you ok? That was quite a fall you took up there," he added.

"I think so," said Jake, and tapped around his body until he came to his head. A decent bump had formed on his forehead but apart from that he felt good. Memories began to pour back little by little. He began to shake.

"Did you see the animal," he asked hoarsely, "the huge dog?"

Guidrius shook his head.

"Didn't see anything," he lied. "Just heard you call out from where I was walking. Came to help as fast as I could."

"What happened?" asked Jake. "How did you get me back here?"

"You don't remember?" asked Guidrius.

Jake shook his head tentatively, pulling at his ponytail gently.

"Not a darn thing," he grinned. "But here am I, missing

my manners!"

Rising he approached Guidrius and held out his hand.

"I'm Jake," he said.

"Guidrius," replied the stranger as he grasped Jake's hand.

"Fancy something to eat? A coffee perhaps or something stronger?" he asked and he moved more steadily now back into the kitchen beckoning Guidrius to follow him.

Guidrius stood in the shadows, testing the gathering strength in his limbs. He wondered how long he could pull this off for, how long before Jake became suspicions. He wondered how he really looked after all this time. The camouflage would work, as long as his strength would last anyhow. He had no plan; that was the plan! It had all happened so quickly! He had saved Jake, healed him when he got him back home but he would not have any memory of that yet. He'd left the harmless bump on his forehead to avert suspicion and it had worked. His stomach growled and he realised how hungry he was. Shielding his eyes from the light, he followed Jake inside.

As Jake moved about the kitchen he could feel something gnawing away at the back of his mind but the memories were elusive. He left them there, turning in circles, searching for answers he had no questions to yet. Long experience had taught him to trust his instincts and there was something here he just didn't get. In the living room Guidrius found himself a soft chair and sank deeply into its folds. His long legs stretched way out in front of him and a large pale hand tapped each arm noiselessly. The comfort was bliss to his tired frame and he watched Jake in the kitchen through sleepy eyes. Stirring to stay awake he gaze was drawn once more to the photos on the wall.

Coming into the room, Jake found Guidrius relaxed and

looking about him inquisitively.

"Family?" he asked, gesturing to the photos.

Jake nodded as he handed him a strong black coffee and some biscuits.

"Three generations of Bell's," he replied proudly, "my daughter, grandaughter, and a much younger me."

Guidrius nodded.

"Do you have any family?" asked Jake, and was immediately sorry for asking as his guest's face registered unbearable pain for a millisecond and then it was gone. It took some time for him to reply.

"A daughter," he said, "lost her when she was a baby. I still can't come to terms with that."

The two men, from very different worlds, sipped their coffee in silence. What was there to say? Everybody harbours personal tragedy and Jake was pleased and surprised this stranger had shared his with him. He knew from experience that talking about it helps the healing process and it looked like this man had healing to do.

From time to time as he prepared dinner Jake looked over at Guidrius but he was still looking at the photos, a deep longing etched on his face and not for the first time that evening, Jake felt pity for him. His distress and loss were obvious and he didn't like to see the man in such deep pain: he had seen enough loss in his time. He noted his odd clothing and worn shoes, not really shoes to go hiking in but it was summer and possible not to wear any shoes at all on the mountain. He could do with a shave and haircut too, thought Jake, rubbing his still smooth chin. And the smell, well, he couldn't quite identify that and he was puzzled. Then all of a sudden it hit him! It's dog! But no ordinary dog! The smell was still fresh in his memory; imprinted for all time. Startled he raced to the door and clicked it locked.

Rushing in to warn Guidrius he found him fast asleep curled up on the chair. Standing back, he drew a hand through his hair wincing as he accidently brushed the bump on his forehead. Guidrius shot awake with a start and as he pushed his head forward into the light Jake saw his eyes for the first time; eyes the colour of amethysts, eyes the same colour as the huge dog's. This was the second time today he had dropped his guard and looking at Jake he saw the realisation dawning in his eyes and the memories come racing back. He was losing his touch around this man!

Silence hung like thunder between them. Guidrius hoped they could find an amicable outcome. He realised he needed this man on his side and held out his hands, palms up, in a gesture of trust and sank back into the chair. He was done with running and searching whatever the immediate outcome. He just didn't have the energy to spar and he sensed a lack of aggression in Jake anyway. There was curiosity and fear but no deadly intent. This was a man who knew how to read others; a man who could take care of himself.

"So," he said softly, "you remember."

Jake was rooted to the spot, his emotions in tumult, indecision playing on his countenance, disbelief shining from his eyes. This stuff in his head seemed utter nonsense. Yet he nodded and the man was relieved. Thrusting his hands deep in his pockets, he saw Guidrius following his every move keenly. But Jake could see no threat in him. But it just didn't make sense! Or did it?

"Look, man," he said, "this sounds a bit crazy coming out like this, but are you. . ."

He just couldn't make himself say it. It sounded too nonsensical. Scratching his forehead and again catching the bump, he winced anew.

Warily, Guidrius watched him struggle.

Clearing his throat noisily, Jake began again, leaning a little forward to catch another glimpse of those eyes, just to be sure.

"You saved me, man!" he said. "I'd be a goner if it weren't for you!"

In reply, Guidrius just waved his hand across his face wearily. He was coming unstuck in this form and needed to let go; it was draining his energy heavily and he needed time to recover. Taking a chance, he said tiredly,

"Do you mind, please," and indicated to Jake to move back a little, maybe even sit down.

Jake pulled a chair from the table to one side and sat down heavily. He had a feeling about what was going to happen and he could sense the familiar churning in the pit of his stomach but this wasn't war, it was something entirely different, and he welcomed the fear. Fear keeps a man alive, he told himself, as he waited.

Guidrius looked deeply into Jake's mind and knew he could trust this man who had protected her as his own.

"I need to explain what will happen so you won't be afraid of me," he said calmly.

Jake nodded slowly and Guidrius continued

"The form you now see is a camouflage, it's not the real me," he continued without rising from the chair. "It's a projection of what you think an odd hobo on the mountain might look like. This protects who I really am but it takes energy to sustain and my reserves are low. I need some decent sleep to renew myself after healing you."

"When I let go this image," he continued, peering closely at Jake, "you will be the very first person to have seen me in my true form in twenty-five years."

Jake could feel cold chills run up and down his body at these revelations and he couldn't repress the shudder that wracked his body. He thought he knew all there was to know about camouflage! But this was something entirely different! His mind was doing double-time and he found he was holding onto the chair with a death grasp. Guidrius sighed. He was really freaking this guy out!

"Are you ok if I continue?" he asked calmly, steeling himself.

This time it took Jake longer to reply then to Guidrius's relief he nodded twice. He realised he really did want to see what this man looked like for real. Guidrius hesitated for only a millisecond then changed.

The transition was close enough to be instantaneous and suddenly a very tall, scraggly stranger was sitting in front of Jake. His faded red hair bunched around his shoulders and his beard was flecked and dirty. His worn and dirty clothes hung off him in tatters and his bare feet stank. But his green eyes were clear, and with a tremendous jolt, Jake made the connection however unlikely to Tullie but brushed it away as quickly as it came. He whistled shrilly.

"Whew!" he spoke through his teeth, "that's incredible, man. But I was expecting something different, you know."

Guidrius did know, and he made one other quick change, and before Jake sat the huge dog, his form spilling over the edges of the seat. Then he changed again and flopped exhaustedly on the chair. Jake remained rooted to the spot, unable to breathe. Guidrius watched him intently through hooded eyes. The oven timer screamed into the deep silence and both men jumped.

"You have time to shower before dinner if you want," Jake heard his voice offering from a long distance off and Guidrius nodded gratefully.

While Guidrius showered, Jake opened the windows and doors and sprayed air freshener around the place to dispel the smell of dog and unwashed body. He tried unsuccessfully to understand the circumstances that led to such lack of hygiene, but he was still shaking his head to dislodge the fairy tale when Guidrius emerged wearing some of Jake's old clothes he had left out for him. He had trimmed his beard and his long hair was tied in a knot pulling it back from his face and revealing more of his features. He moved with ease, almost loped, Jake thought, across the floor to look again, more closely this time, at the family photos. He reached up to touch Tullie and Jake saw his ring and his heart skipped painfully. Here was the answer he had been searching for all these years and now that he had it within his grasp he wished he had never sought it in the first place for he realised that the possibility of losing Tullie was more real than he had ever imagined. But he knew she would want to know the truth, however bizarre that might be!

"Let's talk over dinner, Guidrius," he said quietly, moving back to the kitchen to plate up.

Watching Jake leave, Guidrius bent himself gingerly into the chair he had so recently vacated, stretching his long arms comfortably along its smooth covers. The ring on his finger twinkled in the artificial lights. Jake couldn't take his eyes off it as he called Guidrius to eat. But Guidrius was fast asleep, his head rested forward on his gently rising and falling chest. Without thinking Jake pulled his phone from his pocket and snapped a picture of the ring. Here was proof and he wanted it recorded for posterity. Guidrius slept on, undisturbed.

Leaving the slumbering figure to his rest, he quietly made his way upstairs. A thorough search of the stinking discarded clothes revealed nothing except the evidence of the years of slumming he had endured. Guidrius had cleaned up after himself thoroughly; apart from the clothes there was nothing to suggest he was even there. These Jake carried downstairs and burned outside. Now there was absolutely no trace of the man-dog apart from the picture on his phone and the memory etched deep into his head. He grimaced, heading for the barn. He had some planning to do but first he needed to clear his head.

CHAPTER 11

Jake's body burned as he forced himself past his endurance level time and again in a punishing workout. Sweat poured from his body and he was breathing heavily. One minute break then he started all over again. Finally, when his body could take it no more and his mind was clear, he stood in the shower and let the water wash away the salty sweat and tears. Dressing in fresh sweats he moved further underground, into the heart of the secluded facility. Time slowed as he went through his weapons routine and finally satisfied he selected what he wanted to bring with him and came up to the surface. He was surprised to see it was still dark and he looked at his watch to see it was only three am. Avoiding the main house, he let himself into Anjie's kitchen and made fresh coffee. Taking it back to the veranda he stood looking in at the sleeping Guidrius and tried to make sense of what the future might hold.

As daylight peeked around the mountain, he had only the beginnings of a plan but it was a start. His priority was to get this man away from here, to move the danger away from Tullie. He needed intel but there was nowhere to get it apart from asking the very person he was unsure about! He felt better with the loaded gun at his back and the knife in his ankle sheath but deep down he knew he wouldn't use these against this man but it still felt right to pack. Too many years in the field to go unprepared into the unknown, he acknowledged wanly, moving quietly into the kitchen to begin breakfast. He wanted to be away before Anjie returned. This was his mission, and until he knew more, he would carry the load alone.

Guidrius woke up to the delicious aroma of cooking bacon and the splattering of eggs frying in the pan. He was starving. Instantly alert, he remembered everything that had happened and was grateful for the undisturbed night's sleep. Stretching silently, he unravelled himself from the chair and padded to the kitchen.

"Ah, you're awake," said Jake, and nodded to the table.

The silence at the breakfast table was punctured by the chirping birds outside as they swooped and called to each other. The light rays of the sun penetrated here and painted generous shapes of gold on the table top, glinting off the ring. The bloody ring! Guidrius could feel Jake's eyes following the sunshine.

"You've seen one like this then?" he asked quietly, holding up his hand for Jake to see more clearly.

Jake jumped. He had been lost again in reverie and although the interruption was unexpected, it was direct, an approach he himself would use. He nodded.

"Did you find anything else with it?" Guidrius asked.

Jake nodded, slowly finishing the last of his breakfast, playing for time. Then to his surprise Guidrius took him exactly where he wanted to go!

"Can you take me back there, please?" he whispered, and the father in Jake knew exactly what he meant.

Both men worked in tandem clearing away the breakfast evidence. He didn't want to leave any trace either, Jake noted darkly. Moving to the hallway he found a pair of boots that fitted Guidrius, a pair BB had left behind some time ago. As Guidrius sat to put them on Jake saw that he was roughly the same height as BB too but here all other similarities finished. Lifting the rucksack off the kitchen table, Jake changed his mind and mailed the picture to Anjie and BB as he followed Guidrius out the door.

In the trek up the mountain both men were quiet, locked

away in their own personal worlds that had started to overlap less than twenty-four hours ago. In Jake's mind a new world of inverse proportions was emerging: Guidrius's happiness at finding Tullie again was matched in equal measure to his own dismay. By nine am they had reached the half-way point and they stopped for water. Jake handed Guidrius a bottle from his rucksack which he accepted gratefully and had to force himself to drink it properly and not lap it like he had been doing for decades. Noticing his predicament, Jake turned away to survey the land below to give him time to recover. In a short while they would turn north-east into the full glare of the sun and the reflection off Bear's Lake. Finishing his drink, he reached into his bag for his sunglasses pulling out a wrap-around pair for Guidrius who accepted gratefully. His green eyes were much more sensitive to the light and while he could shield them consciously, he was still not completely restored and wanted to conserve his energy for what lay ahead.

It was close to eleven am when they came to the place where Tullie had been found. No visible trace remained of the recess where Guidrius had hidden her but he reached deep into the earth and felt satisfied that this was the place. Jake watched him uneasily. He wasn't sure what would happen next but he felt the questions coming before he heard them.

"Tell me," said Guidrius, "who else was here that day? I can sense another presence."

"My daughter, Jane," replied Jake, surprised at the direction this was going.

"Why did you take her?" he asked in anguish, rounding on Jake suddenly. "Why didn't you leave her for me?"

Jake rounded back on him in fury.

"Leave her for you!" he shouted. "You weren't here, remember! You abandoned her! You were nowhere to be

80

seen!"

Sparks began to fly in the air but Jake was fearless in his defence of Tullie.

"We searched!" he roared. "Goddammit! We searched and searched and searched but we found no one! Nobody! You hear! You weren't to be found!!"

"That beautiful baby," he was spluttering now, years of anger pouring out, "that beautiful baby was left alone and unprotected! She was hungry and wet. Where the hell were you?"

He moved away from Guidrius, his fists balled tightly at his side, to stop himself laying into the man. But he wasn't finished. Swinging back, he continued his tirade.

"Where were you? Well, let me tell you! You were no-where to be bloody found! And now you come crawling back to her thinking that by flashing your bloody ring, like the one I just gave her for her birthday, that all will be ok. Well, let's get one thing straight! Tullie is my grandaughter and there's nothing you can bloody do about it!"

Fizzing, his body rigid with anger, he stomped away from Guidrius who was just standing there looking at him, emotionless.

"The ring?" Guidrius called after him. "You gave her the ring?"

Jake's years of training registered the fear in Guidrius's voice and it was enough to stop him in his tracks and he struggled to get a grip on his emotions.

"The ring?" Guidrius asked again, coming closer to him. "When did you give it to her?" he probed urgently.

Turning to face him, Jake was struck by the blind panic he saw. An icy premonition encased his body.

"I left it for her birthday, which is tomorrow," he answered truthfully, his voice dropping ominously. He wasn't used to having his decisions challenged. Then when Guidrius said nothing, he put his hand tentatively on the other man's arm for the first time.

"Is there a problem, Guidrius?" he demanded roughly.

Shaking off human contact, Guidrius stomped away from Jake. Time was closing in on them faster than he had expected. The second she put on that ring she was in danger. And he hadn't been able to prepare her. His blood chilled and he rounded on Jake.

"Did you give her anything else, man?" he demanded, grabbing Jake by the arm and leaning close to his face.

"The necklace," Jake replied evenly, eyeballing him coldly. "I gave her the necklace but it is unlikely that she'll wear it. She cannot stand anything around her neck."

Guidrius dropped his arms and sat down heavily on the ground. Thank the Light that was all he had given her. Raising his eyes to Jake, he spoke quickly,

"What else did you find with her?

Jake sat down warily, arms distance away from Guidrius.

"Look, man," he said evenly, returning Guidrius's stare openly, "I don't understand what's going on here but it has to do with someone I love very much, and I think you do too."

Guidrius's nod was imperceptible to the untrained eye.

"So," Jake challenged now, "if I tell you what I found and what I did with it, will you tell me what the hell is going on?"

Again, that funny feeling of time standing still hit Jake as he sat there looking at Guidrius in the spot where he had found Tullie and where Guidrius had left her. At the same time they held out their hand to each other and said in tandem, "Deal!"

For better or worse, they were in this together, for Tullie's sake.

CHAPTER 12

Jane Bell hurried home. One hour was all she had. Quickly she retrieved the plain box from the attic that held Tullie's things. She piled clothes and supplies into a bag in the back of the Buick, dropping her purse on the kitchen counter. She wouldn't need that where she was going. That part was easy. The next was not. She could feel the tears welling up in her eyes as she gathered precious photographs and added them to the pile. Jake wouldn't like it but she was beyond worrying about that now. Choking back her tears, she fled down into the basement and collected the fuel. Twenty minutes. She had plenty of time. She wandered the rooms slowly, liberally sprinkling each, tears flowing unhindered down her cheeks. She was standing in the middle of the living room when the door opened behind her.

"It's time," he said.

She nodded and followed him outside. He disappeared around the side of the house as she retrieved her bag from the Buick and got into the waiting van. All was quiet. It was still early. Nothing much happened here on a Saturday morning, she mused. In the shadows she saw a small flash as he lit the fuse. He got back in the van and they drove away slowly, in silence.

She sat as far back in the front seat of the van as she could and stared ahead not wanting to see any more than was necessary of the destruction of her old life. She opened her mouth to pummel him with questions but he shook his head and she let the silence stretch between them. Gulping down her pain, she fixed her sunglasses on her nose as the tears silently squeezed past her tightly shut eyes.

Big Bob drove languidly around the town making sure he turned up on several CCTV cameras. Pest Control was a legitimate part of his business; that and Rosa's. Nobody would think his routine strange even if they noted it. Finally, satisfied he had done enough, he parked the van outside his old warehouse and they transferred to his car, and made for Traveller's Mountain. He had a lot of explaining to do on the way. For once, Jane listened without comment.

*****

Without warning the ambulance slewed to the left, turning off the road, the pace reducing to a crawl. They could hear the scrape of trees and shrubs against its sides and pebbles rattling against its chassis. Within minutes it came to a halt and the back door opened to reveal the wilderness they had driven into. Anjie motioned Carney out and he went stiffly from being cooped up so long. They were only metres from a sheer cliff drop and he began to sweat in earnest. So this was it then! But Anjie prodded him around the side where he saw, with enormous relief, a mobile trailer parked to the side of the road.

"We take this from here on," said Anjie. "Do as you are told and you'll both be ok. But one word from me and your friend . . ." and he drew a finger menacingly across his throat.

Shaking, Carney nodded. Anjie watched him closely. He would do as he was told.

"Make it ready for her," he instructed, standing back to let him go.

There was a lot of space inside the trailer and in

record time Carney had organised a bed for Tullie, then both men helped him move her and secure her in place. The captives were allowed a toilet break and some snacks before they were arranged as before and were ready to leave. Anjie stood at the door covering them with his gun while the driver went back to the ambulance. They could hear the crunch of the wheels on the rocky ground, then an awful scraping as it cleared the cliff, followed by a series of bangs and one last massive explosion. Anjie turned to drive this time as Cal stepped into the back to take up guard duty.

They made their way languidly down the trail, a family trailer on holiday, taking in the sights. The sun was directly in their eyes as they approached Matheson from the east and they pulled in at a truck stop for a break. Tullie hadn't moved throughout the whole ordeal and Carney was worried about her.

"Keep her topped up," warned Anjie, as he swapped with Cal. "This is no time for heroics."

Reluctantly, Carney reached forward and added more sedative to her drip. Her regular breathing didn't alter, she didn't twitch but somehow he knew she was aware of her surroundings; Anjie's voice had soothed her somehow.

Time crawled by as they waited for full darkness, then they moved back on the road, Cal driving this time. Carney could hear when they made town but Myra was asleep at this stage. He envied her! His eyes were burning from looking at Tullie's drip, fear keeping him on a precipitous edge between the surreal and real; between her life and death, until both blurred and he was her and she was him, her pain was his pain and his fear was hers. Anjie recognised the signals but he was confident Carney would make it. The rest of the team would be there by now and they would take over soon. They could all do with a break! Calmly Cal drove them up the old road, past Rosa's and onto the mountain. Rolling down the window he heard the first owl sounds as they broached the perimeter of Jake's place, and then a huge portion of wooded fence slipped away and they were in the tunnel, the world shut out behind them. He breathed a sigh of relief. Carney could sense the change of surface and Cal slowed down, and then stopped. Figures approached and the door was thrown open and he and Myra blindfolded, were roughly handled out of the van. They were moved forward and he felt the prick of a needle in his arm and blackness claimed him.

CHAPTER 13

Myra's call troubled Matt. It was not unusual to have a second opinion especially if faulty equipment was suspected. But they went back a long way and he was able to read her better than most. After all, she was his first and only babysitter; grandad would not let anyone else into their home. He dialled his boss and called off sick for the rest of the day. Making his way home through the early morning traffic was easy and within minutes of Myra's call he was unearthing the locked box his grandad had left him from underneath the debris in his living room. No one could say Matt was a tidy person but he knew exactly where everything was. All he needed now was the code. He didn't have long to wait. Myra's text sounded like thunder in the silence of his room. Grabbing his kit he strode out of the apartment.

The hospital car park was eerily quiet this early in the morning as he parked his bike in the trees beside the West Exit below Myra's office window. He hadn't opened the box yet. He hoped Myra was being over dramatic, that this was not for real. But he waited patiently, eyes fixed on the window above. That was another thing he could do really well in addition to being the best scientist in the country; young Matt could wait forever. And he trusted Myra implicitly. And he had a great vantage point to see the entire car park manoeuvrings. He didn't have long to wait. An ambulance drove around to the front door and some men got out and went inside, white coats flapping in their wake. A laundry van drove slowly in and went around to the back exit. All routine and normal, he noted. Then he spotted Myra at the window. Hurrying forward he gathered the package safely into his arms and retreated to the shadow of the trees to watch again.

Five minutes passed and he reached for his phone, ready to take Myra's call when she would inform him that all was ok. Six minutes passed, then seven, and he began to worry. It was dead on ten minutes after the ambulance arrived that he saw them emerge. Something was definitely wrong. He was sure of it now. He could make out Carney and Myra but he didn't recognise the other two. He guessed the patient was Tullie. But he waited still. Then she gave the signal and his heart galloped out of his chest in a potent mixture of fear, dread and excitement. Pulling back further into the trees, he let the two vehicles pass within a hair's breadth of him heading eastward. Then he got on his bike and shot westward at breakneck speed. He had to know what was in that box and he knew just the place where he wouldn't be disturbed.

An hour later he was pulling into the small abandoned marina at the base of Bear's Lake. Parking his bike in the trees behind the dilapidated hut that had once served fishing permits, coco cola and ice cream, he walked for half a mile to the old boat. It looked pretty tattered on the outside but he kept it well maintained and stocked. He liked it that way, less likely to be vandalised. Smiling to himself, satisfied it had not been disturbed since his last visit, he went below and stashed his things in the starboard bedroom, then cast off. Brave Betty coughed into life and he caught a whiff of what he thought was possibly sewage from the bilge. He made a mental note to clean that as soon as possible as he chugged forward happily on the smooth waters heading west towards Traveller's Mountain. He reached behind the wheel and checked the radio was off. Swiftly, reaching into his pocket for his phone, he thumbed a quick text before switching it off: he was incommunicado. Swishing calmly forward on the water soothed his nerves and he let the calm descend without interruption as he ploughed forward. There was not a soul to be seen in any direction he looked; just wilderness, water, and

Traveller's Mountain up ahead looming up from the lake at the other end. The turquoise water glinted with silver stars that threatened to blind him and to either side the dark greens of the shadows danced with the bright greens where the sunlight caught the trees. Far above a lone plane trailed parallel white bars in its wake. All was quiet apart from the familiar and comforting creaking noises Brave Betty made as she adjusted to the thrust of water against her hull; they created a symphony with the swish of the small waves she was creating and he felt like the conductor of all he surveyed. As she took him further out in the open lake, she rose and fell slightly and as he began to rethink the events of the morning a sense of surrealism began to over take him. There was the world around his feet as he had experienced it these many years; and there was this secret conspiracy Myra had just made him party too. Slowly and reluctantly he eased Betty back and came to a calm standstill. Lowering her anchor he noticed the increased depth of the water for this time of year but he had enough chain so he was ok. Back at the wheel he reached underneath it for his binoculars and went up-deck to survey the area. Satisfied that he was alone he dragged his feet back to the bedroom and retrieved the box.

The code was one he could have guessed many, many times - 010484, his birthday, but he had given his promise that he would never open the box unless it was absolutely necessary. Matt never broke his promises. A solemn, introverted child, who preferred being with his grandad in the lab as often as he was allowed, he had never known his parents. They had been killed in an accident shortly after he was born and he had been raised by his grandad. The only female influence in his life was Myra. He was in boarding school when the lab accident happened that killed his grandad and he had never gone back to the house that he had shared with him as a boy. The government had appropriated all his lab work; they had cleaned the house of all traces of him, Myra had told him, and he stayed away, keeping the memories intact. But Brave Betty was in his mother's name and they missed that, and it became his bolt-hole. Even after he joined Myra at Matheson's and she helped him buy his apartment, he spent every moment he could spare on the water, alone. He wasn't ready to share this bit of his heart with anyone yet. Only Myra knew where he went.

Shaking himself loose from his reverie he keyed in the code and at first nothing happened. He tried it again with the same result. Frustrated, he shook it and it popped open in his face, just a cheap lock, he noted. One anyone could break if they wanted. Inside lay a folded map and a key, and underneath, hidden in the lining, a small envelope. He turned the heavy key over in his hand, slipping it into his back pocket as he gazed at the open map. He knew this place. He had memories of travelling backwards and forwards as a child here with his grandad, particularly after his parents died. His grandad never let him out of his sight. With his practiced eyes he could see the island in the distance to his right. Heavily populated with trees it had earned its name, Greenway Island. Even the waters surrounding it looked green by reflection. The map had a dot that he took to be the landing point and he memorised this easily. People believed that it was impossible to land there. Rumours abounded that it was haunted and that anyone who went there never returned but his time there was always pleasant, and although he never met anyone else, he had been aware of others talking and working with his grandad.

Leaving down the map he picked up the envelope and slowly unpicked the top. There were several sheets present and he recognised his grandad's handwriting in some of them. Carefully he smoothed them out on the floor and began to read. Two were Lab Reports and he looked at these cursorily. One was from a patient called Man-x and the other from someone called Key-a. He idly wondered why these were here as he picked up his grandad's letter and began to read.

CHAPTER 14

"My dear boy,

If you are reading this then I may well be dead and you may be all alone. For that, I am very sorry. But know this, I have loved you like my very own, and I love you still.

Matt could feel the tears stinging his eyes. He was holding a piece of paper his beloved grandad had held and he was telling him he loved him!

Since you are reading this, I need to tell you straight away that you are in grave danger. This is an IM moment. They will stop at nothing to eliminate you, as they did your parents. Are you somewhere safe, my boy? Go now to Brave Betty if you are not there already. Go east to Portrunning. Turn off your radio and throw your mobile overboard. It will have a tracking device and they will be looking for you. Do it now! Leave this down and get rid of the phone. Do not go near Greenway! You are not ready yet.

Without thinking Matt obeyed as he had always obeyed his grandad. It was the one thing he had insisted upon, training him up to respond instantly to an IM, an Instant Mission as they had called it, one that called for action immediately, disclosure later. The splash of the phone as it hit the water brought him back to reality and he quickly ducked down, raising his head slowly again to survey the shore. It was clear; nothing moved and he heaved a sigh of relief. But inside he felt he was just that little bit melodramatic and the message about his parents intensified the feeling.

What I am about to tell you is painful for me and for you. I do wish I could be there to tell you in person but this will have to do now. Make yourself comfortable; it will take a while.

You were born on Greenway Island on the 1ˢᵗ April, 1984. I was the attending physician; present also were Myra Crawthorne, and my son, Raymond. Your father was in the building but not present at the birth. He remains unaware of your existence. Raymond was unable to father children so I used sperm from your father to inseminate Elizabeth and she became pregnant with you and carried you to term. Neither Elizabeth nor Raymond knew the identity of your real father. Neither does Myra, though she suspects, I think. At that stage I was splitting my time between practicing in Matheson and researching for the government in Greenway; later I moved to the Island full time when you went away to boarding school. I hope you can forgive me in time for what I did back then. It was the cutting edge of research and I so badly wanted to help Raymond be a dad. But you need to know now the identity of your true father. He remains in the facility in Greenway and is known as Man-x. You are registered there as Key-a. I have included your records with this letter. They will tell you much more than I can write in this short space.

Matt dropped the letter and rummaged anxiously for the records. He was dumbfounded! All he could think of was that his real father was still alive, just out there beyond the trees! But his excitement turned to incredulity, followed quickly by a fierce anger, as he read the pages before him. Man-x was unidentifiable, a loner, a creature of unusual powers and passivity. A hybrid: partly human and partly something else. But what? Frantically he scanned Key-a's records. At first, he didn't recognise himself in the data present and he sat back against the side of the boat relieved. But why would his grandad make up such nonsense? Then, as he sat there, bit by bit, fragmented memories came together: he always had his check-ups on Greenway; he always used his grandad's reports for health checks; all his dental work had been done on the island.

He was in such good health he hadn't needed to visit a doctor in years. His eyes were drawn back to the blood group; both his and Man-x's read UNKNOWN. Then it hit him why Myra was so worried. Scrambling downstairs, he gently lifted the vial she had thrown down to him, along with the lab report from Matheson. The word UNKNOWN jumped out at him from the page. So did the name, Tullie Bell. Another shock went through his system! Tullie Bell had been kidnapped along with Myra and Carney. What an absolute mess this was! But he was brought back to earth by the sound of a motor boat approaching from the direction of the island. Quickly hiding the package, he raced up on deck, dropping his jacket across his grandad's papers as he went. Grabbing an empty mug he sauntered out on the deck, stretching lazily. The small boat was coming in his direction fast, straight out of Greenway, way too fast for its size, so he guessed it had been pimped. Too late, he recalled his grandad's warning to go in the other direction. As the craft neared his location it spun off to his left and made shore about a mile away in a clump of trees. Two men got out and disappeared into the wilderness without giving any indication of having seen him at all. A chill ran down his spine despite the heat of the day, a premonition, a warning, and he rushed below to gather his grandad's package with Myra's. As his head hit the water to starboard, he heard the thunk sounding from the port shore and before he could make safe distance from Brave Betty she erupted out of the water behind him with a whoosh of flames, her old timbers flaking apart like confetti and reaching towards him at increasing velocity puncturing his body with a multitude of small cuts. Brave Betty had a full tank when they set out and the fuel was now burning off around where she had stood, the water sizzling and roiling, but here and there were enough small clear pockets for Matt to surface briefly and refill his lungs. His mind was clear of everything but survival and he knew they'd be watching. It was hard to guess where he was heading exactly; his head still buzzed from the explosion. He stilled himself underwater and felt for the current. Bear's Lake was a tidal lake and the tide was taking him southwest, veering him towards the coastline where the two waited. He realised he didn't have a choice. But he also realised that they would certainly look for him on the other shore first in case he made it so maybe, just maybe, he could slip in under their very eyes and make it to safety.

*****

Meryck was in a foul mood when Johnson approached him.

"Hope you've got something useful," he growled.

"Sir," started Johnson. "We've found who owns the bike. One Matthew Raymond Ostenwalder, the senior lab technician over at Mercers. He was at work this morning but went home sick. We've got his address, Sir."

"Well, what are we waiting for," roared Meryck, jumping to his feet and heading for the door. "Let's get over there and see what this young man has to say."

"Sir," called Johnson after the fast departing figure, "I've sent a car already, Sir."

"No matter," waved Meryck. "I want to hear what this punk has to say myself!"

With Meryck driving they got there at the same time as the car and they stood around as the uniforms checked out the apartment. There was no one home but the manager let them in. The place was in an awful mess. Meryck wondered if it had been turned over before they got there but it was too random to tell. It was too early to rule anything out. There was only one photo present and Meryck whistled.

"So, our good friend here knows Myra Crawthorne! Find out who the old geezer is," he said, shoving the frame into a young police woman's hand.

"Well, that wasn't much use," growled Meryck as they made their way back to the car.

Johnson was following behind taking a call. Meryck could make out the phrase GPS so he slowed down to wait for him, keys ready in his hand.

"Well?" he asked as Johnson caught up with him.

"Got the GPS on his bike, Sir. Nothing on his phone so far. They're patching through the info to your car, Sir," he replied stepping past the waiting Meryck and reaching for the radio.

"Let's go then!" said Meryck decisively, going around to sit in the passenger seat and handing over the keys.

Acknowledging the uplink, Johnson settled himself in the driver's seat and pulled away from the kerb.

From further down the street a nondescript pick-up slowly pulled out and followed them at a distance.

CHAPTER 15

It was slow going out of Matheson and they hadn't got far when another call came over the radio about an explosion at Bear's Lake.

"That's where we're going, Sir!" exclaimed Johnson and he turned on his siren as Meryck picked up the receiver.

They arrived to a circus of activity, emergency craft on the Lake, police, ambulance and fire crew waiting by the shore and divers in the water. The fire had been put out and only bits of flotsam and jetsam were left of what was Brave Betty. Meryck and Johnson couldn't make out any body bags but they could hear the plethora of possible explanations that were floating about on the wind. The most plausible was a gas explosion. And the boat hadn't been identified yet so no one knew how many they were supposed to be looking for. But their quarry was further along on the left so Meryck and Johnson sidestepped the yellow tape and headed for the abandoned hut they could just make out among the trees. They found Matt's bike where he had hidden it round back and they radioed for the truck to take it in. They had a while to wait before it could reach them through the throng and they sauntered further along in companionable silence, Meryck indulging in his favourite habit, Johnson waving the air aside in disgust. Half a mile down the track they came to the old jetty where a fresh slick of oil adorned the water along the side. It wasn't rocket science to join the remaining dots and while they discussed the full implications of what they'd just seen, Meryck's cigarette burned down unheeded between his browned fingers. Johnson took out his phone to call in the location but Meryck halted him with a tap on his elbow and a nod into the shade. Silently they crouched down,

Johnson looking askance at Meryck who just pointed across the water. It took Johnson some time but at last he saw them; two figures surveying the action on the water. From the salvage team's perspective, they were nigh invisible but from Meryck's and Johnson's slightly off point of view they were clearly visible. Then Meryck almost knocked Johnson over with the punch to his arm!

"Look!" he whispered fiercely.

Johnson looked just in time to see a slight figure answering Matt's description slip undetected into the rich foliage to safety just above the two watchers.

"Now what have we here?" asked Meryck of the whole world as he strode from cover and yelled, "Hey!" at the top of his voice.

The two watchers froze in place then trained their binoculars on Meryck who waved back cheerfully. In an instant, they were gone but not before the salvage crew had seen what had happened and a police craft withdrew from the search and turned to head for their vacated position.

"Let's see what maggots crawl out of the woodwork now," he drawled as they paced back the way they came.

They had not got far when Meryck's phone sounded across the water.

"Sir, this is Sally again. I'm afraid I don't have any additional news for you. Can't find any birth cert anywhere," she said apologetically.

"But I did find out that the physician that signed off on her health records was one Dr Myra Crawthorne from Matheson General," she added.

"Is there anything else you'd like me to follow-up for you, Sir?" she asked.

"No, Sally. Thanks," he said thoughtfully and hung up.

"Witness Protection, Sir?" asked Johnson quietly.

"Maybe," said Meryck, shaking his head, "or maybe not. It just doesn't add up! Something's not right," and he moved towards the water to get a better look.

*****

Matt was lucky. The undertow drove him right to shore and he squelched his way into the undergrowth on his belly then rolled exhausted onto his back to check out his body. He couldn't see any wounds on his front so he surmised his back had taken the brunt of the impact. He rolled over to see how much he was bleeding but there was no blood on the ground where he had lain. Good, just grazing then, he surmised. That was one less thing to worry about. But he knew he couldn't rest on his laurels and within seconds he was moving forward and upward as silently as he could. He didn't know exactly where they were, just that they were now to his right and below him, he hoped, as he inched his way forward. But he had moved too far downwards in his blind crawl and it was only the arrival of the first response vehicles that had saved him. The two had been coming towards him but stopped and retreated when the police sirens echoed out across the water. Two more steps forward and they would have found him! He lay still as death on the ground hardly daring to breathe! He waited until he heard the first boats being launched and the first diver hit the water before attempting to move again. The sound of the water hoses dousing Brave Betty hissed and splashed on the water covering his hasty retreat. Cautiously, one baby step at a time, he went up the unfamiliar terrain until he was sure he had left them far below. He turned to make his way inland and had not gone far before he heard the call from across the lake. Hiding behind an ancient tree trunk he could just make out the figure on the old jetty waving in his direction. From directly below him he heard the commotion and the two men made a runner down to the boat as the police craft turned to intercept them. Shaking, he lowered himself to the ground. Where to now, he thought frantically?

CHAPTER 16

Jed kept his arm around Jenny as they left the hospital and she relaxed against him for the comfort and protection he offered. He hardly registered her presence and was glad that she was quiet for a change. He lived like an iceberg; only a very small portion of the real man was on the surface. Inside, his mind was whirring with opportunities and dilemmas, and his stomach grumbled reminding him he hadn't eaten in ages.

"Fancy something to eat?" he asked, and she nodded.

"Rosa's maybe, eh?" he said, nudging her playfully.

She nodded again, her spirits lifting a little.

They took his truck, pulling out onto the old road and winding along the corkscrew bends, Jed driving and Jenny leaning back in her seat, eyes closed, enjoying the breeze as it fanned in through the open window. Traveller's Mountain loomed up before them, visible from one angle, then the next, as they continued the long climb up. The car park at Rosa's was deserted. Jed slid into a shady spot and they piled out stiffly, blinking in the brightness.

Inside was cool and welcoming, and they found a window seat near the side where they could enjoy the view and keep an eye on the truck while they ate. Jed nodded to Joey in the kitchen as they passed by, then Darla was there to take their order and pour them their first coffee of the day.

"Well, ain't this somethin'," she drawled, calling out loudly to Joey. "The almighty has honoured us with his presence!"

"And how are you too," drawled Jed right back at her, refusing to be drawn in by her low opening shot.

"And Jenny," continued Darla, "how you doin' these days? Ain't seen you in an age!"

"Hi Darla," replied Jenny, her eyes brightening at the encounter. "Haven't had the time lately. Been busy, you know."

"Ah! Yes! Starbucks!" retorted Darla. "Suppose you won't be wantin' any of my coffee today then?

They laughed easily together.

"How are things with you, Darla?" she asked while Jed drank deeply and held out his mug for a refill.

"Doin' real fine," returned Darla. "Bit quiet these days though. That motorway's taking a toll but BB will never admit to it"

"BB around?" interrupted Jed.

"Nope," she answered, giving him a shrewd look. "Now what business would you have with BB?"

"Not a darn thing," he replied silkily, delighted that she could be riled so easily.

"We'd like the special," he purred, ignoring her question, and Darla just threw him a dirty look and shouted the order to Joey.

Watching Darla's departing back, Jenny was reminded of the happy times she'd had here with Tullie. She'd met Jed here too for the first time. And it was Darla who had comforted her when her parents told her she had to stay in Matheson; she couldn't go to college with Tullie. It was too dangerous. It was Jed who had taken her here to eat when she'd flunked her exams on purpose. She sighed sadly, giving

103

her thoughts free rein at last. It had been so long!

Jed had been aware of Jenny's preoccupation as they ate and put it down to the events of the morning. He was happy to have the time to mull over these himself. Tullie was going to be ok but it would take her a few weeks to fully recover, he knew. His previous anger had dissipated and he realised he needed to look at his situation with new eyes. As long as she was isolated she wouldn't have time to meddle with the picture she'd taken; he felt he could relax about that for the next while at least. And Tullie was Tullie. She hadn't meant anything by taking the pictures in the first place; just zealous to a fault and protective of her new 'babies' as she put it. He knew how quick-tempered he could be and was glad he'd had this space to read the situation differently.

He sighed.

"She's going to be ok," said Jenny, reaching out to cover his hand with hers, reading the situation correctly.

He smiled back gratefully, and the moment was broken by Darla arriving to refill their mugs.

"So, you going to man up and visit him this time?" demanded Darla, taking the latitude that age bestowed to its very limits.

"None of your business, Darla," he retorted shortly and continued to finish his breakfast ignoring her presence at their table.

With a snort and a shake of her head she left them, her parting words hanging in the air.

"One of these days, you'll regret it, your high and mightiness!"

Darla always had to have the last word, and the one after too, he mused, suddenly seeing the funny side of it for the first time, and laughing out loud to Jenny's surprise not to mention Darla's. She hauled her considerable girth behind the counter and continued to scowl darkly in his direction. He smiled back at her, his eyes twinkling. It had been a long time since someone had had the nerve to speak to him like that and he found he was actually enjoying it. Turning to Jenny, he asked her,

"Ever been to Tinakilly?

CHAPTER 17

The drive to Tinakilly was like balm on an open wound. Jenny had fallen asleep shortly after they left Rosa's and Jed relished the silence and the view. As they drove into the uplands the hills engulfed them in calm greens sprinkled with wild reds and yellows in abundance. The turquoise sky, darkened to a sapphire blue by the tinted windows, was a perfect foil to the emerging countryside. As they climbed he could glimpse occasional fields of ripening corn spreading out to the horizon below them; and ready and waiting grain silos glinted in the sun. Patches of blue among the trees revealed small lakes linked by a snaking silver river as it meandered down the valleys. Here and there, kestrels hung on the wind pinpointing some prey he could not see. Sliding open his window a little so as not to disturb Jenny his sharp sense of smell was assailed by the predominance of pine amid azaleas and fuchsias, and the occasional scent of night stock that nestled in almost perpetual darkness beneath the heavy summer foliage. It was a glorious day to be alive!

His thoughts turned to Tullie and the precious cargo he carried in the back. Once he had secured this he determined to go back and wait for Tullie to come around. Despite his rationalising, he was distraught he couldn't get to her personal stuff to retrieve and destroy the pictures; it wasn't possible to bring this up without causing suspicion. They had a low view of him and his activities as it was; one he had cultivated over the years. His phone buzzed; it was a text from Bill. He was sorry for the pain he had caused his sister but it was necessary to keep her out of this, to keep her safe. Bill understood. Although he loved Tullie too, he recognised Jane was too close to her to be objective when the time came. For what, they didn't know yet. But he hoped the cargo he protected would somehow help. Keep your friends close and your enemies closer still, he thought darkly but on a day like today, on a journey through these glorious hills, he couldn't believe Tullie was an enemy. Different, for sure, but an enemy, this special little girl he had watched over her entire life and trusted completely. Until now, a little voice spoke in his mind. Until now!

Grant's Cottage came into view as he crested Willow Hill; a rambling two storey building with random structural additions identifiable by their architectural differences added through the decades. Some semblance of continuity was retained by roofing material but there all congruity ended. Pointy roofs played against triangular ones; flat spaces revealed walls rising behind them to create a whimsical labyrinth of living space before the road dipped down and he lost the view to towering trees that blocked the wind and provided cover for the building. To the casual observer it was a folly; to Jed, it provided a much needed portal to the sanctuary the hidden caves provided at its back. No one was at home as he drove into the yard and around the back, straight for the barn that stood between him and beyond. He knew his presence was being recorded on the unobtrusive surveillance he and Bill had installed. Parking quietly in the barn, he gently woke Jenny.

"We're here," he said softly, and she stretched lazily and looked around her in surprise.

"Just parked in the barn, out of the sun," he confided, as he opened the door and slipped around her side to assist her out.

Outside, Jenny stared around her in amazement. The place was stunning. Over the short fence she could see beautifully landscaped gardens slope down to the edge of the trees. Beyond the gardens, she glimpsed the edge of the tennis court, secluded away behind young pines that blended almost seamlessly with the copse behind. The back of the house was a mixture of brick and stonework; the windows upstairs small and latticed. Downstairs, the large windows doubled as doors that spilled out onto elevated terraces, some paved, some decked, but all replete with varied containers of summer plumage that spilled onto the surrounding ground. South-facing, the sun poured it's bounty on the scene, and green umbrellas added much-appreciated shade while keeping perfect harmony with the natural surrounds.

"It's beautiful," she breathed, her voice flat and deadened in the enclosed calm.

"Yes, it is," Jed whispered back. "It's my favourite place in the whole wide world. I'm glad you like it. And since you like the back, I'm sure you'll love the interior! Come on, let me show you around!"

The inside was even more intriguing. The labyrinthine layout allowed for surprises at every twist and turn: here a nook displayed Asian art while there historical artefacts battled with African art for supremacy; huge silk rugs adorned the walls here, while Spanish tiles worked their magic there; antique furniture pieces rubbed shoulders with functional modern composites. But despite the contrasts, modernity had come to Grant's Cottage in its totality, the kitchen being the ultimate testament to this, chrome taking its pride of place beside pale walls, colourful kitchenware and ceramic hobs, of which she counted two. A serene breakfast area nestled in a window space that opened onto an enclosed garden the size of another tennis court, enclosed by the natural surroundings, and moulded into a Zen garden of brushed stones and water features unadorned by flowers of any kind, its grey and silver stones offering serenity and encouraging contemplation.

While she explored the upstairs bedrooms, all on-suite, Jed made some coffee. Each of the six bedrooms was themed but all were tranquil and beautiful, ready for use, she saw. None seemed occupied which puzzled her. She was intrigued to see that the back had a view across a broad expanse of water that she was unaware of; neither had she observed the hill that she now saw rose among the trees to the left of the shed they had parked in. What a gem, she thought as she made her way downstairs. She could hear Jed talking to someone as she approached; he was on the phone. They were still alone. She paused when she heard Tullie's name mentioned, her heart constricting in fear for her friend.

"Is Tullie ok?" she asked dashing through the doors to join Jed in the kitchen.

He held up his finger for her to be quiet; he wasn't finished with the call. She waited anxiously but the caller continued to talk and with only an occasional affirmation from Jed.

"Tullie is fine," he told her pocketing his phone finally. He wasn't ready to tell her. He had to figure this out for himself first but it certainly put a new twist on things! Keeping calm he asked, "How much did you hear?"

"Oh, I just heard you mention her name as I was coming downstairs," she replied, and her voice trembled, "and I was afraid she'd got worse. She did look terrible, didn't she?"

Reaching over to her, he hugged her small, trembling body to him.

"Ssh now," he said, stroking her hair, "she's fine. She's gonna be ok, just you wait."

Nestling into his chest she could feel the heat from his body envelop her and she lifted her head to meet his lips as they pressed passionately down on hers. All thoughts of Tullie fled their minds as reason slipped away in the moment and their bodies sought out each other, the force of their passion filling the longing that Jenny had harboured since their first meeting. For Jed, it was a revelation, giving and receiving freely something he never thought he would experience in his lonely life; and he cherished each moment, each kiss, and each tender touch. But later, lying satiated in each other arms brought fear, that fear of loss that had haunted his life since losing his mother when he was five, and the fear of not being able to keep Jenny safe. What had he done, he berated himself silently! She was now a part of him he would never relinquish, he vowed, bending over to kiss her brow as she snuggled into his side. Mumbling sleepily she reached for him again and this time their love was slow and gentle and it completely undid him.

"I love you, Jenny," he whispered hoarsely, as he came.

"I love you too, Jed," she said, choking on her emotions.

Later, as they lay in bed, the moon shone brightly through the window bathing their naked bodies in celestial light. Jenny slept deeply while Jed, who only ever slept three to four hours anyway, watched her chest rise and fall with every precious breath while he waited for the earth to turn some more and the moon relinquish some of its light upon Tinakilly. Pulling the clothes gently over Jenny he turned towards the window and dozed a little while he waited. He was more relaxed that he could ever remember yet more alive than any op had ever left him. He would have to go away for a while, he knew, to give Jenny the space she needed to recover from this folly, for already he was moving on, changing his mind, pushing his feelings away, creating the distance that would keep her safe.

It was nearly dawn before his opportunity came and he slipped quietly from the bed and out to the barn, shutting the door fully behind him. It was dark in here but he daren't risk a light so by familiar touch and a little fumbling he found the lever and the cave doors slid noiselessly back and the reflective strips glowed dimly but with enough light to guide his way forward. Slipping into the truck he pushed the start button and it whispered into life. So far, so good, he thought. Pushing the gear shaft into Drive he nudged forward and as soon as he was inside the doors he paused and closed them firmly behind him. He had about an hour,

110

he reckoned, before the natural light might wake Jenny so he had to work fast. Pushing down on the accelerator he raced through the mountain tunnel to his destination.

The sound of an engine starting up roused Jenny from her slumbers. A light sleeper, she had heard Jed move about only moments before but took no notice. But now all her senses were on the alert. Racing to the window she saw that the shed doors were closed but the sound was definitely coming from there. She waited for him to drive his truck out, to open the doors and drive away and leave her alone, but instead the sound faded into quietness and she was perplexed. Slipping into her jeans and top, she tiptoed down the stairs looking for signs of life as she went but she was alone. The shed door slid open noiselessly to her touch and she peered in cautiously but there was no one there! No truck! No Jed! In the breaking dawn light she left the mystery of the missing truck behind her and slid back to bed, sleep the very last thing on her mind now but some sixth sense warned her that this was the best course of action. What did she really know about Jed anyway, she asked herself? That she was in love with him was obvious. But where would it all lead to? Despite herself she slept and when she woke up he was fast asleep beside her, and when she reached for him, he did not disappoint her.

The smell of breakfast roused them at last and they both were amazed to find it was nearly ten o'clock.

"You've worn me out," he grinned at her. "I've never slept this late since I was a teenager!"

"I'm too weak to get up," she purred back. "You'll have to bring me breakfast in bed."

Then her eyes shot fully open.

"Who's making breakfast?" she whispered, sitting up in bed, letting the clothes fall from her curvy frame.

"That would be Bill, I guess," murmured Jed, admiring the view.

"Perve," she pouted, throwing a pillow at his head.

Ducking, he laughed loudly.

"Everything ok?" called a loud voice from bellow.

"Never better," Jed called back, grinning. "Down in a sec!"

"It's ok, Jenny," he said softly, bending to kiss her. "I will bring you breakfast, just this time," and he dragged himself away downstairs and Jenny snuggled back into the covers.

"Bill, my man!" exclaimed Jed, slapping his friend on the shoulder. "When did you get back?"

"Jed," smiled Bill in reply, "just in a few minutes really. You got company up there?" he asked, his eyebrows reaching for the ceiling.

"Yep," replied a cheery Jed. "I'll take her up breakfast and we can catch up on some gossip."

While Jenny ate her breakfast in bed the two men moved out to the Zen garden walking slowly on the loose stones, raking as they went. The sound bounced around the enclosed space, a regular cacophony of noises that insulated them from anyone who might wish to hear what they were talking about.

"Any further news on Tullie?" asked Jed, quietly.

"No, not a thing," replied Bill, his face wrinkled into concern. "No sight of Jake either. You know anything about that?"

"Nope," replied Jed. "Didn't know he was away. Darla gave me a hard time yesterday about not visiting. Even asked me if I was going up to see him. She mustn't know he's not there either."

"Have a detective coming to see me in a few hours," he said. "Man by name of Johnson. Guy in charge of her accident, I believe."

"Thought that was Meryck," said Jed, surprised. "I met him at the hospital. Sharp bloke."

"Apparently, he's off the case," came back Bill. "Don't know the ends and outs of it but something bothers me here."

"Did you hear Jane's house burned down and she's missing too?" he asked after a short break.

Jed whistled quietly and shook his head.

"Is Jake up to his old tricks again, do you think?" he asked.

"Don't know," replied Bill. "In this case, I'd be delighted if it was him!"

They walked around for a while in silence, deep in thought. Jenny watched from the window above, a puzzled look on her pretty face. Something was wrong, she could smell it. Hurriedly, she showered and dressed and went down to find what was going on.

CHAPTER 18

Guidrius led the way forward silently and Jake followed. Up and up they went, Guidrius padding over the ground effortlessly while Jake began to feel every pull and heave forward. Last night's session was taking its toll but he wouldn't admit his frailty, least of all to this man. The air thinned the further up they went and he could feel a slight chill as the temperature dropped. Then when he thought he'd have to give in, Guidrius veered to the right and the going became easier. Occasionally they emerged from the low cloud cover to breathtaking views over the world below but still there was no let-up in pace. Jake began to lose touch with time and place as he followed Guidrius, turning when he turned, going straight when he did, no conversation breaking the complete silence this far up. When Guidrius stopped Jake was glad but he didn't recognise where they were; he had never seen this part of the mountain before. Standing with his hands on his hips, breathing heavily while Guidrius seemed not to be effected at all, he raised his eyebrows.

"North-west," was all Guidrius offered tritely.

Jake hadn't noticed the curve inward on the mountain-side it was so slight. Without any preamble Guidrius walked straight at the hollow and passed through. Breathing deeply, Jake registered this but made no attempt to follow. He wasn't sure he was seeing correctly at this altitude, and in such a stressed state, so he just stayed put, his mind winding its way back home, planning his return alone, in case all of this was just an hallucination. But no such reprieve was about to happen. Guidrius reappeared once he saw Jake hadn't followed him through and, grabbing his forearm, he slowly led him forward. As they went closer to the mountain, the opening became more defined and without any effort they passed through unscathed.

The interior was filled with dark shadows but the feeling of space reached far and wide, up and down so when Guidrius flicked on lights Jake wasn't surprised to see it was enormous, reaching in every direction in odd angles. The ground sloped downwards naturally, and to the right, and once around the corner it rose again and continued to do so for several feet. But it was cool inside the mountain and the air was sweet and the sound muffled and Jake found himself recovering rapidly. Guidrius walked a little behind him and to his left, willing him forward and upward. When they reached the top of the first rise Jake could see other routes leading off in several directions. They had reached a plateau.

A web of frigid air hit Jake full-on as he moved over the rise then Guidrius walked passed him confidently ushering him forward. Several minutes passed as they continued to their left until Guidrius stopped abruptly.

"We're here," he said, his voice deadened in the interior of the mountain.

All Jake could see was a large empty space with a circular platform rising slightly from the floor, in the centre. The ceiling here was high and lost in shadow despite the soft light that seemed to come from everywhere and nowhere at the same time: he had been unable to identify its source. Guidrius walked away from Jake to the other side of the cavern and motioned him forward until they stood on opposite sides of the elevated space. Guidrius moved his arms slightly and to Jake's astonishment several globes began to form in the air between both of them. They were small to begin with but grew and expanded until Jake thought he was looking at several versions of the earth, globe sized, swirling gently in an elliptical fashion about a foot above his head. He felt they were tethered in some way to this space between them but has no way of verifying this. They glowed with energy, filling the cavern with every conceivable colour in the universe. He was mesmerised; they were just so beautiful. So enthralled was he that it didn't register for several moments that they were also producing a faint sound, a symphony of notes, some harmonic to his ears, some discordant. He realised that he could hear the individual melodies from these spheres more clearly as they passed him by and he waited for several full revolutions before being able to recognise the differences fully.

Across the space Guidrius watched Jake carefully. He was pleased with the man's response to the globes, and especially pleased that he had picked up on the melodies they produced.

"You may step inside if you wish," he said, stepping onto the slight platform to be immersed in the light show between them. "They will not be disturbed and you will not be harmed."

Jake watched in fascination as the globes reassembled themselves around Guidrius and reformed their elliptical movement. He could discern no obvious difference in their behaviour so, tentatively, he stretched out his hand to a passing globe. It whispered around his hand, forming and reforming, continuing on its mysterious journey unhindered. He held his hand for the second and the third and they too whispered around his hand in a slightly different tickling pattern and continued on. By round three he felt he could close his eyes and almost identify each one by its sound and the way it tickled his hand. It was amazing. These globes seemed at once ephemeral yet solid; inert yet alive in some way. Closing his eyes, he raised his arms, and stepped, without further hesitation, onto the platform and let his senses lead the way. It occurred to him briefly how bizarre this was; how uncharacteristic his behaviour! It was as if he was thinking from a different space, in another time.

Inside the world of the globes he could feel a slight swish

of power that was hidden from him as he stood outside. The sounds here were louder too, and the tickling sensations stronger; they seemed to pass through the very core of his body. As each globe came closer he thought on several occasions that he could see movement inside but it passed too quickly to be sure. He recognised landmasses similar to earth in each one though, despite the varying colours it represented. At times he thought he could count in excess of ten globes surrounding him but it was impossible to be accurate they moved so fast. His head began to spin and he realised he was reaching sensory overload. Lowering his arms to his sides he crouched down to regain his balance and the globes readjusted themselves to his height, maintaining their movement around him. Guidrius was stunned. He had never seen this response before! Reaching out he helped his new friend off the platform and the globes winked out of existence.

"What happened in there?" stammered Jake. "What were those things?"

He felt the loss of the experience keenly, as if he had left something of himself behind or that they had completed him somehow and he missed the link once it was gone.

"I need something to eat," he whispered, playing for time, and staggered over to where he had left his rucksack.

"Those things," answered Guidrius softly to his retreating back, "are the histories of the worlds."

*****

Myra and Jane sat beside Tullie watching the medic checking her vitals. He nodded towards them, added more sedative to Tullie's drip and left. BB and Anjie strolled wearily into the room and sat down heavily.

"Well, that went well," sighed BB, "now the real work begins!"

Beside him, Anjie nodded as he examined his boots minutely. Myra's presence bothered him. There were too many gaps in her records for his liking despite BB and Jane vouching for her. They didn't bring outsiders to the Mountain easily!

"Carney ok?" asked Myra quietly. "Maybe I shouldn't have brought him into this. He's quite highly strung. But he is a damn good doctor."

Anjie nodded, too preoccupied to get involved in a discussion about Carney now.

"Where do we go from here?" asked Jane. "What'll happen to Tullie?"

BB cleared his throat quietly and got up to get a drink of water from the dispenser. Cup in hand he turned to them and began to fill them in on the news from Jake, or the lack of it. Anjie reached over and drew the covers back from Tullie's hands to display the ring on her left hand, glowing warmly in the soft underground lighting. Myra moved to the bed and checked Tullie's eyes for herself, breathing a sigh of relief to see the familiar green. Of those gathered, she alone knew of the existence of Man-x; it was time to come clean. They all knew Tullie was different but she hadn't shared all the facts with any of them, forging her records to keep the little girl safe as she had done for Matt but he was not her concern now. He'd work it out for himself, she hoped fervently.

Turning from the bed, all in a rush, she told them the story about the night Man-x entered her life. She told them about the similar test results: about her screening of Tullie all these years; of falsifying documents to keep her safe; and of the real threat their beloved Tullie may well pose now to all of them. She didn't know anything about the ring or the visitor Jake had but it was ominous. Whatever they were in, they were in it up to their eyes. Matt's story she kept to herself, for now. Silence filled the room; they were all looking at her bug eyed and disbelieving.

"Is that all?" asked Anjie, dissecting her on the spot.

Myra faltered and they knew there was something else. She hated this man already!

"For God's sake, woman," shouted BB, "out with it! How can we protect Tullie if we don't bloody well know!"

So she told them all she knew about Matt. She told them about Greenway; about his birth and the death of his parents; of the accident that had killed Ostenwalder; and she told them about what she had given Matt; and what she thought his grandad had left for him. The telling was cathartic; it was with relief that all the words tumbled out of her mouth, official secrets or not. She felt cleansed by the process; felt a safety in sharing with these people that she hadn't felt since her mentor had died. And when they thought she had finished she shared one other detail with them. This however was speculation and she struggled to find the best words to describe her suspicions. In the end, all she could do was convey her misgivings:

"The Mallins, they're Witness Protection, I think, or something. I saw the parents on Greenway. I don't think Jenny knows anything," and her voice trailed off, and she sat down with a bump on the couch hugging her arms to herself.

A heavy silence filled the room. Jane was reliving her daughter's life: Myra's mind was blissfully quiet for the first time in years; Anjie and BB worked the angles silently, each to his own strengths, borne out of decades of practice. For Anjie, Myra had supplied some pieces of the jigsaw he had been trying to complete for years; for BB it was hell on earth. Had Myra really forgotten? Should he say something now too?

"We need to talk to Tullie about this," offered Anjie into

the quiet of the room, and BB's moment was gone.

They all nodded, one by one.

"And Jake," added Jane.

They nodded again, together in this.

"What is it you need to talk to me about?" asked a sleepy voice, and they turned to see Tullie smiling groggily at them from the bed.

"Where am I anyway?" she asked. "Last time I remember I was in the back of an ambulance and I could hear you, Anjie."

"I just had a lovely dream," she added, and drifted slowly back to sleep.

The sound of Anjie's phone shattered their frail moment of togetherness. It was a quick call and BB watched him intently.

"Looks like we've got a fix on your Matt," he said to Myra. "Nearly blown to smithereens on Bear's Lake. Now who'd do a thing like that?" he wondered aloud. Myra gasped, her face draining of colour. Jane raced to her side.

"Jane, get the medic back in here. Myra, check on Carney then get some rest yourselves," he added looking from Jane to Myra.

"BB," he said, and with that the three women were left alone.

CHAPTER 19

Jake ate slowly while his mind tried to make sense of what Guidrius had just said.

"Why bring me here?" he asked, wiping his hands on his trousers and stepping back towards the platform. "And where exactly is here? I thought I knew every part of this mountain!"

"The globes contain the histories of the worlds," repeated Guidrius, sidestepping Jake's second question.

"Worlds?" interrupted Jake, sceptically.

"What you have here before you," continued Guidrius, as the globes winked into existence again, "are memories gathered from the beginning of time and reworked into the visual, interactive form you see before you. They show what happened both in time, and through time, and leave the viewer to interpret it for themselves. They are powerful interactive records. You can live the moments but you cannot change them."

"Take my presence in your world, or Tullie's," he continued, fingering the globes speculatively. "We share certain traits in common but I am different enough to terrify the population, to send your world into a spin. Who knows where that might lead! Will everybody respond like you? I doubt it!" he stopped, and looked directly at Jake before continuing.

"You may leave here when you wish. I will not hold you against your will. I pose no threat to you. You may tell others about me but will they believe you? Or if they do, and if you can hold me, what will your people do to me? But more to

121

the point, what will they do with Tullie if they find out she is different?"

Jake's eyes never left his face as he spoke and he saw no subterfuge there. This man was for real.

"If you pose no threat," Jake asked him, "why are you here? Or Tullie?"

"I brought her here to protect her," he answered truthfully. "My world is in turmoil; has been for some ages now. It's time for The Reunion but we are as unprepared as you. Tullie is our ambassador; the one we have waited for, for millennia. She has the capability to bind and release; to create and to destroy. You'll understand better once you have lived your history. There are only a few of us left who know who she is and who can protect her until she comes into her own. I had to get her away. And I am grateful that you have kept her safe. You are a good man, Jake Bell."

"I have known for a long time," Jake mused out loud, looking towards the globes, "that Tullie was different. It was just little things as a baby, then more as a young child. But it was when she had her first check-up that we realised we had a very, very special girl on our hands," he continued, turning to look Guidrius in the eye again. "You see, we couldn't identify her blood type so we falsified the records to keep her safe."

Guidrius could see he was telling the truth. He kept silent. Jake had more to say.

"You may as well know it all," said Jake. "I bought the plot on Traveller's Mountain and built my home there because somehow, deep down, I knew Tullie belonged there. I chose the spot carefully. Beneath the house are caves that nobody knows about but me and a select few of my old team who are sworn to protect her. If anything happens she will be taken there for safety until we figure out what else to do."

Jake was appalled at his disclosure to a near stranger; Guidrius was intrigued and delighted at the man's foresight.

"There's something else I should mention; something that has bothered me for years. There's someone else here like Tullie. He's been incarcerated for all this time on Greenway Island. Poor bastard! They've experimented on him relentlessly yet he remains completely passive."

The look of horror on Guidrius's face stopped Jake in his tracks.

"He's alive?" he asked in a choked voice.

"In a manner of speaking," said Jake. "You know who he is?"

In his agitation, Guidrius began to change forms repeatedly before Jake.

"Hey! Hey!" shouted Jake in alarm. "Don't do that! Stop! Tell me what's wrong!"

Startled, Guidrius returned to his old self and in reply he tapped at a portion of his ring and the memory of what happened the night he fought Man-x appeared in front of Jake like a movie projection. He saw the flash when Guidrius arrived on the mountain, carrying a small baby and some packages, a few feet away from where they found Tullie. He saw the second flash and Man-x appeared. He was a fearsome sight and Jake withdrew rapidly from the vision before him. Guidrius moved beside him and held him steady as together they watched the ensuing fight. Jake saw the two fall over the cliff edge into Bear's Lake. He saw the fizzing and sparkling as Man-x's circuits blew and he watched him drift off with the current restored to the human form he was familiar with from his tour of duty on the island. He saw Guidrius's injuries; saw them heal overnight despite their seriousness; and he could feel his pain cut at his insides as he returned to find Tullie gone.

"Enough!" he croaked. "I've seen enough! Turn it off!"

"Now do you understand?" asked a pale Guidrius. He too had relived the pain of losing her.

Jake stumbled and sat heavily on the floor. What he had feared all his life had come true. Tullie's real family had turned up to claim her. All he could think about was losing her!

"So," he spoke softly, "you're Tullie's real dad?"

"I have a lot to show you about my world, Jake," he said, as he nodded in reply.

"But where are you from?" asked Jake. "I don't understand! And what's this about a reunion? A reunion of what? Tell me. I need to know! "

Guidrius walked to the globes and they spun happily before him. He waited for Jake to join him before answering.

"See this globe here," he said, indicating one that gave off a cool green light, "that's your world, Jake. You should start your search for understanding here."

"This one," he continued, reaching out his hand to caress a silver glowing globe as it passed, "is Silvamon, our home world. Tullie and I are Silvites."

"And Man-x?" queried Jake.

"Ah, that's not so easy to explain," answered Guidrius. "He is from our world but he is not a true Silvite. He's a Halfer; an engineered prototype warrior programmed for destruction, of one in particular – and anyone who stands in his way; then he self-destructs."

"And this act of destruction," asked Jake quietly, although he felt he knew the chilling answer already, "does it have anything to do with Tullie?

Fear and dread gripped his heart as Guidrius nodded solemnly.

It was some time before either spoke again, both lost in their memories of what had been and thinking forward to what might be. The possible scenarios troubled the men, and interlocked as they were, the outcome was uncertain. But they were not alone in this. Others were involved too, on both sides. The waters were muddied, churned up by centuries of ignorance and pride.

"Jake," he said, turning to the man deep in thought beside him, "I need to go and collect the other objects Tullie had with her that night. They're still back there, in the recess."

Jake stared at him for some time as if he had never seen him before, and then nodded.

"I won't be gone long," continued Guidrius. "While I'm away please feel free to work with these," and he indicated the globes.

"They will tell you what you need to know now," he offered. "And when you are ready, together we will work out what Reunion will mean to both our worlds."

Looking back as he passed over the ridge to the outside world, he could see Jake still standing exactly as he had left him.

CHAPTER 20

The pain from his side woke him, his heart thumping so loudly he was afraid those on the lake would hear it! He had no idea how long he had been asleep. His clothes crumpled where they'd dried as he slept but it was summer and they had dried quickly. The police boat was returning empty-handed from the search for the two men he saw in dismay, then realised it was this sound that had really woken him. He had only dozed for a short time. He felt in his back pocket and withdrew the key. He was insanely glad he hadn't lost it in his escape; it would have been so easy for it to slip from his pocket as he swam. He hugged it to him as if it was his last lifeline reliving the last hour in vivid detail before making plans to move on. But his last waking thought haunted him. Where would he go now? Absently he felt around for his rucksack and realised it was somewhere at the bottom of the lake or in pieces floating around below him. Despair threatened to overwhelm him but then he remembered he had not taken the rucksack at all, just Myra's and his grandad's packages. He fished them out of his side pocket, soggy around the sides but otherwise intact and he felt he had got his life back. But this was followed by the dip into despair again as he realised he no longer had a life; he didn't know who he was anymore, and he couldn't help the tears that dripped down his face and splattered onto the packages he held in his trembling hands. He let them come, weeping the shock and pain out of his system as his mind tried to plan the next step. Below him the search was deemed complete and the services began to pull back one by one until, as evening began to draw close, only yellow tape fluttered in the breeze below indicating Brave Betty's last resting place. Emotionally and physically exhausted, and more frightened than he'd ever been, he rolled into a ball and fell into a fitful sleep.

Meryck and Johnson waited for the boat to return. They had no luck; the two had evaded them. They had found no trace of anything amiss so it looked like there would be no witness to what had happened here either. A plank reading part of Brave Betty's name had been retrieved and it had been traced to one Elizabeth Egan married to Raymond Ostenwalder, parents to the Matthew Ostenwalder whom they were looking for to help with their enquiries. Meryck and Johnson were thoughtful as they pulled away from the lake towards home.

"You think that was him up on the skyline then?" asked Johnson.

"Pretty sure," answered Meryck. "No one else around. It's his mother's boat. One thing's for sure though; those two meant him no good!"

"Do you really think it was a gas explosion, Sir?"

"Looks like one, but with those two about there could be a more sinister explanation. Thing that eludes me is, why would anybody want Matthew Ostenwalder dead? What threat does he pose? And to whom?"

Following at a safe distance behind, Rick was discussing these very same questions with Anjie and BB on speaker phone.

"Found evidence of someone coming from the Lake on the south-east edge," he was saying. "Had to call off my search when the police boat took off towards Greenway."

"No, came back empty handed," he continued after a pause. "Yep, north, north-west way. No, can't say where he'd be by now, for sure."

"Right," said Anjie. "Keep the tail on Meryck. I want to know what he finds as soon as he does! We'll do the rest

127

here."

Anjie and BB looked at each other expectantly.

"Yep, I'm on it!" nodded BB.

"Don't forget to pack some strong coffee," Anjie called after him. "We could be out there for a while! I want to find him before anyone else does!"

*****

"We got a tail, Sir," said Johnson matter-of-factly.

"Yup," replied Meryck, picking at his teeth absent-mindedly.

"Head for Rosa's then. Guess we can all do with a bite to eat," and he grinned maliciously. "Put the boot down a bit, Johnson. Don't want to make it too easy for him do we?"

CHAPTER 21

Tullie woke in the early hours with a cracking headache. She wasn't sure where she was. She kept having the same weird dream, and every now and then she heard Anjie's authoritative voice then calm descended once more. Her room was dimly lit yet she could make out the figure of a medic as he sat at the side of the room watching some movie on his laptop. The drip in the back of her right hand hurt as she stroked her bandaged head gently. It was her first experience of IVs and she wasn't sure just what to expect. She tried lifting her left arm but it was bandaged from fingers to shoulder and moved stiffly, like a mummy, she thought allowing herself a small giggle. Carefully she wriggled the right side of her body; that seemed ok, but when she tried the same on her left side she felt her foot was weighed down on the bed from ankle to knee and she didn't have the strength to lift it free. She coughed gently, her mouth and throat dry, and he was at her side in an instant.

"Well, hello there. I'm Adam, your friendly medic," he said smiling, reaching for her pulse. "Welcome back. Can you tell me your name, please?"

"'Think so," she smiled feebly back at him. "Last time I checked I was Tullie Bell. Have I passed the test then, Adam?"

"Yep," he replied, adding the reading to her chart. "Tullie Bell you are, no doubt about it!"

"So, how are you feeling?" he continued, checking her pupils now. "Headache? Pain anywhere?"

"Just my head," whispered Tullie. "Feels like I tried to go

129

through a twenty-foot wall!"

"Not surprised," he returned. "Quite a nasty knock you took back there. Can you remember any of that?"

"Got hit off my bike, right?" she said after a short while. "How are the other guys? Think there was two of them, right?"

"They're doing just fine in a holding cell," he nodded, reaching to add more sedative to her IV.

"What's that?" she asked, alarmed.

"Just something for the headache," he smiled. "You'll be up and about in the morning, right as rain."

"What's wrong with my leg?" she asked groggily. "I can't seem to move it."

"A fracture," he said back. "No need to worry yourself now. Just let the meds kick in and I'll tell you everything in the morning."

Relaxing back into her pillow, Tullie was asleep again in seconds.

*****

Anjie and BB turned off the main road and pulled round the back of the hut well beyond the yellow tape. Silently, they climbed out and moved forward stealthily, stopping at intervals to recce the quiet mountain side. Their night goggles showed no signatures as they made their way around to where Rick had directed them. It was easy going from there. Matt had left clear tracks; he had indeed kept his head down. There was some whispered discussion as they came across the trail of the other two; they had been so close to stepping on Matt! Mission order: rescue Matt first, then they were coming back to find the other two. They moved upwards more alert now, searching for traces of three rather than one.

They heard the snoring from above them in the same second they spotted two figures tracing their steps backwards along the lake edge to find the spot where Matt exited the water. They had to move quickly! Undoubtedly the same two back to finish the job, professionals then, as they had guessed. Anjie skirted to the left while BB went to the right giving a thumbs up when they identified their target. Matt was fast asleep on his back now, arms and legs spread-eagled, dreaming of happier times when the two struck. Anjie pinned him to the ground with his body weight while BB covered his mouth to keep him silent. Matt was terrified as he peered through bulbous eyes up at his assailants. BB raised a finger, nodding his head down the mountainside.

"We're here to help, Matt," he whispered. "We know who you are. Myra told us."

This was no comfort to the panicked young man pinned to the ground like a fly to a board. He had seen Myra kidnapped; her fate uncertain. Anjie looked at BB worriedly. They were running out of time. They had no way of knowing how Matt would respond if they let him go. He looked too stressed out to co-operate. Reaching a quick decision, Anjie held his knife in front of Matt's face, threateningly. Matt suddenly became very still and compliant once BB had complemented this gesture by running his finger across his throat. They would kill him, he realised, if he didn't do as they said.

They worked efficiently and quickly to position themselves favourably, keeping Matt behind them and out of danger as they prepared to take on the approaching two who made no effort at concealment. Matt was definitely a goner if they had not got here on time but they were confident they had left no additional tracks so the element of surprise remained on their side. Attaching silencers to their guns by touch they never took their eyes from the tracks below them. Behind them, Matt was beginning to realise they were taking on the two that tried to kill him earlier, and he crouched low and prayed. There was nothing else he could do.

Emptying his mind, Anjie prepared to take the kill shot. Gesturing to BB, he trained his gun on the second man and fired. It was a direct hit and he tumbled with a crash down the trail. Cursing, the lead man hit the ground but not before BB's shot got him between the eyes. Matt registered the pops and heard the crashing just below where he hid and he covered his head with his arms and bent lower than he thought possible into the shrubs and grass, rocking back and forth, whimpering in distress. He heard Anjie and BB slip away yet he stayed where he was immobile with fear and dread. Why did these people want him dead? And who were these sent to protect him?

Training their guns on the bodies they checked their handiwork and nodded to each other. Turning them over they saw firsthand what they had been up against and they were right to be cautious. They had seen shadows like these two before but never at work so close to home. Crouching down close to their face BB's phone flashed twice. Pushing them hurriedly into the brush, they collected a very shaken Matt and headed for base.

CHAPTER 22

Johnson powered the car up the old road, Meryck cursing profusely at each hand break switchback.

"You ok, Sir," called Johnson gleefully. For once he was having some fun.

"Watch where you're going, you young git!" roared Meryck. "I told you to put your foot down not break the bloody sound barrier!"

Johnson laughed.

"He's still with us, Sir!" he shouted again above the sound of the tortured engine. "He's one good driver!"

"Start to slow down from the next bend," instructed Meryck breathlessly.

"Good," he added a little later. "Now get ready to pull tight around the back, let me out, go park in the trees and stay put."

Johnson did as he was told and Meryck disappeared in the back door of Rosa's as he brought the car to a halt by the trees. Looking in his rear mirror he saw the trailing car nose around the corner and park a little ways back in a solid vantage surveillance manoeuvre. The waiting had begun. But not for long!

Meryck dashed swiftly through the restaurant, flashing his ID to Joey and Darla as he went. Within seconds of Johnson parking up, Meryck was knocking on the side window of the trailing car with his gun. Johnson revved the car backwards to block a forward exit. Ken whistled! He didn't think the old geezer still had it in him. He rolled down the window.

"Hello, Ken," growled Meryck. "Wondered what that bad smell was!"

"Nice to see you too, Vince," replied a smiling Ken.

"Fancy a bagel?" asked Meryck.

"Like old times then!" said Ken as he got out of the car, hands in the air.

Meryck eyed him distastefully while a much-puzzled Johnson looked on.

"No running this time," said Meryck directly.

"No running," he agreed, turning towards the front door, "best friends, and all that."

"Search her thoroughly," Meryck instructed Johnson before following Ken inside.

*****

Darla had seen enough in her time to pour their coffees and leave them be. Joey took a cigarette break and peered around the corner at Johnson going through Ken's car with a fine toothcomb. Thumbing through his address book, he got a pick up on ring three.

"Ken's been rumbled," he said without preamble. "He's here with Meryck. The other one is going through the car." Then he hung up and went to sit in the sunshine to finish his cigarette.

"Years been kind," nodded Ken, sagely.

"Cut the crap, Ken!" snarled Meryck, never taking his eyes off him for a second. "Why are you following me?"

134

"That I can't actually tell you," drawled Ken. "Matter of national security, and all that."

Meryck reached across the table suddenly and hauled Ken out of his seat by his tie.

"Don't bullshit me!" he hissed. "Last time you had my tail I barely came out alive."

Feigning innocence, Ken kept his hands loose and his body floppy. Meryck wasn't at all deceived. This man was deadly. Officially, he didn't exist. Officially, he knew just about everything there was to know about killing a man. Officially, thought Meryck, looking into those cold eyes, I'd be dead right now if I was the target.

Meryck's phone went.

"That'll be for you," smirked Ken into his face.

Letting him go Meryck answered the call. He didn't have to say a single word. He'd been pulled from duty. He was to let Ken go. The shadows had spoken.

Johnson was still working through the car and didn't see them approach. Ken held out his hand for the keys. Johnson looked at Meryck, and he nodded. Together they stood and watched Ken drive away. Johnson's expression was puzzled but Meryck's was coldly inscrutable. Joey watched them warily. Meryck had always been trouble. This wasn't over yet.

From his position in the corner booth Rick made an educated guess at what had just happened. Flipping open his phone, the conversation was brief and one sided.

"Bingo! The eagle has landed," he said. "Watch your backs up there."

*****

Johnson was full of questions on the way back down the mountain but Meryck stalled him with a wave of his hand.

"National security, lad," he said dryly. "Best not know any more than that."

Then after a while he told Johnson he'd been pulled from the case and that he was going to take some well deserved holiday time.

"Pull over here," he instructed. "I need a breath of fresh air."

They walked down the valley in companionable silence until they reached a small stream trickling faintly through the lush vegetation. Then confident they weren't been observed or overheard, Meryck turned to warn Johnson.

"Listen," he said quietly. "This mess we've got involved in goes much deeper than we thought. We've got to be very careful; very careful indeed!"

Johnson went very still.

"Dangerous?"

Meryck nodded.

"How dangerous?"

"Life or death: this is organised, and it's big, if Ken's involved. Make no mistake, Johnson; in this, we're the expendables."

He dropped his gaze and looked around searching for the right words to warn Johnson yet keep him on his side. He could hear him sucking in air through his teeth as he steadied himself. When he felt the time was right he turned around to face his young colleague again.

"Me and Ken go back a bit," he finally said. "We worked

Special Ops way back in the time. He's a killer; shrewd, fast and above all loyal to his superiors, if you can figure out who those are. Had my back last time out. Haven't seen him since. Didn't know he was dancing to a different tune and it took me two years to fully recover. Paid off quietly; moved into police work after that; then moved out here to live the quiet life after Becca was killed in a hit and run. She was the same age as Tullie Bell, give or take a few months."

Keep the info on a need-to-know basis flashed through his mind and his voice faded away for a while and Johnson let him be. He had enough to occupy his mind with what he just heard. He had suspected Meryck had a different career path to him; men his age could be expected to have. It explained a lot; the lack of following protocol, for one.

"Guess you found nothing in the car?" he asked at last, and Johnson shook his head.

"Look for adjustments under the drive shaft next time," he advised. "But getting back to where we are now, there's something big going down and I bet my life on it that the girl is somehow involved. And that Matt guy. Keep an eye on those two and you'll make progress, mark my words!"

"But, Sir," interrupted Johnson, "I'll need your guidance on this one. I don't have enough experience to go it alone."

"Oh, they'll assign you a new lead, don't you worry," replied Meryck. "Someone you've never seen, don't know and who'll keep you running in circles until this dies down. They're not interested in solving this, Johnson; just burying it. Deep! It belongs up the ladder! Mark my words!"

Johnson wasn't very excited to hear all this, he could see, but who would? A young detective starting out on his career. Messed things up, did he? Aw, what a shame! Better he move back to uniform then and not create any more messes. Meryck had seen it before but he really thought those days were over; that things were more transparent now. Well, apparently not! But two could play this game!

"I'm thinking I'll head to Skyway for a break," he said, a twinkle in his eye.

Johnson smiled for the first time since they began their conversation. He had only worked with Meryck for less than six months but it was a marriage made in heaven!

"By the way, did you ever find out where Tinakilly is?" he asked as they made their way back to the car where he scribbled something on a scrap of paper and handed it to Johnson before pulling out a different phone and sending a quick text.

CHAPTER 23

This time when Tullie woke, she was alone. The events of the past twenty-four hours passed clearly across her mind and she wondered where she was. It didn't look like a hospital although it had all the facilities, she noted. Flexing her fingers and toes she found she could move them freely; all of the earlier stiffness and pain had gone. Lifting her right hand to her head she felt around for the sore spots but it too felt normal. Even the drip in the back of her hand didn't bother her any more. Slowly she eased herself upright and was delighted to find she had lost none of her strength either. Moving the bedclothes down she saw the cast on her leg for the first time. So that was what was weighing her down last night! Gingerly she swung her legs over the side of the bed. So far so good! She examined her left arm in detail and slowly began to pick at the bandages to see her injuries first-hand. The drip hindered her progress; she could feel the long needle deep in her tissues forcing the back of her hand flat making her movements awkward. Liquid was still dripping through but she ignored it and continued unpeeling what she could. Bit by bit she got it unwound and the skin underneath was unblemished apart from some faint thin silver lines she could see trailing up from the ring on her finger. Her dreams tumbled back to her all at once and while memories tickled the edges of her consciousness she was unable to pinpoint the link she was searching for. But she was grateful for the strength that flowed through her body and put it down to the meds they were pushing into her system.

Turning her attention to her leg she realised she wouldn't be able to remove that herself. It was way too thick and strong. Like the drip, she'd need assistance with removing that. Looking about her she mentally measured the distance to the water dispenser in the far corner. She was parched!

Moving lower on the bed she found that the drip was on a moving stand and not fixed to the bed as she had first thought. Grabbing the stand firmly and holding onto the end of the bed with her other hand she pushed herself upwards. It was a bit awkward at first but in a short time she was bending down to pour herself a drink when the medic returned. He looked at her in amazement, noting at once her bare arm and her easy stance.

"Well, that was a short bit of shut-eye," he said calmly, making no movement to help her.

"Hello to you too," she smiled back before drinking her first cup of water in one gulp and turning to fill another.

"I see your arm has healed well," he said moving across to her to check it out.

"Amazing!" he mouthed, reaching for the chart to fill in his records.

"Hey, listen," Tullie said. "Can you remove this needle now, please?"

"Might as well," he said, "seems you have no further use for it now."

She hobbled back to the bed and he quickly removed the drip, pushing it away to the side out of the way.

"Any chance of removing this too?" asked Tullie, sticking out her left leg and brandishing the cast in his direction.

"Hmmm," he said. "Let me have a look at that."

He bent down and gently rotated her foot.

"Let me know if it hurts at all," he asked.

She nodded.

He pulled her foot towards him, and then pushed it

away, his thoughts rioting in his head. He'd heard rumours about spontaneous healings but had never experienced one up close himself. The foot was perfect; there was no doubt about it!

"Yep," he grinned. "That looks great too. I'll need some tools to remove the cast. I'll be right back. Just rest up there and I'll be back in a jiffy with my machine saw!"

Dashing down the hallway he wondered about the correctness of what he was about to do. He had been instructed to keep Tullie sedated but it was just not working. She was awake and healed despite his pumping sedatives into her system, enough to knock a horse out! Anjie and BB were away and the two women were asleep. The only other one who could offer an opinion was Carney. Making his decision alone he turned sharply and went to get the doctor.

Handcuffed to the bed frame, Carney was sleeping fitfully. The small room was dark and he had no way of knowing where he was, or whether it was night or day. His slumber was broken abruptly by a medic looking for his assistance with Tullie. He guessed correctly that this was outside the man's skills set and his interest was piqued.

"What's wrong with her?" he asked roughly.

"Well, that's just it," he replied quietly, standing in the shadows, "there's absolutely nothing wrong with her. She's completely healed."

"That can't be right," said Carney, sitting upright on the bed and pulling at his cuff. "Those injuries of hers are nasty. It'll take a few weeks to recover; six at least for the fracture, then physio."

"You'd think so," was the reply back. "The bandages are off her arm and it's perfectly normal. I'm about to cut off the cast now."

"Are you mad?" demanded Carney. "You'll cause more

damage!"

"Want to help then?" asked the man in the shadows. "No nonsense though."

"Now?" asked Carney.

"Now," he replied, moving towards the bed, holding out a key, his eyes waiting for the answer he hoped.

Nodding, Carney held out his hand and felt the key gently touch his palm.

Tullie was surprised to see two men return but didn't mind who removed her cast as long as she was free of it. Carney picked up her chart and looked at it for a long time before committing to the removal. They plugged in the small saw and began to cut away the cast to reveal an absolutely normal foot with no signs of trauma whatsoever. The medic pulled out his phone and snapped a picture for the records and then Tullie jumped from the bed and skipped freely around the room. Carney made additional notes on the chart. It was three am on Sunday morning, twenty hours exactly since the accident.

"Tullie," said Carney, "I'll need to take a blood sample to wrap up the procedure."

The medic watched impassively. It was a good move, one he should have thought of himself but he was flabbergasted, entirely out of his comfort zone. And he had the additional worry of what to do with both of them now.

"Any place we can get something to eat?" asked Carney as he held out the sample for the medic to store watching closely while Tullie unwound the bandages from her head. A sliver of a scar was all that remained; even the stitches had dissolved!

*****

Anjie and BB wasted no time in getting Matt back to base. Now they had him they weren't too sure what exactly to do with him. He was muffled up in a sleeping bag in the back of the car still shivering with the shock of his second near-death experience. BB handed him the flask of strong, sweet coffee and Matt spluttered through the first few sips but gradually calmed down and managed a whisper of a thank you as he handed it back.

"You doing a bit better now?" asked BB.

"We've got you. You're safe with us," interrupted Anjie.

BB was surprised with Anjie's speech. Usually his friend was the ultra-silent one. But Matt seemed to have got under his skin in a good way, mused BB. Anjie liked to look after strays. Matt was lucky to have him on his side.

"Who are you?" whispered Matt, unsure if he even wanted to know the answer.

"We're friends," shot in Anjie before BB could reply. BB smiled.

"Matt," he said quietly, "we know about Greenway. We know about Tullie, and Man-x. But we didn't know about you. Not until Myra told us. Then we heard about the explosion and we knew you were part of all this somehow; enough for someone to want you dead. Why, we're not sure. Maybe you can help us understand that. One thing we do know is that you're in danger and we can protect you, if you let us."

Matt digested this in silence for several minutes. They thought he might have fallen asleep again but he surprised them by leaning forward and asking loudly,

"But who are you guys? How do I know I can trust you?"

"That, is the sixty-four thousand dollar question," said Anjie, "but remember, you are alive because of us. That must count for something. The rest will have to wait 'til later. Ok?"

In his rear view mirror, Anjie saw his nod and the rest of the journey went quietly.

CHAPTER 24

Jo Meryck got the text from her husband and left the house immediately. BECCA meant only one thing but they were prepared for it. She had lost her heart for this sort of work when their beautiful daughter was killed but her training kicked in and she went on autopilot. She drove to Becca's grave and retrieved the locker key from her safekeeping. The rest was plain sailing and by the time Vince was turning in his gun and badge she was well away. For how long, well, that was anyone's guess, she sighed. So the Greenway Conspiracy is real, she shuddered. Then Becca hadn't died for nothing, she sighed sadly.

Meryck wasn't surprised to be ushered upstairs on their return to base. Holiday leave, they put on his form, and accepted his gun and badge shamelessly. The shadowy tendrils went deep and accountability was unquestioning and complete. Only the fall guys were visible; the expendables, Meryck reminded himself again. Downstairs was as quiet as the grave as he collected his personal stuff, what little he permitted himself, then he sauntered between the desks jauntily, a man without a mission it appeared to all but Johnson. He no longer existed; the name on his door had already been replaced by one Inspector A. Gross.

When Meryck got home Jo was already gone and he breathed a sigh of relief. With the events of the past twenty-four hours he didn't want to take any chances. Ken turning up like that had been a warning shot, he reckoned as he checked out if Jo had left anything to eat in the fridge. The first bullet missed him by a whisper as he ducked his head inside. He threw himself against the wall searching frantically for the whereabouts of his assailant. Silencer! He was close! He tried rolling towards the dresser where he kept his spare weapon but was pinned back by persistent fire. Sprinting low he went in the other direction and the shots shattered the window from the inside out as he passed.

Rick heard the window shatter and knew immediately something was wrong. As he tiptoed around the back the pattern of sound confirmed it. Meryck was in trouble. Someone was shooting at him from inside his own house!

"Meryck?" he shouted, ducking low under the window sill, "are you ok in there?"

A splatter of shots peppered his position giving Meryck valuable seconds to find a better vantage point. He knew that voice!

"Here!" he yelled, and Rick reached up and threw a spare gun to him through the shattered window following up immediately with cover fire.

"Thanks, buddy," yelled Meryck, and he ran for the backdoor firing off rounds towards the area he suspected his assailant to be.

Ken hadn't prepared for this, and cutting his losses he smashed through the front window and fled, wondering who the help was.

They heard him go and knew it was useless chasing him. He was gone. Turning to Rick, Meryck offered him his gun back.

"Thanks," he said. "I'd be a goner without your help."

Rick nodded.

"We gotta tidy up here," he said indifferently. "Best you go away for a while, I think."

Meryck nodded.

146

"Would I get a proper answer if I asked what you're doing here?" asked Meryck, "Or why you're following me around?"

"I promised Becca," was all the reply he got, and needed.

"Johnson could do with you covering his back," said Meryck softly, looking him in the eye. The nod was almost imperceptible.

"Take care, man," said Rick, patting Meryck on the arm, where they both remained crouched on the shards of glass beneath the shattered window, "you've upset somebody real bad."

"Wouldn't be the first time!" grinned Meryck.

"Yeah, but they want to make it your last," replied Rick calmly, pushing home his concern.

"I've got Johnson," he added as he slid away into the night leaving Meryck with the distinct impression that he knew exactly whom he had upset. Meryck also felt it was the same one he was thinking of, and felt glad that someone out there was looking out for him, for a change. Memories of Becca rose unbidden to his memory as he remained hunkered down under his own kitchen window: playing chess together; her graduation; returning from her first undercover assignment elated and exhausted; her funeral; and he could feel the fierce anger return and he let it. It washed over him, lashing him from the inside out, until his resolve was renewed and he limped forward to begin his new life – again! Damn, he thought! His body ached from the thrashing around. He wasn't getting any younger, he realised grimly.

He wasn't sad about leaving this time. Neither was he surprised that no one came to see what the noise was all about and he reckoned no one would turn up anytime soon to check out the fire either! There was nothing left but a shell by the time Rick returned following Johnson next day. The young lad had taken his tail in his stride; Meryck had a good one here.

CHAPTER 25

The early dawn disappeared behind them as they drove into the tunnel, Matt fast asleep in the back of the car. The satisfaction of a job well done warred with the responsibility of what they had to do to accomplish it. Both thought this was in the past. Yet they had bent to their task willingly and skilfully and it would take some time for the adrenalin to disperse.

"Let him sleep," said Anjie.

"Keep an eye on him, Cal," instructed BB. "Let us know when he wakes up."

And they headed inside for some fresh coffee and a debrief.

*****

Adam led the way to the kitchen, Tullie and Carney following behind in single file. When the medic flicked on the light they were delighted to see a fully equipped kitchen before them with the smell of real coffee floating in the air. Carney went straight to the water cooler while Tullie followed her nose. Adam shut the door behind them and sat with his back to it. Looking around Carney saw it was the only exit but he wanted answers more than he wanted to escape right now. And he wanted something to eat. Tullie was happily rummaging in the cupboards and within minutes was pouring fresh coffee into three mugs for them.

"Anyone for sugar or milk?" she asked, heading for the giant fridge that sat in the corner.

Both declined but she proceeded anyway. She wanted

to see what there was to eat in this place. Pretty cool for a hospital, she thought.

"Is this the staff kitchen then?" she asked as she pulled out bacon and eggs and moved around looking for a pan.

"Sort of," grinned Adam, admiring the view. Carney just grunted as he downed his third cup of water before reaching for his coffee.

"Careful! That's hot," she said, turning to the stove top to start cooking.

While the pan was heating up she searched around and found some biscuits in a barrel tin on the counter.

"Want one?" she asked, holding out the tin in their direction, noticing the tension for the first time.

"What's up?" she asked, her mouth full of biscuit, as she swept her hair back from her face and tied it in a rough knot at the back.

"Oh! I'm sorry," she suddenly realised. "I haven't thanked you guys for helping me out. Thank you! I really appreciate you looking after me."

Carney and Adam exchanged glances. She doesn't know anything, thought Carney.

"You're welcome," they both said in tandem and Adam vacated his position and joined Carney at the table making sure to remain between him and the door.

The sound and smell of frying breakfast filled the room and nobody was prepared to make the next move until they were fed.

"Can I help?" asked Carney, rising and going to stand by Tullie.

Behind him he could feel Adam tense.

"Some plates and cutlery would be good," replied Tullie, smiling at him.

Carney found he was beginning to admire the young woman before him and hurried away to lay the table to cover his confusion. But when it seemed he knew more about her than she did herself he decided to just go with the flow and see what would happen. He saw Adam's tension increase when he appeared at the table with a fistful of knives and forks. The young man hadn't thought about that, had he! The kitchen was well stocked and he had no trouble sourcing bread, butter and jam and some yogurts to go with the meal.

"Adam," called Tullie unwittingly, "can you top up the coffees please? I'm nearly done here."

Carney watched with deep amusement as Adam weighed up his options. He'd have to go by Carney to get to the coffee pot leaving the way to the door clear. On the other hand, nobody seemed in any hurry to leave. He made a calculated decision to trust that Carney wouldn't do a runner without Tullie and she seemed completely oblivious to what was going on. Moving to the stove he collected the coffee but never took his eyes off Carney. Having refilled the mugs, he left the pot on the table. He wasn't going to risk that situation again. Tullie plated up and they all sat down together to eat in silence. Through the huge windows they could see the first flush of dawn appear.

Finishing her food first, Tullie cradled her coffee mug in her hands, leaned back in her chair and fixed them both with a stare.

"So what's up, docs?" she asked, grinning and patting her stomach. "I really enjoyed that! Now, when are you going to tell me what's wrong? This isn't the hospital, is it? And you are the strangest doctor I've ever met, Adam!"

151

"And you, are you real?" she asked Carney direct.

"Well, Adam," said Carney silkily in response. "Would you like to go first?"

Adam was completely taken off guard; he didn't know what to say.

"Afraid, I can't comment at the moment," he said, stumbling on his words.

"So, what's wrong with me then?" she asked turning to Carney.

"I can't say," he replied truthfully. "Apparently nothing! But less than twenty-four hours ago you sustained serious injuries in a road accident; the kind that keeps you off work for at least six weeks, yet here you are, perfectly healed and cooking us breakfast!"

Tullie rubbed herself all over to check if she really was ok. Sticking out her leg she considered what she had just heard.

"Now, where is here?" she asked quietly, turning the full glare of her emerald eyes upon them.

"And who exactly are you guys?" she continued, pushing her chair back to stand over them both.

Pushing back their chairs too the two men stood united now against what they saw as a common foe. Then the door crashed open and a tired Anjie and BB stood in the kitchen trying to make sense of the scene before them.

CHAPTER 26

Jake watched Guidrius go and he was glad to be alone. So much had happened since this man had walked up to him on the mountain he didn't know where to start. With the memory of Man-x strong in his mind again he rose and approached the platform. The globes winked into existence for him as they had for Guidrius and despite his troubled mind he felt the awe and wonder rise from deep within him and entice him forward once more onto the platform. It felt like coming home to safe, comfortable surroundings now and he reached playfully to the spinning orbs. They caressed his outstretched hands, hummed to him and followed his every move as he casually strolled about the contained area. He stepped outside and they stopped at the perimeter without faltering in their orbit. Stepping back in again he focussed on the one Guidrius had identified to him as his own world and one by one the others winked out of existence. His globe, the one Guidrius had said carried the memories of this world, expanded around him to encircle him. He was now its centre, its core, its heartbeat, he thought with wonder.

It was like being surrounded by thousands of tiny windows each pointing to a different place and time. Reaching through one directly over his head it expanded to fill the area above him. Moving his hand down, it spun with him to position itself where he indicated, the whole globe spinning around to keep in alignment. Opening his arms expanded it further and flinging his hand wide made it encircle him completely. Reversing his hand actions collapsed the area back to its original position. He spent several minutes pitching and rolling individual panels around him until he could see that those at the bottom reflected earlier times and the top ones, nearer the present. He was amazed at the detail presented but disappointed they were just static images; he had expected them to be interactive. Didn't Guidrius say they were? Searching around for the very first window Jake wondered how he could interact with it. As he passed his hands over the remaining ones an image began to hum lightly and rise up to his waiting hand, as if he had called it. He had the beginning! Now he just needed to figure out how to be part of it. The solution was so simple that when he first thought of it he dismissed it outright! But opening the first window around him, he drew his arms back into his sides and stepped forward.

It was like being present in the moment in every way but not visible. Reaching around him, he touched living things now lost to antiquity. Familiar plants felt, and smelled, just as he expected; the sun beat down upon his bare head, making him sweat but a cool breeze from the globe cooled him so that no particle of moisture fell from his body into this memory cell. He could walk and run, shout and laugh but nothing was disturbed and nobody paid him any heed. If he wanted to travel faster, he just had to think it and it happened, and at times it was hard to say who moved, him or the globe. Places he wished to explore just appeared; but up to a point only. Once he tried to go forward beyond a century he was blocked. He had his timed reference point! Each window encapsulated one hundred years; like a child's buried time capsule but complete in every way. He could even hear thoughts if he wished!

Pacing his search, he found life to be much as he expected. There were forests, mountains, oceans, grasslands, deserts; every kind of possible habitat was present, and with every habitat, every form of animal life he had ever known, and more. There were species now extinct that moved him with their love of life; species that remained extant but varied in size and colour and habits than those he knew. Humans were present too in every shape and size and colour, but all living in harmony with each other and their natural surroundings. Babies were born, but in that first century he could see no death, and could discern no living memory of it in the people either. Moving to the waters, he found them teeming with life; many he recognised as precursors to what lived today but many also were completely different. And everywhere he went, he saw evidence of complex communication. This was a world without strife or discord: a perfect Eden. Pulling back from his immediate surroundings, he sought to get an overview of where he was and was surprised to find he was on a large island entirely surrounded by ocean; an enclosed perfect habitat, one he couldn't place in today's world.

While his brain marvelled at this early beginning, his critical faculties argued that this was infantile. Conflict existed forever, didn't it? Pushing these thoughts away he chose to explore a shore-side community first. He moved among them, invisibly and silently, selecting individuals at random to follow and observe. He had been following a young man from the coast for a while when a transformation occurred that he wasn't prepared for. Wading into the water, the youth dived beneath the waves and the globe's memories followed Jake's direction. He saw the youth form instantly into the shape of a dolphin and play with a pod that seemed to be waiting for him. There was no doubt about it! The young man had changed into a dolphin! Jake followed him underwater but was unable to make sense of their interactions, and then, after several minutes, the young man reformed and re-entered human life exactly as before. Others on the shore took no notice. It struck Jake that this was unremarkable to the people there. Continuing to watch he saw the same event happen again and again; and its reverse! Dolphins emerged from the ocean to walk shakily on human legs and commune with those on the shore.

Turning from the shore, Jake went inland to the central plains. Here too, he saw evidence of transformations but there were so many different types, it confused him at first. Then it hit him! Here, there were many different forms

155

of animals and humans, and the connection suddenly became clear! At the coastal village he had observed the people there were all similar in form and colour: here on the grasslands he saw different shapes, sizes and colours of humans among the many different shapes, sizes and colours of animals. Hour after hour he watched for evidence to support his view and it came, slowly at first, then with increasing frequency as night followed day in his enclosed globe. Moving to the uplands he saw the same pattern until his brain was buzzing with questions. Shaking his head he replayed the scenes slowly again, following different individuals for longer until another observation jumped up and hit him square between the eyes! As well as differences in body shape and form and colouring he could plainly see different temperament traits in those humans transformed from different animal species, and different physical abilities. The correlation was plain to see; so plain it shocked him to the core. Dolphin-humans were peaceful and playful and had an affinity for water. Cat-humans were lean and observant, loners for the most part, and controlling any social interaction when it occurred. They were lithe and lean and moved with ease and power. Goat-humans were sure-footed and fearless in scaling heights; wiry and strong, and stubborn and territorial. As at the shore, all could change forms at will. And with his trained eye, the potential for conflict became obvious.

*****

Guidrius moved quietly past the engrossed Jake carrying a small parcel that he had retrieved easily. Slipping it into Jake's rucksack he crept silently away again, his destination Greenway Island. He had to see Man-x for himself, to ascertain the level of threat that he now posed first hand. Maybe he could eliminate the threat once and for all, he grimaced. He knew the way. He had searched the Island after losing Tullie but it was deserted then. Slipping into his dog form he padded softly from the cave.

The nearest way down the mountain to Greenway Island was steep but this was no trouble to Guidrius. Where footfalls didn't exist he simply created them; at times, if observed, he could be seen to walk on fresh air alone. He timed it perfectly; night was falling as he approached the shore. Now there was nothing between him and Man-x but a mile of water and impenetrable night. Lying down, his massive head on his front paws, he observed the island for some time until he was sure he could sense where the movement was within and what security he might face. They wouldn't be looking for a dog; that was his element of surprise. Satisfied that he had gathered all the information he could, he rose slowly and paddled out on the water.

He felt the tingle of the force field as he approached the island and gently let himself sink to establish its depth. It was deep and he had no way of knowing if there was an entrance at land level so far down. Surfacing, he paddled water around the field until he found a part of the island that rose sheer out of the water offering no chance of access without special gear that would leave any intrepid intruder at the mercy of the island security. But he didn't need any special gear. Yet he did need to get through the distance of the force field without arousing any suspicion. He needed a distraction; a natural way to take down the field for the short time he needed. Sending out a call, he felt the shrimp approach. It would be an unusual event, talked about for many years to come but it would serve his purpose well. The shoal buffeted the force field, swelling inside it and pushing holes through its deadly net, leaving small floating bodies in its wake. He moved them with his mind left and right in a randomised pattern that criss-crossed just enough to pave a narrow path for him to the cliff. Leaving them continuing their movement around the island he ploughed forward.

From the top of the cliff Guidrius could sense the breaks in the force field and the massive reduction in the shoal he had summoned. He had no time to waste. Slipping silently

157

through the trees, his great paws took him swiftly to the hillside where the scent of Man-x was strongest. But he was presented with a problem he hadn't anticipated. The facility that was holding Man-x was underground. Sniffing around, he found the well-hidden air vents. They were too small for him to pass through whichever form he took. But he had to know! Drawing his energy around him he sent out a link to Man-x, and it hit home swiftly! The ruckus started immediately almost right beneath his feet. Man-x shot awake from where he had fallen asleep in despair after losing Tullie's link again and went berserk. He could feel the link with Guidrius and it infuriated him, drove him to madness, to a depth of blood-lust he hadn't experienced in years. Then Guidrius broke the link but not before Man-x knew he was nearby and he intensified his efforts to escape. Doors that previously had held him now smashed before him and the alarm sounded loudly deep in the mountain. Guidrius had learned what he'd come to find out. He slipped away and was gone before anyone else noted his presence.

*****

Exhausting the first century, Jake hurriedly sought for the second and the third and beyond, one by one, time passing in a blur as he delved into the mysteries of the world not revealed in this way before. The more he saw, the more he realised he didn't know at all, how ignorant he really was. His whole world was being reformed inside his mind and he knew he'd never look at life in quite the same way again. The first battles weren't long in coming and they were painful to watch; skirmishes really but enormous in their portent: the very first time human harmed human. It seemed to open the floodgates. In a blink of an eye all the world was engulfed in a struggle for dominance but not just dominance within the species but dominance among the human species. Life on human legs had evolved superior reasoning ability, and he watched in fascination, witness to the moment of exaptation; the point of no return; the point when the human species took form in isolation from its animal partner forever. Within the shortest of time spans, this was observed and quantified by the most intelligent and acted upon by the most physically powerful. The survival of the fittest, thought Jake grimly, where we come in, rather than the survival of the smartest. Sometimes they did survive too by becoming submissive or complaint but it was always the bully who won out; rage over reason; might over right so often that Jake wept for the world that could have been. And to his immense surprise evolution didn't stop. Man continued to grow in ways Jake didn't recognise anymore but animals stopped transforming to human form, preferring instead to stay away from conflict and live in peace. Some humans joined them, returning to their primeval form rather than engage in the ravages of advancement. Before his eyes, he was watching his ancestors evolve and the world change in ways that were totally different from the world of today. Their mind-power was exponential; their intelligence unfettered! They used natural resources in a way no scientist had ever thought to in his time: the very same resources that existed today but were overlooked, misused or abused. How fascinating, he thought! But, as in the world surrounding him, this very power was used for opposite ends: the building up and the tearing down. Is there anything new under the sun, he asked out loud, but there was no answer to be heard, only time moving inexorably on. As he was reaching the last panel Jake could feel the cataclysm that was approaching and he baulked for the first time in his viewing. Did he really want to see this immense power play unfold to the last? The globe slowed down while he decided if he wanted to go on. But he still had questions; questions about his own life, his own world and Tullie's. He opened his arms and the battle commenced all around him. It was ferocious! It raged all over the world, millions vaporised in the blink of an eye until every bolt was shot and every switch flipped. The last scene was of a landscape broiling with black-as-deepest-night hate-energy where a handful of dissonant groups faced-off with what weapons remained at their disposal. They were all that was left of a world of awe and splendour, and evolution beyond the wildest of dreams. Then when Jake thought that mankind was doomed to extinction, this pinnacle of evolution of the species being its greatest moment and its darkest hour, a tall, thin man appeared on the open killing ground, held up his arms and the entire universe became deathly silent.

"Friends," he called, "we must stop this now or we will all be destroyed!"

"It's Gellon!" called one voice tremulously, then another called out and another, and the people began to emerge from their combat zones, lifting their weapons into the air.

"We thought you were all destroyed," wept one, rushing to the tall man and embracing him. "We thought all was lost!"

"Hush, my friend," said Gellon, "we survived but are much diminished. As are all you I see," he added looking around the motley bunch that had staggered into the daylight. Raggedy and starving, they were a piteous sight but deadly too, he knew.

"Come on out, every single one of you," he called out. "There is not much time left!"

As Jake watched, he saw Gallon's call carry across the world and from hidden places, high and low, they came, starving and cowed and dying. Who was this man, he wondered? Then he was speaking again.

"You have a choice today," he called, "to live or to die. There is no going back now only forward! If you choose to fight, turn away from me now. Go from here. Take your fight someplace else."

"But if you choose to live," he spoke softly now, "throw down your weapons now and go and be with your kind, because today I offer you small hope for your species that life may go on."

160

As Jake watched, nobody turned away, instead there was a shift forward and soon a huge pile of weapons - Jake could only guess at their capacity they were so different from what he knew, lay at Gallon's feet. He felt himself being drawn forwards too and he went unquestioningly, his mind dully registering the mesmerising effect Gallon was having on all in earshot, and beyond, he realised as well. This man had compelled them all whether near or far, and he had reached far beyond time and space to him! Such power was awesome, and dangerous beyond qualification in the wrong hands. How many more like him existed, he wondered. And as he looked at Gallon's face up close, he had the answer to his question in a heartbeat. Then Gallon began to speak again and Jake was free.

"You have chosen well. Life will go on," he sighed gently, "but the earth is ruined beyond recovery this time; she will rest no longer. As I speak, she is roiling and turning in her depths. This world is about to pass away and we must find new homes."

The distress of the people was evident. How different was this from death? Where could they go?

"I hear your questions," Gallon said. "I will build a world for you to live this time out; a separate world for each species where you may lick your wounds and recover, and find your true way again before we come back together to live in harmony once more. Seek out your kin now; you have six hours, and meet me here at sunset. I have much work to do."

Then he was gone as suddenly as he had appeared and the people milled and thronged together and Jake waited with bated breath for hostilities to break out again but they didn't! The peace held and groups began to form around the place, first one, then another, until there were more than twenty groups. Newcomers poured into the area and seemed to flow directly to their own until the killing field pulsed with life of every sort in a large circle around the growing heap of weapons. Exactly six hours later Gallon was back bringing with him the remnant of his own people.

"Choose again," he called loudly. "Choose a new leader to bring you through this time; a person of peace to atone for the leadership of war. Make it quick! Our time is nearly up!"

But nobody moved; nobody spoke. What he asked them to do was anathema after all the destruction. Give up their power for peace! The hate for the other, the blame for the other, rose in their throats and it was as much as they could do to stay quiet. Gallon looked around then spoke again,

"Come forward, leaders!" he shouted, and from his own tribe a woman called Garwa stepped up to stand by his side.

As if woken from their slumber, one by one, a woman from each group stepped up beside Garwa while their tribes gasped in astonishment and ire but did nothing to intervene. Gallon looked directly at each one as if plumbing the depth of their decision, then nodded, satisfied. Reaching out his hand towards the pile of weapons before him, a ray of pure energy shot forward and ignited it and it pulsed with every colour of the universe. Reaching in his hand, he nodded to the women to do the same which they did without hesitation. Several seconds passed and they stood there, their left hands immersed in the inferno, invisible to the world, while the onlookers stood stupefied by the scene before them.

"Enough," said Gallon clearly, and they withdrew their hands, holding them aloft for all to see. Fastened around their ring finger was a ring that matched Tullie's, one to each species, similar but differing slightly, Jake saw.

"These rings forged here today, in your viewing, hold the history of this world and your individual tribes for posterity, lest you forget where you have come from and why you are

leaving," he said. "Guard them well, for if you lose them, you will lose part of your soul forever."

"Return to your people," he instructed the women.

In the silence that followed he waved his hand and out from the inferno rose tendrils of air that meshed together to form a series of globes that bounced gently in the rising heat, Jake saw, one for each assembled group. Looking towards his own people he motioned Garwa to lead them forward, and reaching up he guided a globe the colour of silver downwards and opened it to reveal to the assembled people a world identical to the one they were about to leave but unsullied. Gasps of astonishment echoed around the place, and smiles replaced frowns. Gallon raised his left hand and Jake could see the ring that sat there clearly and it made his heart skip a beat.

"Each world is made to meet your every requirement," he called out, "but it is not forever. It is made to sustain you until you are ready to return to the earth once more. Your development is limited here; you must live and work with what you have now. That is the price you must pay for what you have brought about today."

As Gallon spoke the earth heaved throwing many people off their feet.

"Quickly," he called, and Garwa bravely led her people forward into the globe. Gallon reached into the inferno and forged a seal which he used to close the globe then it folded in on itself and winked out of existence and he threw down the seal and broke it into pieces on the ground. The earth shook again and the people surged forward, keen to be away from the danger that threatened all their lives. One by one, the women led their people inside their globes, and one by one, Gallon sealed each globe before it disappeared, then smashed the seal before him. The earth was breaking open about him as the last globe was sealed. He stood alone on the shattered and broken earth and wept for the

life that was lost. Reaching for the broken pile of seals,
he grasped then in his arms and travelled, gathering to
him the wounded and the infirm and the abandoned that
weren't quick enough to make it.

Jake followed him with interest and saw he was heading
for an island where a small tribe of people who had sat
out the war lived; blissfully unaware of what was about
to engulf them. Gallon touched down milliseconds before
disaster struck and sucked them into an unready vortex;
then the waters crashed down and Jake could see no more.

Jake paled at the destruction that ensued once they were
gone. The whole surface of the world broke apart and lava
spurted and flowed like bright blood against the churned
mix of stone, soil, sand, and green debris, hissing furiously
where water and new land met. Animals screamed with
pain and rushed for the ocean. Great trees fell helplessly,
broken asunder by the anger of the earth, bursting into
flames. The whole world turned upside down; and Jake
cried in despair, for there was nothing he could do but
watch the thrashing and the breaking, and close his ears
to the moaning, and the hissing, and the grinding down,
and the smashing. And the fires and the smoke were
everywhere! And then the planets themselves shifted and a
very long night set in. There was nothing left to see. A deep
sadness engulfed him and he let the globe slip away from
around him. There was a light tinkling sound of something
having fallen and when Jake bent down to look he found
two rings identical to Guidrius's and Tullie's but these were
made of what looked like yellow gold and emeralds. They
felt so light to his touch when he held them and without
thinking he tried one on his right hand but it wouldn't fit.
Disappointed, he tried it on his left hand, and it slid into
place perfectly. He raised his hand and the emeralds moved
in the light, like trees waving in the wind.

Guidrius watched from the shadows and smiled. He had
his first Keeper.

CHAPTER 27

"What the . . ," began Anjie angrily, but BB cut across him.

"Tullie," he excitedly, "you're up and about!" and he rushed across the room to crush her to his chest in a huge bear hug.

Grinning happily, she snuggled into his embrace. He was her saviour from these two. Now, at least, she knew she'd be safe.

"Am I happy to see you too!" she squeaked into his jacket, pushing herself away from his chest a little so she could breathe.

She wasn't to see the thunderous look that crossed Anjie's face as he took in the scene before it vanished and he faced Adam coldly.

"Care to fill me in?" he asked icily.

"Sir?" asked Adam, as he looked askance at the others.

"No need for any secrets now, is there?" commented Anjie, and he careered past Adam and the petrified Carney who was eyeballing his combats and weapons, to the window beyond.

"Get the women," he flung at Adam, and he pressed the remote that opened the blinds to reveal a direct line-of-sight to Greenway Island.

"Sit!" he instructed Carney who gratefully collapsed onto his recently vacated chair.

Grabbing the coffee pot off the table he moved past BB and Tullie to make a fresh brew, stopping to ruffle her hair and pat her on the back affectionately. BB was still holding her as if he'd never let her go again and Tullie was quite ok with this.

"Come," said BB softly. "I love this view Tullie. Let me show you," and he walked her past Carney to the window.

The dawn had broken with a blush of apricot from the east and the right-hand side of the island was bathed in beautiful soft light. The west side that was flanked by Traveller's Mountain looked dark and damp by contrast but that would change as the day grew older. BB felt it when Tullie recognised the place and he looked down at her and motioned for her not to say anything. She looked up at him incredulously mouthing Traveller's Mountain in complete surprise. BB looked up and down in quick succession and she knew exactly where they were; under Anjie's quarters on the mountain. She was home but not as she knew it. She rested quietly against his shoulder, the sedatives rolling over her in gentle waves. There would be plenty of time for questions.

Behind her, Anjie poured fresh coffee for himself and BB and he poured one for her as well. Ignoring Carney, he came to stand the other side of Tullie, nestling her in between them both and let the dawn, and the coffee, wash the events of the night away. Before long they were interrupted by Adam returning to say the women were on their way, and Anjie promptly sent him away to collect Matt too. BB nodded over Tullie's head; it was a tactical decision and one he approved. Get it all out into the open, all at once; use the element of surprise. Shake the tree and see what falls out. Suddenly, Anjie tensed and grabbed the controller urgently, and the view before them zoomed fourfold and Greenway was nearer. Tullie felt BB freeze and she first looked up into his face and then back at the window in the direction of his gaze. Shocked at the changed view she looked to Anjie, saw the controller, and understood. There was no window. What they were looking at was a live feed from an outside camera or maybe more, she mused. But it was so clever! She was certain she had a direct view out.

"Something's not right," murmured Anjie, and he began panning left to right, zooming into immense detail here and there.

"There!" indicated BB. "Pan back! The water is different."

Anjie moved closer still, and they could see the dead shrimp on the surface, thousands of them. He flicked another button and the view was overlaid by a criss-cross pattern that was not exactly uniform any more.

"They've damaged the force field," he whispered to BB, "but I don't see any activity."

"Give us an aerial," said BB, and as Tullie watched the view spun up above the Island.

To her, it seemed uninhabited. There were no identifiable man-made structures, no roads, and no human presence of any kind. Anjie spun the view deeper and deeper down and now she was able to make out earth mounds that could be bunkers, they seemed not quite in keeping with the surroundings. Then she spotted the air vents and her skin began to crawl. She could feel herself beginning to freak out. BB felt it too and he hugged her tightly, rubbing her arm gently but never once taking his eyes off the scene before them. She didn't know what they were looking for so she waited patiently and securely in BB's embrace.

"There," he whispered finally, and when Anjie rotated to the spot they all stopped breathing. The massive paw prints had left their clear marks in the soft earth.

*****

The door behind them swung open with a bang and

167

Anjie let the view return to normal. Light that wasn't light streamed in through the window that was not a window. The three turned to face the newcomers and Tullie was engulfed in her mother's arms, BB reluctantly relinquishing her from his care. Carney bounded up when he saw Myra and was anxiously asking her if she was ok, drawing her away from Anjie's stare. Then the door opened again and Adam led in a sleepy and disorientated Matt. Drawing away from Carney, Myra moved towards Matt but he resisted her attention, pulling back towards the door and freedom. Adam swiftly moved to block his retreat. Finally, they were all here, thought Anjie. Now for some revelations!

"Sit," instructed Anjie, seating them in a semi-circle facing the kitchen.

"I think fresh coffee would be in order," he nodded to BB.

Drawing up a chair, he sat and faced the group.

"Time to talk," he said.

"First, let me introduce everybody. I'm Anjie and this is BB," he said, indicating behind the counter. "The guy by the door is Adam."

"This here is Tullie, and her Mum, Jane. Then we have Doctor Carney, Myra and Matt," he said pointing to his left.

"Where we are is unimportant. What is important though is that here you are all safe. Our mission," he continued, indicating BB, Adam and himself, "is to keep you that way."

"I'm sorry we had to take you here by force, Tom, isn't it?" he said, looking straight at Carney. "We needed you to take care of Tullie. We needed her, first and foremost, to be safe. That is our prime objective although anyone helping us do this will also be added automatically."

"So, you see, Matt," he continued, turning to Matt

168

now, "you have become, for us, one of this group. We are pledged to keep you safe."

There was silence as BB handed around fresh coffee and biscuits. The glow from the window continued to build as the time passed.

"I have a question," Tullie's voice sounded loud in the silence.

"I imaging you all have questions; many, many questions," replied Anjie. "I know I do. But before we get to that I need to explain something else to you. You all have a choice to stay or leave right now. We will not hold you against your will. On the other hand we will not disclose what is going on without your consent to secrecy. You are all here because your lives are in danger, and this danger is somehow linked to this," and he indicated Greenway Island framed as a window in the panel behind him.

"Tullie is special," he continued, his voice softening. "She is the main link." At this Tullie looked at him, shocked.

"Yes," he continued to faces all curious now, "she knows nothing of this. But if she is found, she will be incarcerated for life somewhere like the Island. She will be subjected to unheard of atrocities; exploited and unable to stop any of it. She would be better off dead! We're here to make sure that never happens, and we will stop anyone who gets in our way."

His voice conveyed clearly the deadly intent behind the words. No one was under any illusion. These men would kill to protect Tullie like they did for me, thought Matt. Why did he not find that comforting, he thought. But Anjie was speaking again.

"Jane is an accessory to the fact. She is expendable like Matt's parents and grandad," he added factually.

Now it was Matt's turn to gasp and all eyes turned in his

direction but he didn't see them as he was staring angrily at Myra.

"You knew!" he accused her. "You knew all this time and never told me!"

"I didn't, Matt," she cried. "I swear!" but he drew the crumpled letter from his pocket and waved it at her.

"Grandad said you knew!" he shouted, agitatedly. "You were there when I was born! How could you not know!"

Coming up behind him, Adam laid his hand on his shoulder pressing him back into his seat. Matt shrugged him off angrily.

"Get off me," he cried. "Leave me alone!"

Watching carefully, Anjie waved Adam away and continued as if nothing had happened.

"Myra is expendable immediately. There is undoubtedly a contract out on her already. She's been through something like this before. She can't be let live. Too dangerous," said Anjie.

Tullie, Jane and Matt looked shocked at this but Carney only looked at the floor, following the pattern with his eyes, his ears wide open. Myra was in tears. Her life was truly over. A whole range of emotions were playing out on Matt's face but he controlled himself and looked longingly towards the window.

"And Dr Carney, Tom," he added, "I'm afraid we have put you in additional danger by abducting you although you were in danger the moment you ran the IBB screen. There's a tap on the database that locates any such queries and shadows move quickly to neutralise any threats. We cannot be sure what'll happen to you if you go back. You'll be interrogated for sure; maybe even locked up. We can't protect you out there. And we could do with your expertise here."

"IBB?" queried Jane.

"International Blood Bank," answered Matt. "They carry thirty-two blood type records. Anything outside of this creates interest as it might compromise national security. Right Myra?" he asked.

She nodded.

"Mercer's database has the Langereis and Junior types upgrade since last week," she explained. "We'll be integrated by the end of the month too. Wouldn't solve anything though, but we had to go through the motions. Protocol . . .," and her voice trailed off.

"Ryan?" asked Carney shakily. "Where's Ryan? What's happened to him?"

"Still at work, I expect," shrugged BB. "He signed the Official Secrets so will come to no harm as long as he keeps his mouth shut."

"I got another question," interrupted Tullie, more loudly this time. She didn't like it when Anjie ignored her. "What's with the IBB stuff?"

But Anjie jumped in again before anyone could reply.

"Decision time," he said. "You can choose to leave now before you hear any more. We will return you to a place where you can re-enter your life or start anew. We will provide funds for you, and documents, if you need them. You will never see us, or hear from us, again."

He paused for this to sink in.

"Or you can commit to secrecy," he continued. "Anything you hear from now on will remain within this group. You will commit to keeping Tullie and each other safe; to help

171

us determine the true nature of the threat against us; and to work together to combat this threat. You will be under our protection at all times. Any breach of this commitment thereafter will be met with the ultimate penalty."

"Come," said Anjie to BB and Adam. "Let's give them some space to decide."

He stopped at the door.

"We'll be back in fifteen minutes for your decisions," he said calmly.

Tullie looked thunderously at his departing back. Why couldn't he bloody-well give her a straight answer, for once!

CHAPTER 28

Meryck wanted nothing better than to have a cigarette but he was afraid the smoke would give him away. Lying flat on his belly above Bear's Lake where he had seen the two men tailing Matt he thought for the umpteenth time about the two dead men he had come across earlier. Trained killers for sure, they weren't long dead and had been hidden hurriedly among the brush but the broken shrubs and grass told its story to Meryck as clear as if he had been present at the shooting. Clean hits, he saw. They didn't know their assailants were there, he concluded. Matt had found a comfortable spot he noted as he wriggled around appreciatively. And he had friends; powerful friends. But where was he now? And where was Tullie? And why did the shadows try to take him out? Focusing, he trained his sights on Greenway again. He had enough supplies for a few days before he headed for Tinakilly. By then, Ken should be off his scent. But he had the distinct feeling he would find the answers he was looking for on the island.

The morning passed uneventfully and Meryck dozed for short periods waiting for Johnson's call. He'd got no sleep last night following the fire as he travelled around in random patterns setting a false scent. The sound of his phone reverberated around the mountainside and he cursed. He was certain he'd turned the setting to silent vibrate! Grabbing his handset he hit the answer button but the sound continued. Flinging away his phone suddenly he grabbed his rucksack and emptied the contents on the ground. Swearing anew, he saw Tullie's bag tumble out. The sound was coming from there but it stopped before he could answer it. Quickly he checked the caller. Jed! Again! Thumbing through the settings he clicked vibrate and slid back into his lair sweat pouring from his body. Cautiously he peered around his position checking for any signs of urgent activity but there wasn't any. He lay crouched like an animal for another thirty minutes before relaxing to breathe freely. He had an escape route worked out but he was relieved that his position was uncompromised. Leaning back, his eyes were drawn to her bag once more. Reaching for it he decided to check it out more thoroughly now that he had all the time on the world.

The necklace was simply lovely nestling among the fabric in the decorative wooden box. Lifting it up slightly was all it took for the sun to glint off the precious stones. It felt so light in his big, gnarled hands. A birthday present, he wondered? An expensive birthday present, he corrected. But he concluded that it would certainly look wonderful against her pale skin. Pointing his phone he snapped a shot of it before returning it safely to its box. The faded envelope caught his attention next. It looked important, like a Will or Property Deeds. Its seal was still intact so she hadn't looked at this, he surmised. Reaching for his knife he skilfully separated the seal from the paper and gently extracted the contents. The paper was silky yet strong but the writing undecipherable. Two, he reckoned, were identity documents or deeds as these had ornate swirls and colours, while the others all closely resembled each other; even, monochrome writing throughout. These he had no idea about whatsoever. Turning them over and over in his hands, the writing seemed to be the same whichever way they were turned. But taking no chances he snapped pictures of both sides, and of the other two, before replacing them in the envelope. Johnson could help him with these and he didn't have long to wait, just enough time to check out the rest of her stuff which was all ordinary and everyday.

"Johnson," Meryck answered. "You ok? Is your tail still with you?"

"Sir," said Johnson at the same time. "You ok Sir? Can you talk?"

"Shoot," said Meryck softly, "this line's safe. I'm good to talk. You burned the note? Memorised the number?"

Johnson's speech went on for some time. As they had suspected, a new supervisor had been provided for him, one no one had ever heard of or seen before. Worse, she didn't show up on any regular database, coming up as classified every way he searched. His following friend was with him wherever he went; always just out of direct contact but within quick reach should he be needed.

"Is it really necessary, Sir?" asked Johnson again. "It's creepy having someone like that about all the time."

"Trust me, Johnson," said Meryck. "I wouldn't have asked him if I didn't think it was absolutely necessary!"

"Any news on our missing friends?" he continued.

"Nothing," replied Johnson. "They've just disappeared off the grid! And the funny thing is; there's no ongoing investigation! I'm on my way to Skyway now, just like you said, to interview Bill Boyd"

They both were quiet for a bit as they thought things through.

"Mmm," said Meryck. "How long will you be there?"

"Just for as long as it takes, Sir," replied Johnson. "I've been in touch with Bill Boyd and he knew nothing of what happened. Jane Bell hadn't been in touch. Got an appointment tomorrow morning when they dock. Funny thing about her, Sir. What do you make of it all?"

They tossed the circumstances of the past twenty-four hours about for a few minutes but were no closer to an understanding of what might have happened than before.

"Johnson," said Meryck, "there are a couple of things I want you to do for me; under the radar for both our sakes, of course."

"Go ahead, Sir," he said, "but be quick. I can see Godzilla looking around for me!"

Meryck chuckled. He got the picture clearly and was glad the lad's sense of humour hadn't abandoned him.

"I've got a few pictures I want you to have a look at," he said, "from the envelope in Tullie's bag. See what you can make of them. And the jewellery; see if you can trace its provenance. And Johnson, use Rick, not the usual channels. Let's keep this off the grid for now."

Hearing Johnson's intake of breath he knew he wasn't impressed with him interfering with evidence in this way and in another life they would have indulged in a good argument the outcome of which would have been Meryck conceding defeat, he knew.

"I'm sending them now," he added.

"Ok," said Johnson shortly. "Gotta go, Sir,"

"And Johnson," said Meryck in a parting shot, "if you hear anyone mention Greenway Island, any snippet or passing reference at all, let me know immediately!"

CHAPTER 29

Anjie strode ahead down the corridor followed by BB and an anxious Adam. Turning to the left, he indicated both of them to follow him inside. Adam had never been in this room before and it took his breath away! It was a central Intel hub lined with screens on every side, and computers gathering and processing information on an unprecedented scale. Scenes from all over the world ran beside database revelations and real time snoop scenes. As the door whisked shut behind them Anjie spoke for the first time.

"We're good," he said. "You can speak freely here."

"Care to fill us in?" he asked, turning to Adam.

"Sir!" shouted Adam, and saluted.

"Just tell us what happened," replied Anjie tiredly. "How come Tullie is up and about so soon? And what happened to her cast? And why the hell is Carney involved? He's compromised now."

They listened carefully as Adam recounted the events of the previous night. He left nothing out; he wasn't a qualified doctor after all just a trained ops medic and Carney had been the one who treated her initially. He'd made a choice, one he thought best in the interests of Tullie and he was not about to back down on that one.

"I see," said Anjie. "You made a good call."

Adam nodded.

"Dismissed," he said curtly, looking intently at the room

they had just vacated on one of the screens. "Now go back and stand guard. No one leaves," he nodded to the room.

"Sir!" replied Adam, but when he got to the door he couldn't open it.

Anjie waved his hand and the door slip open noiselessly.

*****

"So, it's all going to come out now," said BB wearily, sitting down heavily.

"Looks like it," sighed Anjie, rubbing his face.

"What do you think they'll decide?" asked BB, nodding towards the screen that was alive with activity.

Anjie shrugged. He was a man of his word but he hadn't filled in all the gaps. The arguments were in full flow. Looking at his watch, he realised they still had a full ten minutes to go. Time passed slowly when you're exhausted, he thought ruefully.

"Let's check who's up and about while we have the time," he smiled at BB. "Who knows? Maybe Jake will have turned up by now!"

Together they viewed the house above them but no Jake. The mountain was quiet and deserted as they panned around, the lake serene in the dawn flush. The yellow tape lay limply around the site of the explosion as they inexorably moved to the site of last night's fight. They stayed on the scene for some moments, then Anjie began to play it backwards checking they had got away clean. Sleep began to creep up on them and he sped up the replay. They had to go back in the room in another three minutes anyway.

"Hey, Anjie," said BB, suddenly fully alert. "Did you see something? Up there, exactly where we found Matt?"

Anjie focussed the feed and readjusted the trajectory so they were now looking directly down on the spot from above. A man lay snuggled into the hole Matt had carved out for himself, talking on his phone.

"I know him," said BB excitedly as they zoomed in on his features. "That's Meryck, the guy in charge of Tullie's accident."

"Not anymore," growled Anjie who was already processing his details, the phrases OFF THE CASE and CLASSIFIED flashing now beneath a recent picture of the man they were looking at on the mountain. A short while later the name Johnson came up: Meryck had been talking to Johnson.

"Know him too," said BB. "It's his young side-kick. Nice guy."

"Time to go back in," nodded Anjie casually. "Let's see how this plays out. No doubt about it; the vultures are gathering. The CLASSIFIED run should be through by the time we've finished."

As they got to the door another message flashed on the screen. Tullie had missed another call from Jed!

More alert now than they'd been on the mountain, they made their way back to the kitchen.

"That was close," whistled BB. "Meryck just missed us by a whisper!"

Beside him, Anjie nodded. He wished Jed wasn't in the scene. It complicated things more than he wished. Too much uncertainty, by far!

CHAPTER 30

Jake was surprised to see Guidrius waiting for him. Blinking in the strange light, he staggered off the platform and realised just how exhausted he was. It had taken all night!

"You need rest," said Guidrius, coming forward to help him. "That was a mega sess by anyone's standards!"

"You think!" slurred Jake. "What do I do with this?" he asked, holding out the second ring, stupid with tiredness.

"Keep it safe," smiled Guidrius as he guided him forward. "We'll talk about it when you wake up."

Jake crumbled onto the floor and Guidrius drew a light blanket over him.

"Sleep now," he said. "I will wake you in a little while. We have only a short time and I have other things to show you before we leave this place. And you'll have questions, no doubt," he smiled.

But before he even turned away, Jake was snoring gently, one new ring shining on his finger, the other clasped in his fist which he held close to his chest.

*****

Back in the kitchen Carney was staring out the window, deep in thought and oblivious to the rest of the room. Occasionally a word or a phrase would make its way through to him and he would turn briefly to cast a worried eye over the gathering. Matt was tearing into Myra, expelling years of pent-up anger and anxiety, blaming her for everything he could think of. Myra was letting it all happen, waiting for the moment when the tirade would blow itself out so she could try to explain. It didn't seem as this would be anytime soon, he grimaced. Jane Bell was talking a storm, trying anxiously to build bridges with Tullie whose whole profile was set in deep disbelief and incredulity. In the melee, he was forgotten, a casualty of happenstance, an expendable. What did he want to do? His overwhelming feeling was one of betrayal: Myra had betrayed him and hung him out here to dry. But he'd been happy enough to go along for the ride; an entirely different type of ride for sure, but he was happy to be complicit after the fact only a short while ago. He vacillated between feeling he had everything to lose and everything to gain; and in the end fell afoul of the fact that the decision wasn't a real decision at all, just a choice between survival and extinction, and in cases like this people always chose survival, didn't they? So what was there to fret about? Who'd miss him? No one! No one home! No home – period! Did he want to be part of this big party? It certainly was intriguing! His scientist's senses were in overdrive. But could he trust these people? After all, they had just kidnapped him, forced him to administer drug amounts he did not feel were safe. But Tullie had recovered overnight! How did she do that? Could others do this too? Would she share her secret so he could help others? He began to pace back and forth, back and forth, running his hands through his hair in agitation, Myra noted absently.

Matt was winding down thankfully. She couldn't blame him even though some of the things he had to say were wildly off the mark, and hurtful. Her heart went out to him. He'd had some very difficult things to deal with these last twenty-four hours. He was lucky to be alive. How could she comfort him? What solace would he take from anything she had to say right now? Maybe in time! The main thing was that he was safe. He didn't seem to realise he had nowhere to go though; whether he liked it or not he was a part of this big picture now. He had a part to play, she realised, a much bigger part than she had ever imagined. All those

181

years ago she had pushed all her anxieties about Elizabeth's pregnancy and her delivery on Greenway away, happy that her new friend was finally going to have the family she longed for. But she did have doubts; no, questions really, ones she never asked. Ones she didn't have the courage to challenge! She sighed. Something died that night twenty-five years ago; she felt her very soul had been questioned and she had faltered in the face of the unknown. She had let Man-x down. And now she had let Matt down. And Elizabeth. And look where that had led her; and them all, she asked herself as she looked around the room. She was tired of keeping things bottled up.

Matt had retreated behind the counter in search of more food when she followed him.

"Do you think it's been all hunky-dory for me then? Well it hasn't!" she screamed at him.

"For years I've lived in fear of them returning; afraid I'd be 'disappeared' because of some whiff of impropriety," she yelled into his face.

"For years I've stood in front of the mirror every morning afraid to look myself in the eye in case they had changed colour overnight; that I was becoming like him!" she cried.

"I've watched out for you! Looked after you! Kept you informed when you didn't want to come home!" she continued, fury blasting its way through years of captivity, and Matt recoiled before it; before a Myra he didn't recognise at all.

"I treated you like my own son!" she shouted, tears pouring down her face, "and this is what I get called for my troubles? Liar? Cheat? Betrayer?"

They all turned to look in their direction; it seemed like this last word unlocked a whole world of emotions in all present.

"Well, I was betrayed too," she sobbed. "Your grandfather left me in the dark too. I didn't know! I really didn't!"

"Well, you should have asked, shouldn't you," Matt found the energy to shout back but it was a pale shadow of his earlier anger. "How the hell can I trust you after all this?" and he threw up his arms in defeat.

"That's enough, all of you," Tullie said loudly into the pregnant pause that followed Myra's outburst, standing up and looking them all in the eye. "It seems like all this comes down to me somehow; this all would have remained underground apart from my unfortunate accident. I could say I was betrayed too but what good would that do now. What's done is done. We need to find out as much as we can about what's really happened to bring us all here together. But we need to use that information to move forward not go around and around in circles of recrimination. Whatever we know now, or don't know, does not change the people we are, or were. It only influences how we look at things from now on, and that influence is our choice. We get to decide from now on."

Jane Bell watched her daughter turn the tumult of emotions in the room towards herself; saw her work the same magic she had witnessed time and again since she was a child, since she was able to talk really. She had cut through to the core of why they were all present without negating anyone's experience. They were all looking at her now, a burgeoning empathy visible on their faces, their own fears subjugated to her plight. In one short speech she had them to her side, soothing away the difficulties that threatened to overwhelm them. They spun around her energy wordlessly and with the same astonishment she always experienced in these moments, Jane watched as Matt reached out his arms to embrace Myra, healing the pain and separation that had sprung up between them and restoring trust and love. Carney was next. Moving from the window he reached out his hand to Tullie and she grasped it firmly, shaking on an undeclared bond that would last for as long as they lived.

"I'm glad you're ok," he said softly.

Tullie turned to Jane Bell, the only mother she had known, and an unbidden memory of a figure with her back turned towards her rose in her mind, an image from that dream; a woman she had reached out to but couldn't remember what happened next, and she pushed it down as she took Jane in her arms and they clung together as if this was their last embrace on this earth.

*****

Anjie pushed open the door and BB followed him in.

"So, you've come to a decision, I see," said Anjie, looking slowly around him, taking in the calm expressions and the positive body language.

Tullie nodded, coming forward to stand before him, speaking for the rest.

"Yes, we have," she articulated clearly, looking back over her shoulder for nods of affirmation.

"But," she continued, "we want some answers. We want to know what you know, all of it, no more secrets, and we want to know what it all means for our future, how we're going to live from now on. It's all or nothing. Agreed?"

Anjie nodded. He had the outcome he had hoped for. They would lose no one today. Tullie had worked her magic again; it was what he had bargained on. She was his best asset and his greatest challenge.

"I need a few hours to put the last of it together," he said firmly in a voice that booked no argument. "I promise you that everything I know I will share with you. And I promise that we will explore every possible outcome for all of you."

He moved among them, shaking on a deal that sealed them to each other for life. None demurred; all grasped his hand firmly and he could sense the deflation and relief as each body shrunk with fatigue, and relaxed in hope, and trust, and safety, for the first time since the accident.

"Get some rest," he ordered. "After lunch I will show you what I can, and tell you what I can't show you."

"Myra," has asked, "can you show Matt to a room please? There are supplies of spare clothing in the locker rooms should anyone fancy a shower and a change of clothes. Can I leave this to you as well, Myra?"

She nodded.

"Jane," he continued, "show Tullie to her own room please. I'm sure you still have much to talk about."

"Tom," he said turning to Carney, "we are delighted to have you on board. I know you're exhausted but I'd like to show you around myself before you have a bit of kip, if that's ok?"

Leaving BB to tidy up and get lunch started, they all trooped out, going their separate ways once outside the door.

*****

Carney followed Anjie down the corridor and into the lift that carried them further downward to another secure floor. Handing him a pass, Anjie led them through heavy doors into a spacious lab. Carney couldn't believe his eyes. He was standing in a state-of-the-art lab.

"I trust you'll find everything you need here," said Anjie, grinning proudly. "You may not be familiar with every piece of equipment; some of this stuff is military standard,

185

you understand. All the manuals are in hardcopy as well as digital, just in case."

Moving through the lab he pointed out several machines that Carney did not recognise, explaining their function in detail, without reference to any prompt sheet whatsoever. Turning a corner, they came to another door. Beyond the door were complete hospital facilities including an operating theatre, ICU and other smaller units.

"These are secure units," indicated Anjie, offhandedly.

"Prison cells?" queried Carney acidly, remembering his own recent experience.

"If you wish," answered Anjie, not rising to the bait.

"And here," he continued, "are your own quarters," using his pass to open another door into a self contained, spacious apartment.

Leading the way across the room, he grabbed a remote control and the end wall flicked to reveal another view of Greenway Island from a more lateral position than that viewed from above. Throwing it across to Carney, he moved to the window and pressed a concealed button and the fridge swivelled out from the wall to reveal a door. He opened the door to reveal a stairs going down.

"Fire exit," he said shortly. "This leads to the lake, and a boat, should the need occur. I would caution you against using this until I have explained it further though."

Carney joined him at the top of the stairs and the two men stood there, looking down in silence for several seconds.

"I'm not going anywhere," said Carney, "but thank you," and he thrust out his hand to Anjie.

"Apart from Jake, BB and myself," said Anjie as they

shook hands, "you're the only one who knows where this exit is. And you're the only other one with access."

"Now get some rest," he added, "we'll meet at two," and he was gone down the stairs, and the fridge swung silently back into place.

CHAPTER 31

Ben Smith wiped the sweat from his forehead as he followed the progress of the boat on his left monitor. They were a fine pair, those two; their very presence chilled him to the core. He pitied the poor bastard on the boat who had wandered this close. Damn! He had even anchored! Didn't he know where he was? He pushed a button and the portion of the cliff that shielded the deep entrance into Greenway slipped back into place. All was contained once more. Glancing around the screens he checked on the inmates one by one. Man-x was sitting immobile as always; that one puzzled him, and worried him, and excited him, in equal measures. The new research was bearing fruit. At long last, something good to come out of this hell-hole, he thought grimly. He badly wanted to be away from this place; to take Kate and Jenny and disappear again, somewhere where they wouldn't find him this time. I'll make it happen if it's the last thing I do, he swore into the empty space around him.

The old geezer was sitting cross-legged again, a chess board on the floor in front of him, moving the pieces with his mind. His appearance was a shambles but Ben knew his mind was razor sharp. Those purple eyes bore deeply into the minds of anyone who crossed his path and they would scream in pain at the intrusion as he cackled with mad laughter. His eyes turned to the camera boring straight into Ben's now. Distance provided no safety barrier but he was used to it now. He was sorry he had come to this but it was his own fault. Nobody had seen his intent to test the DNA derivative on himself but something seemed to change in him since the accident. He guessed the Club was involved, and Ben knew he was correct in this assumption, and the old guy knew he knew. He had read his mind many, many times. Ben let him. It was the only link with the outside he had but even that hadn't been interesting of late since Ben hadn't been home in weeks. He too was a prisoner now, the eyes bored into his skull, and Ben knew they wouldn't let him go freely. They had Kate and Jenny tagged to keep him quiet. One false move and they too met with an unfortunate accident. Shaking, he slipped the phone out of his pocket and powered it up, frantic now to check they were ok. Kate was at home, he sighed in relief, but Jenny's dot was scarily close to the boundary they had afforded her. Panning in, he recognised the place instantly. Tinakilly! What the hell was she doing there? Swearing, he realised he couldn't call her from here. Personal calls were blocked. His heart pounded in his chest as he slid the phone back into his pocket and continued his checks. She was on her own, he realised, as tears trickled down his gaunt, unshaven face.

Turning back to the screen he watched the progress of the two as they pulsed across the water towards Brave Betty. The old guy became agitated, the chess board flying into the air, pieces cracking against the walls and ceiling. But then it veered away and he felt himself breathe again but the old guy became even more agitated. Turning to the other cells, Ben watched sadly as the inmates sat immobile and dribbling on their bed-chairs, their appearance unkempt and their frames bony and frail. They hadn't eaten or drunk since the recent round of experiments; their very soul seemed to have abandoned them. They would eat if instructed, drink if instructed, do anything they were directed to do, and in between they sat and waited, human robots devoid of will or feeling. If left alone, they would simply fade away and die.

The hospital ward was calm; the patients dozed in their beds, the IVs administering a strong sedative along with the test fluid, the monitors purring their data quietly to the nurse's station in the corner. To the right, two doctors in protective suits monitored three patients in ICU. He was restricted from seeing much of what was going on there but the excitement was evident; hence the big visit tomorrow and the extra security on the water. Wrong place, wrong time, Brave Betty, he sighed, and looked around for a vacant unit for the newcomers but there was none! The three spare units had been kitted out for the ICU patients already. So, they expected the healing to be that fast, he gasped!

The restricted zone area was out of bounds but he knew that another surveillance system watched over it. He had installed it himself and knew all the fail-safes and weak spots. Blocking the screen in front of him with his body, he typed the code and the zone flicked into life. He had only five seconds but it was enough. 4.5 seconds later he exited, shaking. The human forms were visible now and he shuddered, wiping his brow. Transgenics! They had to be from their size; and their eyes! Quickly, he counted. Six! So they were what they were coming to see!

Turning to the screen on his right, he saw the kitchen was busy. The new chef, well not really new now, but certainly much newer than any of the rest of them, was good. She had not complained over living in and was pleased with the apartment they had provided for her when off duty; all under surveillance, but she wasn't to know that. Her heart must definitely have been broken bad for her to incarcerate herself away in this place but she wasn't to know the half of it! The kitchen was well equipped, the food fresh and plentiful, the whole thing presented as an island retreat for some poor unfortunate and his family. They had done well to trawl so far afield for her services. She was a good find even if she did keep to herself; well to the kitchen staff anyway. Make lunch be soon, his stomach grumbled. His breakfast had sat badly in his belly with the boat's arrival in their waters.

The explosion caught him unawares, the sight erupting on the screen to his left with a force that threatened to wipe out all about him too. His heart stopped in his chest! Here we go again, he almost wept! But he was distracted by the old guy going berserk, flinging himself at the door in a desperate attempt to escape, something he had never done before. Ben's hand trembled as he pushed a button and an odourless gas hissed quietly into the room. He knew what was happening, Ben saw, as he flattened himself against the door, as far away from the inlets as he could, and covered his mouth with a raggedy sleeve. But he knew it was useless; he had used the same control against Man-x in his time and to Ben's astonishment he saw his resistance time had doubled, no quadrupled! He had to let go of his old friend; he had become someone entirely different, he had been told. The Club was probably right. He needed to be hammered down for everyone's sake. But pictures of Kate and Jenny flashed across his mind and deep inside he knew he could never give up on anyone. As long as there was life, there was hope. As the old guy slid into unconsciousness, both of them were smiling grimly.

*****

Ben was sleeping in his bunk off the Control Room when all hell broke loose. His young assistant was frantic. Alarm bells were going off everywhere and when Ben looked at the screens two things were seriously wrong. Man-x had erupted uncontrollably, his raw power seeping through the buildings enervating everyone in his path as he smashed all before him in a blast for freedom. Ben hit the red button and heavy steel doors slid closed in his rampaging path, trapping him in an unused part of the building. He had been heading for the air shaft in the next section Ben was sure, watching where Man-x was looking. A few strides would have seen him free! His hand shaking, he released gas into the area and Man-x gradually collapsed unconscious on the floor. He'll stay there tonight, thought Ben. We don't have the manpower to move him now since the two haven't returned yet.

The critical moment over, Ben turned his head to the second alert. The force field had been breached in several places. It would take all night to get it back up. Panning around the island he could see the destruction was mainly in one area and relaxed a little; that area was inaccessible anyway, the cliffs were too sheer for anybody to climb. Still, he directed the security detail while he delved deeper for the cause of the breach. The pictures from the underwater cameras were stunning! Thousands of shrimp floated dead on the water! It looked like a whole shoal had come in through the bay at high tide and got battered against the force field knocking out several pockets. He began to breathe normally again; a natural disaster then. He stood down the alert and set to repairing the code lines. He had until mid-day to get it done before the hot shots showed up.

*****

Man-x heard Guidrius call his name and his head exploded in pain. His reason subverted, he smashed his way to where he could sense him, to the left and above. The pain intensified as he got closer but he was puzzled. Guidrius stood still; he wasn't moving away as Man-x was programmed to expect. Reason warred within his skull: he could remember no direct order to terminate this man but some memories flashed through his brain; he was a threat somehow. Searching above him for a way out, he spotted the air-vent. It was small, too small for him to pass through he realised in frustration and he roared out his anger volubly; then the security door crashed down in front of him, cutting off his progress and he slammed his body into it with all the force he could muster as the gas began to fill the corridor. He'd experienced this many, many times before and knew the more he struggled the faster the impact so he slid down the side wall slowly, feigning submission. Let them think they have me, he thought, elated. He'd found his mission again and these humans would bother him no more.

CHAPTER 32

Matt felt human again after a shower and a change of clothes. Curling up on the bed in the small windowless room, he unfolded the papers and began to read from the beginning just to make sure he had it right, hoping against hope he had misunderstood. But no, it was as he remembered.

He was not his father's son.

Elizabeth was his mother.

Man-x was his father.

His blood group UNKNOWN.

Sighing, he put down the sheets to let the truth of his old life slip away before turning to the new one he had agreed to a short while ago. Surprisingly it wasn't as difficult now as he had experienced earlier on Brave Betty but then he was alone; here he had a new family, albeit a rather strange one, but a family nonetheless. And there was the big revelation to look forward to. And there was Tullie. She looked so forlorn; he was drawn to her, he realised. She was pretty too, no beautiful, he corrected. In fact, he couldn't remember seeing any other girl more beautiful that her. And she spoke out to gather them together even though she must have been in turmoil herself. How brave was that! Pushing aside her memory was tough but he wanted to finish the letter. There was a lot more to read yet.

When your parents died I suspected the Club was behind it and the years have confirmed it. My job at Greenway has become my whole life; they will not let me leave the island now. My job here is controversial. You may not like me much for this, my boy, but please hear me out.

Matt shuffled uncomfortably on his bed when he read this. Somewhere deep inside it linked with ancient memories he hadn't realised he had, and they were unpleasant. Getting up, he wandered back to the kitchen. He wanted to read this in daylight. Making himself some fresh coffee, he sat at the table and opened the letter again.

We don't yet know where Man-x comes from; he is silent and withdrawn and non-communicative no matter what we do to him. It seems as if he has shut down; has removed his consciousness from the present moment, as if he is waiting for a command. But we have discovered many wonderful things about him. He heals within hours. His strength is immeasurable. I believe he is telepathic, that he can communicate beyond mere words. In all the time he has been with us, he has not aged one single bit. We cannot identify any implants though I feel they exist; a technology beyond our capabilities sustain him, I'm sure. A silver compound runs through his blood; and yours now, the code may well be hidden there. I don't know what it means for you, I can only guess, I'm afraid. I have watched your progress and I have seen the beginning of these signs: you heal quickly; you are strong; you prefer being alone because you create deep empathetic bonds with those around you. You are intelligent, I believe, way beyond what is normal. You see patterns in things others don't; intuitively finding solutions where conventional wisdom fails.

Matt put down the letter again and drank deeply from his mug. What his grandad had said about his personality came as no surprise to him; the only surprise really it was articulated clearly and objectively like that. In fact, it explained a lot really, especially his feelings for Tullie. With a start, he realised where he was going with this and backed away swiftly picking up the letter hurriedly and continuing reading.

My job here has been to experiment on Man-x; to see

194

what use we can make of the information he provides
for us. The government is involved deeply but plausible
deniability is the order of the day. They have handed
over the running of the facility to the Club, a collection of
individuals whose agenda is singular and brutal; exploit
Man-x for all possible military advantage. Failure is not an
option. After my first breakthrough, they had me moved
permanently here; I am a prisoner as much as Man-x. But
this I swear: they do not know about you. That was work I
did in secret at the beginning; I doubt I would have done it
later. It was risky and untried but your mother was willing
and desperate to have you, my boy, and despite what
lies in your veins, you are my flesh and blood, and I will
do everything in my power to keep you safe. When they
were killed I sent you away to a very public place for safety
though it broke my heart to part from you. I told them
here you were adopted from the start and that seemed to
suffice. Thankfully, their focus was elsewhere and as long as
I produced the goods, they left us alone.

It was that last trip your parents made to the island
that sealed their fate, I'm afraid. Can you remember that
trip, for your fifth birthday? You were happily playing in the
lounge with your dad and your mother wanted to see your
real father. There was nobody about and I foolishly took her
to see him. I wanted to see his reaction as much as hers.
He came to the door and looked at her for long minutes,
something he had not done with any other person before,
even me, whom he saw several times a day. She looked
back sedately, picturing in her mind all the features of this
strange man she had passed on to you with her own genes.
When she put her hand up to the glass, he covered it with
his, the only gesture of emotion I have ever seen from him. I
feel he knows he has a son. I also feel he will love you to the
last. It is my belief, that no matter how strange this man is,
he will do you no harm, ever.

But I had made a huge mistake letting an outsider see
Man-x. The cameras saw it all in silence and a week later

your parents died in that car accident. They interrogated me after that visit to Man-x and I explained your mother was the first female he had seen since we incarcerated him here. They brought in other women then to test his response but he just sat in silence and ignored them. That was really when they began to see your mother as a threat. Your father, well, he was a warning to me, I think. I hope you can forgive me, my dear boy.

The mug was empty as Matt lifted it to his lips and he didn't have the energy to go for a refill. The pain of the accident pierced his heart afresh and he put his head down on his arms and let the tears come. In Anjie's Control Room, the sobbing filled the silence but there was no one there to witness it. He was spared that, at least. Gulping air, he let them subside and reached for the letter again. It was nearing the end, the writing more hurried and scribbled now.

You know that my home was ransacked by the government after I died. The thing is, my boy, my death was a fabrication. I had become way too valuable to them to let me ever go free and they needed to cut you lose from me; another of their warped management strategies. It is nineteen years since I 'died'; I am still at Greenway but am much changed. I have a friend and ally on the inside. I cannot name this person in case this comes into the wrong hands but if you are ever in need or trouble find a Detective Meryck. You can trust him completely. Show him this letter. He will believe you.

I must go now. I do hope we can meet again someday, my boy. One last thing: when they searched my house they were not looking for any of my work; they were looking for the letter your mother wrote to you before she was killed. They must not have found it or you would not be alive still.

I love you, Matt.

BE certainly courageous always!

Ever yours, Grandad xxxxx

And there the letter ended. Matt was stunned. Standing, he walked to the window and looked out on Greenway Island. It was entirely possible his grandad was still alive over there: he now knew his dad was; he could feel him in his core. And a letter from his mother! How wonderful! He had to find it, to hold in his hands something that she had touched after all this time. He suddenly realised he was crying again but his time they were gentle tears, and he let them flow, washing away the loneliness, the uncertainty, and the pain of the last twenty years.

CHAPTER 33

The moment Guidrius touched him Jake came awake instantly. A reflex born of decades of survival swung into action and he caught Guidrius unawares for once; sitting up and holding the knife skilfully to his throat with one slick movement.

"Not a good move," he said coldly, and let his hand drop.

"Hmm," said Guidrius, rubbing at his throat reflexively, "that was fast," and turned away unconcerned.

"Time to get up," he called over his shoulder curtly. "We need to be away soon."

The air between the two was charged as they finished off the rations from the backpacks.

"What's this?" asked Jake, pulling a small bundle from the bottom of his.

"The rest of Tullie's stuff," he replied. "Leave it for now, there's something I need to tell you."

Jake turned to him, waiting patiently.

"You know I mentioned that things in Silvamon were in turmoil," he began, looking away into the distance beyond Jake's right shoulder.

"Well, that's a bit of an understatement!" he concluded. "The whole world is about to blow itself apart. Once Tullie is ready, I have to take her back."

Jake's chin bounced off the floor.

"You're thinking of taking Tullie back into the middle of serious conflict?" he demanded.

Guidrius nodded.

"Like what I saw at the end there?" he croaked.

Guidrius shook his head.

"No," he said, "worse."

"Well, that's not going to happen, I tell you!" Jake shouted into his face. "Over my dead body, I tell you!"

Guidrius was stumped! It appeared he had lost his power over Jake for the first time. The experience in the globe had changed him, that was only natural, he granted. He now had a Keeper on his hands and he didn't know quite how to deal with him. Gallon had not shared that wisdom.

"Tullie's not going anywhere without me too," he added softly, in a voice that brooked no further argument. "If she needs to go back, we will both take her!"

"But . . .," began Guidrius, and Jake held up his hand.

"No buts, Guidrius," he said forcefully. "No buts!" and gathered up his stuff, ready to leave now.

Guidrius was still standing stock-still, trying to fathom what had just happened. He had been gazumped! He felt the chuckle build in his belly and he didn't try and hold it down; he hadn't felt like this in years. Throwing back his head his laughter guffawed around the cavern. This was fun! The years of planning and hiding, of running and checking, had made a dull creature out of him. Finally he had someone who could stand up to him; be a friend and a foil at the same time, a comrade and a pain in the ass. He had forgotten how engaging being a human was.

Jake was really annoyed at Guidrius's response and the

more angry he looked the more Guidrius laughed.

"What's so blood funny?" he growled.

"You! Us!" hiccupped Guidrius, bending over now to catch his breath, and biting his lip to make the laughter go away.

"Jake, you are perfect!" he grinned, straightening and meeting the man's cold stare.

"I promise you," he added, solemn again, "we will do this together or not at all."

They shook hands then; another pact, another bond.

Trudging up the incline out of the cavern, Jake realised what was bothering him.

"What do you mean before – that Tullie has the capability to change things? What kind of capability?" he asked.

But he felt he knew the answer even though Guidrius hadn't spoken a word.

"Did you just mention Gallon?" he asked aloud.

Guidrius grinned. It was beginning to work. His grin widened.

"Did you just call me an asshole?" he asked Jake, and his laughter echoed around the caves again.

"I really do need to show you how to control those thoughts, Jake," he puffed.

"Laughter suits you," Jake said sarcastically. "It has taken years off you! You should get out more often, you know!"

Guidrius broke out into peals of laughter again. It was as if the cork had been blown clean off his laughter bottle and all the contents were bubbling out unhindered, lightening the heavy load he had carried alone for years. It proved way too contagious and before they had got very far they both were chuckling; two grown men with the hearts of boys, moving quickly down the mountain.

*****

Tullie lay awake on her bed, alone at last. Her young body buzzed with energy, her mind somersaulting with ideas, her stomach lurching with emotion. And beyond all that, were the memories that seemed as clear as to be real. Who am I, reverberated through her body, a question she seemed incapable of switching off. And she knew she never would until she found the answer, Jake had taught her that. Never leave a stone unturned, cross all t's and dot all i's! She wished Jane could have told her more but she didn't even know where the ring came from. Jake! He must have answers for her! But where was he?

Surprisingly, she didn't feel as bad as she thought she would about Jane not being her birth mother; Bill, her dad. What pained her more was the knowledge that she had been abandoned but she pushed this away for the moment. While she loved Jane she had never formed a strong bond with Bill, she mused, preferring Jake's presence to his until he just gave up. Then came the divorce. Now Tullie understood his animosity towards her, and now she could finally understand why Jane couldn't tell him, wouldn't tell him, where she found her. She was so sorry for the pain she'd caused them both. Maybe now she could bring them together again; maybe he still loved Jane; she felt Jane had lost none of her love for him despite her deepening friendship with BB. The fact that Jed featured in their breakup bothered Tullie. Why would he do that? What had he to gain from it all? And did he know more about her than he was willing to share? Maybe he knew her real parents? A small glimmer of hope and longing escaped from her heart and again the lake dream came to her mind unbidden; the woman with her back to her, who was she? Was she real?

Fingering the ring, she drew herself upright to sit cross-legged on the bed. She'd not sleep now she knew despite all the sedatives they'd pushed into her system. What did UNKNOWN really mean, she mused, and her thoughts turned to Matt, and began to wander. About the same age as her, he was a good-looking bloke with a fine temper, she thought. He'd certainly had a rough time. And he wasn't who he thought he was either! A kindred spirit maybe, she hoped, and felt the loneliness threaten to overwhelm her. Sometimes, she just felt so alone, so out of step with the world around her. And this was one of them. Where are you Jake, she cried, and reached out to him. In her mind she saw him on the mountain with a fellow companion, a tall guy, laughing companionably as they hurried towards home. Dressing quickly she made her way to the kitchen to help BB with the lunch and tell him Jake was on his way, that he was ok after all.

But it wasn't BB that Tullie found in the kitchen; Matt was there looking out the window towards Greenway Island.

"Ah, sorry to intrude," she said, "I couldn't sleep and I thought I'd give BB a hand with the lunch."

Turning towards her, she could see he had been crying; no, he was still crying.

"I'll come back later," she said softly, reaching for the door handle. "Sorry."

"No! Wait, please," he said, wiping the tears away with the back of his hands and reaching for some kitchen paper. "I could do with some company really! And there's lots of fresh coffee!"

"I could do with some company myself," she mumbled, closing the door and crossing to the counter to help herself.

"Can I get you some?" she asked, making time until he

had composed himself again.

"Yeah, please," he smiled. "No need for a new mug though. This has seen a few brews in the last hour," he said, walking over to the table to retrieve his used mug.

He's nice when he smiles, she thought, liking the way his mouth curved upwards and his eyes crinkled at the corners. Grey eyes, she noted; warm grey eyes, she corrected.

"We haven't met properly," she said, offering him her slender hand. "I'm Tullie."

"Matt," he replied, taking her hand gently yet firmly.

"Bit of a rush earlier," he said. "Sorry for all the shouting. Don't normally do much of that," he added apologetically.

"No problem," she replied. "Sounds like your world has fallen apart too. No way to know how anyone will respond to that sort of thing. No way to know how you'll respond yourself," she added slowly.

He watched her appreciatively. She was lovely, with a haunting loneliness not unlike the one he was feeling right now. He could only guess at her deep distress, she was hiding it so well, but he knew it'd be there. How could it not be? Despite whatever results came back, they were both human, weren't they?

"You doing ok?" was all he could think to ask.

"Sort of," she told him, "though I don't know whether I'm looking forward to or dreading the meeting. I just want to hold onto the me I know for a little bit longer."

"I know what you mean," he said, "but I'm the kind of guy that can't leave a stone unturned, I'm afraid! Natural curiosity my grandad nurtured in me, I guess."

"Me too," she grinned weakly. "My grandad wouldn't let

me away with not solving a puzzle either!"

"And we've got a big one here," he replied, ruffling his dark hair.

"You think!" she shot back a little too quickly. "Sorry. I'm not really myself at the moment."

"Hey, listen," he came back at her. "Let's just talk about the weather, or the holidays, or anything but this morning. Let's make a pact to not mention a single thing about all this while we have coffee in our mugs! Agreed?" he asked, picking up the coffee pot to refill their mugs.

"Agreed," she said, laughing for the first time and holding out her mug willingly.

They had exhausted the weather and were onto football when BB returned, their coffee untouched. Matt was delighted that Tullie was interested in sports; he liked nothing better than a good game of footie, whether watching or playing, and Tullie had played in her university women's soccer team as a striker. She was delighted in the non-condescending way he discussed it with her; most blokes thought girls ignorant about football. A few minutes later and BB would have undoubtedly found them kicking cushions around using the furniture for goalposts! But then, he'd probably have just joined in, she grinned. Leaving their mugs down side by side they stepped behind the counter to help with lunch.

"Great news, BB," she whispered. "Jake's on his way back. Should be here for lunch."

BB dropped what he was doing instantly and gave her his full attention.

"Is he alone?" he asked, urgently.

She shook her head, sending her curls into a riot of movement. Matt watched mesmerised. What would they feel like to touch, he wondered. Definitely silky, he decided and blushed, turning away quickly to find more plates. Sounds like they'll be more for lunch, he thought.

Giving Tullie a quick hug, BB left in a hurry to find Anjie.

CHAPTER 34

Bill drove slowly back to Skyway for his meeting with Johnson turning over and over in his mind his conversation with Jed. He was nonplussed to find out that it was Jenny who was with him; she was young enough to be his daughter which he told him in no uncertain terms later. He was startled to see how naturally close they were though; he felt Jed was genuine for the first time ever about any woman. But it didn't clarify anything about the missing women; rather it clouded things further, complicating events that were better kept simple. They had left just before him, heading for Traveller's Mountain, and some answers, they hoped. But the one thing that intrigued and worried them was the lack of uproar in the media. Who was powerful enough to hush this all up, and why? Bill worried about Jane. He missed her terribly and was surprised he felt the same about Tullie. If they were with Jake, they'd be fine. If not, well, he just didn't know what they'd do then. He was sure Jed was involved somehow. Damn the man! Where Jed travelled, murky water flowed close behind.

He was parking the car as the clock hit eleven. The deserted Golden Belle lay in dock, her deck scrubbed, her nets cleaned and stowed, ready for the night's work ahead. Walking up and down the quay was a young man in shirt sleeves, his police badge clipped to his belt, talking on the phone.

"No, not yet," he heard him say as he approached; then on seeing him he spoke into the phone again, "I'll get back to you later, Sir. Mr Boyd is here."

"Mr Boyd?" he enquired, thrusting out his hand to grasp Bill's firmly.

"Pleased to meet you, Detective," replied Bill. "Now how can I help you?"

"Is there somewhere more private we can talk?" asked Johnson, and Bill nodded to the Golden Belle.

"Please, call me Bill," he said and led the way aboard.

Johnson climbed on deck gingerly. The boat swayed slightly in the water and he was afraid he was going to be queasy.

"Not got your sea legs yet?" asked Bill, grinning, and led him to the foredeck where they could sit outside and enjoy the morning air.

"Never been good on water," gulped Johnson. "Thank you. Outside is good."

"When all this is over," smiled Bill, "come and find me and I'll take you out and help you sort that out."

He went below to grab a beer and a soda to give the young bloke time to gather his senses. He could murder a beer anyway after the morning he had: and the night before. They'd had no luck at all last night. For some reason, the shrimp had deserted their spot and his was not the only boat to come back empty.

"Now, how can I help you, Detective Johnson?" he asked again, handing him the soda while he pulled the tab on the beer for himself.

"That ok?" he asked, indicating the soda. "Good for the stomach, plus you're on duty."

"Perfect. Thanks Bill," replied Johnson, and he cradled the can in his arms.

"I need to ask you, Sir, about Tullie. What can you tell me about her disappearance? Any idea where she might be, and who might want to kidnap her?" he asked, all of a rush, keen to be off the boat.

"I have no idea, son," replied Bill, settling back and taking a deep slug from the can. "The first I heard of any of it was when you called. And I still haven't heard from Jane, before you ask. Bloody awful business! House gone too! Have you any further information?" he turned to him hopefully.

Johnson shook his head. There was nothing to tell.

"Can you describe Tullie for me please?" he continued, "When I last saw her she was unconscious. What kind of young woman is she? And your wife, Jane, Sir? Do they get on?"

"My ex-wife, you mean," he replied sadly. "Where do you want me to begin?"

"Where was Tullie born, Sir?" asked Johnson. "I know it's a long way back but the more details we have the better. Was she born in Matheson?"

Bill was silent for so long Johnson thought he hadn't heard him. He was just about to ask him again when he started talking.

He didn't know where Tullie was born. She was not his child at all, apparently. Johnson winced at the pain in his voice when he said this but kept silent and let him talk. He had only found out a few years ago.

"How?" asked Johnson.

"Jed," replied Bill, and continued with his story.

He'd left Jane when he found out. She wouldn't tell him anything. If she'd told him he could have got over it; he could have stayed, and they could have worked through it. Maybe Tullie was BB's: Jane was pretty close to him, always had been, but he was just thinking aloud. Jane would never have slept with BB while Maggie was alive; just not that kind of woman. He'd always believed he was the only man in her life until then.

Tullie was a fabulous daughter. She was kind, funny, and intelligent; and she loved the water as much as she loved the dusty puzzles her mother worked on, and the cryptic ones Jake set for her. She was very close to her grandad and she worked with her uncle. They were always a tight family. But him, well, he was just an outsider.

"Will she be alright?" he asked Johnson tremulously, close to tears. "I'm not welcome there anymore," he gulped. "Said some nasty things, and all that, you know . . ."

"She was in safe hands when I last saw her," said Johnson quietly, "and the doctor that was looking after her is missing too. We think they took him to look after her."

Bill got up and walked about for a bit and Johnson watched him carefully and felt he was telling the truth, but not all of it. He made some notes as Bill stepped below for another beer. He was nearly done here. Then the boat began to rock in earnest and Johnson looked about for the cause of the disturbance.

"Aw, the rich and famous have come to town," explained Bill, coming back on deck with an open beer. He pointed to the newcomers who were tying up across the narrow inlet from them.

"Here, have a gecko," he smiled, handing Johnson a pair of battered binoculars.

The smell of fish was revolting and dried scales flaked away from the piece as Bill handed them over but Johnson's curiosity was greater than his discomfort and he gladly accepted.

Raising them to his eyes, he adjusted the sights to read the name Glory Rising. Panning upwards to deck he found he was an object of scrutiny too. A burly sailor was taking the measure of them both.

"Seems like they want to make our acquaintance," he nodded, handing the binoculars back to Bill to have a look too.

"Can't see why they'd want to do that," replied Bill sharply. "We're just shit beneath their shoes. You are looking at the erstwhile owners of Greenway Island known hereabouts as the Club!"

"Not good news then?" asked Johnson cryptically.

"Nope," replied Bill solemnly.

*****

The first phone call Johnson made was to Meryck who was very interested to hear who had come to town. It had been a few years since he had first made their acquaintance and he'd prefer it to be many more. They were bad news, he told Johnson. Keep your distance, and some more, he advised. The news about Tullie made sense, he thought, but it brought him no closer to any solution as to her whereabouts now. Pass on the news about the Club immediately, he told him. Finishing the call, he reached into his other pocket for his work phone.

"That Meryck you were talking to?" asked Rick coming up to him in the shelter of the Belle.

Johnson nodded.

"Told him about the Glory?" he continued quietly.

Johnson nodded again.

"He tell you to stay well clear?" he continued.

"Yes, he did," replied Johnson, finding his voice.

210

"They're very bad news," said Rick, looking him in the eye steadily. "Very, very bad news. Ca'piche?"

"So he says too," said Johnson evenly.

"You got something for me?" asked Rick.

For a moment Johnson had no idea what he was talking about, and then he remembered. Thumbing the phone again he passed Meryck's pictures to Rick who quickly scanned the images to his own hand-piece which was like no phone Johnson had ever seen.

"Be seeing you," he nodded, and he was gone as silently as he had arrived.

From the deck of the Belle, Bill had heard the one-sided phone call with concern. He was about to call Jed when the conversation started below. Peering over the side, he caught a quick glimpse of the man who had approached Johnson. Their conversation was short but Bill heard enough to recognise that he and this Meryck were protecting the young man who had just interviewed him. Don't blame them, he thought. I tried to warn him too.

*****

Traveller's Mountain was deserted when they got there. Driving around to the side, Jed parked the truck by the shed and went to have a look around. There was no security in the place; Jake was his own security, a very robust one too, Jed remembered darkly. Jenny headed straight for Tullie's bathroom to make some adjustments to her dishevelled appearance. Her bed had been slept in, she noted, and all her stuff was still in the bathroom. She quickly ran a brush through her tangled hair and applied a dab of eye-shadow and mascara and felt a lot better. It was eerily quiet and she felt unnerved all of a sudden. Where was Jed? She couldn't hear a sound! Tiptoeing downstairs, she came face to face with Anjie.

"Jenny," he exclaimed, surprised. "What are you doing here?"

"Hi Anjie," she said happily. She liked the guy even though he had hardly spoken ten words to her in all the years she had known him. "I came with Jed."

"What the hell's he doing here?" he fired at her, his mouth opening and closing like a fish out of water.

"When we were up in Tinakilly, we heard from Bill that Tullie and Jane were missing so we came right over to ask Jake what we could do to help," she stammered.

He looked at her for a long time, and Jenny suddenly felt unnerved. What did she really know about Anjie anyway? She rushed outside, brushing past him and called, "Jed? Jed? Where are you? Anjie's here!"

Anjie followed her outside and stood beside her, and Jenny was relieved when Jed sauntered around the side of the house.

"Hi Anjie," he said amicably, reaching out to shake hands.

"Jed," replied Anjie. "To what do we owe the honour after all this time?"

"Not you too," grumbled Jed. "Darla gave me a real hiding yesterday about not coming up to visit. So, where is he then?"

"Jake, you mean?" asked Anjie shortly.

Jed nodded.

"Away, I guess," he added. "Haven't seen him around in a while. You planning on staying around?" he asked sourly.

"Nope," replied Jed. "We're done, I guess. I'll be taking Jenny home now."

"Anjie," whispered Jenny, as he followed them around to the truck, "is Tullie ok? And Jane?"

"They're fine, don't you worry," replied Anjie, to Jed's satisfaction.

He was pretty sure he knew who had them now; he smiled as they got in the truck.

Anjie watched them go with a glint in his eye. Jenny had given him the information he had sought for a long time! He now knew for certain where Jed's lair was!

CHAPTER 35

Johnson was annoyed. While he appreciated all the warnings he didn't like being treated like a child! And to cap it all, when he'd called in the Glory Rising, he'd been given time off. Not dismissed but not wanted in the frame either! He punched the steering wheel in anger; he was now in down time and he'd bloody-well do what he wanted to! The countryside was no panacea in his present mood; he needed speed. Pushing his foot down on the accelerator he went westwards towards Tinakilly, keeping the sea to his right. Even the sparkling water couldn't restore him. He needed to work this out of his system the only way he knew how!

The accelerator needle rose swiftly and he could hear the growl kick in from his pimped car. Illegal, but who was keeping track, he thought sourly. Sometimes your old life can rescue your new, and he drew on it deeply. Rick had real trouble following the kid. He really knew how to drive, he gave him that. Where had he learned how to do that, he wondered? Flicking on his phone, he called Meryck.

"Kid just pulled off the job," he said. "Heading for Tinakilly, and trouble."

Meryck wasn't surprised to hear the news. He just didn't expect it so soon, he thought, as he strolled down the High Street. Tinakilly was a secluded jewel, he decided. Small and pretty yet full of surprisingly good shops and cafes. Settling himself under an umbrella in the corner of the square he ordered a latte and two almond croissants, thankful for the shade, and the view that drew the eye east and west along the one lane road that split the town in half. This was a far more civilised recce point than his previous, holed up in Matt's Place, as he had come to call it. The croissants were fresh and buttery; the latte hot and foamy, and he sat back and relished his late breakfast. Glancing at his watch, he unfolded the paper and prepared to wait.

From behind his paper, he heard two voices join him on the square, keeping to the far end, which suited him just fine. Throwing a glance in their direction as he turned a page, he saw two young men, twenties he reckoned, and he absently wondered what two young men would find interesting in this old people's retreat. His interest was piqued further when they began asking directions from the waitress.

"Which direction is Willow Hill, Miss?" asked the blonde one. "We're looking for Grant's Cottage. Must have missed it."

"Which way did you come?" she asked, and when they pointed east, she nodded.

"No, you haven't missed it," she replied, pointing in Meryck's direction. "Continue west. That first hill you climb there is Willow Hill. Grant's Cottage is on the right as you go down. You can't miss it. A jumble of a house. But there's no one home at the moment. I saw Bill leave earlier."

They thanked her and when she'd gone they began chatting again.

"Who's Bill?" asked the dark haired guy. "Thought the place belonged to Jed."

"Previous owner," said the other, "but he sold out to Jed years ago. He needed money for the divorce. Expensive, those things," he said with feeling.

"Drink up," he continued. "Let's get this stuff over there and be gone. This place gives me the creeps!"

*****

215

As the two left, Meryck heard rather than saw Johnson arrive. Tearing into the town, disregarding speed limits, he parked within a foot of the cafe and climbed tiredly out looking back to see where Rick was. Nowhere in sight, he grinned, and suddenly felt much better. Moving forwards, he grabbed a chair and reached for the menu.

"Just coffee, to go; make it two, please" said a familiar voice as the waitress approached. "Put it on my tab too."

Johnson could feel his anger returning as Meryck joined him.

"And hello to you too," he growled.

"So, you're off the case," muttered Meryck, looking past Johnson to see the two get into a blue van.

"Well, I've got another for you," he continued, following the van out of the town as it began to climb Willow Hill.

Johnson looked at him, then at where he was looking, and his usual good humour was suddenly restored.

"What's up, Boss?" he asked.

Paying for the coffees, Meryck walked Johnson around to the back car park where Rick was waiting in the shade as if he'd been there forever.

"Get in," he instructed and leaving Johnson to the back, he climbed in beside Rick, handing him the coffee.

"Pretty cool wheels," Rick nodded to Johnson.

"Pretty cool driver, you mean," Johnson retorted.

"Well, now that you two have got that out of the way, let's get to work," said Meryck blandly unfolding a detailed map of the area. A paper man he was, and a paper man he'd remain, he glared at the grinning faces.

216

"Two guys just left here making for Grant's Cottage. A delivery for Jed, I overhead," he told them. "Apparently, Jed now owns the place. Bought it from Bill who needed the cash for the divorce," he explained.

Rick was already driving out of the car park, turning right without need for directions.

"You know this place well then?" Meryck asked.

"Fairly," was the reply, "but I didn't know Jed was the owner. Bill's name is still on the deeds."

Rick was good at his job and he calmly cruised past the two men who were unloading crates into a large barn at the back. Taking a bet that they would return the way they came, they drove back to Tinakilly, parked at the side of the garage and waited for them to show up. Sure enough, they hadn't been lying, they were keen to be away, and the van drove back through the town within fifteen minutes. Either they were very good at their job or they didn't have much to unload, Meryck thought. Giving them a few minutes grace, they pulled away, heading back to Grant's Cottage.

The place was deserted, and Johnson thought he had never seen such an oddity before. Meryck was mentally exploring all the hiding places inside; he'd not be caught out again. Rick was harbouring similar thoughts as he viewed the tree line but no one replied to the bell and the silence continued unabated, butterflies fluttering across their path, and bees checking out the newcomers who had strayed onto their path. The gate was well oiled and swung open silently, and they followed the tyre tracks in the gravel through to the barn. Deep grooves, noticed Johnson. Big barn, thought Meryck. The door was padlocked but Rick was prepared for every eventuality and within seconds they were cautiously peeking around the open door into a dark interior. When their eyes adjusted to the lack of light, they made out four crates by the back wall. Rick was the first to move, palming back to them to wait until he gave the all clear. He suspects something we don't, Meryck thought, glancing to where Johnson was hunkered down on the far side, and shaking his head. Rick's progress was slow. His neck swivelled in all directions while his feet padded softly on the cement floor. The rest of the barn was empty, and when he reached the crates, he beckoned them forward, but motioned slowly and to keep alert. They were big, chest height, Meryck realised, as he drew near. The paperwork on the side was from the Naprstek Museum, Prague to an address in Lagos, Nigeria, said to contain works of art from Europe, Asia and Africa. How the hell have these turned up here, thought Johnson, but Rick didn't give them a second glance, Meryck observed.

"Fake?" asked Meryck quietly, indicating the documents.

"Fake," replied Rick.

Johnson peered around while Rick did his thing with his funny handset. Meryck was engrossed in the crates, guessing at what they might contain before Rick offered his expertise. There wasn't much to see and it was too dim to really see far anyway. Moving out of Rick's way, he looked at the tyre tracks again and saw that they continued under the crates. Stepping lightly behind the crates he thought the marks went right up to the wall. What sort of a vehicle could do that, he thought, intrigued? Hunkering down, he checked more closely, just to be sure. The marks really did go straight up to the wall; he could discern no breaking pattern. Padding back towards the entrance to the barn, he followed the faint marks outside. They disappeared underneath the van threads by the corner of the house and he was now certain he had two sets of prints. Choosing the clearest he could make out he snapped a picture on his phone and crept back to the crates to snap another by the wall.

"Found something?" asked Rick.

"Maybe," replied Johnson. "Tyre prints seem to go right

through the wall, right there," he indicated.

"You got good shots?" asked Rick.

"As good as I can," he replied.

"Let's go then," whispered Rick, suddenly shifty.

Back in Tinakilly they ate in the car, the music blaring, windows up so they could chat in private.

"How do you know these marks go straight through," asked Rick. "Could be some flat-backed vehicle."

"None that exist," replied Johnson confidently.

"How can you be so sure?" asked Meryck, zooming in on the tyre marks for a better look.

The old geezer knows his way around this technology, Rick and Johnson grinned to each other.

"What? Think I never used one of these before, do you?" grumbled Meryck to their feigned innocence.

"Yeah, Johnson," picked up Rick. "How can you be so sure?"

When Johnson didn't reply soon enough, they both turned to look at him. They sensed a good story and weren't going to let him off the hook. Johnson could feel the colour rising up his face.

"Come now," laughed Meryck. "Can't be that bad?"

"Wouldn't be anything to do with a particular smash shop?" asked Rick smoothly and he was rewarded by Johnson's face going white.

"Now what have we here?" asked Meryck. "Secrets, is it?"

But Johnson wasn't budging. The statute of limitation wasn't out on this one, and he'd be booted off the force instantly.

"We all have secrets, Jim Boy," said Rick. "Sometimes our old life comes back to bite us in the ass; sometimes not. Your secret is safe with us. If you say a vehicle drove right through that wall, I believe you. Now, can you tell which vehicle?"

To Meryck's astonishment, Johnson rattled off a list of about twelve vehicles that might fit the bill, plus any pimped ones that could also. Rick busily clicked on his handset while Johnson talked and they narrowed it down to three possible models.

"Any of those registered to Jed or Bill?" asked Meryck.

Rick shook his head, disappointed. He was sure one would have.

"So, what's in those crates then?" asked Johnson. "Share and share alike, right?"

"Wrong," replied Rick, grinning, as he reached to answer his phone. His face became serious and they knew something was up and kept quiet. As usual, the call didn't last long but when it was finished Rick got out of the car agitated and walked around a little mumbling under his breath. Shoving his hands deep in his pockets he kicked at the ground viciously, sending sprays of pebbles against the side of the car.

"Whoa, what have we here," whistled Meryck. "Don't say a word, Jim Boy!" as Rick kicked the front tyre before getting calmly back in the car, the outburst over.

"There's been some developments," he said slowly. "I need you two to follow me. Ok?"

"Reckon you can keep up?" he grinned at Johnson, but

Meryck thought he registered some desperation in the man's eyes; and he never looked in his direction, not once. Something was up, for sure, and he didn't like it one bit!

CHAPTER 36

The lunch began rather awkwardly; no one had anything further to say so they just milled around exchanging inane comments about the weather, and the food; anything but why they were here. Anjie was relaxed and upbeat, moving among them with ease, checking that everyone was ok. BB's food was delicious and plentiful and everyone ate gustily, having seconds and thirds to postpone the moment of truth. But Anjie wasn't one to renege on a promise and with the coffees came the explanations, or what they could share at this point.

"BB and I are undercover agents working with Jake," he began to everyone's surprise. "Twenty-five years ago, as our unit was withdrawing from Central Africa, an event occurred that had the military in a flip. An 'unknown' was discovered right here in Matheson, at Myra's hospital, your grandfather's hospital, Matt, and a certain commander, I am not at liberty to disclose his identity, whisked him away for reasons of national security. Following a change in government, this military unit was disbanded but since the records of Man-x, as he became known as, were strictly on a need-to-know basis, not many knew, and his whereabouts slipped through the net."

Matt was looking at him open-mouthed, he saw, but he continued, looking forward to what he might have to contribute later for he was certain now he knew something.

"We tracked the commander's activities to an underground facility on Greenway Island and set up our observation post here; one of many on the mainland. We are unable, as yet, to pinpoint the exact location of Man-x but we have identified peculiar activity on the island

222

including the disappearance of several key scientists, and one of our operatives, who was working undercover there. Then there were the accidents; coincidental maybe, but we think not."

At this point he was interrupted by the arrival of three men who slid to the back and kept silent. Jane's face registered shock, and Meryck and Johnson gawked back but held their peace.

Nodding to the newcomers, Anjie continued.

"The presence of a sophisticated force field around the island has confirmed our suspicion that something odd is going on there. It was breached lastnight by a strange occurrence; a shoal of shrimp somehow got drawn in at high tide. But we don't think this is a coincidence either. We have observed unusual activity on the island, something we cannot identify clearly yet but we highly suspect that the breach was deliberate but to what end we do not know. Coupled with the attempt on Matt's life and the arrival of the Glory Rising off Skyway we are on full alert."

He stopped completely as two men entered and walked to the front.

"What's going on?" asked Jake, and Tullie rushed to the front and threw herself into his arms, followed quickly by Jane.

"Where have you been?" she cried. "We thought you were in danger!"

"Hey, I'm ok," he stroked her hair, and whispered softly. "Belated Happy Birthday, my dear!" but over her head his eyes questioned Anjie.

Drawing back, Tullie regarded the stranger with Jake openly, searching his hand for evidence of the ring. Bowing his head, Guidrius sent out a greeting and Tullie gasped audibly, quickly withdrawing to the security of the group.

Jake watched her go and his heart sank. Beside him, Guidrius was euphoric! He'd found her! And she'd registered his greeting! This was better than he'd for!

"The Glory Rising," Anjie's voice cut across them, "is registered to a businessman named Randell Kane whom we believe to be the head of what we call the Club, a collection of interested parties of dubious intent. We believe they are on the verge of a breakthrough in militarising weaponry from their experiments on Man-x. Their presence here would indicate this is imminent and that the proof is indeed on Greenway. We are building up our forces for an assault on the island hoping to catch them in the act. Their security has been seriously beefed up for the visit and we want to minimise damage. The Glory Rising itself will be boarded once they reach port. Our mission is to rescue the hostages, and to recover and destroy Man-x, and any experimental evidence from him."

"You can't do that!" Matt shouted, standing up and shaking the letter at Anjie.

"And why would that be?" asked Anjie, waiting expectantly.

"Leave it," said Myra, reaching across to him. "It doesn't matter now!"

"But it does," he cried back. "It does! And it's time we all knew!"

Beside him, Jake could feel Guidrius still, ready for a strike.

"Wait," he whispered. "I sense no immediate danger," and he felt him relax just a fraction.

"What should we know, Matt?" asked Anjie again. "Stay out of this, Myra. You've caused enough trouble already!"

Matt struggled to contain himself as all eyes looked on,

waiting for him to speak. He drew himself up to his full height and walked up to Anjie, turning to look back at them all.

"You see, you can't take out Man-x and any experiments you find," he said calmly, "because if you do that, you'll have to start with me. Man-x is my dad: and yes, he is on the island," handing Anjie the letter.

"So, it's true," Myra whispered, to no one in particular.

Rick was upon then in an instant, grabbing the letter from Anjie, and scanning it frantically. The whole room was in turmoil, and Myra was looking at Matt with deep sorrow in her eyes. The man who had come in with Jake never took his eyes off Matt for an instant. Jake surveyed the room critically, caught Meryck's eye and nodded imperceptivity. But Johnson caught it.

"You two know each other?" he whispered into Meryck's ear.

"Long story," he replied. "Good man though."

That was enough for Johnson and he visibly relaxed. This whole scene was bizarre but the men in charge were sound so he had no need to worry.

But now Rick was looking at Meryck, and calling him forward, he handed him the letter.

"Is this what I think it is?" he asked, pointing to the line above the signature.

Meryck could feel the blood drain from his face and Matt looked at him anxiously. He was going to pass out, he thought, and his medical training kicked in. As he made to approach him, Rick held him back.

"He's ok," he said testily. He was not about to let an 'unknown' near Meryck! "Give him some space."

225

Meryck moved behind them all and sat down heavily, his world in a spin. The letter was recent; how recent he wasn't sure, but Becca was alive, and on Greenway! Rick was waiting, watching him solicitously. It was a hard blow, he knew. He wished with all his heart that they wouldn't have to bury her for real this time. Looking up, Meryck nodded.

Anjie was unsure where to go with this so he motioned to Rick to fill in.

"Hi, I'm Rick," he said. "Three years ago we were getting close to the Club up north and they sussed us, taking out three agents, one of which was Becca - Vince and Jo Meryck's daughter; a reported hit and run too, but yours was accidental, Tullie," he interjected quickly, then continued. "We had him transferred here after that, he and his wife Jo, who also works for us; he thought he was going out to pasture but we felt we might need him here. Becca didn't die, though she was critically injured, but he and Jo were told she had, and they thought they buried her here. She recovered and we gave her a new identity, and a new look, and a new occupation," here he paused to look back at Meryck. "She infiltrated Greenway as their new chef, and we haven't had any contact with her since, until now."

"Do you have any more of these, Matt?" he asked.

Matt shook his head. He was glad the focus was off him for the moment but felt heartedly sorry for Meryck. He knew how he felt.

"Do you think they are still alive?" he asked, gruffly.

"They?" said Rick.

"Becca, and my grandad, whom I buried too," he whispered, looking to Meryck for support.

Pushing himself upright, Meryck came forward and put his arm around Matt.

"We'll find out together, my boy," he said shakily, "and don't you worry; nobody's getting killed on my watch! You're safe with me! Come on," and he led him back to his seat, settling himself down beside him.

In the stunned silence that followed, Jake stood up and went to talk quietly with Anjie. Anjie's gaze flicked continuously towards Guidrius, his years of training unable to conceal his incredulity. Tullie watched Matt closely, while Guidrius watched her. He didn't know whether to send her another greeting or wait for Jake's intervention but before he could decide Jake had turned and addressed the group.

"I am sure you have many questions, and I will try my best to answer these to your satisfaction once I have completed what I have to say," he began. "My story starts with Tullie, and ends with Tullie. Whatever else you have heard today is an adjunct to her. Man-x is here solely because of her."

He paused for that to take effect, and noticed with satisfaction that there was no element of fear or suspense as everybody looked her way, interested but unconcerned.

"Twenty-five years ago yesterday Jane and I were walking on the Mountain when we came upon Tullie, apparently abandoned."

Tullie's ears picked up sharply. Did he really say 'apparently?"

"We took her home and she became Jane and Bill's daughter but despite all searching and looking, and believe me, what my databases can't find, can't be found, no records appeared. We found her the night before Man-x entered the scene; we only made the connection a few years later through a random blood test. Do you remember, Tullie, when you fell off the climbing frame and grazed your knee? I routinely screened for bacterial infection and turned up the link. I went to Myra to confirm it."

227

At this, Anjie scowled deeper than ever at Myra. What else had the woman not told them!

"Now, I want you to see this," he nodded to Guidrius. "A picture can convey much more than I can say at this point."

"I'm sorry, Tullie," he continued. "This will hurt but it will also explain a lot."

Stepping to the side, Guidrius strode forward and they registered his striking physique for the first time. Tullie moved to stand by Jake at the side, watching Guidrius closely. There was something about him that was familiar. As he held out his hand to display his fight with Man-x, she knew. And he knew she knew, and played the scene sadly, yet hopefully, that all was not lost.

Gasps of horror and astonishment sounded around the room; suddenly the space seemed way too small for them all, too claustrophobic by far. But Guidrius only had eyes for Tullie and she, him. Rick measured up Man-x endlessly before turning his full attention on Guidrius. While not fully understanding exactly what was playing out before him, he could see from his countenance that he was only interested in Tullie; this man was their ally. Myra sat stonily through it all; she finally had the answers she had sought all these years but they did not bring with them the closure she had expected. Matt was transfixed; he carried part of this machine of a man in his DNA. Could he trust himself, even if these others did? Sensing his mood, Meryck patted his knee sympathetically. Anjie and BB were with Rick on this one; measuring the threat yet looking at a solution, speculation replacing anxiety on their faces. Carney was flabbergasted. His face registered enough shock for all of them combined. Could he really have been foolish enough to think he could work with such, such . . ., words failed him! He was way out of his league! These people were mad! Stark, raving mad! Johnson wouldn't have necessarily disagreed with him there but it was no time for hysterics.

"So, where exactly do you come from?" he asked Guidrius calmly, keeping an eye on Carney. He looked like he was about to unravel.

"And what do you want with us?" he added.

Meryck harrumphed. Thrust the innocent to ask the searching question we were all thinking but were too afraid to ask, he thought admiringly.

PART 2

CHAPTER 37

Randell surveyed the saloon with distaste. Greedy blood-suckers, the lot of them, he grimaced with distaste as he sipped his cocktail delicately. Mahler was salivating over the mass destruction stats, while Boris stood to one side apparently disinterested but taking in every detail on weapons development. Carla was draped across the sofa, her red dress a welcome splash of colour in the beige surroundings filled with suits. He wasn't sure which of the two called the shots, her or blonde Bowen, but it didn't matter; it was their money that gave them the right to be here. From the bulge inside the Arab's jacket, he knew he was packing, but he didn't mind. Every one of his waiters was chosen with care. He carried no excess baggage of any kind despite the calm opulence in which they were being entertained. Five present, he rolled off their real names again in his head: one to come; and he hadn't heard from Ken yet either. No move would be made without those two being reckoned with. The time had come to trim the unnecessary; a demonstration, as it were, he grinned. He was going to enjoy this. He had them all exactly where he wanted them!

Ken watched the car drive up and Oswald Balmier, III, got out and went aboard swiftly. The minions had gathered then, and it was time to report in. The taste of failure didn't sit well in his mouth; he hadn't found Matt or Meryck and he had lost Winton and Connor, two of his best men, years of planning gone down the drain! Jed would be rightly pissed off, he knew! He didn't know if anyone had survived the explosion but he did know who the boat belonged to now. They wouldn't take kindly to his oversight on that either. All in all, he couldn't think of a single good reason to go on board apart from his pay check and the promised payback. Wandering along the quay with his fishing rod and bucket, he was surprised not to be stopped. Where was the security? Every sense heightened, he pressed himself against the hull. Something wasn't right!

Oswald strode on board the Glory without a concern in the world, his hands pushed deep into his pockets, the crew on deck following him below, where he greeted everyone by name saving Kane for last.

"We are most grateful for your efforts today, Randell," he said smoothly, and everyone applauded. "Without your devoted support, we would never be so close to achieving our goal."

"But we've been compromised," he spoke testily now, looking around every face for the element of surprise.

Randell nodded to his staff and they drew their guns covering the group. Angry murmurs spread like wildfire as they were deprived of their concealed weapons, then Randell showed his hand, something Oswald was hoping for. Randell reached behind him, picked up a gun and pointed it directly at him.

"Time to say goodbye, Oswald. Out with the old and all that," he purred, satisfied that all had gone exactly to plan, and pulled the trigger. The click from the empty chamber echoed around the saloon. Nobody moved a muscle.

"So," said Oswald, looking into the nozzle of the empty gun, "time to say goodbye, is it?" and he nodded. A single muffled shot rang out and a small red spot blossomed through Randell's white jacket and, open-mouthed, he toppled backwards and hit the floor with a thump.

"Get him out of here," he shouted, and the crew hurried to obey.

"Now where were we?" he asked, turning to address his stunned audience. "Ah yes, we've been compromised!"

234

"Secure the room," he instructed. "I'll deal with them later."

"Get us out of here," he bellowed into the intercom.

Ken heard the clinking as the anchor was raised and voices sounded on deck again. They were leaving, he realised, as the engines reversed, pushing back into the inlet to turn. Dropping his fishing gear he ran at headlong speed for cover as puffs of dust bit his heels.

"Enough!" he heard Oswald roar. "Do you want the whole bloody world to know what's going on!"

*****

As everyone waited for Guidrius's reply, Rick fingered his earpiece, nodding to Anjie. The scene in the window changed and they could see the Glory Rising manoeuvring out of Skyway for the open sea.

"You'll have to wait for your answers 'til later, JB," he said quietly, turning to follow Jake quickly out of the room.

"Well, come on then," he stopped to add, indicating to Meryck and Johnson, as he let Anjie and BB out before him.

The three women and the three men who remained looked at each other, and then back at the screen, their eyes following the movement on the water. They could only guess at what this might mean but for Matt it signalled a reprieve, and he breathed a little more easily. Gathering his courage, he strode up to Guidrius and introduced himself. He wanted answers badly and he felt this man could provide them. Guidrius was nonplussed. Halfers didn't approach; they waited to be instructed, but he wasn't sure just what Matt was. Halfers offspring were state property; they were engineered, not let develop naturally. His eyes bore deep into Matt and he felt no resistance. But then he realised with a shock Matt was tapping him too, riding the energy wave he had directed at his mind to search his depths also.

He chuckled, caught in the act, and Matt reciprocated. Then he got serious as he realised just why the Silvites had engineered this trait out of the Halfers. It was a control technique; the Halfers weren't naturally dangerous, just naturally curious. The danger came later, he realised, with a shock. Blocking out the ability of the Halfers to read Silvite minds meant that they lost contact with Halfer minds too; and suspicion between the two groups had grown over the years. Matt wasn't dangerous. He was just different, as when they left earth in the first place. Guidrius was shamed by this revelation, and contrite. Matt was intrigued.

Tullie watched the two men stare intently at each other and she could sense a bond developing between them. As the energy opened up around them, her lake dream came back to her forcibly and she was struck again by its tangibility, its presence. The man on the shore, so ready to help her, was the same man communicating with Matt, she was sure. Was he really her dad, she wondered. So much had happened since she left work only two days ago! It was just too much to take in and she could feel herself shut down. She had answers to questions she hadn't asked; answers she didn't want to explore right now. Why couldn't everything be simple and straightforward and open? Why were there always twists and turns and complications, she sighed? Turning away from the two she vaguely wondered where Salvie was. What would she give to be away from all this right now, riding the winds or closeted with a demanding puzzle!

"Mum," she asked, turning to Jane, "what happened to Salvie? Was he badly damaged?"

"No, love," said Jane, coming over to give her a hug, "not really; just a few scratches Jake can sort out for you in a jiffy when the police release him."

"Do you have my bag?" she asked, relieved that Salvie wasn't seriously damaged.

"No," replied Jane, thoughtfully. "I'm not sure where it is, now that you ask. Maybe the police have that too. We must ask Meryck when he gets back."

"What do you think?" she asked, nodding towards Guidrius. "How do you feel about all that?"

"How do you?" asked Tullie back, her eyes clouding over. "Some dad, eh? What the hell does it make me?"

*****

"So, what do you think?" asked Myra, making her way over to Carney, her fingers itching to hold a cigarette.

Carney wasn't in the most communicative mood. Secretly, he could murder Myra for unsettling his life so badly, and he still felt she was holding back something.

"So, when was it you painted me into this pretty picture?" he asked coldly.

She looked at him, derision plain to see on her face.

"Painted you in?" she cried sarcastically. "Well, that's gratitude for you!"

"Gratitude?" he roared at her. "You expect gratitude from me for dropping me in this?"

He was beside himself with anger, the sparks flickering around the room, and all heads turned to watch.

""Well, it's what you always wanted, isn't it?" she shot back, the lack of sleep and nicotine pushing her over the edge. "If only we could find a cure for cancer! If only we could manipulate DNA to stop the cancer cells turning off healthy cells! If only . . . ! If only . . . ! I've had it up to here with your 'if only's!' Now you have a chance to work with new possibilities and you belly ache! What sort of a fool are you anyway?"

"What else haven't you told us, Myra?" he yelled at her, "What else, eh? Every time there's a new revelation you somehow know about it already! Anjie's right to be angry with you!"

"Anjie's a fool," she shot back. "They could still be alive, in there with all that horror, you know! And he waits for proof!"

"Who?" asked Matt, engaging now despite his best instincts.

"Yes, who," added Guidrius, stepping up behind Matt.

Myra stopped suddenly, realising she had given herself away. They were all looking at her now.

"Who, Myra?" asked Tullie, forcefully.

"Becca," she whispered back, scared now, "and Ben."

"Who the hell is Ben?" asked an angry voice from the door. "No more secrets, Myra! Not now! Not ever!"

Anjie was furious; striding into the room, his face thunderous; his hands balled into giant fists that curled and uncurled by his sides.

"Ben," she stammered, looking at him fearfully. "Ben Smith, Jenny's dad."

"What the hell has he got to do with Greenway?" he stormed.

"He's a software engineer," she whispered. "He develops the systems there. Has done for the last ten years. But he hasn't been home in months. I think Jenny and Kate are tagged."

"Tagged?" he asked incredulously.

She was beaten, and it was all her own fault. She dug

deep for the other shameful secret she had kept hidden for years.

"Tagged," she explained slowly, "as in electronic tags."

"Like Elizabeth and Raymond," she whispered, her breath petering out. Might as well get it all out now.

No one moved. No one made a sound. Guidrius was frantically scanning her for implants.

"Go on!" demanded Anjie.

Looking up into his closed face, she knew she would get no sympathy.

"Once Elizabeth and Raymond were found on Greenway, in a Restricted Zone, they tagged them and gave them a travel limitation," she said jaggedly. "The day they were killed, they had made a bolt for freedom not realising the implications. Nobody knew back then."

The silence was total now, each digesting what they had just heard.

"How do you know this?" he asked.

"I did the autopsies," she said, "and found the implants. Ken explained what they were."

"Ken?" asked Anjie.

"He was around a lot back then," she answered, colour seeping up her face.

"And Ben?" interrupted Tullie. "Is he tagged too?"

Myra nodded.

"And who else?" demanded Anjie, but Myra began to cry and wouldn't answer.

"She is," Guidrius said softly, into the silence. "It's our technology. I'm sure of it."

So that's why she never ran, thought Anjie, and the smallest bit of compassion for her leaked into his heart.

"Active?" he asked Guidrius.

"Don't think so," he replied. "The implant hasn't lasted well; it's degraded in parts. Different materials. Still sending some information though but I doubt they will regard it as accurate."

"Can you locate it?" he asked.

Guidrius nodded.

"Extract it?" he added hopefully.

"Pretty sure," replied Guidrius, "but there may be complications. I'll need assistance, in case."

"Do it!" instructed Anjie, to Myra's astonishment. "Carney, show Matt and Guidrius where to go."

CHAPTER 38

Matt's eyes were on stalks as Carney guided them through the facilities underground. Guidrius was thoughtful, while Myra was downright scared but Adam's presence made any chance of escape impossible. Besides, she felt Carney would shoot her himself if they'd given him a gun!

"You'll be fine," said Guidrius, taking her arm and leading her forward, and she did indeed begin to feel more and more relaxed, fading into a deep trance. He caught her as she crumbled towards the floor.

"There!" said Guidrius minutes later and Carney and Matt saw the foreign article hidden behind her left elbow. It was deeply embedded and the edge had attached itself to the bone years ago becoming part calcified and rendering its operation unreliable, they saw with relief.

"Stop!" called Guidrius suddenly, and Carney paused in the extraction instantly. "There's a problem. It's modified in a way I don't recognise. Looks like it might combust if it comes in contact with air."

Matt and Carney looked at each other closely, sweat beading their foreheads. That was close, they thought. Another second and . . . They weren't sure what exactly but Guidrius was worried!

Myra mumbled gently as Carney swabbed the wound. Small as it was, copious amounts of blood not quite as it should be, was leaking out and dripping onto the floor despite his intervention. He motioned to Matt for a sample container and while Guidrius pondered their predicament, the liquid flowed swiftly in, filling it in seconds.

"Guidrius," Carney nudged, indicating the flow. "We have another problem. She's bleeding out too quickly."

"Let it flow," he replied.

"Have you any transfusion supplies?" he asked Matt suddenly.

Carney nodded. They were well equipped.

"Anyone know her original blood group?" asked Guidrius, and Carney called urgently for Adam.

"Check her records," he shouted, and Adam spun away to the computer station and within seconds called back with the answer, then he was away, running to storage as fast as he could.

"Stand back," said Guidrius, when the IV was in place, "and be ready to start the drip on my mark."

They felt an energy pushing them aside as Guidrius enclosed Myra and himself in an air bubble, holding up his hand, ready to signal. Matt saw the air began to ripple and he realised he was replacing the oxygen with carbon dioxide. Myra's vital signs began to get weaker and weaker as her oxygen began to run low and to Carney's surprise, the flow from her arm slowed and began to solidify. Matt could feel Guidrius begin to struggle to breathe too but he held on and on, Myra's rasping breath resounding around the operating theatre, tensing them for action. Then in a flash, Myra stopped breathing and Guidrius lunged, ripping the implant from her body and crushing it in his massive hand, before signalling to start the IV and letting the bubble go. Matt lunged forward with oxygen for Guidrius while Adam rushed to resuscitate Myra; Carney starting the IV and checking her vitals.

"That was close," whistled Matt as the machine bleeped into life.

"Yes, it was," coughed Guidrius, opening his hand to reveal a tiny object, part organic, part mechanical. Sticky red blood oozed from around its crushed body. They stared at the dead modified parasite, and their imaginations ran riot. Adam alone had the sense to fetch a glass container. Guidrius relinquished his find gladly.

"Here," Adam said to Matt, handing him the jar. "You're the expert! I've got work to do," and he rushed from the scene, pulling the packet of cigarettes from his pocket urgently. For once, he didn't care who saw him, as with shaking fingers he flicked his lighter once, twice, before he got it lit.

*****

Jake's head swivelled as he checked the monitors, calling to BB and Rick for clarification. Meryck and Johnson watched bug-eyed. The scale of the operation was enormous; beyond anything they had ever imagined. These guys were serious! Something big, real big, was going down here, they realised. BB glanced at Jake, dying to know where he'd been and who the hell Guidrius was, but more importantly, to see if he was ok. He seemed fine but he was making connections none of them had come up with before. Was he party to some new intel, he wondered. Maybe Rick had something to do with it too, he reasoned. Heads down now, they all gathered around the central bench which displayed live shipping maps of all quadrants out of Skyway. The Glory Rising wasn't the only boat around. There were several small and medium sized pleasure craft pulsing around, all identified, and discarded within seconds. A passenger ferry rounded the point and made out to sea. On the horizon, several cargo ships droned by in well-beaten lanes. There was no way to tell where the Glory was headed exactly though her current course indicated she would cross the cargo lanes. It was wait-and-see time. A flicker of a blip moved to intercept the Glory; a sub, Meryck surmised, and he traced their trajectories to an intercept point in open water.

"Will you still board?" he asked, and all heads swivelled towards him.

"What would you do, Vince?" asked Jake.

"Track 'em; see where they lead us," he shrugged. "They're spooked. Possibility of mistakes, and all that. Need to know what set them off too."

Rick and Jake nodded assent. Meryck was right. They'd only get part of the picture if they went in now. There was too much at stake to act rashly.

"BB?" asked Jake.

He nodded too. He agreed with Meryck. The game had changed and they needed to change with it.

Picking up the phone, Jake called off the mission, downgrading it to an eyes-open only.

"What's that?" asked Johnson, who was watching the Glory up close while the others studied the map. "Any way we can rewind this thing?

BB was on it instantly. Not only did he rewind it but he panned in closer still. They watched for the splash Johnson had mentioned; everyone recognising a weighted body bag when they saw one.

"Mmm," said Jake, "trouble in paradise," picking up the phone again.

CHAPTER 39

Ben watched the Glory Rising manoeuvre to leave port with a mixture of feelings: relief that he wouldn't be found wanting since security still wasn't up to scratch; Man-x remained in the corridor; the two hadn't returned yet either; and concern that something worse was afoot and he was marooned here to rot among the unmentionables below. His body wracked with shudders every time the thought of them growing serenely; monsters who would change the world. More likely annihilate it, he thought worriedly. He wished he had never looked now but once he had found them he couldn't help returning to see what was happening regularly like a moth drawn to the very light that would destroy it, he realised. Thumbing his phone he was relieved to see Jenny was back home with her mother. Then the quietness struck him and he realised Myra's dot was missing and his heart contracted. Not her too, he moaned. When will it all end, he wept. In his cell, the old geezer registered the despair and wept for Myra too. He was sure she would be ok after all these years. With no one left to protect now, he had nothing to lose. It was time to leave, one way or another.

The new arrival time sprung up on the screen: midnight. He relaxed a little. The force field would be finished in an hour so he had plenty of time to test it. The workmen repairing the damage Man-x had sprung on them could assist in moving him back to his reinforced quarters, if necessary. The few hours reprieve meant he could have the situation in hand. Exhausted, he pushed through the last of the repairs and moved to the test phase.

The kitchen staff weren't best pleased that the visit had been delayed. They had worked from early morning to put out a delicate and complicated menu, one suitable for the visiting dignitaries, and many of the creations wouldn't keep well. They'd have to start again in a few hours time plus find a way to dispose of the food before it spoiled. Even the regular meals were disrupted with all the additional work. Someone suggested a buffet in the kitchen and the idea was rapidly taken up by the chef. Some of the food would be issued to the guests and their carers first of all, and then the workforce could come and eat whenever they were ready. The only element that would be held back was the alcohol. That would keep until later.

Ben read the call for volunteers from among the kitchen staff with dismay. Being cleared for work outside their usual zone would make them vulnerable to additional restrictions but they needed as many hands as they could get to restore the place to complete functionality before midnight. Scanning the list of duties to be filled, he saw that feeding some of the less active guests was on the list, including the old geezer. A wild idea formed in his head and he picked up the phone and volunteered to help as soon as the test was through.

*****

Oswald plotted a course through the cargo lanes and went below. The saloon was very much as he had left it; everyone had stayed where they were, no doubt pondering their next move, or his. All heads swivelled to glare at him as he entered. The hostility was palpable; their looks hooded and cold. He threw the pact they had just signed with Kane down in front of them and he was gratified to see some surprise leak through.

"So, you're done with me then," he said steely, looking each one directly in the eye.

Mahler shrugged.

"Business is business," he said. "You know how things

246

are."

Boris just looked right through him without saying a word. The Arab played with his beard while regarding him evenly, not a hint of emotion visible on his face. Carla crossed her knees and flicked her nails. Bowen played with her hair, ignoring him altogether.

He retrieved the pact they had sighed before he got on board, a five-way split, and tore it into shreds before them. Then reaching into his pocket he produced another document and flung it across the room to Mahler.

"I hope you like doing business with this one," he grunted. "When you're finished signing, spread it around. Let's have a party!"

Grabbing the papers, Mahler started to read and they all watched him intently. He'd be as white as a sheet right now if he could go pale, Oswald grinned. Instead his hands shook and his eyes bulged in his face.

"You can't be serious!" he bellowed, shaking the pages in the air.

"I'm perfectly serious," he replied calmly. "Sign it or . . . ," and he shrugged leaving them to fill in the obvious.

"What does he want, darling," purred Carla, rising and moving across to Mahler to plank her red talons on his sleeve.

"Ninety percent," spluttered Mahler, showing her the papers.

That had an immediate effect. Boris reached over and grabbed the papers from Mahler. The Arab and Bowen rose too but made no attempt to close the gap.

"What the hell do you think this is?" growled an infuriated Boris.

"That," said Oswald smoothly, "is the price of a life; mine, to be precise! Take it or leave it. I'll be back in five to collect."

It wouldn't be happy families ever; he smiled grimly, as he climbed up on deck. But he wasn't bothered; he'd have his ninety percent or their lives. They knew what they were getting themselves into and the rewards would be well worth it. But he'd make them pay for crossing him! Idly, he wondered why Ken had done a runner. Lucky man or he'd be fish food too beside his friend Randell. He wasn't bothered; he'd deal with him when the time came. And that was coming fast. He tapped away the five minutes looking mindlessly out to sea. The day was good, the visibility clear; a day when things in the distance look closer than they actually are. Greenway Island was straight in his line of vision as he turned to go below again. He regretted he couldn't be there right now. It had been some time since he was at liberty to visit and he let his anger at this interruption in plans mount as he climbed down. He wanted only those who were prepared to pay dearly to be on his side with him tonight.

This time, they were grouped together against him, and he held out his hand for the document. Not one had signed it.

"Nobody wants to do business then?" he asked smoothly. "Last chance?" he asked, singling out the Arab, but including them all in his casual look.

They shook their heads, adamant they wouldn't be the first one to break rank.

"Fair enough," he said, drawing his gun and shooting the Arab at point blank range.

"So, Mahler," he crooned, "You're not signing either, right?" and he levelled his gun at him.

"No, wait," he screamed, throwing up his arms, sweat beading oh his forehead. "I'll sign! I'll sign!"

"Good choice," said Oswald, handing him back the papers and carelessly waving his gun around.

When Mahler had signed, Oswald slid the papers towards Carla with the tip of his gun, never taking his eyes off her face. She reached for them hurriedly and quickly signed her name in a flowing hand beneath the shaky signature Mahler had appended.

"Now, just two to go," he said silkily. "Which of you gentlemen is next?" slamming the papers down with a bang in front of the two. Boris glanced at him with deadly intent but swiped his name across the page under Carla's. Bowen was in no state to resist but he wrote his name firmly beside Carla's for all that, he noted with interest.

"Gentlemen, and Lady," he smiled, picking up the document and pocketing it, "we have a deal."

"Now enjoy the cruise," he continued. "Cocktails are being served up top to celebrate," motioning for them to move. "We make berth at Greenway at midnight."

*****

Ken lay panting in the summer grass watching the Glory pull out of port. The last bullet had grazed his shin as he had dived for cover, head first, over the railings that separated the quay from the encroaching summer wilderness and he could feel the blood trickling down his trouser leg. Damn, he thought! What was that all about? It was bad enough doing business with that snake Kane but Oswald was another thing altogether; and it seemed like he was the one calling the shots on deck. Where were the others? And why were they leaving? Rummaging through his pockets he fished out a less-than-clean handkerchief and used it to staunch the flow; not big enough for stitches, he noted, so

he held on until the bleeding stopped and then headed for
his car, and for the back entrance to Greenway.

CHAPTER 40

Tullie and Jane looked in dismay at Anjie as Myra was hauled off; they didn't recognise this man before them.

"Come on," he said. "Let's go join the others. There's something I need your help with," and he held the door open for them.

Jane was full of questions as they walked along one corridor after another but Tullie was silent; she let them talk, vaguely noting the main details. The more they walked the more afraid she became of what was going to be revealed next. She wished fervently she could turn back the clock and start the weekend again! The size and contents of the room they entered did nothing to calm her either. Rick was manoeuvring photos around a high-tech table screen and the results were individually reflected in the many screens around the room.

"Where did you get those pictures?" she demanded, aghast, as she stared at the enhancements of the pictures from her phone.

"Guilty, as charged," said Meryck, kindly, stepping apart from the group to let her have access to the table.

"You have my phone?" she asked, sharply, "and my bag?"

He nodded.

"And my laptop?" she continued.

"No," said Anjie. "Your laptop is over there," pointing to the corner.

Rushing to where he pointed, she grabbed her laptop

and held it tight to her chest, looking around with eyes the size of saucers, like a rabbit caught in the headlights.

"What are these, Tullie?" asked her Mum, running her fingers gently along the digital images, feeling for the groves and spirals that weren't there, the puzzle genie overwhelming her maternal instincts.

But Tullie didn't reply at first. Despite her circumstances she was drawn to the images all around her and remembering her first impressions about the names. They let her be, watching and waiting for her input; recognising she was deeply engrossed. Handing her laptop to Johnson, she returned to the table and began to defragment the aggregation they had amassed until the individual pictures were spread starkly around the room. After further close scrutiny, she moved them again and again until satisfied they were in order, a different order than previously, but she knew this one was correct; she could feel it!

"This is the work I was doing for Jed just before I came home," she said dreamily, ignoring them all as she continued her scrutiny.

"But where did he get these?" asked a gobsmacked Jane. "They look very, very old to me!"

"They are," droned Tullie, "and there's a few pieces missing. Just one big one though from this Alpha piece."

Behind the women's backs the three men glanced at each other meaningfully while Meryck and Johnson looked on. Jed's name was all it took to take the day's business up a notch. What was he doing with these anyway? And what had they to do with Tullie? Or Greenway?

"But what are they about, Tullie?" asked Johnson. "Are they valuable?"

"I don't know yet," she began.

"But I think I do," said Jake suddenly, just as the door opened and Guidrius and Matt walked in, and the moment passed.

"Do you have my bag here?" she asked Meryck, breathlessly. "I have an idea!"

He nodded and left to fetch it from his car while Tullie marched around the room anxiously. Guidrius watched her closely. She couldn't have made the link, could she? And where did she find the fragments anyway? In all his travels he didn't find one whiff of them! Then here they are, right in their midst! What other mysteries does this place hold, he wondered? Was he underestimating these people, his observations blighted by his finding Tullie safe in their care?

*****

"Did you know about these?" he asked Jake, quietly.

"No," back came the reply.

"What are they?" asked a new voice, and they both turned to Matt, stunned at the unexpected intrusion.

"We'll tell you later," smiled Guidrius, at a very confused Matt, who hadn't spoken a single word.

*****

"How did it go?" asked Anjie, moving his gaze from Guidrius to Matt.

"Here's the evidence," replied Matt, holding up the container for all to see. That drew everybody's attention! They approached, curious to see what they were dealing with.

"And Myra?" asked BB, shivering.

"Still unconscious, but stable," answered Matt. "We'd

have lost her without Guidrius; possibly us too," and he did a short recount of the past forty-five minutes.

"We've got to get these out of Jenny and Kate," interjected an appalled Johnson, and nobody disagreed.

"So what's the plan now, Jake?" he added.

Jake turned to the one dark monitor in the room and pushed a button. Multi images filled the screen, and touching the one in the centre, Greenway Island leapt into full view.

"We go in at midnight," he said tersely. "That's not going to change. But we may have to amend our strategy in light of the new information we have gathered today. The details are on a need-to-know basis so we'll leave that for the moment. Not all of you here need-to-know."

"Are you still planning to eliminate what you find there?" asked Matt in a strangled voice.

Jake let his eyes wander over the group in front of him until they came to rest on Rick.

"What do you think?" he asked him. "What elements need changing in your book?"

All eyes turned to Rick now.

"Did you know Becca well?" asked Johnson pointedly when he made no move to answer Jake.

Rick nodded.

"How well?" he continued when Rick didn't respond further.

Rick looked uneasy now, as if he had some great secret he didn't want to share.

"I'd like to know that answer too," added Meryck from

254

the open door, where he stood holding Tullie's bag under his arm.

"Becca's my wife," he answered calmly, turning to face his father-in-law.

Before Meryck could find his voice, he continued.

"We were married in the hospital after her accident. We had a date set and were going to tell you and Jo that weekend. She was pregnant with our son," he stumbled over the details before continuing, "and she wanted to make sure I had full rights if she didn't make it. But it didn't work out the way she thought it would. She made it and he didn't, and something snapped in her. When I came through surgery, I was seriously hurt too, six of us were," he explained, looking around solemnly, "she was gone. Signed up for reconstructive surgery; vanished into thin air. Left to finish what she had begun, they told me. I knew she went to Greenway but had no proof she was still there, or still alive, until I saw your letter, Matt."

"Look, I'm sorry, man," he said plaintively to Meryck. "I couldn't tell you. I'm not the best person to make suggestions about Greenway right now," he offered to the rest, slumping into a chair and holding his head in his hands.

"Hey, man. We'll work it out when you're ready," said Johnson, moving over to sit beside him and tap him comfortingly on the shoulder. "At least you know she's definitely made it in now."

Meryck was rooted to the spot, his limbs incapable of movement, his brain whirring. In the last few minutes he had learned that Becca was alive, and married, and was about to give him a grandson. His thoughts whirred from Jo to Rick, and Becca, and back. They had a son-in-law! And their daughter was alive! Though in serious danger! Tullie reached forward for her bag and he was released from his spell. Stumbling over to Rick, he sat on the opposite side to

Johnson, and reached out his hand to welcome his son-in-law to the family. No words were needed. They understood each other perfectly, Jake saw. Time to bring Jo home, he decided.

CHAPTER 41

Guidrius watched closely as Tullie withdrew the necklace and moved back to the table. She had got the main part correct: the central amethyst was indeed what was missing from the Alpha piece but she was unable to complete her work because she only had digital images, she needed the real fragments themselves for the link to be made. Frustrated, she made her way around the rest, making the links with the other small stones, but again unable to complete the process.

"I need the real thing to make it work!" she whispered fiercely.

"Make what work?" asked Jane, puzzled.

"I'm not sure!" replied Tullie. "This is driving me crazy!"

"Tullie, we need to talk," said Jake, calmly. "These are much more than you think they are."

"What do you know about them?" she asked, curiously, the memory of his earlier comment coming back to her now.

"Do you have something to do with these?" she continued, turning to address Guidrius for the first time.

"Sort of," he replied softly.

"Is this yours?" she asked, accusingly, waving the necklace in his face.

"No," he replied softly again, "that belongs to your mother."

Something about his answer drew her up short. Did he

really say 'belongs?'

"They're the Seals, aren't they?" asked Matt suddenly, staring intently at the biggest one, the one Tullie called 'Alpha'.

Guidrius looked at him curiously. He had inherited the memories, well, some of them, he realised. Could he possibly be the one? A Halfer's son? Tullie's Protector? There was only one way to be sure. Slipping off his ring, he offered it to Matt who didn't hesitate in taking it, slipping it onto his left finger where it snuggled happily into place. He had his second Keeper, Guidrius realised exuberantly! Yet, why did he not feel good about all this?

*****

Jed dropped Jenny home and drove straight back to Tinakilly. The four crates stood silently where they had left them and he made short work of moving them inside the mountain. Parking his truck in the open space beside the small lake, it took him ninety minutes to waterproof the lot, and then he sat down to wait. But he didn't have to wait long! Something's wrong, he thought, reaching for the gun at his back, but it was Ken who emerged from the water and he relaxed a little. It was still too early though.

"What's up?" he asked, without preamble, rising to greet him but keeping his hand on his gun. "You're early."

"Change of plan, my man," replied Ken, changing quickly into the dry clothes Jed had provided. "Glory Rising has left dock, heading straight out to sea, as the crow flies! And not a sign of Mahler but a whole lot of eyeball on Oswald!" he added grimly.

"What's with the bandage?" asked Jed.

"A small going away present," said Ken. "Looks like I'm not welcome at the party no more," he added, brushing his hair with his hands.

Jed whistled. This was a new development; completely unexpected and not entirely welcome.

"Catch," he said, throwing Ken a flask. "Looks like you could do with some sustenance."

While Ken knocked back the hot coffee, Jed pondered their options. They'd lost the current address of the Club but they still had the entry card into paradise. They just had to find a different way to align the two, he thought.

"I'm getting too old for this shit," said Ken, dropping down to rest his tired body against the wall.

"Me too," replied Jed. He feared they were both losing their edge. He reckoned they had one more shot at equalling the score before they bowed out of circulation on some remote island and had a life for a change. With Jenny, came to mind, but he knew that was impossible. She'd never forgive what he had to do.

"Think they suspect anything?" he asked.

"Nope!" answered Ken, tiredly. "Hey! The sooner I'm done with all this, the better."

"So, what's with this vendetta with Meryck?" said Jed, rounding on him. "Bit public, wasn't it?"

"And who was the bloke that intervened?" he added, in a rush.

"Did you know Joey was in the Club's pocket?" Ken asked in reply, and Jed's eyes widened.

So, he didn't know then, he thought with satisfaction, own backyard and all.

"And Darla?" asked Jed, open-mouthed.

Ken shook his head.

"Squeaky clean," he answered shortly. "Doubt she knows a thing about Joey."

"And . . .," prompted Jed, rattled now.

"Only got part of the story, I'm sure," replied Ken slowly, "but there was a bit of a mess up at the hospital, Matheson's, with some query to the IBB on a blood test from Tullie. Club onto it like a shot: apparently, some vague link to the geezer on the Island. Hit and Run. Accidental, I believe. Meryck was the senior in charge. Now he must have some murky background because they wanted him off the case pronto, one way or another. Looks like they might be right! The Club took out an outfit few years back. Happens one was his daughter. Mrs did a runner, didn't she; clean as a whistle. Not the first time, I'd say. So I tailed him to Rosa's; him and that side-kick of his. Great driver, that one. Anyway, Joey saw us talking and called it in. I was ordered to do the biz, you know."

"And the helper?" asked Jed, undeterred.

"No idea," was the frank reply.

They sat in silence for a while, each going over every detail minutely.

"By the way, another stick for the fire," said Ken. "Winton and Connor bought it on the mountain. Clean. Professional hit. And no bloody idea who," he finished forcefully.

Jed sucked in air through his teeth at this revelation.

"Are we compromised?" he asked quietly, moving slowly around the area.

"Doubt it," Ken replied. "But we are on our own now, that's for sure!"

"Plan B then," sighed Jed.

"Plan B it is," answered Ken.

CHAPTER 42

"Time to regroup," said Jake, stepping forward to take charge once more.

"The way I see it, we have three fronts we need to cover: Greenway; Jenny and Kate; and retrieval of the Seals."

"Four," interjected Matt. "I think there may be more letters for me at grandad's house. I'd like to have a look before any final decision on Greenway, please," he begged.

Meryck and Rick looked up sharply.

"I'll go with you," they offered in tandem, looking at each other solemnly.

Jake looked around the room for any comments or dissents but all seemed to think this was a good use of time, a worthwhile and necessary job to cover every possible angle.

"Ok," he replied, "four fronts then."

We'll leave right now," said Rick jumping up, his vigour returned when he realised there could be more news from Becca.

Watching them go, Jake was pleased his old friend finally knew the truth about his daughter: however painful it felt it was better to know the truth of it all. Rick would look after him and he would look after Matt. And Jo would be here by night fall. He sighed silently. His own situation wasn't the best either, he knew, looking at Tullie and Guidrius.

"Jane," continued Jake, "go along with Carney, Guidrius, and Johnson to Jenny and Kate's. They know you so they'll trust you. Once the tags are removed bring them back here secretly and keep them in the kitchen. They don't need to know where they are. Got it?"

"I've met Jenny at the hospital," interjected Johnson, pleased he would see her again so soon.

Jake nodded.

"That's good," he said. "You'll need to work out a plan and let me know what you decide before you go," he added. "I want to be kept in the loop at all times. We're in murky waters here."

Jane nodded. She knew exactly what he meant.

"We have 'til midnight," he said. "Why don't you see how Myra is doing," he added, but they all knew he really wanted to know how Carney was faring; he was the true maverick and they didn't know how he'd fare in the long run. Jane knew she had some explaining to do to get him to trust her too. This was the perfect opportunity.

"Let's schedule your planning session for 4pm in the kitchen," he said to Jane as she reached the door. "Don't forget this," and he tossed Matt's container to her.

Nodding, she left, holding the vial at arm's length, her disgust evident on her face. Adam was waiting outside to take her to the hospital cum lab, and Myra, and Carney.

"Do you know where the Seals are? Did Jed move them?" Tullie asked, looking at Jake.

He nodded twice.

"Jed moved them yesterday morning to Tinakilly, Tullie," he replied. "We'll need to send in a team to retrieve them but it's not as simple as it sounds. Would you like to fill us in Anjie, please?" he asked.

"This is a bit awkward, Tullie," said Anjie. "I'm afraid you're in for another shock."

She shrugged. She could take it, couldn't she? How much further apart could her world fall?

Seeing her response he looked around for support and BB went and sat down beside her, taking her hand in his. Guidrius watched longingly. He had a lot of time to make up! Would he ever be able to comfort her like that, he thought.

"We've been watching Jed for some time now," began Anjie. "He was honourably discharged from the military some years ago, after a stint in Africa, not far from where we were originally. Change happens slowly there; well, positive change anyway. Most of his unit was wiped out in a surprise attack, or so the story goes. The truth is murkier than that though," he paused.

"I never knew he was in the forces," whispered a surprised Tullie.

"I know you didn't," interjected Jake. "He was undercover, and we respected that. Very few know, and it stays in this group," he added looking around at them all forcefully.

"Only one of his unit survived along with him," continued Anjie. "They're both here, and we feel working together again."

"Who is he or she?" asked Johnson. "Anyone we should be worried about?"

They looked at his innocent face but knew he had a right to know. Doubtless Rick was filling Meryck and Matt in as they travelled.

"Ken," said Jake. "Ken, the assassin, the weapons expert, the explosives expert, do I need to go on . . . is Jed's partner."

Johnson was stunned. What sort of hornet's nest had he stumbled on? They're all mad, for sure, he gave them! But now Rick's tail was beginning to make sense, and to introduce some believability into this whole debacle.

"So, it was you who sent Rick to watch our backs?" he asked Jake.

Jake shook his head but Anjie nodded before continuing, letting Johnson sort it out for himself. He's a shrewd guy, he reckoned; another good pair of eyes to have on board despite his youth.

"Jed and Ken have a contact from their time overseas, an arms buyer," he said. "We think he is part of the Club but we're not sure. We don't know his name either. But we do think that the Seals are part of a ruse to get closer to somebody either on Greenway or the Glory. They're planning an assassination or something big."

"The four crates you found," he said to Johnson, "contain enough explosives to blow the mountain to smithereens and everybody and everything within a fifty mile radius."

"Uncle Jed would never do that," cried Tullie, aghast.

"I'm afraid he would," answered Jake. "But you were always safe with him until you took these pictures. You know he has a second surveillance system at work, just where you work?" he asked her.

She shook her head, her brain whirring. So he would know about the pictures.

"Check your phone, Tullie," said BB softly, putting a protective arm around her now. "There are loads of missed calls from Jed, not to mention the texts. He wanted to get in touch with you very badly."

Nobody spoke as she thumbed through her phone letting the impact of what she had just learned sink in with the realisation that BB was right.

"We think Jed is supposed to trade the Seals to someone on Greenway or the Glory but he will substitute them for the four crates of high explosives the guys found today," he said softly.

"We must not let him blow up what's on Greenway," said Guidrius suddenly, and they all turned to him. They had forgotten his presence in their individual involvement in the story.

"Why?" asked Tullie, addressing him directly.

"The implants and modifications won't be destroyed by explosives, just splintered," he explained, "and they will grow wherever they come in contact with organic material. You'll just multiply your problem exponentially but with a twist. There's no way of knowing what the splinters will evolve into if left to themselves. They were always monitored carefully on Silvamon."

"Are you telling us we can never destroy those things," asked Johnson, gobsmacked, "that we cannot neutralise the threat to life no matter what? And what's this Silvamon thing?"

Guidrius looked at him oddly.

"Sorry, no offence intended," Johnson apologised.

"None taken," he replied for both him and Tullie, and Matt. "Silvamon is our home world," he explained, indicating himself and Tullie.

"What is the best we can expect, Guidrius?" asked Jake.

"There is one person who can neutralise the threat or manage it to everyone's benefit," he offered quietly, looking directly at Tullie, "but I'm not sure she is ready."

Surprised eyes turned in her direction.

"Why are you all looking at me?" she asked, sharply. "I've nothing to do with all this!"

"I'm afraid you have, Tullie," said Jake calmly. "You have everything to do with this."

"BB, Johnson," signalled Anjie, "I think it's time we reviewed the Greenway Plan. Don't know about you but I could do with some coffee! Coming?" and he led the way out of the room, and Tullie was left alone with Jake and Guidrius for the first time.

CHAPTER 43

Carney looked up as the doors swished open to admit Jane and Adam.

"To what do I owe the honour?" he asked sarcastically.

"I know we got off on the wrong foot," Jane said apologetically. "I'd like to explain, if you'd let me, please," she continued, holding out Matt's container to him.

"What do you expect me to do with that thing?" he asked, alarmed. "That's Matt's department!"

"Well, he can't do anything with it right now," she told him. "He's off site, visiting his grandad's old place, something about more letters from Greenway."

Carney shuddered. He was still not over the drama Guidrius had played for them; his thoughts were running riot in all the wrong directions.

"Get a grip of yourself," she said sternly and nodded to Adam to sling his hook. He had no further need to be here.

Carney began his pacing the minute the door closed behind Adam, and Jane began to worry she had sent him away too soon.

"Where's Myra?" she asked calmly, and he pointed to a door on her left.

Myra was resting quietly; Jane had to look closely to see the rise and fall of her chest, but she was breathing easily despite her porcelain look and the blood seeping through her bandaged arm.

"How many units have you pumped into her?" she asked alarmed.

"Three; that one's four," he explained. "Her bandages have to be changed every thirty minutes. I can't isolate the compound that's causing the free-flow," he added.

Gently, Jane brushed her brown hair back from her forehead. She felt warm, even hot, despite her colour.

"She's very hot," she said softly, and Carney nodded.

"Running a fever," he replied, "but I think the antibiotics are beginning to kick in finally. Been a bit worried about that too."

"Doctor," she called to him as he left, "may I join you, please? I have something to tell you."

Stopping, he held the door for her, and he followed her back to the lab where he stood with his arms folded, waiting.

"Let's grab a seat," she said. "This could take a little while."

"We've got ten minutes before I need to change her dressing again," he replied, testily, staying exactly where he was, not entirely trusting her, she noted.

"Well, it's like this," she began, "we've got two more with these tags; more recent ones so likely to be fully functioning. We need to work out a way to remove them before midnight. Their lives are in danger if we don't," she added.

He said nothing but just looked at her with his mouth open for a very long time. Jane felt like waving a hand in front of his eyes to see if he was present at all! Geez, he really needs to get a grip, she fumed silently.

"Two more," he suddenly repeated. "How long 'til they get here?" he asked.

"They won't," she replied calmly. "We have to remove the tags in situ. We cannot risk their being traced here."

"In situ," he parroted back.

"In situ," she confirmed, looking him straight in the eye.

"Who's the 'we'?" he asked suddenly, catching her off guard.

"You, me, Guidrius and Johnson," she told him frankly.

"And where will 'we' be?" he added.

"In Myrtle Avenue," she answered, "44 Myrtle Avenue, Matheson, to be exact."

He didn't blink an eye, she saw. He was processing all this in his own way. He hadn't said no so far!

"And who are the two in question?" he said quietly. "And how do they fit into this entire debacle?" he added.

"We're talking about Jenny Smith and her Mum, Kate," she answered truthfully. "You may remember Jenny from the hospital? Tullie's friend?"

He shook his head.

"But this has nothing to do with Tullie this time," she clarified. "It has to do with Greenway and Jenny's Dad, Ben Smith."

Ah," he said dramatically, starting to pace, "the plot thickens, my fair lady. Pray tell me more!"

"No! Hold that command," he gestured theatrically. "Let me guess! Ben is an amazing astrophysicist and they're holding his family to ransom so he will do their dirty work for them on the island! How am I doing?" he shouted to the unseen audience. "How good am I?"

Jane watched him without reply. He wasn't far out but she wasn't going to confirm or deny anything while he was so strung out.

"Tell me," he spluttered, running his hand through his hair while he ranged backwards and forwards in their enclosed space, "tell me, how do you guys live with yourselves? What sort of people are you? How can you be so placid with all this stuff going on?"

"What do you think is going on?" she asked him directly. "Tell me! Explain to me what I'm obviously missing?"

"I don't know what you're bloody missing," he retorted bluntly. "You sit there, high and mighty, with your alien daughter, and your explosive people tags, and expect me to act as if this is all normal. Well, it might be for you but it bloody-well isn't for me! I don't know what to bloody-well think!"

She was saved from answering by the bleeper and she was glad to see him race off to change Myra's bandages. Quietly she crept after him and watched through the glass. He was so gentle with Myra despite his outburst. He really cares for her, she realised. He must be very worried. Myra always had a way of looking out for stray dogs, she thought. She knew what the feeling was, poor thing. Grabbing the sample off the counter she headed for the nearest microscope. She mightn't be a scientist but she was good with patterns and puzzles. Maybe she'd be lucky. She certainly wasn't getting very far with Carney.

*****

Brierly Hall was a fine old pile, built at the turn of the century by an eccentric millionaire looking for some peace and quiet for his erstwhile hobbies, evidence of which still adorned the entrance hall. To Matt's amazement his key code still worked both at the gate and at the Hall itself. To his continued amazement the place was well kept; the lawns mowed and not a speck of dust anywhere. Rick was uneasy. He hadn't expected this either. It was too easy. He was right to be concerned. They stepped into the kitchen to come face to face with a shotgun.

"Hands up where I can see 'em," a voice rasped, and Matt was too dumbfounded to speak at first.

"Miller?" he asked, at last. "Is that you Miller? I thought you'd be dead by now!"

"Matt?" replied the extremely elderly man behind the gun. "I thought you'd gone down with Brave Betty," and he lowered the gun and moved into the light to get a better look.

"Well, so 'tis," he said in amazement. "Even gramps thought you were a goner!"

"What do you mean?" asked a shaken Matt as he held the old man at arm's length after a prolonged hug. "How would gramps know? Is he still alive then?"

Miller chuckled.

"You and your friends better come with me," he grinned, and they followed him down the stairs to the cellar.

"What are we doing here?" asked Meryck.

"Keep your shirt on, Mr Meryck," said Miller, "and close that door behind you, boy," he ordered Rick.

"How do you know me?" demanded Meryck, but old Miller just waved him away as he fumbled with the wine rack. Suddenly Matt remembered seeing something he wasn't supposed to see many years ago as a boy. He'd seen his parents appear out of nowhere when he was playing hide and seek. He thought it was just part of the game back then but now he wasn't so sure why they had banned him from playing in the cellar.

"I always reckoned you suspected," chuckled Miller as Matt's eyes gleamed in the half-light as the rack slid back to reveal a passage.

"You know where it goes?" he asked.

"Nope," replied Matt truthfully.

"Well, there's a world of wonder in there, young Matt," he said, "but you'll have to find it for yourself. I'm not too good at the stairs these days."

"Don't worry about getting back out," he wheezed. "It'll all open for you. Was meant for you, you know. Always meant for you. Hoped you'd come home sooner," he swiped at a rogue tear.

"Gentlemen," he said, stepping back, "I'll be in the kitchen when you need me."

"Matt," he called after him, softly, "your mum always kept her special cookies in her favourite tin; you remember, the one with the . . ."

"Blue rose," filled in Matt, wonderingly, looking back. He was surprised he'd remembered; it had been so long.

Miller's old face folded into wrinkles as he smiled fully for the first time in years.

Downstairs was dusty but ordered. The lights flickered into action instantly illuminating a large area divided into several discrete labs. A second later the extractor fans hummed into life, inviting them in. Matt expected the place to be completely trashed; there were signs of damage here and there but as much as possible had been repaired and what couldn't be repaired had been replaced. But the models were out of date; at least ten years old, he noted. Still, it was pretty exciting to find his grandad's lab functional after all this time. Was it Miller who had cleaned up, he wondered, and then dismissed this immediately. Some of the machines were way too heavy and too complicated for an old man like him to position. He was even old when I was young, he mused.

"Miller!" he shouted suddenly, and Meryck and Rick jumped.

"What is it?" asked Rick excitedly. "Have you found something?"

"No," laughed Matt as he headed for the stairs, "but I know where to find everything now. Come on!" he called.

Miller was patiently waiting for the kettle to boil when they reached the kitchen.

"That didn't take long," he smiled wryly. "You figured it out then?" he directed his question at Matt.

"Kinda," replied Matt, and reached above the cupboard for the biscuit tin with the blue rose.

"Tea?" Miller asked the guests politely.

They shook their heads.

"Any chance of a coffee?" asked Meryck. "Black and strong," he confirmed.

Old Miller shuffled to a large cupboard by the solid fuel cooker and pulled out a cafetiere and a bag of ground coffee.

"Not sure how to work this thing," he said, handing the lot to Rick. Meryck grinned. Some things never change. Rick looked askance at Meryck.

"Be a good boy and make mine with an extra kick," Meryck smirked, and he joined Matt and Miller at the worn kitchen table.

Matt sat looking longingly at the tin, wanting desperately to open it yet now that he had it in his hands, wanting to prolong the moment for as long as he could. Miller stood behind him, his hand on his shoulder.

"It's ok, lad," he said, shakily. "She loved you more than life itself. She knew they'd find out about you if they stayed."

"Are you saying she knew they were tagged?" he whispered hoarsely.

Miller just continued patting him on the shoulder, his eyes misting over with heavy memories.

"Open it, man," said Meryck. "Please, Matt."

Matt could hear the longing in Meryck's voice and he heard Rick coming to the table with the coffees.

"Here, Matt," he said strongly. "Drink up. This'll help," and he pushed a steaming cup of sweet black coffee under his nose.

Matt wrapped his hands around the mug and sucked at the coffee greedily. It burned as it slid down his throat and he was glad at the pain. Here was something he could quantify, and measure, and heal. But this other pain that had risen since entering the lab was an entirely different beast. He felt powerless in its grasp and it was suffocating him, crushing his chest slowly but inexorably. He couldn't get a breath! His coffee mug smashed into smithereens as it hit the paved floor and Miller jumped back in fright.

"Bag!" shouted Meryck catching Matt before his head hit the table.

Rick was there in a second, pulling Matt's head back and

holding a paper bag over his mouth.

"Breathe, Matt!" he said sternly. "Breathe! In. Out. In! Out! That's right! Keep going!"

Gradually the colour returned to Matt's face and they all breathed more easily.

"What happened?" asked a groggy Matt.

"You hyper-ventilated," Rick explained. "It's nothing to be concerned about. I imagine it's something to do with how you feel about that," he indicated the tin.

Matt nodded. He was right, he knew. And now it really was time to know. Cradling the tin, he took a deep breath and popped the lid.

Miller was the only one not surprised by the emptiness inside.

"Let me see," he croaked, and he withdrew a pair of ancient glasses from his pocket and perched them on his nose, reaching for the lid that was discarded on the table.

"Ah, yes!" he said quietly, "all in order, from the edge of this one to here," he said, pointing to a place half way down the stem. "This is the last. Put it there myself a week ago. Here, have a look," and he passed his glasses to Rick.

Excitedly, Rick grabbed the glasses and the lid and peered feverishly at the rose. Meryck watched him anxiously while Matt sat dejectedly, his head in his arms. He would never hold her letter, he cried inside. There wasn't one. He had been a fool to get his hopes up.

"Micro dots," Rick whispered to Meryck, passing on the glasses to him to have a look.

Meryck's hands were shaking too much to hold the lid so Rick held it for him. The silence in the room finally got

Matt's attention.

"What?" he asked to their gleaming faces.

"We have more than one, Matt," laughed a relieved Rick. "We have at least ten!"

"Eleven," interrupted Miller.

"This one down here," he said softly, pointing to what looked like a smudge in the grass, "this one is young Matt's here."

He shook his head as they looked at him questioningly.

"Not the time," he whispered, "you need to go now. Right now!" and he ushered them out into the hallway, holding tightly to Matt's arm.

"Leave it a while, then come back," he whispered for his ears only, "at night."

Matt hugged him tightly. He understood perfectly. After all, he could read his thoughts clearly. He'd be there at midnight!

CHAPTER 44

A heavy awkwardness filled the room after Anjie, BB and Johnson left. Jake expected Guidrius to take the lead, and Tullie expected Jake to. They looked from one the other, each waiting for the opening the other would provide but no one spoke. It wasn't helped by the fact that they each knew already what the other was thinking.

"Oh, for Pete's sake," grumbled Tullie, fixing finally on Jake, "out with it!"

"I'm not sure what to say," he spoke softly.

"Why don't you start with why it has taken you all these years to tell me?" she demanded crossly. "Did you think I wouldn't want to know, or what!"

He shook his head.

"No, Tullie," he replied, "it's not like that at all."

"You see," he continued slowly, "I didn't have any answers for you, until this week. I desperately wanted to tell you but I didn't know how or what," he petered out.

"But I did make a start this year," he followed up, lamely. "Whatever I knew, you would know, no matter if I lost you or not. You deserve to know."

"You won't lose me, grandad," she whispered. "You'll never lose me. I love you, you know that!" and she reached out and hugged him.

"I trust you despite all this," she whispered into his jacket.

"Now tell me the rest," she insisted, pulling back and looking into his face.

Guidrius watched with aching heart as Jake explained in his own words what had happened that day they found her on the mountain. Tullie watched Jake's face keenly, drinking in every syllable and consonant, every nuance. Guidrius watched as her body tensed and relaxed, tensed and relaxed in rhythm with the highs and lows of Jake's story, her life.

"I never opened the envelope," she mused, drawing back from Jake and looking in her bag.

"No need," he said, and touched the screen again, and the pages flickered onto the table in front of them.

"Sha-ma Endora," she read, solemnly.

"Sha-ma Endora," said Guidrius, "a noble fire."

"Sha-ma Endora," she continued reading, "royal daughter of Guidrius and Zarma Endora," and they were all quiet as the final piece fell into place.

A strange peace settled inside her as she read a language she had never seen before. The truth of her heritage could no longer be denied; in fact, she no longer wished to deny it. The reading worked as a calling card, and suddenly she longed for a home she had only seen in her dreams and a woman with her back to her. Guidrius watched his daughter step into the shoes of her ancestors, and hope began to flicker in his lonely heart. Jake felt his grandaughter slip away from him and prepared for the blow that never materialised. He found he was able to slip with her; to move towards her world while remaining firmly in his. She was surprised to feel Jake move with her; then delighted. She wouldn't have to lose him; it wasn't a choice of one or the other. This was the pinnacle of what Guidrius had hoped for; what he had given up his life to achieve: unity of the people. And it had begun with Jake and Tullie. He closed his eyes savouring the bitter sweet moment. It had been a gamble. And the cost was high.

Across the room Tullie looked at her father for the very first time. Jake stepped back. It was their time now.

"Thank you so much for everything, Jake," she whispered, giving him a huge hug. "I need to spend time with him now," she added, "but we're still good too."

"I love you, Tullie," he said. "Go and be all you can be. I'll always have your back!"

"I love you too, grandad," she replied. "We're a family, always!"

Guidrius turned away from their embrace, pushing all personal feelings aside, and giving thanks that the mission was successful. He could bear the cost; it was worth it.

A slight hand halted his progress and he turned to see Tullie looking up at him and Jake closing the door on the way out.

"Father," she said, "I think we have much to catch up on."

Tears spilled down his face as he grasped her to his chest, their hearts beating as one for the first time in years. And closeted in the purple ocean, Zarma felt their joy and it broke the chains that bound her. Turning, she faced the others. Together they moved the ocean so its waves swelled and swelled. Finally, their time had come. Sha-ma was alive!

*****

"What the hell do you think you're doing?" roared Carney, as he crashed into the lab, pulling Jane away from the microscope.

"Well, you weren't going to do anything," she retorted

sharply.

"You don't put the whole thing under there," he sighed, infuriated.

"What do I know?" she said in mock modesty, rolling her eyes to the ceiling.

"Why don't you just keep your nose out of this?" he challenged, working expertly at the specimen, slicing it into slivers and shoving slides agitatedly under the scope. Flicking a switch, a screen lit up to their left and Jane could see the results plastered across it in vivid detail.

"That's how it's done," he shot at her.

"Well, bravo!" she clapped. "The mighty has spoken!"

But he was captured by the detail on the screen and ignored her. Pushing more and more slides under the scope, he lined them all up on the screen and began to shake his head from side to side. Jane was ignoring him too now. The detail was terrific, the specimen magnificent. She followed the colour trail as it spiralled deeper and deeper to link with the paper thin chip, interlinking several key nodes. As if reading her mind, Carney magnified the chip again and again, reading the mineral output on the bottom left of the screen with interest. Jane could see where the suckers locked onto its target; Carney could see what it was that caused Myra to bleed out; what was thinning her blood.

"Look," they both said together, pointing to two different things. It was an awkward and exhilarating moment; enemies achieving success together through the most unlikely route. Carney held the upper hand.

"Look!" he said again. "That's what's causing Myra to bleed out. I can stop it now. Hang on. I'll be back," and he rushed out the door. The door slammed shut behind him leaving Jane alone, then it opened again just as suddenly.

"Thanks," he said, embarrassed, and this time the door remained shut.

Jane remained, evaluating the information on the screen and guessing wildly at how these could be removed from Jenny and Kate.

CHAPTER 45

Anjie turned away from the window as Jake entered.

"Tullie ok?" he asked, and Jake nodded.

"You ok?" asked BB, and again Jake nodded.

"What have we got?" he asked.

"Pretty much as before, Jake," answered Anjie, without preamble. "Everything is in place and all primed for midnight."

"But?" asked Jake, sensing his hesitation.

"We need to know what Jed and Ken are planning otherwise we could be walking straight into hell," answered Johnson for him.

Anjie and BB agreed. The time had come to place them fully in the frame, and time wasn't on their side.

"Well, what are we waiting for?" asked Jake. "Let's go! Johnson, you hold the fort," he ordered. "Work out your plan with Jane and Carney while we're away. Adam will show you to the lab. Then consolidate it with Guidrius here at 1600 hours. If we're not back by nightfall, take Rick and Meryck with you for protection."

Johnson nodded. He liked nothing better than a mission he had charge of! Finally, something he could get his teeth into. Then, there was Jenny of course. He could feel his face redden as Jake looked at him intently.

"You'll be fine," said Jake, and he called Adam.

"Johnson has free rein," he said. "Whatever he needs . . . ."

"Sir!" saluted Adam. Jake shook Johnson's hand as he left before turning to his old friends.

"Now, what have we got really?" he asked.

*****

Jed and Ken knocked back the cold rations with distaste. They had grown used to better fare over the last few years. This just brought back unpleasant memories best forgotten.

"Let's get started," grunted Jed, throwing the remnants of his meal in the disposal bag.

"We have time for a hot coffee, at least?" grumbled Ken. "Got to cut the grease. That food was crap!"

Jed relented. He wanted one himself badly. Might as well, he thought as he nodded to Ken; could be a long time until the next one!

They shared out the hot brew while they mentally prepared for the task ahead.

"When is Bill getting here?" asked Ken.

"Midnight," said Jed.

"He's not helping us then?" asked Ken, staring at the materials spread around them.

Jed shook his head. "Told you before! He's our way out, man!" he emphasised.

"Let's go over it again," said Jed. "Might as well use the time profitably."

In between sips, they rolled off the order of operations: first, move the detonators, then the cabling. While Ken moved these across, Jed's job was to redistribute the explosives into smaller packages, fish sized, and string them into beads capable of being hauled behind the submersible. It would take them three hours to complete, they reckoned, going at a sedate pace so as not to be picked up by the radar; then two more to complete setup and they were ready with part one. Then, they waited; the hardest bit of all Jed knew, to wait and keep alert.

"Right! Let's go," he said suddenly, chucking the last of his coffee on the floor.

*****

Rick drove slowly away from Brierly Hall, Meryck in the front seat clutching the lid to his chest. Matt watched the Hall fading from view as they drove down the short driveway, Miller waving enthusiastically from the doorway.

"He knows Matt's alive, doesn't he?" asked a calm voice from the shadows.

Miller nodded to his wife. He could feel gramps rummaging around in his mind as well, and he let him. Nothing much left in there anyway.

"What's he planning now?" she asked quietly. She had only a faint sense of him; he hadn't given her as much as he had her husband. She was more frail and he didn't want to damage her. The results were mixed. She had the longevity her husband had but not the strength of intuition. In many ways, this was a blessing. What he saw in that prison was not for the faint-hearted.

"He's reviewing the situation," he told her. "Thinking about bringing Ben out with him but worried about the girls."

"Anything we can do to help?" she asked. There were days she wished she hadn't been so keen to live forever. This was one of them. Besides, she didn't relish what was coming.

"I know, dear," he said sadly, taking her hand, "but you know we cannot leave. We wouldn't get any further than the front gate."

"Can't Matt help?" she asked desperately.

*****

"Stop the car," shouted Matt. "We need to go back. They can help us with Jenny and Kate!"

"They?" asked Meryck while Rick did a u- turn.

"Miller's wife is alive too," explained Matt. "They're tagged, like Jenny and Kate, but they have a way to remove them."

"How do you know all this?" asked Rick but Matt just shrugged. He wasn't sure himself.

"What's the Club holding onto them for?" asked Meryck.

"Dunno," was all the answer Matt could provide.

Miller wasn't in the least bit surprised to see the car pull up in front of them; he hadn't moved an inch but his wife was now beside him at the door.

"Matt," she said happily, as she hugged his strong frame against her frail body.

"Meme," he sighed. "I'd feared you had died too!"

"Nah," she laughed, "you know me. I'll live forever!"

"Come on," she added, taking him by the hand and leading him inside again. Miller indicated to Rick and Meryck to follow, but remained behind to watch. They could sense he was anxious. Something was bothering him but Meme was already moving so they followed her inside.

She led them back down to the Lab.

"Miller doesn't come down here much anymore," she explained. "No, not because he's old, but because they're monitoring him very closely," she added. "Twice in one day would just raise suspicion. Me," she continued, "well, they've given up on me! I do a very good senile impression," she laughed.

Matt couldn't see what they could find here that would help Jenny and Kate; the equipment was simply too antiquated. But Meme wasn't deterred. She marched straight through all the rooms to the end, then winked and pushed at the far wall. The wall slid silently aside and they were in another passage, the door swishing closed behind them, and low lights winking on to guide their way. She moved with the ease of many years of practice and their confidence grew. Down here, her frailty was replaced with a certainty of purpose. The corridor split and they followed the left fork to another dead end which opened, with her touch, into a very modern lab indeed.

Matt whistled. Meme smiled affectionately and led them forward without delay.

"This is what you need," she said, removing an object that looked like a laser pen from a cabinet to their right.

"This will incapacitate the tag, making it lose its grip" she said. "You will then have ten seconds to extract it and kill it," she explained.

"We may not want to kill it," said Matt, "just incapacitate it enough to safely remove it; then introduce it to a new host."

"A new host," she asked sharply. "Do you know how horrible these things are?" she said, patting her left arm.

"A cat," Matt said quietly. "We were thinking of putting it into the cat so we can remove the women from the scene but leave the live tags still in the house. We need to buy a few hours time."

Rick and Meryck looked at him sharply. They hadn't discussed this part of the operation at all but he had figured it out well, it seemed. Meme wasn't too sure that it was a good idea at all but she wanted them safe, regardless.

"Then, you'll need this gadget," she said sadly, making up her mind, and handing him what looked like a reinforced syringe.

"While they're alive, they're very pliable," she explained, flatly, "it only takes a little prick and they're transferred."

Matt understood instantly. These things had been developed by his beloved grandad right here. They were all his work; his fault.

"I'm sorry, Meme," he said. "He shouldn't have done that to you!"

"It's ok, Mattie," she said, patting his arm affectionately, "We agreed willingly. How many can say they have a chance at living forever! But there's always a price; there's always a price; and sometimes it's just too high," she sighed.

"You must go now," she said, hustling them upstairs, "Quickly. It's nearly time for our daily check-in!"

"Just one question, Meme," Matt said, looking back at them both as they reached the car. "Where does the corridor on the right lead to?"

They both shook their head but it was too late; the underside of Greenway filled his vision, one he recognised instantly from his childhood. He now knew what the key in his pocket opened.

"Hey," Rick called across to them as he got in the driver's seat, "how do you guys get food and stuff if you cannot leave the grounds?" but they didn't reply, just waved them off frantically.

Half-way back to Traveller's Mountain they met one of BB's vans. Slowing down as it drew near Rick waved to Joey, then pulled away and kept going. Joey watched the strange car accelerate away and continued unconcerned on his mission.

"That was Joey!" exclaimed Meryck. "What's he doing out here?"

Rick slowed down at Meryck's tone and watched the van in his rear-view mirror disappear around a corner.

"Trouble?" he mouthed.

"He was there when Ken drove away," Meryck recalled, "having a fag break."

"Coincidence?" asked Rick.

"This whole thing is one big coincidence," growled Meryck.

"Right," said Rick, and pulled the car into a u-turn. "Let's see where your Joey is going, shall we?"

Cautiously, he pulled the car around but there was no truck to be seen anywhere up ahead. Matt whistled. Meryck's face became a study in concentration.

"Pull over here," said Matt. "You can see the front of the house through the bushes, or at least you could do."

As soon as the car slowed down, Matt jumped out of the back and sprinted for the spot in the hedge that he had crawled through on many occasions. It was packed tight; he couldn't see a thing, the new growth over the years doing its best to take over its neighbours. Motioning the car nearer, he climbed on the bonnet, and then the roof. Crouching, he peered over the hedge. Sure enough, Joey was unloading boxes of groceries to a stooped-over Miller. Nodding, he got back in the car and they headed silently for home each constructing possible links and affiliations from what they had just discovered.

"That was close," said Meryck, finally breaking the silence.

"Yeah, but where does it leave us?" asked Matt.

"Mmm," said Rick, "rather, where does it leave BB?"

CHAPTER 46

Ben walked slowly along the narrow corridor towards the kitchen, his footprints marking every step on the dusty floor. The holes in the walls had been repaired and painted but the ongoing sound of the hammers reverberated above the powerful extraction fans working at full throttle to clear the dust and smell. The kitchen was busy to overflowing; the new meals being prepped while the old ones lay spread out for distribution and consumption. Several tables were occupied by workmen and security taking their breaks which cut down the working space for the kitchen staff but they didn't seem to mind. In fact, a jovial camaraderie echoed around the room, something he had never experienced in the place. Off to the right sat a group of medics or scientists; it was hard to tell exactly from his vantage point but there seemed to be more and more these days, he mused. Even the colour of their tags didn't identify them any more since they were all digitised now, iris and fingerprint access all over the place.

"Help yourself, Sir," said a young man in an apron, handing him a tray and pointing to the service line.

"Thanks," he nodded absently, noticing how hungry he was for the first time.

Moving along the line, he piled his plate high with food meant for kings and grabbed some coffee from the large pot at the end. But then he realised he had a dilemma: he didn't know where to sit. He knew no-body and wasn't really in the mood to make new friends. You just didn't make new friends here anyway, he thought, and looked around for a quiet, isolated spot to eat.

"Why don't you come and join me," said a voice from behind and he turned to see the new chef holding her tray, ready to eat too, nodding to a small table behind the counter away from the hustle and bustle.

"Welcome to my office," she said, pushing her laptop to one side to make room for them both.

"My name is Ella," she said, holding out her hand once they had secured their trays. "I hope you like my food!"

"Ben," he said back, grasping her thin hand and shaking it firmly. "It smells delicious. Can't wait to get started! I'm starving!"

"Yeah, been a busy day," she said, between mouthfuls.

"Busy night too," he said, then clammed up. Not supposed to talk about your work here!

"I heard," she nodded, throwing him a wide smile. "Not much escapes us here even though we're not supposed to know anything."

"So, you married, Ben?" she asked innocently, sitting back, drinking thirstily from her mug.

He nodded, chewing thoughtfully. So, nothing much escaped then down here, he thought. Wonder how much she actually knows?

"Yep," he said finally. "Married now for nearly thirty years; one daughter, Jenny."

"And you wife's name?" prompted Ella, quietly.

"Kate," he replied, attacking the last of his food with gusto.

"And does Kate work here too," she asked, conversationally, "or Jenny?"

He shook his head, settling back now with his own drink, patting a pleasantly full belly.

"You married?" he asked back, and wished he hadn't as her face crumpled for a millisecond.

"Was once," she answered, "briefly."

"Kids?" he prompted, gently.

She shook her head not trusting herself to say anything and he let the moment pass without further comment, and she was grateful to him for it.

"I'm sorry," he said quietly. "I didn't mean to pry."

She smiled her wonderful smile at him again and he ignored the extra brightness in her eyes as he reached over and patted her hand.

"Fancy meeting someone as nice as you in a place like this," she whispered, shaking her head. "That's the first kind act I've experienced in all the time I've been here."

"Why do you stay?" he asked, bluntly. "This is not a nice place to be. Isn't there somewhere better you can go?"

"Maybe," she said sadly, "but the routine tends to take over after a while. Routine is good for the soul, don't you think?"

He said no more. So it was true, he thought. She's been hurt bad. But there's a time to move on too. He knew all about that!

"Why do you stay?" she interrupted his reverie. "Isn't there somewhere better you can go?"

He smiled. She had him there!

"Maybe," he replied sadly too. "Maybe one day I can put all this behind me and start again. I'd like that."

"What's stopping you?" she continued, genuinely interested.

"You know the way work creeps up on you," he said slowly, "responsibility and all. Well, I'm kinda in the middle of something. Got to finish what I started."

"Don't we all," she said, sighing.

"Well, Ben," she added, rising, "been really nice meeting you but got to get back to work. "

"Me too," he said, holding out his hand to shake hers gently this time. "Got some meals to deliver."

"Not you too," she grinned, moving towards the News Board. "Let's check out the list. Who knows; maybe you'll be stuck with me for a bit longer!"

Following her, he thought that would not be a bad outcome at all. Maybe, just maybe, he could get her to come away with them.

*****

The group on deck spread themselves as far away as possible from each other; killing time wasn't the only thing on their mind as the Glory slid through the sparkling afternoon water. Oswald kept his distance but instructed his staff to follow every move and nuance, and report anything out of the ordinary to him; anything at all, however small. There was no way of trusting them. A cornered animal is a dangerous animal, he scowled, and he was far from through with them yet; or one, at least. His eyes, hidden behind his sunglasses, roamed the deck, focusing on one, then another before moving on. Carla was the only one nursing her drink, he noticed. He had to act fast.

"Madam," the man said, "Mr Balmier would like to see you in the Saloon."

Carla looked right through the man while Bowen's eyebrows did a wonderful journey across his forehead.

"It's ok, darling," she said huskily, "I'll be right back," and she swayed slightly as she walked slowly to the gangway, the man right behind her to assist, if necessary.

They all watched her go lazily; no one inclined to intervene, even Bowen had slunk lower in his seat after she left. Walking away from them, she never saw them collapse, neither did she hear them fall or their glasses shatter. A slight prick was all she registered on her arm.

"All out, Sir," the man reported, as he carried the unconscious Carla carelessly over his shoulder into the room and dropped her unceremoniously on the couch.

"Good, good," muttered Oswald, stroking his chin reflectively. "Now begin the search, her room first. Don't forget her handbag. And check her jewellery; every hairclip and toe ring. Check for implants on them all too. Don't forget her nail art! And put everything back the way you found it! I don't want them to know we know, just yet," he finished forcefully.

"Don't forget to open the umbrellas over the sunbathers," he called up to the crew on deck. "Wouldn't want them to get too sunburned now, would we," he chuckled as he picked up the phone.

*****

"Well, look at that," grinned Ella, pointing to their names at the bottom of the list. "Apparently, you are stuck with me for another while."

"Will be my pleasure," smiled Ben, checking out their route. Ella watched him covertly. She was pleased she had made contact. It certainly is an ill wind that doesn't benefit someone, she thought. Last night was exactly what she needed to move her plan forward. She hoped the information had got through; surely they would be following the Glory at any rate. This was the only man in the building who could open the doors for her, delivered up to her like dinner on a plate, she grinned. He'd be out of a job when she was through with him; maybe she could turn him. It was a calculated risk, she knew, particularly so close to the culmination of her mission. The old geezer seemed to trust him though. But he had been a bit mad these last few days, had to be sedated. How much could she trust him, she wondered? There were so many uncertainties, way too many, she realised for the umpteenth time. Who was she to stand alone against such a flood? It had been easy in the end to arrange the duty list; they'd asked her to do it and she was careful to leave herself until the last hoping he'd turn up. And it had worked. And now that he was standing beside her, she knew her time here was at an end, one way or another. He'd be dead meat if he stayed. Maybe, just maybe, she could convince him to leave with her.

CHAPTER 47

"I've got a birthday present for you too," said Guidrius in a choked voice, and he pulled away from Tullie and rummaged in Jake's backpack for the small package.

"It's a little late," he smiled as he handed it to her. "It was meant for your first birthday."

"They're beautiful," she whispered as she gently extracted three thin, white gold bracelets, holding them up to the light to admire them fully.

"Thank you, father," she said, and rested her head on his shoulder as they both admired the handiwork, Guidrius lost in memories of another woman, another time. The thin bands had tiny symbols crafted along their lengths, both inside and out.

"Where do I wear them," she asked, "this hand or this?" holding up her right hand followed by her left.

"Both!" he said. "Let me put them on for you."

Selecting one, seemingly at random, he fitted it around her right wrist where it curled itself softly to the contours of her arm and melted into her skin to look like a feathery silver tattoo; tiny leaves sprouting from a skinny vine, almost imperceptible to the human eye.

"Wow!" she whispered excitedly, "did you see that?"

"Yes," he replied, excited too, "it fits perfectly. I hoped it would! Do you feel anything?" he added.

She shook her head, her lively curls bouncing around her pretty face. She may as well be one year old, how young she still looks, he thought.

"Good," he said. "That's perfect."

"Is it supposed to do something?" she asked. "Am I supposed to feel something?"

"Only if danger is present," he explained, smiling, "danger to you, that is. You'll work it out for yourself."

"Man-x, you mean?" she asked searchingly, and he nodded seriously.

"Do you really think he will try to kill me?"

"That's what he's been programmed to do."

"The part I really don't understand is me, where I come in," she said, reading his face intently.

"Let me help you put on the rest of these," was all he replied. "They'll help with the answer."

Lifting the two up, he choose one again, and she held out the left arm this time.

"Do both of these two go together?" she asked, excitedly.

Smiling, he pushed the bracelet up her arm to just below her elbow. Like the previous one, it settled into place gently and melted into her skin to form a single line tattoo of white silver with amethyst bands, exactly like the ring, tingling as it rested there, sending shivers up and down her lower arm. She shook her arm and he smiled.

"Felt something that time?" he asked, and she nodded.

"Ready for the last one?" and she smiled. Lifting her hand gently, he draped the last bracelet over her hand and onto her wrist where it too snuggled like its twin further up; same markings, same tingling.

"Wow!" she said, when they had finished tingling, holding up her arm and admiring the markings they had become. "They are so beautiful," she added, "and so light! They're like silver tattoos!"

"Rub between the two with your right hand," he instructed. "Make sure to touch each with the other band, like this" and as she did, the markings extended themselves to cover her entire lower arm with a peculiar mesmerising pattern, solidifying into the same metal and stone as the ring.

But it didn't feel heavy, or awkward, she thought. It didn't get in the way or feel inflexible at all; it was like a second skin, and it felt good.

"Now, rub up and down your arm with the right band," he instructed, and this time they returned to what they were before; two separate bands, separated by an expanse of arm.

He watched her repeat the actions a number of times and he was relieved she was finally wearing them.

"What else do these do?" she queried dreamily.

"The bands, combined with the ring, identify who you are to the world," he answered. "They can only be worn together by one person; any other putting them on would be killed."

"Now you tell me!" she admonished him, punching his arm playfully.

"And the arm shield, or whatever it's called?" she said, "what does that do?"

"That concentrates your natural capabilities, some call it power, in one place," he replied, "your power to create or destroy; to heal or confuse; among others. It is an awesome responsibility, Tullie."

"What if I don't want this power or whatever it is?" she asked, sharply. "How can I get these things off?"

"You can't ever remove them, Tullie," he replied sadly. "They're meant to be part of you; to complete who you are. They're passed from mother to daughter in perpetuity."

"Does that mean . . .," she began, her eyes widening in shock, but he forestalled her. He didn't know her fate for sure himself!

"But you do have a choice, Tullie," he continued, softly. "You are the first leader in millennia to have any choice at all. You can accept who you are or turn away. If you turn away, these marks will fade and you will forget they are there at all. But they will always protect you; alert you to danger and direct you to safety. You will gradually forget about today; your memories will fade. . ."

"And I will forget you too?" she interrupted.

He nodded.

"I don't want to do that," she said slowly, "ever!"

Struggling with his feelings, he continued, "If you accept, then I will teach you how to use these gifts wisely, as much as I can, because, in the end, the journey is yours, the choices are yours."

"Who am I really?" she asked. "The full truth this time, Guidrius, please."

"Your official title here is The Ambassador of Unity," he began, "but first and foremost you are my daughter and Queen of Silvamon. You must fulfil this destiny first of all. . ."

"Is my mother not Queen?" she interrupted. "The women in the Lake, they were all previous rulers, weren't they?"

"You know of the Lake?" he asked in a strangled voice. "Going there is death for the uninitiated!"

"I spoke with them in my dream," she told him, "when I was in the ambulance on the way here. But I tried to talk to this woman who had her back to me," she continued. "She was so sad. She seemed bound in some ways."

He was looking at her with admiration.

"Did you enter the Lake?" he asked.

She nodded.

"You waited for me on the shore, ready to save me when they rose to touch me," she smiled.

"Tullie," he said softly, "that's what happens at an initiation. Except usually only one comes to speak to the initiate; their mother, the one they are taking over from. Only those with a direct link get to share their wisdom with the new Queen. This is unheard of - that the others were able to reach out to you too! "

"But what about the woman who was bound?" she asked again.

"I don't know," he told her sadly. "All through your grandmother's reign there was increasing trouble; dissension in the ranks over succession. It had been going on from the beginning in some small ways but came to a head when she died; or was killed, as some believe. The rule has always been that a female succeeds to balance the years of war under male leaders on earth. But it didn't sit well with the men; they grew tired of peace and prosperity, and power struggles began to surface. Not all men, mind, but enough to shift the balance."

"Since the beginning," he continued, settling himself in a chair, "a Queen had only one child, a girl, so there were no questions, no dissensions. Then a few centuries ago, Queen Satya gave birth to a boy, Zellon, and Silvamon was turned upside down. Some saw it as a sign that it was time to return to earth; others argued that it was a time of testing to see if we could continue to live and develop in peace regardless of who sat on the throne, Queen or King. We certainly saw what happened with that one! Rumours started that the child had been genetically engineered; it was certainly possible to do that at that time. The Council was asked for a ruling, the first ever, and they decided that Satya should have another child to decide the outcome. If she had another boy then the direction was clear; millennia of succession would change. If she had a girl, then the boy child had been engineered and he would not succeed. Satya was isolated throughout the entire time and she gave birth to a girl, your great, great grandmother. Zellon was exiled. But rather than uniting the people, this caused a schism. People began to take sides. And the Council was asked more and more to decide on matters as the Queen pined for her exiled child. She became isolated by choice, this time; sidelined in matters of state. When she died, your great grandmother fought a valiant battle to restore power in the royal lineage and she did indeed make progress. But when your grandmother took the Throne, she was not as strong; it was as if the line was indeed failing bit by bit. By the time she died, your mother knew she had a tough battle on her hands. She was right. She had read the signs correctly. She knew her life was in danger. If she was killed before giving birth, your line would fail and Zellon's would ascend."

"I was your mother's Protector since she was born," he continued, quietly. "When your grandmother died, I took her in secret to the Lake. What she learned there, she never shared with me or anybody but when she came out she told me we had to flee, that her life was in danger. I had gathered as much from palace intel and was sure the people would still protect her, but she was adamant. We fled that night and spent the next three years moving constantly as the world fell apart. Zellon's grandson took the throne and started to bend everyone to his will. We weren't safe. He looked for us everywhere."

"Your mother never once used her powers to protect us or harm anybody," he was far away from her now Tullie could see, lost in a world she had no part of, yet was there in some ways. "She knew the second she did, Zucon, Zellon's heir," he explained, "would be on to us in a flash. When you were born, she gave me these gifts for you and sent us both away, to keep you safe. Zucon was close, very close, those last days."

"Now you see how Man-x fits in, Tullie," he finished sadly. "Zucon wants to eliminate the female line entirely. You're the last of the first line of female Ancients; the last one who can take us back, take all the worlds back. Without you, Silvamon is lost for sure; and it is unlikely the other worlds can survive either. Whether Satya's son was engineered or not, we were nearing the end times again. The signs were there for all to see."

"Were the moons part of these?" asked Tullie, to his immense surprise. How did she know about those, he wondered?

"I saw them," she explained, "when I was in the Lake; I thought they were too close together."

"What else do I need to know?" she asked.

In reply, Guidrius let a small silver globe form in the palm of his hand and he motioned to Tullie to put her hand in his, and the two were enveloped in their home world.

*****

Man-x sat quietly in the corridor, his senses honed, following the movement around the building closely. He had fully recovered long ago but preferred to remain docile and compliant, something he could do forever, if it served his purpose. They were nearly finished with the repairs; he couldn't make out exactly why the visit had been postponed, maybe because of his burst for freedom. If only they knew, he thought! Freedom was a vague dream, something experienced briefly as an infant before he was harvested. His entire life was programmed for his task ahead; he had sensed her again briefly nearby then she had gone cold, her presence shielded by the royal shield. He wasn't worried; he'd find her. And when he found her, he would kill her. Then he would be free! But it was a bittersweet release he faced. Something had changed the day the woman came to see him; he wasn't sure what or how but he knew life had changed for him somehow. He felt a bond with her. But no matter how hard he tried, he couldn't figure it out. It annoyed him, causing his systems to overload which filled them with heartless concern. They didn't care about him! Nobody cared about him, not even the old geezer who was as close to a friend as he'd ever have, he reckoned. He felt it when she was killed; so did the old geezer. But they were both good at shielding their thoughts; he got no further with him yet he still tried. Something was different about him these days. He felt he had come to some decision and he wondered if he could ride the outcome. His knew if he was going to escape it would be from here, this corridor. He had to be ready when they came for him.

*****

Ben and Ella worked in tandem to organise their lunch round. They had the entire Second Floor, the living-dead, they called them, those poor unfortunates waiting for something. They would have to instruct them to eat otherwise they would just sit there and fade away. Ben felt sick at the thought; Ella, angry. Nobody had the right to do this to another human being. They piled their carts high, each serving numbered for identity purposes. The medic for their floor added a small cup of meds to each tray, carefully marking off each delivery, and they were ready to go.

"What do you think those meds are for?" whispered Ella

as the lift doors swished shut.

"Not a clue," replied Ben, surprised she spoke so freely, "Don't really want to know either! Let's just do this and be away," he added forcefully.

"Ok, ok!" she said. "Keep your hair on! Didn't mean to upset you!"

"I'm not upset," he whispered fiercely as the lift arrived and the doors swished open, "I'm disgusted! And a little bit frightened," he added weakly. "I'm not sure this has been a good idea to volunteer," he continued as they pushed their carts towards the first room. "It's one thing seeing all this on screen; quite another to come face to face with one of these!"

She stopped her cart suddenly, slewing it around to face him and he nearly bumped into her.

"One of these!" she hissed at him, really angry now. "What do you think they are? They're human beings like you and me that have been tampered with! People! Real people, you know!"

"Keep walking," he instructed her quietly, bending to straighten a wheel that was perfectly ok. "We're on camera! Always on bloody camera!" he whispered, fiercely.

"Thanks," she said in a strangled voice, and they moved forwards again slowly, one to each side of the corridor. There were no security personnel down here; this was a low-risk area. Their new passes opened each of the twelve doors and they delivered the trays silently except for the instruction to eat. Ben was humbled by what he found; Ella nearly in tears. Vacant eyes started out of shrunken faces perched on top of shrunken bodies yet each did as they were told without question or comment; food, water, meds, all were consumed with equal indifference, slowly and meticulously. Each doorway scanned them in and out; there was no way to interfere with any tray should they have wished. For the duration, they were automatons with only a slightly higher nature; they had chosen their task. Beyond that, they did what they were told, exactly.

The old geezer heard them coming from his room at the end. They would both reach him at the same time. He was intrigued. What was Ben doing down here? He wanted to meet Ella in person for once. She was the key to the next phase of his plan. He began to pace but thought the better of it immediately. They would never let anyone in if he was agitated, and they would gas him again, and he would have to pretend again. He had learned this little trick from Man-x. He could sense him in the corridor; imprisoned where he fell. There was a different energy about him today; whether this was good or bad, he couldn't tell from this distance.

"Good afternoon, General Ostenwalder," said Ben cheerfully, as he delivered the lunch tray to his old friend.

Ostenwalder watched him with hooded eyes from the far corner of his cell but said nothing.

"You're not supposed to talk," Ben heard.

"Fuck them!" he replied back. "I haven't seen you in person in years!"

"Careful, Ben," replied the old geezer, "that is danger talking."

"I've had enough," cried Ben silently, as he waited for his old friend to eat. "I'm out of here as soon as I can!"

"Don't look surprised," munched Ostenwalder, "but Matt and Myra are both ok. They took out Myra's tag. They know how to do it! They're going to remove Jenny and Kate's at nightfall."

Ben had to steady himself against the wall briefly. The information had reacted explosively with his gut, exhilaration replacing the constant worrying that gnawed at him night and day.

"I'm leaving," said Ostenwalder. "Going at midnight when the Glory arrives. Going to use Man-x to blast my way out. You gotta keep him in that corridor, Ben. If they return him to his quarters, I have no way out!"

"You can't do that," said Ben, hotly. "He's dangerous!"

"I know," he replied, tipping the meds back his throat, "but I also know how to handle him, I think," he added.

"Now, do you want to come with me or not," he asked.

Ben's mind was in turmoil as he picked up the empty tray. He had the opportunity he was looking for and he could see he had thought it through, as far as he was letting him see. With Jenny and Kate safe, he had nothing to lose.

"What about Ella?" he asked, as he moved towards the door. "Can she come with us too?"

"If you can make her," he answered, chuckling. "Good luck with that one."

CHAPTER 48

At the next intersection, Rick took the fork for Skyway, driving away from Traveller's Mountain at an increasing pace.

"Where we going?" asked Meryck, jolted awake by the sharp turn.

"You want to go back and share these with BB without further clarification?" said Rick, in reply.

"What do you think we have here?" asked Meryck, quietly, glancing over his shoulder at a distracted Matt.

"Dunno," was the reply. "I'm pretty sure BB is above board: if not, we're all compromised. It's too big a risk to take."

There wasn't anything else to be said until they could decipher the information in the dots and get some intel on Joey. Meryck dozed fitfully, making up for lost sleep, while Matt snoozed gently, content to be back in his family bosom again. Rick's mind worked overtime as he tried to make sense of what he had seen at Brierly, both inside and out. Clearly, there was some continuing link with Greenway but Matt's grandad had died years ago - or had he? And Becca had died too, he remembered. Sometimes things just aren't as they seem. But why hold these two old people in situ? How old were they anyway? He badly wanted to wake Matt up and ask him but stopped himself. He'd have those answers soon enough, he knew, as he pulled the car around the last corner and Skyways came into full view below them. He loved this trip down the hill, the sea sparkling in front of his windscreen, the road disappearing from beneath him with each upcoming twist and turn. Johnson would love this ride he thought, and he grinned, and put his foot down. The zigzagging of the car woke his two passengers and they grabbed for the nearest handhold to steady themselves.

"What are you doing?" roared Meryck. "Do you want to kill us all?"

Rick laughed. Becca didn't like the way he drove either.

"Hang on," he called as they hit the last stretch, a straight run down to the horizon with a hairpin bend at the end. Gathering speed on the descent, he approached the bend fast and jammed on the brakes, but nothing happened. Hitting them again and again did nothing! They could tell from his face that something was wrong.

"The brakes," he yelled. "The brakes are gone! Brace yourselves!" and then the car hit the bank at the bottom, tipped straight up in the air and plunged, backwards, down the cliff to hit the water with a massive impact. Within seconds, the water came streaming in through every crack and hole in the old vehicle and it began to sink. Kicking viciously at the front window, Rick looked to see Matt do the same with the back, and he thumbed the alert on his watch. Matt's window went first and water poured in accelerating the descent. He climbed out and hung onto the side of the car, pulling with all his might at Meryck's door as the front window gave. The car was wobbling now and Rick was afraid it would go over on its side but when he swam around, Matt was already tugging a sagging Meryck out of the car. He grabbed him from the other side and they rushed him upwards as the car, completely filled now, sailed regally downwards to the depths, and out of sight.

They broke water, gasping for air. Meryck was alive but unconscious, a large gash on his head; they needed to get him to shore fast. Luck was with them; the tide was coming in and they used the current to their advantage pulling themselves up on the sand as a dingy came rushing around the point, making straight for them.

"More trouble?" gasped an exhausted Matt.

Rick shook his head. Help was nearly there. Now that the danger was over, he let the pain in his right leg and shoulder overwhelm him, and he crouched on the ground, groaning. Matt watched him with alarm. Then the dingy pushed up onto the beach beside them and two burly guys were beside Meryck and Rick in an instant.

"You ok?" the one checking Meryck over shot at him.

Matt nodded.

"What happened?" asked the other, gingerly laying Rick flat on the sand.

"Brakes went," gasped Rick.

"Didn't we tell you to scrap that heap of junk," said the other, grinning.

"But you don't ever listen, do you" added his mate, stretching Rick's leg gently into place as he gasped with pain.

"Looks like you took a tumble with this one," he said, smiling. "We might get to sign our names on you again!"

Rick's pale face looked back at him thunderously.

"That's not an option," he said between clenched teeth. "Operation is at midnight. Hit me with the best you've got," he added as the man loaded a syringe.

"Shoulder gone too," he added a little later, applying a sling to Rick's right arm. He was sitting up now, his right leg braced from hip to toe, stretched straight out in front of him.

"How's he doing?" he asked, nodding to Meryck, who was semi-conscious by now, the oxygen pulling him out of the deep hole he had sunk into, a bulky bandage surrounding his head holding a large dressing in place over his left temple.

"He'll be ok in an hour or so," said his carer. "I'll sew him up when we get back. He's lucky. Could be a lot worse!"

"Here," he said to Matt, "give me a hand, will you? We'll load him first," and together they hauled Meryck to the dingy, laying him down in the bottom, before going back for Rick.

"This'll hurt, man," said the other, as the two grabbed Rick while Matt looked on and hauled him upright, holding him steady on his feet. With super-human effort, Rick ground his teeth, and stumbled between them to the dingy where he sank gratefully onto the floor beside Meryck.

"Now you," indicated the shorter one.

"What," said Matt, "you want me to lie down too?"

"Yup," they said, in tandem. "Two out, two in," and he realised what they meant.

It was cramped on the floor and he was afraid he was going to hurt either of them but Rick reached out and grabbed him and he fell sideways over him.

"Go," he shouted through clenched teeth.

The journey was blissfully short but each bump as they skirted the waves jarred his bones. No painkiller could deal with this and by the time they slowed to a crawl and the boat house roof covered them, Rick was awash with sweat. Climbing off him gingerly, Matt apologised.

"It's ok, kid," he replied. "Just be thankful to be alive! You've more bloody lives that a tom-cat!" and his head fell back, suddenly.

"Just in time," said the two, looking at Rick as they

helped Meryck up. "He'd never make it out under his own steam!"

They were well prepared. Within seconds of arriving Meryck was slumped in a wheelchair under Matt's care while they lifted Rick out of the dingy floor with extreme care and placed him on a gurney.

"Follow us," they called, as they headed for a lift in the back. "It'll only take one load at a time," they said, pushing Rick in and getting on board. "Hit 3 when we're out," they called, as the doors swung shut.

"You ok, Matt?" coughed Meryck, looking more alive now that they were alone.

"I'm ok," said Matt. "I had the whole back seat to lie flat in. How are you doing? Are you hurt anywhere else? We were very worried about you!"

"Nothing that I can grumble about," said Meryck, gingerly moving his body. "I remember us hitting the ditch then cracking my head as we spun up but nothing else until I came around on the sand. Is Rick ok?"

"Some fractures they suspect," explained Matt, watching the lift come back down. "They haven't stopped him though and his temper is definitely not improving any time soon!"

He pushed Meryck in and punched number three and the lift slid silently upwards.

"Here," said Meryck suddenly, handing Matt the blue rose lid. "Look after this. I hope it hasn't been damaged!"

He had just enough time to slip it under his soggy shirt before the door opened. The smaller of the two was waiting for them.

"This way," he said, taking Meryck's chair and pushing him along swiftly. "We need to get you out of those wet clothes."

"There's a shower room over there you can use, Matt," he pointed. "Use whatever you find."

Matt nodded.

"By the way," he called after him, "I'm Will Buckley, but everyone calls me Bucks. Come and join us when you're ready," and he disappeared around a corner.

As he was left alone, Matt suddenly realised why everything was all so rushed. He was freezing. His clothes sagged with salt water, but he knew it was not just that that made him feel cold. He was going into shock. A warm shower would help, he realised and he slopped forward leaving a wet trail on the floor behind him. Turning back, he could see where they had taken Rick and Meryck; similar trails led straight ahead and to the left. The shower room was functional but adequate. Letting his mind go blank, Matt stood under the scalding water for as long as he could tolerate then lowered the temperature and stood some more.

"You ok?" called Bucks. "You've been in there a long time."

"I'm good," spluttered Matt, "coming out now."

"I've left you some clothes," called Bucks. "I'll be waiting for you outside."

Matt was grateful for the space and the clothes. They were a good fit and he could feel the warmth gradually returning to his body. Reaching into his wet gear, he slipped the lid under his floppy top, and crammed the two instruments Meme had given him into a back pocket.

"These fit great, thank you," Matt said to the waiting Bucks who scrutinised him closely.

"Wouldn't blame you for being a bit shocked," he said companionably, as he led the way forward. "Three times in three days!" he whistled. "Someone wants you dead real bad!"

Matt stumbled and Bucks turned to offer assistance.

"Didn't think they were after me," he said weakly, accepting the support gratefully.

"Only one place those brakes could have been tampered with," continued Bucks. "Only one place the car was left alone for a length of time."

Matt was still looking shocked as they entered the room where the others were.

"You can't mean Brierly?" he whispered, stopping Bucks with a hand on his arm.

"Wouldn't do that too often!" growled Rick. "You're bloody lucky Bucks didn't take you out," he continued, hobbling forward to check he was ok. "Glad you're ok, boy," he smiled.

Matt quickly withdrew his hand and looked in fright at Bucks, then to Rick.

"Aw, come on, Rick," said Bucks. "Give the kid a break! He's shocked enough as it is!"

"You're safe with me, Matt," he said, putting a hand around his shoulders and drawing him across the room to where Meryck was sitting, his head wound now covered by a simple large plaster.

"Six stitches," mouthed Meryck, grimacing, and patting his patch gently. "Hope you're good at sewing," he smiled at Bucks, "don't want to spoil my good looks!"

"I'm the best!" replied Bucks, sitting Matt down. "Plenty

of practice!"

Rick watched this scenario unfold and a memory crossed his mind of Meryck looking out for Matt too. It seemed that this boy brought out the very best and the very worst in people; but who was meant to die, he couldn't really say.

"This is First Class Paul," he said, as the second guy who rescued them came into the room carrying a tray of hot coffee, the enticing aroma preceding him.

"Only ever travels First Class," explained Bucks from the door. "In fact, only ever does First Class in everything; the finest coffee, designer clothes, and you should see his sunglasses collection!" and he whistled appreciatively, the sound being cut off instantly as the door swung closed behind him.

Paul ignored the comment and shook Matt's hand in welcome, handing him a steaming mug.

"Not bad for a rookie! Not bad at all!" and he whistled too. "Three out of nine gone!"

"Rookie?" asked Matt, wide eyed, looking around in confusion.

"Seems like you've been made an honorary member of this rogue band of Rick's," smiled Meryck, pleased. This way, the boy had a fighting chance at least.

"We're just waiting for one more," said Rick, gingerly lowering himself into lounge chair. "Not broken after all, thankfully," he grinned. "Out of place and bloody painful but I can function." Then the door swung open again and Bucks was frog-marching a very frightened man into the room before them.

"Meet Bill Boyd," explained Rick to Meryck's astonishment.

"I think we have everything we need now to work out what the hell is happening," he continued as Bucks pushed Boyd into a chair and moved to the side to help Paul with the equipment bank. Matt's head was aching from the swivelling it was doing to keep up with all that was going on.

"What are you going to do with me?" cried Boyd, to the blank faces watching him.

*****

From the wheelhouse of the Glory, through his binoculars, Oswald watched the car gunning down the switchback road, going a darn sight faster than the dot on the screen suggested. Going to Brierly had been their first mistake, and their last, he hoped, as he waited for the denouement. The crash was spectacular; he had never seen a car jackknife straight up and over in such a way; it was so satisfying to watch. He could almost hear the crunch as it struck on the way down, somersaulting until it finally hit the water with an almighty splash and sinking instantly, the dot dying on the screen in tandem with its occupants, he hoped. But he was prevented from any further viewing as the Glory entered the cargo lane and a giant ship pulled across his vision.

"Keep watching," he growled, handing the glasses over. "I want to know about any activity of any sort in the vicinity," and he went below to mull over the search results.

They had turned up absolutely nothing. Either these four were very good or very stupid, he couldn't decide which. He was sure Carla or Bowen was hiding something, but then, they were all hiding something, he spat. Well, he'd bloody well know where they went from here out, he fumed. They would never know they were tagged, he'd seen to that, working the tiny procedure while they were out. They milled about the canapés on deck, ignorant of what had just happened to them. He watched them on the monitors; looking for the unusual gesture or pose or posture that would give him a way in but there was nothing. Rings of smoke rose from Mahler's cigar as he stood by the rails; Carla's red nails flashed as she delicately downed some caviar, Bowen fingered his glass and didn't eat at all. Boris sat to eat and was tucking in with gusto, enjoying every morsel, and washing each down copiously. Oswald didn't mind; it wasn't his stock and Randell wasn't going to miss it. Randell, he thought!

"Have you searched Kane's quarters?" he called suddenly.

"No," replied his unfortunate assistant, timorously.

"Well, what are you waiting for?" he asked silkily, and she paled. She'd better find something or he'd really take it out on her, she knew.

"You and you," she pointed, "you're with me," and they hurried out.

Sweeping the counter clear in his anger, he left the debris behind him for some minion to clear up, and marched up stairs.

"See anything?" he barked.

"Just some pleasure boats," was the reply, "and one dingy; went behind the Point," he indicated in between two large cargo boats.

"How many on board?" barked Oswald again.

"Two, Sir," was the reply, "two out and two back."

"Time?" he asked more quietly this time, internalising the information.

"Ten minutes max," he was told.

"Now what could be of such interest that would take ten

minutes only?" he mused, aloud.

"What's around that point?" he asked. "Houses? Hotels?"

"Nothing, Sir," was the reply.

"Nothing?" he queried, eyebrows raised.

"Just a small beach, Sir," he was told.

"Well, that's not nothing now, is it?" he asked acidly, and went below again. There was a chance this was nothing, but it could mean something. Turning on his heel, he returned upstairs.

"Did you see where it came from?" he demanded, "or went?"

"No, Sir! Sorry, Sir!" was the reply.

"You will be, you young fool!" he called as he went below again, "if it turns out to be something!"

He was only partly mollified when his assistant handed him what she had found in Kane's quarters. He was completely mollified by the time he had finished with it.

"Good job," he said to the quivering woman. "Get Mahler down here, will you! Now!"

CHAPTER 49

Grant's Cottage was quiet as they approached on foot. They had decided not to wait for Rick to return; they had no word of how they were doing, and the longer they waited the less chance they had of putting the best finishing touches to the night's plans. Years of working together kicked in. Jake took the lead, Anjie to his left and BB to the right. They travelled lightly but were prepared for any eventuality. The trees provided excellent cover; they crept up to the side of the barn, approaching it from three sides. The fourth, the front, had been rescued from incarceration; no part of the greenery was allowed here, but this was not the entrance they sought. From up on the hill Anjie could see that the ridge the barn abutted onto extended circuitously to Bears Lake. Below, Jake and BB acknowledged his signal and continued their search for another way in; the cave had to be around here somewhere, thought a tired Jake. BB's warble called them to the south-west and they hunkered down within sight of a slight opening. They could see no signs of recent access, no tracks of any human or animal except their own which they had minimised as much as possible. Creeping forward, BB signalled the all clear; they had found what they were looking for. But the opening was tightly bound with thick briars and tree roots; they had a bigger job on their hands than they had expected. Extracting his clippers, BB got to work stealthily, Anjie joining him while Jake kept lookout.

*****

Jed worked at breakneck speed on his part of the task; he couldn't wait to get this stuff parcelled and away. Be quick, accurate, and away; his personal motto when in the field, and never more so that when dealing with this stuff.

Ken came and went at intervals; Jed practically ignored him, only briefly acknowledging his presence each time he climbed out of the water. For his part, Ken had worked with Jed long enough to know he was in the groove and he let him be; he was intensely present and focused, and when he was in that space he was also deadly if approached or interrupted. One more trip should do it for these then onto the explosives; Jed should be finished by then, he thought, as he quietly attached the penultimate load, slipping back into the water without looking back. The blackness was broken by the powerful beams from his headlights but he could travel this stream blindfolded, he had done it so often. Monotony fought with alertness on these last two journeys. They were close to achieving something they had been working on for ten years and a certain lethargy was kicking in the closer he got to completion. There and back; there and back! He preferred the adrenalin rush of the face-to-face kill, relishing the look of astonishment and fear on his victims face before he pulled the trigger. This was so mundane and ordinary by comparison; logical and distant. He would not get to see anyone's face this way as they said hello to death. His only gratification would be the explosion; that would be heard for miles around and the fallout would be talked about forever! But that was more Jed's thing, he mused, steering the submersible expertly around a trio of turns. He was a distant assassin; a sharpshooter par excellence, keeping well away from up-close combat. They made a good team; no, they made the best team, he decided happily, as his destination opened above him.

Stretching, Jed got up and walked around the enclosed space. He was done, and Ken had only one more load of cables to shift too. Perfect timing, he thought, smiling wryly as he surveyed the last of their deliveries, the explosives. They would work these together, he decided. He needed a break. Stretching out on the floor, he let his mind go free, far away from where he was, and he was both surprised and pleased that it was Jenny who filled his vision, and not the faces of his downed comrades. Chewing absently on his gum, he pushed her to the side and brought them forward again, his small band of operatives, walking confidently into the small village to exchange their prisoner for the pieces of rock hidden right above where he now lay. Ken was covering the rear while he was hidden in the trees, on lookout, and he had spotted no deception although he had been in place for twenty-four hours previously. He could do nothing to save them as they were all gunned down, prisoner and soldiers alike; the gunfire warned Ken and he managed to evade their attempts to corner and kill him, meeting up with Jed back in Lagos twelve days later. Jed had hung onto his position in the tree for a further twenty-four hours. The place was deserted apart from the bodies which they had left for the wild animals. They wore no ID tags so he had nothing to retrieve; silent in, silent out. But he took the bracelet from the prisoner and had worn it ever since. He'd hang it on his wrist before he killed him personally! And he had found the chest with the rock pieces; they had abandoned it! It was of no use whatsoever to them apparently yet they had killed eight of his men for the pleasure of killing the prisoner. And they had walked away laughing! Clapping each other on the back on a job well done! He could feel the anger returning and he nursed the small embers into a raging furnace. He felt it viscerally; his stomach clenched and his whole body shook and he rolled into a ball, clenching his fists tight to his body storing the energy until he needed it, like his school yard fights long ago. He rocked backwards and forwards, backwards and forwards, the momentum settling him into the routine for the hours to come. Returning for the last load of cables, Ken ignored him. He'd been there before. Jed's personal preparations were nearly complete by the time Ken slipped away once more. Suddenly, he was desperate for some fresh air. He always felt better in the open air and this was his last chance. Grabbing his phone, he slipped quickly away to the Cottage.

*****

The cave opening was narrow but they were grateful that it was only the entrance itself that was covered in. After the first few feet they could see animal tracks but they were old and they moved more quickly and confidently now, Jake bringing up the rear, replacing a cover of greenery behind them. The air was fresh but earthy and the passage high enough for them to walk upright as they squeezed by gnarled rock protrusions that threatened to obscure their way. At first, the going was straight but gradually it began to slope downwards and before long they the way underfoot became wet and slippery. Roots still penetrated here, grasping for the best hold on the mountain, and muffled oaths whispered along the passageway as one, then another, tripped and fell, or bumped their head, or slid forward ungraciously on their backside. It was dark as night and they risked a low headlight; they had no idea where this would emerge or what might be waiting around the next corner. Downwards they trudged, and forwards, in this singular cut through the mountain until time blurred. The sound of falling water roused them and they squeezed through a low opening on all fours to emerge in a cavernous underground opening whose bottom was entirely water; a pond really, fed by the mountain streams that kept Bears Lake hunger at bay all year round. Stalactites dripped from the roof while stalagmites pushed themselves upwards like meerkats on duty. Such deep beauty transfixed them all and they stood for a minute to take it all in.

"Lights," hissed Jake, pointing to the water, and they quickly doused their headlights, following the trajectory in the water coming their way.

Ken hauled himself carelessly onto the landing bay and discharged his last load of cables beside his first load, the detonators. Bundles lay where he had thrown them; he'd disperse them later. No use in repeating effort was his motto. Do it once; do it right! He'd land Jed's stuff over there. Pushing back without delay he sank back into the water. They watched him go from behind a promontory, noting his direction. He had passed directly below them, back the way he came.

"Ken?" Jake asked them both, and they nodded. They had one part of the puzzle.

"Where exactly are we?" he asked Anjie, who was moving about trying to get a reading, shaking his head in disbelief. They watched him silently; he'd let them know when he knew.

"Doesn't make sense," he growled, slapping and shaking the instrument around. "Must be broken! We haven't travelled that far, surely!"

"What does it say?" asked BB, stretching his body and yawning.

"Look," pointed Anjie and Jake joined BB for a look.

"Can't be," whispered Jake.

"That's what I think too!" replied Anjie. "We can't have come that far, can we?"

BB was walking around now, searching, and then he stopped abruptly and pointed.

"See that!" he called. "That's the old smugglers bell! Pinged it myself a number of times as a youth! But I never came in this way before!"

"You saying we are under Greenway Island?" asked Anjie, stunned.

"No, not exactly under, not yet," he replied. "See those rocks there? Behind those are a series of tunnels that will take you under Greenway; right through to the sea!"

Looking where BB was pointing, Jake and Anjie set their bearings while BB cavorted about delightedly. He was like a kid with a new toy pointing out one landmark after another.

"Here! Here is where we came in as kids," he explained from diagonally across the pond. "It's a bit of a climb up from the sea, and you have to be small," he grinned.

"Bit of a rite of passage, for us boys and tomboys too," he laughed. "Not supposed to give the secret away but every year, at Halloween, when I was a boy, someone climbed in here and rang the bell. The sound comes out all over the mountain but especially on Greenway. Nobody's been able to ring it since they took it over," he explained, jovially.

"Come and see," he said, climbing with agility towards the bell. "I even carved my initials on it. We all did."

The bell was a mess of initials, some rusted over through the years, the newer ones higher up, as the first come, first served, scratched theirs in the more accessible places.

"You were BB back then too?" laughed Jake, running his hand over the top of the bell.

"Over here," said Anjie, suddenly. "Didn't know you wrote yours too, Jake?"

"I didn't," he replied coming over to see his initials scratched as new on the very top of the bell.

"Might as well have written 'Jed wuz 'ere'," he spoke slowly, looking up the tunnel towards Greenway.

"We've seen enough here," he continued slowly. "BB, have you ever gone up there?" he asked, pointing upwards.

"A long time ago," BB said quietly. "Takes about thirty minutes; bit of a crawl in places, both up and down but it's possible."

"And it comes out . . .," prompted Anjie.

"In a disused storage bay, right under the generator," he explained, thoughtfully. "You'd never hear any activity down there; it's too noisy. No cameras either as they're sure it's inaccessible except from inside."

"It'd go up instantly!" swore Jake. "One small series of detonations and Greenway would just crumble into the sea!"

"Or a strategically placed cache and it'd vaporise into space," added Anjie. They looked at each other for several seconds, weighing Jed's options silently.

"Up!" offered BB.

"Up!" they agreed, worried; Jed always liked a good demonstration.

"Guidrius won't like this," said Jake.

"I don't like it either," added the two in unison.

Jake turned to BB.

"Any other way in, man?" he asked.

"Not that I know of," he replied.

"Anjie?" queried Jake.

"Nothing on the detector that I can fathom," was the answer.

"Wait or go options?" asked Jake.

"Both," they replied in unison again.

"My feeling too," added Jake. "We've only got another part of the story here," he continued, and they looked at him sceptically.

Palms down, he acknowledged their scepticism with a

grin.

"Anjie, you head back," he instructed. "Inform the team. We'll need to go in earlier, be there before the Glory docks. One team from here, and one as agreed earlier. Make a third by sea. Work with Rick on that."

"BB and I will stay here and see how this plays out," he continued. "We'll need support. Send them here asap. Don't wait 'til nightfall. Work with Guidrius as to how we can minimise the damage should we fail to stop the explosion."

"Be careful, Jake," said Anjie, as they shook hands before leaving. "He may be your son but he has no respect for you. He always ran his own agendas, that one. Not to mention his sure aim. Keep your head down on this one."

Jake watched him go, his emotions in turmoil. BB watched them both, caught between a rock and a hard place! He had to find a way to tell Jake, and quick!

CHAPTER 50

"Would somebody mind filling me in too?" shouted Matt. "What the hell is going on?"

Boyd squirmed back in his chair, trying to get as far away from Matt as he could.

"Keep him away from me," he shouted, pointing frantically at Matt. "Get me out of here! I've done nothing! Let me out!" and he began clawing at Bucks in his terror to be away from Matt.

"Well, that's what I call a good reaction," drawled Rick. "Get him out of here!" and Bucks quickly led a slobbering Boyd away, and all eyes turned on Matt.

"Hey! What did I do?" he shouted, waving angrily. "I'm the one that nearly got killed – again!"

"What the hell is wrong with him?" he ranted, unappeased.

"Matt," called Bucks loudly as he opened the door, and Matt stopped immediately, working hard to get a grip on his emotions.

"Ok! Ok!" said Paul, intervening. "Let me try and explain, Matt, as far as we can fathom. We know that you concentrate more energy around you than most. This attracts more and it repels more. Something in you reacted to something in Boyd and we need to find out what. Do you know?" he asked quietly.

Mat shook his head.

"I don't get on well with a lot of people," he explained.

327

"That's why I work alone in the lab, mostly. Dead samples can't argue with you," he grinned weakly.

"Mind if I run this over you?" asked Paul, politely, approached Matt calmly with a scanning wand.

"Please," he said wearily. "I want to know more than you!"

"Gee Whiz!" whistled Paul, as the machine roared into life. "Your mirror neurons are firing in all directions! You just amplified that guys feelings right back at him! And there's something else I can't fathom! Your energy readings are off the chart! "

He punched a series of button and the readings spun up on the monitor behind them.

"Do me a favour, Matt?" he asked, monitoring him all the time. "Go stand by Rick and tell me what you feel?"

Matt moved towards Rick and stood close by him, elbows touching, watching the display on Paul's machine. His body showed up pulsing with colour all around while Rick's displayed gaps where his injuries were. Instinctively, Matt reached to the screen and redistributed some of his energy to Rick. Instantly the gaps disappeared while Matt showed no reduction in intensity or variety. He heard Rick gasp beside him and Bucks moved in to support him but Rick palmed him off.

"I feel great," he gasped, shrugging his damaged shoulder and pulling up his pants to remove the support on his leg. It was perfectly restored; not a bruise or a scratch in evidence. Rick hopped on it around the room, kicking at the furniture, and thumping the walls. Matt looked on open-mouthed!

"You bloody-well healed me!" Rick shouted at Matt, grabbing him in a huge hug. However Matt was pulling back, aghast!

"There's something wrong!" he croaked. "I can't do that stuff! Get off me!"

"But you can, Matt," said Meryck, pulling off his bandage to reveal a completely healed forehead, not even the slightest scar remained. "However you managed it, it's a good thing. And, thank you, I'm grateful too."

"Now, put that away, Paul," he continued. "We've had enough fun and games for today. Let's get to work on the micro dots. Time is running out! Matt?" he coaxed, and in a stupor, the boy handed him the lid from under his top.

"Bucks," said Matt, all eyes on him now in the descending calm, "I'd like to meet Boyd again, if I may. If what Paul says is true, I want to see if the process can be reversed."

Meryck watched them go with concern, Paul with anticipation. Rick rubbed at his healed shoulder deep in thought. Meryck grunted and Paul shot to work, the soft purr from the machines breaking the spell.

"All the accidents are accelerating his capabilities," explained Paul quietly as his hands moved at breakneck speed across the pads. "We're not joking about the nine lives thing. Maybe he has nine, maybe more, but each trauma will release more energy. He's a walking time bomb."

Rick and Meryck glanced at each other covertly. Matt's demonstration troubled them both equally. Paul could well be right. They may indeed have a situation of unknown proportions on their hands.

"But he's our time bomb," said Meryck decisively. "We'll let Jo take care of him once we get back."

Rick nodded slowly. Becca could help too, he thought. And they had Guidrius. Paul didn't know about him yet, he realised as they turned to dots on the screen. They needed all the help they could get!

Carney was unusually quiet when he returned.

"How is she?" asked Jane.

"Stabilised," he replied quietly, running his hand through his hair.

"Look, I owe you an apology," he offered. "I'm kinda out of my depth here."

"We all are," she replied. "It's been one hell of a rush! Apology accepted though," she smiled, and held out her hand to shake his warmly. "But we're not aliens or monsters," she corrected him, "just different, you know."

He smiled shamefacedly at her.

"I should have known better," he answered. "People are amazing; all things are possible! I'm glad Tullie is ok. She's a nice kid. She's lucky to have a mother like you."

"Begin again?" she offered, and he nodded enthusiastically.

"Deal," he said, shaking her hand this time.

*****

Myra lay drowsily on the bed, looking at the patterns on the ceiling above her. She couldn't remember where she was or how she got there but she felt good, though tired. Her left arm ached a little and she gingerly rubbed the light bandage that covered the area around her elbow. The back of her hand felt stiff where the IV was attached and she watched the fluid drip slowly and regularly done the tube – plop, plop, plop, she counted along with it until her eyes grew heavy and she slept.

In her dream she was climbing a beautiful mountain. The

sunshine was bright but not glaring; she didn't need her sunglasses at all. Big, colourful butterflies flapped around her, wheeling in a lateral cone ahead of her, enticing her on. Birds flitted around her, chirping to each other and she felt she could hear them call 'Come on! Come on!' to each other, and to her, as they passed. Laughing, she held out her hand and the occasional bird perched on it tentatively. Then her tears came and the more they poured down her face the lighter she felt. She was free! But free from what or who, she didn't know but she pushed the thoughts away and enjoyed the beautiful countryside, and the seaside beyond. Lounging on the soft, warm sand she heard someone calling her name quietly but insistently. Looking around she could see no one but the calling continued and she suddenly understood she was asleep and she needed to wake up.

"Myra!" called Carney. "Wake up, Myra. Come on now. It's time to open your eyes."

Gradually, slowly, she found the strength to open her eyes. It was like reaching up from the bottom of a deep pit, trying to see who was at the top peering down.

"Hey," he called to someone she couldn't see. "She's back!"

"Myra!" he said. "Can you hear me, Myra? You've been unconscious for some time now."

He shone a light into her eyes and checked her pulse but she didn't know who he was. He could see her confusion and tried once more.

"Myra," he said, gently, holding her hand, "nod if you can hear me."

Slowly, she nodded.

"Can you talk?" he asked, and she nodded again.

"How do you feel?" he asked but she just shook her head.

"Where am I?" she whispered. "What happened to me? And who are you?" she asked.

Carney looked sideways and Myra followed him with her eyes. A woman she had never seen before was sitting at the other side of the bed.

"Myra, this is Dr Carney, your friend," the woman explained, pointing to Carney.

"Who is Myra?" she asked back, confused. "What am I doing here?"

Carney and Jane exchanged worried glances. Myra had experienced memory loss and there was no way of knowing immediately if it would be permanent but it certainly was serious.

"Can you tell me the last thing you remember," Carney began but Myra began to cry uncontrollably.

"I don't remember anything," she sobbed into her pillow. "Leave me alone!"

"Myra," said Jane, "you're with friends. We've been friends for years! You're safe. You had a little operation but you're safe now!"

"Leave me alone!" hiccupped Myra, and Carney added a sedative to her drip.

"And I'm not Myra!" she trailed off as the sedative took hold.

*****

Bucks laid a hand on Matt's arm before they reached Boyd's room.

332

"You up to handling this?" he asked, straight up. "What's the plan?"

Matt looked at him directly and Bucks could feel his mind tingling.

"Stop that!" he shouted, crossly. "Stay out of my head, you hear!" and he thumped the wall beside Matt's head.

"What you do that for?" growled Matt, his anger engaging instantly. "I never even looked inside your bloody head!"

"Matt!" roared Bucks, and instantly Matt recognised the pattern. Paling, he slumped against the wall and slowly slid downwards into a half-sitting, half-crouching pose.

"I'm sorry," he whispered. "What happened? What did I just do?"

"You don't know?" asked Bucks testily.

"No!" whispered Matt, his head sinking lower and lower on his chest, his energy draining from around him leaving him high and dry, and exhausted.

Bucks slithered slowly down beside him but avoided looking him in the eye.

"You looked directly in my eyes, mate," he explained quietly, "and I could feel you moving around in my head, penetrating the wall I thought would block you from my mind."

"I didn't know," whispered a contrite Matt, looking beseechingly at him and Bucks strained to keep his gaze averted.

"It's your gaze, Matt," he said in a strangled voice. "One look and you're in! I'm not sure I can keep ahead of you. If I can't I'm no use to you at all!"

"Look at me!" instructed Matt, thrusting his hand at Bucks. "Look, and I'll stay out of your mind! Promise!"

Ever so reluctantly Bucks raised his head to meet Matt's gaze. Electricity sparked between them instantly as brown eyes challenged grey then the moment passed and they were just friends communicating at a level Bucks had never experienced before. His eyes widened and Matt laughed, humour restored, and leapt up pulling Bucks with him.

"So this is what telepathy fells like," he thought, and Matt nodded.

"Now I can only hear what you want me to hear," explained Matt, "'though I can pick up some emotion too. How about you?"

Bucks walked around a bit testing out this new form of communication from all body postures. He was absolutely intrigued to learn that he could still hear Matt loud and clear whether he was near or far, facing him or with his back to him, eyes closed or open.

"Distance doesn't matter," confirmed Matt as Bucks ground to a halt in front of him.

"I can hear when you speak, Matt," answered Bucks, "and I can also feel your emotions. Will I be able to reach you when they're fully fuelled?" he added, thinking of the previous encounter with Boyd.

"You have full access," smiled Matt. "Of course, there may be times you will have to let me be and block the experience," he added, grinning.

"How can I do that?" mused Bucks.

"I'm not sure myself," answered Matt truthfully. "This is all new to me too! But I kinda picture a switch in my head that I can turn on and off."

Suddenly Bucks's head was silent; Matt was gone. From the look of surprise on his face Matt guessed what had happened. Grinning back at him, Bucks threw his switch and it was Matt's turn to look surprised.

"So, back to normal then," commented Bucks aloud and Matt looked at him searchingly.

"Bucks," he began, tentatively, suddenly feeling very alone and vulnerable.

"It's ok, my friend," interrupted Bucks, the words moving silently between them again, "I've got your back. I'm going nowhere," and he meant it with all his heart.

Matt dipped his head against the wall and let the feelings come. Years of loneliness flashed across Buck's mind; feelings of being unwanted and never fitting in screamed in the emptiness; then the switch was shut again and Matt stood and looked him in the eye.

"I've never had a friend 'til now," he whispered aloud holding out his hand. They shook solemnly and the friendship was sealed.

"I've got your back too," Bucks heard Matt whisper.

They walked along companionably until they reached their destination, Bucks sharing snippets of his life journey with Matt. They had much in common. What separated them was environment and opportunity. With every step, they bonded more.

"By the way," said Matt, stopping Bucks this time, "why is he here? What's he done?"

"We found him nosing around just before Rick called for help," explained Bucks. "We couldn't ignore him and we didn't have time to scare him off, so we grabbed him. He's frightened. But we don't know where he fits in; just that he's hiding something, for sure."

Boyd looked up warily when Bucks entered first, and then his eyes bulged when he saw Matt.

"It's ok," said Matt, holding out his hands, and staring at him closely, "I'm not going to harm you. I just want to talk."

Buck suppressed a chuckle as Boyd visibly relaxed. Matt was consciously working his magic. This was by far the best way forward.

"Ok," he nodded, amicably.

"Listen, man," began Matt, "why are you here? Who are you looking for?"

Boyd answered immediately and truthfully.

"I followed that guy who warned the policeman to keep away from the Glory," he replied. "What's the man's name? Ah, yes! Johnson! He was right to warn him. Bad news, those guys. Wanted to tell him there was a fracas after they left. They were shooting at some guy that got away. I've seen him before; man by name of Ken something or other. Equally bad news. Thought they were friends. Saw him many's a time on board," he petered out.

Matt looked at Bucks, eyebrows raised, but he only got a blank look in response though he felt he knew more than he was letting on. He had learned to use the switch well, Matt grinned.

"Let me talk to him," he begged. "He'll understand! Look," he continued, "I need to get out of here. The Belle sails at eleven and I have a shitload of stuff to take care of beforehand. I was just trying to be helpful, is all!"

"I'll see what I can do," promised Matt as he headed for the door. Turning he added, "Listen, thanks man," he added. "It's good to look out for others," he smiled.

Boyd beamed back, Bucks noted. Bet that works well

with the girls, he thought!

"And by the way," he said offhandedly, "what was all that about upstairs? About me, I mean?"

Boyd scratched his head, thinking.

"I'm not sure," he answered thoughtfully. "I can't think what got over me. I'm sorry. I didn't mean to hurt your feelings. I guess, I was just scared and I felt you were too."

"It's ok," smiled Matt. "I meant you no harm and I don't think these guys do either. They just like their privacy, and you were snooping around."

"I guess I was," smiled Boyd.

"I'm sorry, man," he said to Bucks, "but can I speak to your guy now, please? I'd like to tell him myself."

"I'll send him down," promised Bucks and joined Matt in the hallway.

"Nice work, Matt," chuckled Bucks.

CHAPTER 51

Silvamon welcomed Tullie into its fold seamlessly. With her hand in Guidrius's she felt she had never left, that her life on Traveller's Mountain was the dream. She could picture her life growing up from the visual of her mother's life; the Palace, the lifestyle, the lessons she had never had but were a central part of her heritage. She could visualise Guidrius watching every step her mother made; could see him whisk her to the lake without anyone knowing, and bow to the wisdom of his mistress, and flee without warning or preparation. Guidrius liked to be prepared, she learned; liked to be forewarned. He was intense in his own training, chosen because of his prowess and his knowledge. She watched the power plays develop and the darkness and pain spread across a peaceful land. The memories didn't present all she would like to know about Zellon and Zucon; nothing about these two was recorded. They were left out of history as if by their absence they would be negated, disappear, be unmade from human consciousness and consequences. This absence of knowledge bothered her. She was like Guidrius. She wanted to be prepared, to know as much as she could about what was different in her society, all the stuff that didn't come to the surface readily. It left her wondering if it was right to have so much power concentrated in so few, and with such bias, gender or otherwise. It left her wondering about Zucon, her cousin. Could she be a better ruler? What would she do differently from her predecessors?

The world around her changed with her questions and she saw the machinations of the Council for what they were; power manipulations centred around Zucon, as figurehead. What he was now was uncertain; the knowledge ended with their coming to Traveller's Mountain. The world might be hugely different now, she hoped, but that was a whimsical thought from someone who always wished for the best in everyone and everything. Moving backwards and forwards through the records, she saw the increase in fear, the disappearances, and the put downs. She also recognised the increase in power among the few and the disempowerment of the masses. Life itself was becoming a dispensable commodity in the hands of the powerful and able. Slowly and surely, society was being turned, and the turning was backwards for the masses.

She thought of the Lake and it emerged before her but it was no longer the sanctuary she had envisioned in her dream. The waves rolled high on the shore as if driven by a mighty wind but the trees were still and calm, not a leaf moved. She heard Guidrius's sharp intake of breath.

"What's wrong?" she asked, and her voice sounded light and airy to her ears. "It wasn't like this when I saw it last!"

"Me neither," he answered, and she heard his voice as a deep boom in her mind.

"Sha-ma," the waves sounded. "Sha-ma! Sha-ma!" as the swash raced up the shore to peak further up each time, like the incoming tide, and then backwash back to the depths.

Instinct made her look under the waves to meet the smiles of generations of rulers welcoming her once more. To the front was the woman who had her back to her previously, Zarma, her mother.

"Welcome, child," she whispered. "It is time to come home," and the waves now whispered, "Sha-ma home! Sha-ma home!"

"They're calling me, father," she whispered to Guidrius, and he nodded back. He had never seen anything like it! The secret world of the Lake was hidden from all but the Queen. But now he was party to it too! So it really was true, he thought. The time had come, and Zucon was completely unprepared!

Above the Lake the two moons were almost touching now. She knew instinctively what would happen once they overlapped.

*****

Zucon was having a bad dream. Silvamon lay under feet of water the colour of midnight. It lapped at the Palace doors and flowed menacingly through the streets looking for victims. The people fled to higher ground but the waters just kept rising. Screams of the dying filled his head and he pushed his fists to his ears but he couldn't escape the sound. He rushed up the stairs but the water followed him, a stream separating from the bulk of the water trying to ensnare his heels and bring him down. The view from highest turret was grim. Bloated bodies festered in the brine while the two moons, almost one now, mocked him from the heavens. He searched desperately for the plug to let the water go but he couldn't reach it, it was too deep and too strong to pull.

"Help me!" he called, feverishly. "Help! Help!" but there was no answer except the increasingly loud splashing of the waters as they rose to reach him the further up he went.

He pressed himself against the ledge as the door began to buckle and bend, fear crippling him as he sank to his knees. The water gushed in, sweeping him over the edge and he plummeted down, down into the depths where slender white arms reached for him holding him under, dragging him further and further down until he could breathe no more. He rose, shrieking, from his bed, gasping in the bountiful air, thankful to be alive.

"Sha-ma! Sha-ma!" he whispered into the darkness. She had finally come for him after all these years.

*****

Man-x accepted his meal in the corridor with complete indifference. He was bothered by the new images in his head that he couldn't make any sense of. He didn't like water; he knew that for sure. It interfered with his pathways, damaged as they were now. He savoured the new emotion he had experienced, rolling it around in his head until he found a name for it: fear. It seemed to have a way of changing the course of a person's life, making them soft and vulnerable. He wasn't sure he would want to be that vulnerable; he wasn't sure he could be even if he wanted. He wondered absently what else would make a person feel like that and the memory of the woman came to his mind. She felt vulnerable, he now knew. But she was strong too; there was another emotion present he didn't recognise but it felt – good. And this made her vulnerable; not fear. There was so much he didn't understand; didn't recognise. But he recognised one word perfectly: Sha-ma. She was his target, his Queen and his salvation all rolled into one. Now, what about all that made him feel good? Crouching low in the corridor trying to make himself invisible, he wondered what good felt like anyway.

*****

Ben was silent all the way back to the kitchen and Ella let him be. Relinquishing their trolleys he made to go but turned back.

"Do we have time for a quick coffee?" he asked. "I'd like the time to apologise."

"I'd like that," she smiled back at him and collected two mugs from the shelves.

They sat comfortably in the now almost-deserted eating area, sipping their hot drinks appreciatively as free people. As free as you can get in here, he growled silently.

"I don't know what came over me," he began finally, unused to this role. "I'm sorry. You were right. I was an ass!"

"Accepted!" she replied warmly. "Now let me apologise for getting angry and nearly getting us into trouble! I just lost it for a mo. Sorry!"

He raised his mug to hers and they clinked, sealing their friendship, and silence descended once more. He was desperately seeking for the words to open the dangerous discussion about leaving with her while she was weighing up the options of coming clean with him. The risks were huge, she realised, maybe too huge.

"Ella," he began tentatively, "can I ask you something personal?" He groaned; this was not what he wanted to say at all!

"Depends," she answered slowly, and he kicked himself inwardly for his lameness.

"Um, if you could go," he began, "would you? Leave permanently, I mean?"

He was treading on thin ice they both realised but as she looked at his face she could see he was deadly serious. That's part of the problem, she sighed, deadly serious. Prevaricating, she nodded slowly, letting her eyes see deep into his soul. He looked back without guile and smiled wanly.

"I hoped you'd feel like that," he whispered now. "I felt it was worth the chance asking."

"Would you?" she asked, interrupting. "Leave permanently, I mean?"

He nodded slowly too.

"Up until a few minutes ago I thought I could never leave, ever," he whispered shakily.

"Because of Jenny and Kate?" she took a chance in asking.

"How did you know?" he asked aloud, surprised, and then looked around quickly to see if he had been overheard.

"Kitchen gossip," she lied, and he decided not to challenge her. It was enough that they were on the same page with this.

"We're tagged too, you know," she spoke quietly for his ears only. "Everyone here is."

His wide eyes told her what she wanted to know; he didn't know he was tagged but he knew his wife and daughter were.

"Then there really is only one chance," he acknowledged.

"One chance?" she encouraged.

He nodded slowly. He didn't seem to like his options though.

"What chance?" she whispered eagerly, leaning forward. He was taking her exactly where she wanted to go, and on his terms. Another gift! She could hardly contain her excitement.

"Ostenwalder is leaving tonight and wants us to accompany him," he explained briefly.

"Us?" she asked, paling. "What did he say about me?"

"Nothing," he said casually, "except I could bring you too if I could persuade you. But he didn't seem too hopeful of that. He treated it as a great joke, really."

She exhaled a breath she hadn't realised she was holding and reached across and patted his hand.

"Funny," she smiled at him. "I was just going to ask you if

you wanted to leave with me tonight! May I share a secret with you?"

Ben didn't know whether to be relieved or worried with the revelations from Ella; relieved that his plan was safe with her but worried about what she had asked him to do.

"It will be tight," she was saying. "You'll have to wait 'til the last minute. But I will make sure you get out, get a new identity, and be safe for the rest of your life."

What the hell, he thought! What have I to lose: a lifelong vacation chez Greenway? And Oswald!

She was looking at him closely. He seemed to have gone into shock. She was worried she had shown her hand too soon.

"Ben?" she called softly. "Are you with me, Ben? Can I count on you?"

His eyes cleared and focussed on her thoughtfully. He nodded.

"Yes, Ella," he said without hesitation. "You can count on me! Let me be the very last of your worries!"

"How much do you know about Oswald?" he asked her. "If he gets away none of us will ever sleep quietly in our beds again!"

"How much can you tell me in ten minutes?" she asked, looking to the clock on the wall.

Nine and a half minutes later she was very pleased she had asked, and very worried she wouldn't be able to warn them in time.

CHAPTER 52

"It doesn't make sense," Paul was saying as he ran the intel again from the dots. "This last one, from last week, points to today's visit but it doesn't indicate why she would have taken such a risk to send stuff we can readily observe!"

"But that's it," shouted Meryck, excitedly. "That's exactly it! She couldn't know we're watching the Glory. This is to make sure we do! The Glory has a more important part to play in all this than we thought! Greenway Island could be a decoy meant to keep us off track!"

"You're right!" added Rick. "Although Becca loves puzzles she only ever sent straight messages when stuck."

"Yes! Yes! Yes!" agreed Meryck, reconsidering, tapping his fingers on the table. "But sometimes she meant the exact opposite of what she said too, just to throw someone off course!"

"Geez!" said Rick, breathing loudly. "You're right there as well! What's on the others, Paul? Let us have them in order, last first!"

Paul lined up all the ten words going back over the last three years; one dot, one word only when she had all the space in the world. Maybe she didn't have all the time?

"How did she get these out?" asked Paul, and Rick and Meryck shook their head. They didn't know.

"I think I know how," said Matt. He and Bucks had snuck in; they were too absorbed to notice them until now.

"I heard from Miller that gramps is definitely alive in

there," he said as he strode forward. "There's this telepathic thing going on between them. Can't hear him myself yet but I did get to listen in on Miller."

They were looking at him curiously now, each shielding their thoughts as much as they could.

"Don't worry," he laughed. "I won't read your thoughts; not sure I know how anyway; seems to just happen."

"So that's how you knew about the tag remover?" asked Rick.

Matt nodded.

"I could hear Meme talking about Jenny and Kate," he said. "She was desperate to help."

"I think Becca might have communicated through gramps to Miller," he continued. "Maybe Miller can only pick up one word at a time, or encode one word at a time."

"That makes sense," interrupted Paul. "These encodings are rough, shaky really."

"Shaky?" queried Matt. "Can I see?"

Paul displayed the words, one by one, going back through the years, and Matt looked at them thoughtfully.

"They're not Miller's work," he said after a while. "I think they're Meme's." He was thinking of something Meme had said earlier but the connection seemed vague.

"Meme said they monitored Miller closely," he thought out loud, and Rick could see where he was going with this. "They didn't monitor her that closely because they thought she was senile, remember? The communication – it's not through Miller, it's through Meme!"

"Paul, can you enhance each letter in the last word?"

asked Meryck, but he was already zooming in on the G, and he found what they were looking for! All along the letter were further instructions, camouflaged perfectly in the old woman's hand!

"Give me five minutes," said Paul, and he set to work with gusto.

"I've printed yours out," he said to Matt, nodding to the printer in the corner, without even looking up.

Retrieving the pages with shaking hands, Matt stood uncertainly in front of his new friends.

"Whatever they say," he said, pointing to Paul, "you need to know, gramps is breaking out at midnight. I promised Miller I'd be there! That's all I know, honest!"

"It's ok, lad," said Meryck, patting him on the shoulder. "Don't worry. Thank you for telling us. Now why don't you find a quiet spot and have a read for a few minutes. We'll call you when Paul is done."

Matt looked at him gratefully. He could feel the tears forming behind his eyes but was determined to hold it together.

"Come on, Matt," said Bucks. "I'll show you where you can have a few minutes privacy."

"Rick," he called back. "Can you look in on Boyd? He has something to tell you."

*****

Mahler stood bullishly in the Saloon watching Oswald pour himself a drink.

"Want one?" he asked, smiling genially.

Mahler ignored him completely but he couldn't ignore

347

the sudden blow to his back that had him tip forward onto his knees despite his best efforts.

"Now boys, be gentle with our guest," smirked Oswald, sipping slowly from his cocktail glass and dabbing at his lips effetely with a small napkin.

Grabbing his hair from behind, they pulled his head back until he was looking directly into his host's face.

"Now, my dear boy," sprouted Oswald, "I hear you like to stir things up a bit in your part of the world."

"Don't know what you're talking about," was the curt reply which was met with a swift thump in the mouth.

"Tut, tut, boys" said Oswald, handing Mahler a silk handkerchief. "Do you really have to be so hard on the poor man?"

"Keep it," he continued. "It's one of Kane's. Found it right next to this folder actually."

He was gratified to see Mahler's eyes widen slightly then resume their indolent look. So, he did know about Kane's records!

"Seems like you two were going to play a little war," he asked silkily, "and with my weapons too! Tut! Tut! Not good!" and he waved his hand and his boys flayed into Mahler, kicking and punching him until the white carpet resembled a dalmatian coat, albeit a red and white one.

"So, a billion here and a billion there, and live long and prosper!" he flung at the downed man.

"And if that's not enough," he continued, "you say here, you will provide the antidote too! Tut! Tut! How very naughty of you!"

Mahler just glared at him through his one open eye; the

348

other was bloody and swollen but he could take it. Oh Yes! He could take it! And when the time came he would dish it out too! This buffoon would not live to see the new day!

"And this antidote . . . ," began Oswald but Mahler declined the invitation to comment and was beaten soundly again for his indolence.

"Not to worry! No hurry!" he said. "We have the next six hours to discuss this like gentlemen. Take him away, Boys. Let him have a wash," he laughed.

*****

Ben saw the incoming call from the Glory to the hospital and against his best survival instincts flicked the switch and listened in.

"Is it done then?" he heard Oswald ask.

"Yes, Sir," was the respectful reply. "All went according to plan. We're ready to deploy at your command."

"Good! Good!" sounded a very satisfied tyrant.

"Now, we'll need a little demonstration when I get there," he said smoothly. "Make sure you have everything packed for distribution but leave out two packs. Understand?"

"Are all the funds in?" he asked, hanging up the phone.

"All but one," was the reply.

"Mahler?" he guessed.

*****

Matt sat on the bed, eyes shut tight, grasping the pages to his chest trying to breathe in a scent that wasn't there. He felt if he could try hard enough he could make it happen. He wanted the words on the page to be handwritten so very badly but he knew no matter how long he sat there it was just wilful thinking. Lifting them to his lips he kissed them gently, hoping that somewhere out there, wherever she now was, she would feel his love. Lowering his hands he looked at the letter Paul had printed for him - two A4 sheets, broad spaced. He had more than he ever hoped for. Checking the time, he was surprised to see four minutes had passed already. They would call for him soon. Tentatively and gently he straightened the sheets and began to read feverishly.

My beloved Matt,

I don't have long to write this as I feel our plans have been discovered. If all goes according to plan we will meet again in a few years time but for now, for your safety and ours, we must part. We have arranged that gramps will send you to boarding school to keep you away from Greenway. I fear that after we go they will incarcerate him on the Island anyway, and that would mean you too if you don't go away. I love you so much Matt, as does Raymond. I guess what we did was very unconventional and you are indeed a very special person. I long to see you as a young man! Will you look like me at all? Or how much of your real father is showing through?

I went to see him, you know, before we left. When he first came to us he was such an amazing creature, docile throughout, but strong and reserved and clever. But there seems to be some disconnect in his brain; some implant that we have been unable to fathom. He recognised me as special when we met but I am unsure what exactly that will mean for you when you meet. You must go to him, Matt. You are the only good thing in his lonely life on this planet. If anyone can reach him, you can.

350

*I want to tell you a little more about our
tags. Gramps designed them for Oswald Balmier,
ostensibly as a way of invisibly tagging prisoners.
But who knows who he has had tagged to date!
I don't know if you remember him coming to
Brierly. Remember the day we met you in the
cellar and banned you from playing there ever?
Well, Balmier was there that day and while he
knew we had a child we most certainly didn't
want you two to meet ever! He's bad news, Matt,
very bad news indeed. The good news is that
there is an antidote that will disable the tags; a
small amount at present, but it exists. We have
chosen to trial it. Time will tell if it's effective.*

*Coming back to the cellar, I want you to know
that there is a passage that goes right through to
gramps lab in Greenway from the lab in Brierly.
It is an extension of the main passage but it is
entirely separate. Remember the word games
we used to play on the fridge in the kitchen?
One magnet would always slip around the side,
almost out of reach? I'm sure you know what I'm
talking about! Meme is the only other person who
knows. You can trust her with your life.*

*The time is going fast; your father is calling me
to leave. I need to tell you one more important
detail before I finish. It may mean something
to you or it may not but you should be aware
of the possibility anyway. Do you remember
that lovely Diner we used to have breakfast at?
Rosa's? Remember Maggie who was very ill?
Well, she's not ill anymore. Tissue from Man-x
cured her completely although I never saw her
outside Greenway since. You see, Matt, there is
a good chance you will be able to heal people too.
If you find you can, don't fight it! It is indeed
a wonderful gift! I hope I can be there to see! I
believe your father is a healer, Matt, from a
very long line of healers. Naturally, I believe he
is incapable of taking a life; if he is forced, it will
kill him, for sure. The internal conflict will be too*

351

much. Got to go!

I love you with all my being,

Mum xxxxxx

"Matt," called Bucks, knocking on the door just as he was finishing the letter. "We're ready! Going in five!"

But Matt sat mesmerised on the bed, transported to the cellar in Brierly where she had written this letter, sitting in front of the fridge, he had no doubt. He knew now that it was Meme who carried the messages, ancient Meme who came alive in the passages beneath Brierly. And he had a link to his growing abilities. Bucks had to call a second time before he stirred. As he left the room his thoughts were not on his mother but on Maggie. He hadn't heard anyone mention her so far!

CHAPTER 53

The Cottage was empty without Jenny. Jed walked around each room, each space they shared, and the ache grew. He had allowed a Jenny-shaped hole to develop in his heart and he was paying the price. Suddenly the cost of revenge was too high by far and he had a euphoric moment where he withdrew from the whole thing and rode off into the sunset with the love of his life. But the feel of the band around his wrist brought him back to reality. Mahler would pay! Then he'd see what was left. He was used to living on the edge. If that was what it took for the rest of his life, he could handle it. But his thumb stroked her number on his phone and without warning he could hear the dial tone sound loudly in the house.

"Hello," said a quiet voice. "I thought you had forgotten about me!"

"Hi, Jenny," he answered, his heart beating loudly. "Just been busy. You know how it is. How are you? And your Mum?

"We're fine," she said, "just being busy. You know how it is," and she laughed and the ice was broken.

"Are you guys at home?" he asked, looking at his watch and wondering if he had the time for a quick visit.

"Why?" she asked, grinning. "Want me to put the kettle on or something?"

"Something, for sure," he replied, smiling, "but not on!" and he could hear her laugh, and his heart felt like breaking,

"Well, come on over then," she purred, "and I'll see what

I can do!"

"Give me five and I'll be on my way," he said, heading for the shed.

Jed was nowhere to be seen when Ken returned and he methodically began to shift the explosives by himself, trailing them carefully behind his submersible so none would catch on the edge as he went under. The dial glowed eerily in the depths reading 4pm. He's be finished in fifty minutes or so, give or take, then Jed had better be there to begin Step 2. There was no way he was hauling all this gear up that tunnel alone! The two lines should do the trick; they'd gone over it often enough.

Jed gunned his truck towards Matheson, and Jenny. At least this way he'd get to say a last goodbye. The clock hit four as he began the descent into Tinakilly; he'd be there in twenty, all going well, all thoughts of Ken and the mission pushed into the back of his mind. Reaching for his sunglasses, he looked around appreciatively. The day was fabulous; a true summer's day full of beauty and life, and he wondered how life could go on as normal when he felt so very different; when he was planning to bring it all to a close. How did the world not know what he was up to; what was about to happen? The disconnect was severe but he recognised it for what it was. He'd used the same strategy many, many times while carrying out his missions; it was the only way to survive, to stop the horror from integrating into one's life and destroying what value was left. He'd given up counting the number of locked doors in his mind! Some days, only some, the dam threatened to burst, and today was one of those. He had reached the outskirts of Matheson when he came to his senses. What on earth was he doing! He couldn't go to Jenny! Not now! Not ever! Breaking hard, he pushed onto the hard shoulder, blue smoke filling the air behind him and the smell of rubber creeping into the cabin. He beat the steering wheel hard, time and again, until the pain inside subsided, overtaken by his badly bruised and bloody fists. It was difficult to send her the text for two reasons: his laboured breathing forced him to stop every few seconds, and he had to wipe the blood from the phone after nearly every word. When it had gone, he stripped the phone, chucking the sim card out the window viciously, and turned back to Grant's Cottage angry and dangerous.

*****

Jake and BB watched Anjie's light fade into the rock face and the silence was complete. The weight of the mountain pressed down and they felt its presence all around them, threatening to engulf them, bury them alive.

"Let's see what we've got," said Jake, and BB jumped. They made their way around the water steadily. The rocks here were wet and slippery and neither of them wanted a dip at this stage. It would be a long wet wait if they did. The detonators were packed expertly, in fact, the whole lot was packed expertly, the cable lengths trimmed and ready for go, and it heightened their awareness significantly. These two knew what they were about. Seeing it just confirmed the danger they were in. They meant business, serious business. And they had the capability to deliver.

"One of us needs to go up there and check that the passage is open," said Jake, looking at BB.

He took the hint; Jake wasn't ready for the climb.

"Find a place to hide further up, if you can," called Jake to BB's disappearing rear. "And be careful!"

BB climbed quickly, his breathing even and steady. There was a small nook to his left half-way up but it was no good; too shallow. The one to the right that he remembered had been colonised by roots too thick to remove and besides, there was nowhere to hide any excavated material. It was straight up, right to the top, no place to hide or languish for any purpose. The room at the top was smaller than he had remembered but he was fourteen the last time he was here! It was still in good shape but there seemed to be something missing. It took him a while to figure out what! It was the noise! There was no sound from the generator. Maybe they weren't using this one anymore. Pushing his ear against each wall in turn he could hear no sound nor sense any vibration. The air was still good, he sniffed; there was still some circulation in here but where was it coming from? Taking a chance, he detached his power light from his belt, and the beam cut the darkness illuminating the room fully for the first time, and the air was the last thing he needed to consider! Small piles of rubble lay strewn about but their positioning was too random, too contrived. They had prepared the walls, he saw, counting more than twenty gouged out indents. This place was going up from here, for sure, he had no doubt. They could finish this part quickly. Switching off the power light, he slithered unceremoniously down the tunnel, all thoughts of stealth mode disappearing behind a screen of fear.

Jake heard him coming but ignored him. He was deep in thought, lingering on Jed's early years, trying to work out where he'd gone wrong as a dad. But the answer was obvious. He just wasn't around; wasn't there for him. He'd put the mission first, and it had saved millions, but it had not saved his own from himself. In trying to be so very different from his dad, Jed had ended up in exactly the same place, pushing the same agenda, and here they were, on different sides, scoping each other out with their finger on the trigger. He shook himself! He was being melodramatic, he knew. But he also knew there was always a strong dose of reality in melodrama – one best listened to.

"Jake?" whispered BB urgently. "Jake?"

"Here," said Jake, switching his light back on.

Making his way carefully across, BB shared his intel; one way up, no place to hide, either on the way up or at the

356

top. Jake digested this in silence. He had thought as much. It confirmed what they had to do. They had to stop Ken and Jed right here. As if in collusion with their thoughts, the light appeared underneath them again, and they hid, suddenly concerned they may have left footprints in the wrong place. But they needn't have worried. Ken dropped off his load and without delay set off back the way he had come again. Instinctively, both men set their watches, deep in their own thoughts as they watched the fading light.

"Let's see what he's brought this time," said BB, and he was off at a lope, swiftly covering the distance to the drop. Jake watched him go. Better to conserve energy, he thought.

"Explosives!" whispered BB, sliding in beside Jake again. "All prepped and ready for connect! Should only take a short time to finish the job once they get the stuff up there."

"Well," said Jake thoughtfully, "we must make sure that never happens. How long 'til the reinforcements get here, do you think?"

*****

Anjie made short work of the journey back to Traveller's Mountain. They were gathered and waiting; just the final prep and they'd be off. He watched them go with a growing sense of uneasiness. He couldn't shake the feeling that he had missed something vital; that they all had. He used these feelings to keep himself super alert even if they came to nothing in the end. But all the same, it wouldn't take too long to go over the plan again. He wanted to make sure they had every hole plugged.

CHAPTER 54

Paul drove slowly through Matheson, around by Rosa's, doing a quick stop for some take-out.

"Stay in the truck," he ordered as he and Bucks went inside to collect, hefting rucksacks on their shoulders.

"We ordered some for you too," said Meryck conversationally to a subdued Matt.

"What?" he asked, absent-mindedly tuning into the company for the first time. "Where are we?" and he started to roll down the window for a better look.

"Stop!" shouted Meryck, and he pulled him away from the window in alarm. "Do you want to get us all killed?" gesturing to where Joey was taking his usual fag break.

Matt shrugged free and stared about him wildly.

"Rosa's!" he shouted, waving at Rick and Meryck. "That's it! Rosa's!"

"Calm him down!" whispered Rick from the front. "He'll blow the beans for sure!"

"No! No! No!," whispered Matt back fiercely! "You don't understand! Rosa's the link! Or rather Maggie is!"

"Who the hell is Maggie?" asked Meryck as Rick turned to look Matt in the eye.

"What do you mean Maggie is the link?" he asked so quietly both of them had to strain to hear.

"Maggie's not dead at all," explained Matt, trying hard

to remember what she looked like. "The letter. My mum's letter. She talks about Maggie. Here, see for yourself," and he handed him the crumpled pages.

Rick scanned the writing quickly and they watched his eyebrows shoot through his hairline. He whistled!

"Now that's something we sure don't know," he said. "That explains some things but not everything. Good to know though," he said as he handed the pages back. "Thanks, Matt."

"Can I?" asked Meryck, holding out his hand and Matt let him have it. He took longer over his reading, noticing all the nuances and implications before returning it to its restless owner.

"It's taking too long," whispered Rick, rolling down his window a fraction and risking a look out. Meryck heard the concern in his voice and his head swivelled to take in the car park noticing the nose of a car peeking out from behind the building that wasn't there when they entered.

"You might be right," he said evenly. "We've got company at nine o'clock."

"Trouble?" asked Rick.

"Might be," said Meryck. "Let's give it five more."

"Make that two max and we have a deal," grunted Rick, delving in the glove compartment.

"Let me go and see," offered Matt. "Nobody will remember me here. Been too long."

"Too risky," they both said as one.

"Look, Joey's gone back in now," said Matt. "I can at least have a look in the window!"

"Ok," said Rick. "Just a look then," and as Matt left to walk nonchalantly to the Diner, Rick shuffled into the driver's seat throwing a semi to Meryck.

The scene inside was quiet. The two guys waited for their order, deep in discussion with Darla while Joey helped in the back. Matt was about to give the thumbs up when he spotted the toe of a very shiny shoe protrude from the back stall, directly in line with Paul and Bucks. They weren't going anywhere because they were being prevented from doing so, he realised. Rick noticed Matt turning, then stopping and looking back again and he slid the van noiselessly alongside him.

"Get in!" he hissed. "Now!"

They drove sedately around the building, noticing how empty it was, before slipping onto the road up Traveller's Mountain. In the rear mirror, a car slipped from behind the building and followed at a sedate pace.

"We've got company," Rick said into his phone, and Meryck and Matt slunk low in the back seat.

"Time to get rid of that letter, son," said Meryck, handing him the matches.

"What?" asked a stunned Matt. "Burn it?"

Meryck nodded, taking a small tin box from his pocket.

"Paul has it on file, Matt," he said. "You can access it any time you like. But for now, wouldn't be good to find it on you!"

It look some time for the truth of it to reach Matt and by then Rick was gradually building speed to put distance between them and their tail but it was no use.

"Quickly now," said Meryck and he held out his hand and together they tore the letter into tiny pieces and burned it in the tin.

"We're done," said Meryck to Rick, pocketing the tin while Matt sat back listlessly. For a very short while he had it all; now he had nothing but memories again. He could feel his anger building and did nothing to diffuse it as they rounded the bend to come face to face a road block. Rick pushed hand on the brakes and they slid to a halt only feet away from the police cars.

"Quick," said Rick, "the gun!" and Meryck slid it under the seat to him.

"I'll get this," he said calmly, as he stepped confidently out of the car.

"Detective Inspector Meryck," said a high pitched voice, and he turned to see his female replacement stepping delicately over to him. "You are a hard act to follow," and she grinned at her own double-entendre.

"Ms Gross," he said, extending his hand. "The pleasure is all mine. Now, what can I do for you?"

She high stepped it past him and looked in the car.

"Let me introduce you to my son-in-law," said Meryck, "and a friend of the family," but she had already moved away, disappointed, he felt.

"Let them through," she called, and an opening formed immediately before them.

"Drive safely now," she chimed, waving them off and turning away to speak into her cell phone.

*****

Joey watched the police tail the two guys into the Diner with apprehension. He thought they had sorted that out; that he wouldn't be bothered no more. Taking his usual fag break, he thumbed his phone.

"Got the police here again," he mumbled. "The new woman who replaced Meryck and her crew. Interested in two young geezers collecting a take-out. Just tailed their drive up Traveller's Mountain. Got a road block three clicks up, I heard them say."

Finishing his smoke, he went back inside to help with the order, to Darla's relief. It was hard work chatting up the two, and it didn't help with the pair watching like hawks from the back stall. But Joey seemed to be on a go-slow and the time dragged. She saw their ride pull out of the car park; they saw it too but did nothing. Then the undercover car slid by in pursuit and they casually ordered two coffees and decided to eat in after all, sitting themselves down in the table directly in front of the others in the practically empty Diner. She slid two mugs of hot coffee in front of them and looked over to see if the others wanted anything but they waved her away with their eyes. Joey dragged his skinny form out of the kitchen with two heaped plates of their best Specials and they got stuck in straight away, chatting happily about their fishing plans for the next day.

"Can you get us the others to go?" called the tall one to Joey. "It's a long hike to the top!"

"Can you drop in a few cold ones too, please," asked the other, kindly.

"Coke be ok?" asked Darla.

"Make it half-n-half," he shot back, "two water and two coke. Don't worry about a bag: got plenty of room in here," and he kicked his rucksack before returning to his food.

To the side, a phone went off and a short conversation ensued, and the two got up lazily from their seats and left without a single glance at anyone. Paul and Bucks continued eating as if nothing had happened; their jokes getting louder and cruder by the minute.

"Keep it down, lads," said a scandalised Darla, glancing around at the empty room.

"Sorry, Ma'am," said Paul in his best drawl.

"Come on, mate," he said to Bucks. "Let's take this outside and give the lady her space!"

"Thanks, man," called Bucks to Joey as they left. "See you on the way down!"

They watched them move freely up the trail, laughing and joking as they went, their rucksacks weighed down by the extra supplies.

"That went well," grinned Paul.

"Sure thing," drawled Bucks, checking his phone.

"Interesting," he mused, handing the phone to Paul. "Know a Ms Gross, by any chance?"

CHAPTER 55

Johnson strode into the lab purposefully but there was no one there. The screen flickered in the corner and he got a first-hand education as he gawked at the finer details of the tag or bug or whatever that thing was! Senses on alert all day, he felt rather than heard the door open behind him and he spun around to confront an astonished Jane and Carney.

"What are you doing here?" asked Carney, suspiciously.

"How is Myra?" he replied, looking from one to the other, taking in the slope of their shoulders and the worry lines across their forehead.

"Alive," was all Jane said as she pushed passed him to sit down heavily at a table in the corner.

"Alive?" he asked Carney.

"She has no memory of who she is presently," was all he contributed, joining Jane at the table.

Johnson stood looking at them both, his mind whirring.

"Are you saying that this thing was somehow caught up in her memories?" he asked, thoughtfully.

Carney shook his head.

"We don't know," he answered truthfully, "but it would be more like her memories were caught up in it, if you get my meaning."

"We just don't know what has happened," added Jane, "except, right now, she's a woman without a past."

"Or a future," injected Carney, rubbing his tired face. "We can't do this to the other two women!" he exploded, suddenly.

"Better like this with a chance at recovery than dead," shot back Jane.

These two were sparking at each other again, Johnson saw, and he couldn't decide if this was a good thing or bad. Sometimes anger is good, and there had been way too little of it today despite all the revelations. Revulsion – yes, but anger – no! His thoughts wandered to Matt. Now he had a right to be angry but at who, he couldn't say for sure. Jenny had a right to be angry too, he reckoned, but she had a right to life as well. He turned away from them both and went to look through the door they had come from. A humped figure sobbed on the hospital bed, the blankets moving with her gulps for air. Pushing the door, he entered slowly, walking loudly so she would hear him, and not be startled. He needed to see first-hand what she was going through.

"Hello," he said quietly, "may I sit down?"

There was no response.

"I'm sorry," he said. "You seem very upset. Can I help? I'm Detective Johnson."

There was no response for some minutes but he waited. He was good at that. Give people enough space and they would respond, he knew. Everyone had their own timeline. He reached for the tissues as a streaked face appeared from beneath the bedclothes.

"Here," he proffered the tissues. "Looks like you could do with these. If I were in your shoes, I'd definitely need them!" and he smiled at her.

She looked wretched, her face blotchy and swollen from crying but her eyes shone their thanks and he knew he had made contact with whoever was home now.

365

"Thank you," she hiccupped, struggling into a sitting position and drawing the clothes up to her chin. She rubbed her left elbow absentmindedly.

"Does that hurt?" he asked, carefully.

"What?" she replied, looking at him fully for the first time. "Oh, this?" she added, following his gaze. "No, not at all, just a little itchy," she said. "Must have grazed it or something."

"I'm glad," he smiled at her. "I hate hospitals or bandages or whatever may be under them. I'm a chicken really when it comes to that sort of thing!"

She smiled at him. Somewhere inside, she knew what he was talking about. She knew about people's feelings when it came to hospitals.

He held out his hand.

"I'm Jim," he offered, smiling.

"Myra," she replied happily, taking his hand in her right firmly.

"Pleased to meet you, Myra," he continued, trying to keep the triumph out of his voice. "Now, can you tell me what is the last thing you can remember?"

"I'm Myra," she said slowly, ignoring him altogether and sitting bolt upright in the bed. "They said my name was Myra and I didn't believe them! Who am I really, Detective? Jim?" she asked, fixing him with her big blue eyes.

"You're Myra Crawthorne, last time I met you anyway," he smiled at her.

"So you know me?" she asked, testily now.

He nodded, watching the colour creep up her neck. She

was going to blow! But she surprised him. She surprised them both. She doubled up laughing instead and the sound reverberated around the empty room. Outside, Jane and Carney heard her laugh and pushed through the doors excitedly.

"It's ok! It's ok," she gulped. "I remember! I remember!" and tears of laughter and relief poured down her face.

"I'm free," she hiccupped! "I'm finally free! And I'm alive! I'm alive!"

"Can you tell us what you remember?" pressed Johnson now. "Anything at all? Anything that can help us with Jenny and Kate?"

"Jenny and Kate?" she parroted back, her eyes glazing over.

"Stay with us!" shouted Carney, rushing to her side and grabbing her shoulders, shaking her none-too-gently. "Myra! Myra!"

She shook herself awake and glared at him.

"Well, that's what you get for pumping me full of that stuff," she threw at the IV. "Get it off me now and I might be of some use to you!"

"Strong coffee coming up, Myra," said Jane, as she headed for the door. "We all could do with some!"

Carney gently withdrew the needle from the back of her hand replacing it with a small plaster. She flexed her fingers appreciatively then lifted both arms above her head. Satisfied that all was good, she threw back the clothes and sat gingerly on the side of the bed, swaying a little.

"You've lost a lot of blood, Myra," Carney told her gently, holding one shoulder now in case she toppled forward. "You may feel a little dizzy."

"How much did you give me?" she asked, fuzzily.

"Enough," he replied cautiously.

"How much do you remember?" he asked quietly.

"Everything," she nodded, heavily. "Every single thing!" she reiterated. "And, Jim," she added, turning fully to him at the bottom of the bed, "they're all tagged, not just Jenny and Kate. Everyone who works at Greenway is tagged; every last one of them!"

"And, Jim," she continued, "nobody ever survived; at least, not until now!"

*****

Anjie prowled the Control Room, looking at the screens, concerned. Tullie and Guidrius had long vacated, heading to the kitchen for some food and time-out to offset the effects of their intense experience together. He had watched them go and was pleased that at least they had one happy ending today. He should have heard from Rick and Meryck by now at least! And there was this thing with Jed and Ken, or rather Jed and Jake, that just wouldn't go away! He spun around at the interruption, tense for action to come face to face with Jo. She was exactly what they needed right now; no, he corrected, she was exactly what he needed right now!

"Jo," he said in welcome, stepping quickly towards the open door to embrace her.

"Anjie," she sighed back. "I thought I would be out in the cold for much longer. I'm really glad I'm not! It's not much fun anymore! Not on my own anyway," she teased.

"I know," he cradled her in his arms, "but am I glad to see you again!"

"Must be something very important to bring me here like this," she glanced down at her pyjamas, smiling, "not even time to get dressed!"

"Oh, I'm sorry," he said, aghast, holding her away from him at last, blushing.

"Got you!" she grinned, stepping away from him. "You really need to lighten up, you know," she laughed and he grinned back. He missed her. He always missed her. He was devastated when she married Meryck; he had gone deep under cover and wasn't planning to return. But Becca was born and he couldn't resist returning to see her daughter.

"I really could do with a shower and some fresh clothes," she hinted. "Not to mention a bite to eat!"

"Of course," he shot in, shaking his head, distracted. "This way, Jo," and he led her to Meryck's room.

"He's here too?" she asked, her eyebrows shooting up.

Anjie nodded.

"There's been some new intel, Jo," he began, and she read his hesitancy perfectly.

"Becca?" she whispered.

He nodded.

"And . . ." she prompted.

"She's alive, we think," he whispered back, and she fainted in his arms.

"What on earth is going on here?" demanded a stunned Meryck, watching Anjie cradling his wife.

"I've just told her Becca's alive," he whispered, his voice breaking in emotion as he laid her down on the bed and moved towards the door.

Meryck nodded. He knew Anjie had a thing for Jo, and he

respected his space. Jo was always safe with him; Anjie was a gentleman. He respected personal boundaries above all else.

"She just get here?" asked Meryck, and Anjie nodded.

"We've got a lot to share," added Meryck, moving towards Jo as she began to come around. "Meet you in the kitchen in twenty," he said. "Make sure everyone is there."

*****

"He's not coming, mum," said Jenny in a strangled voice, and Kate moved closer to comfort her. "And I'm not getting any dial tone from his phone either!"

"It's ok, love," said Kate comfortingly. "Men do strange things when they are in love."

"But it's just that, mum," replied Jenny, shaking. "I don't think he really loves me at all," and she began to cry.

"There, there," said Kate, rubbing her back gently. "Let it all out! No harm ever came from a good cry!"

The sobbing sounds filled the room and Kate wished Ben could be here; he'd know what to do! Jed was almost old enough to be Jenny's dad but they'd been good friends for so long. She'd never seen it coming!

"Have you talked to Tullie about all this?" she asked, gently. "She knows Jed better than anyone, working with him and all."

Jenny shook her head.

"It's all happened so suddenly," she gulped. "I never knew I loved him until now! And he seemed to love me too! Now why would he say he's coming then send me this awful text?" she wailed, and began to cry earnestly again.

"Shh, love," said her mum. "He's not worth all this! Let him go! Forget about him!"

"But I can't," sobbed a distraught Jenny, "I can't!" and she flung herself out of her mum's arms and flounced upstairs. Kate heard the bedroom door crash shut and sighed deeply. There was nothing she could do! She was stuck here without Ben. Bloody men, she fumed, kicking savagely at the dog's bed!

CHAPTER 56

"Well, shall we have tea and croissants and talk like civilised men now?" asked Oswald, genially to a drowning Mahler.

He heard him distantly above the roar in his ears but he was not about to give in to this pig. They lifted his head out of the water momentarily and pointed him in Oswald's direction. He wanted to spit at him badly, to spoil those obscenely shiny shoes he liked so much, but it came up as bile that dribbled ineffectively down his chin as he doubled up with the effort.

"Pity," said Oswald, reading the situation perfectly, and nodded towards the water again. It closed over his head and he struggled to breathe once more, darkness creeping ever closer at the edge of his vision. He closed his eyes and let himself go.

"Resuscitate him!" growled an alarmed Oswald, kicking out at the nearest lackey. "Keep the bastard alive!"

Returning was excruciating! Mahler writhed on the deck gasping for air, unable to prevent himself displaying this much weakness. He heard the clink of metal and he was alone, handcuffed to the nearby railings but he was too weak to capitalise on the situation. Then he heard them returning and he was hauled into a sitting position and propped against the side of the boat. Keeping his eyes shut, and letting his body go limp, he feigned unconsciousness, playing for time.

"Wake him up," he heard one of them say and they slapped him across the face, his head bouncing from side to side with the impact.

"He's out cold," his assailant said, but slapped him again for good measure. His face stung and his head reeled from the assault but he kept to his subterfuge and was rewarded with a sigh from the leader.

"Get some water," he instructed, and Mahler was hosed down right where he lay but he still didn't respond.

"Is he alive?" shouted an irritated Oswald from above them.

"Yes, Sir!" shouted his assailant, "but he's unconscious, Sir!"

Oswald spat and a flurry of abuse flowed from his tiny mouth.

"Get your sorry asses up here!" he roared. "I'll deal with him later!"

With relief, Mahler heard them go. He had been given a reprieve. But he knew his time was up if he couldn't make good use of this welcome opportunity. He began counting slowly as his ears listened for every sound and movement; by the time he reached a hundred he was ready to move.

*****

Jake and BB watched Ken come and go a second time and they knew they had six minutes max. Scurrying down the steep slope they finished their task with time to spare but they were still sweating profusely by the time they reached their retreat again. They sat breathing deeply, their backs against the rugged wall, staring into the darkness.

"Four minutes, fifty," whispered BB, and Jake could hear the smile in his voice.

"Not bad for an old pair," he offered in return, and they shook hands vigorously. "Now all we have to work out is how to stop them going up the tunnel at all."

373

BB shifted slightly beside him but Jake paid him no heed. It was uncomfortable and cramped but it would serve its purpose well and keep them awake and alert in the deadness.

"How long 'til the crew get here, you reckon?" asked BB, again. He was awfully concerned with this, Jake thought. But then BB never was at his best in these enclosed situations. He was a rangy sort, best suited to the great outdoors. Nothing bothered him there; he was equally at home and resourceful in extreme weather as well as extreme situations. It was just the small spaces that caused him difficulty. But he would rise above it, Jake knew from experience. He couldn't wish for a better wing man than BB.

"Another twenty or so," responded Jake, calmly. "What had changed up there?" he asked to keep him occupied.

BB didn't reply for a while and Jake thought he may not have heard him. Then he began to talk of his youth in the area, about meeting Maggie for the first time, their absentee romance and eventual marriage. He stopped when he came to the point about her illness and Jake patted his arm. It was never easy to lose someone, he knew. BB had been there for him when his wife died many years ago; he'd be here for BB whenever he needed him. He was only sorry he was away when Maggie died; all of them were away, Anjie too. BB was entirely on his own.

"I'm sorry, man," Jake said quietly. "We should have been there for you. No one should go through that alone."

BB said nothing but his chest heaved and Jake knew he was trying to hold back the tears. They were saved from further introspection by the light in the water again and they drew further back into the blackness waiting for Ken to come and go as before. They sat still, monitoring the movement below by sound alone, waiting for the splash that sounded when Ken submerged again. But it never came. Instead the whole space before them burst into searing brightness and two voices could be heard on the small shore; two angry voices they heard at the same time as they heard the click of the safety being removed.

"Come out," shouted Jed, spraying the cavern liberally with bullets, while Ken looked, mesmerised, at the footprints in the sand.

BB reached for his gun, he had a direct shot, but Jake reached for his hand, preventing him.

"However this works out," he whispered sadly, "I can't let you do that! He's my son after all. Keep your head down!" and he was rising slowly, his hands in the air, calling to Jed. Jed watched his father rise from the slope above him and hate burned deep in his heart.

"You!" he spat, pointing the gun coldly at his head, slanting his eye for the kill shot.

"No!" shouted Ken. "There's something not right here, Jed. Things aren't as I left them! Don't kill him! I need to talk to him!"

Reluctantly Jed lowered the gun and watched dispassionately as Jake slithered down the slope with his hands in the air. Failing to keep his balance he toppled over and rolled down the final decline to land unceremoniously at Ken's feet.

"Get up," growled Ken, kicking him in the ribs. Jake doubled over and above him BB fingered the trigger anxiously.

"Where are the rest?" asked Jed coldly, prodding the muzzle of his gun into his chest.

"It's just me," gasped Jake, and Jed hit him in the mouth for good measure.

"Just one set of footprints," nodded Ken. Jed had not

taken his eyes off Jake, not for one second. He was not convinced.

"The rest?" he asked again, his voice dropping a decibel into the danger zone, Ken noted.

"We need him, Jed," said Ken.

"It's just me," said Jake again, "for now! You'll not get away with blowing up Greenway, Jed!"

But Jed just laughed in his face.

"And who will stop me?" he joked. "You or the three goons at the Cottage? Missed the surveillance, did you? How careless of you! Oops!" and he pulled the trigger and Jake fell back, his right leg torn open by the high velocity round, bright red blood spurting freely onto the ground. Pushing Jed to one side, Ken grabbed Jake and quickly put pressure on the wound to stop the bleeding.

"Are you crazy?" he roared at Jed. "What part of 'I need him' did you not understand? What the hell are you talking about! Get me my rucksack, pronto!"

Jed casually strolled to the submersible and detached a bag and tossed it to Ken.

"Open it, you fool!" he roared. "Hand me the first aid pack!"

"How many?" asked Jed again, standing over Jake now as Ken worked frantically to staunch the flow. He pointed his gun at Jake's other leg.

"Ok! Ok!" said Jake. "I'm not sure. Maybe five; maybe ten."

"How long 'til they get here?" he inquired calmly.

"Anytime now," replied Jake, equally as calmly. Ken was

nearly finished. The only reason he was alive was because of the sabotage.

"Which way?" he asked icily, and Jake had no option but to point out the route. He hoped BB had time to move.

"I've got him," called Ken, and Jed was away, stooping low beside the water to grab a handful of explosives.

Further up the trail, the team Anjie had sent stopped dead in their tracks as the sound of shooting and angry voices floated up the ravine. Something was wrong!

"Back up! Back up!" indicated the lead. "We're sitting ducks here!" and they withdrew hurriedly and not before time! A bright light was sneaking through the darkness towards them, then it stopped, and they held their breath.

"Retreat!" roared the lead, stealth mode abandoned. "Retreat! Explosives!" and the tunnel ahead disintegrated into a cloud of dust and boulders, and deafening sound.

"Report!" he shouted into the thick fog that enveloped them. They were all present and accounted for; just minor bruising and some jagged cuts from flying debris.

"We're done here," he called, "no way forward. We'll have to regroup and find another way in," he called to the back.

*****

Dislocating his thumb, an old trick of Mahler's, he wriggled free of the cuffs and slipped quietly over the side into the choppy water and made his way around to where the dingy was secured. He could hear Oswald on deck bellowing at the unfortunates who had been his support group just a short while ago. Ignoring the pain, he pulled himself on board, slipped the tie and the Glory rode serenely away without him. He held his breath until he was a reasonable distance away before starting the motor. It kicked in at first turn and he grinned mirthlessly, pushing his hand between his knees as he clicked his thumb back into place. The darkness threatened to claim him again but he held on. There was nowhere on his body where the pain did not reach but he didn't fight it. What doesn't kill you, makes you stronger, he parroted time and again, as he slipped further and further away from the Glory.

"Dismissed," reared Oswald suddenly and they stole away gratefully to find their charge had absconded.

"Sir!" called one urgently, trembling in his boots. "He's gone, Sir! Mahler's gone!"

"So is the dingy," reported the other, searching the surrounding seas urgently, and spotting it disappearing behind a massive cargo heading out to sea.

"So he is," smirked Oswald, and to their immense relief he turned and went below.

"Got him?" he asked, absent-mindedly, and his assistant nodded at the screen.

"Lit up like fireworks!" he said.

"Good! Good!" grinned Oswald. "Now let the Belle know we're on track."

CHAPTER 57

Jo and Meryck walked into a crowded kitchen and Rick was the first to reach them.

"Jo," he said in greeting, his face a mixture of emotions, as she reached out to hug him soundly.

"I'm just so happy you're my son-in-law," she whispered for his ears only. "And remember, once my son-in-law, always my son-in-law," she finished forcefully.

"Everyone," said Anjie brusquely, "this is Jo." He had just received news of the happening at the cave and he was in full work mode.

"We have several situations developing simultaneously," he continued. "Let's start with the last first: Jake and BB have been rumbled. The passage has been closed by an explosion. Several shots were heard, and angry voices," and he triggered a switch and the recording played throughout the kitchen.

"That's Jed," identified Anjie.

"And that's Ken," growled Meryck. "I'd know the bastard anywhere!" and Jo snuck her hand gently into his.

"Guidrius?" asked Anjie, playing a hunch.

"Jake's been injured," he replied slowly, looking at Anjie thoughtfully. "He's been shot – right leg, but he's ok. He and BB have sabotaged the detonators. They don't know about BB yet."

A relieved murmur passed through the group.

"We have to find another way in," Anjie continued, "and quickly! BB knew of another way in, underwater," he added, bringing up Bears Lake on the screen, "but he said it was only suitable for good swimmers to access." He looked around the room anxiously but nobody fitted the bill.

"I think I know a way," interrupted Guidrius, confidently, pushing forward to have a look. "Let me have a closer look at that waterway. I didn't see a way in the last time I was there," and he zoned out at the edge of the group, looking for BB's entrance.

Anjie nodded gratefully before turning back to the rest of them.

"Becca's intel is recent," he intoned slowly, letting the words sink in before he added the icing to the cake, "from last week!"

A buzz of anticipation passed through the crowd, and Meryck hugged Jo and Rick anxiously.

"We have recovered a series of ten communications going back over three years," he continued, flicking on another screen he and Paul had prepared earlier. Paul took it up from there.

"The first, was recorded three years ago this November and then at every five or six months intervals since then. So, last first:

☐   34 M-X PROJECTS

☐   TAG PROGRAM SETUP

☐   M-X CLONE TRIALS BEGIN

☐   CONTROL TAGS WEAPONISED. TRANSGENIC PROGRAM FAILED

☐   WEAPONISED TAGS DEPLOYED. WORLD

LEADERS TARGETED. 12 HOSTS ON FLOOR 2

☐ THE CLUB TAKES OVER RK CJ AB AD GM BZ. OB DENIED MEMBERSHIP

☐ OB HELD IN ALBANIA. GLORY RISING TAGS FISH

☐ SUCCESSFULY TAG ANTIDOTE DEVELOPED. OB GRANTED MEMBERSHIP.

☐ TROUBLE. GM SELLING COUNTERFEIT ANTIDOTES. RK HAS UNIVERSE KEY.

☐ TRANSGENICS SUCCESSFUL. TO BE MOVED TO GLORY NEXT VISIT. OPS BEING MOVED ELSEWHERE. VIABILITY OF GREENWAY IN JEOPARDY.

The silence was total in the room, everyone processing the bit that they could understand best. Then the energy moved and Anjie could see that a flood of questions was imminent. Stalling them, he held up his hand.

"Matt has some additional stuff to share with us," he informed them, and Matt stepped forward to face the group.

"We found a few things at Brierly in addition to these," he began, placing Meme's instruments in full view, and he became the very centre of attention in the room; even Guidrius turned to observe him closely. He was changing fast, he saw.

"There are two direct ways into Greenway through the cellar at Brierly," he informed an astonished audience. "One is known to Oswald – the one Meme uses; the other is not. This other one links between two labs, my grandfather's concealed lab at Brierly, and his personal working lab in Greenway."

"This is invaluable intel," Anjie cut in. "We have amended

our plans to include an arrowhead assault through these passages. This is the intel the authorities were looking for when they thrashed Brierly after Ostenwalder died. Lucky for us they didn't find the second tunnel!"

"Well, here's the thing," interrupted Matt, "he hasn't died. It was all a fabrication. He's still alive." Conversation buzzed around the room. The Greenway conspiracy was like an onion, Jo thought, shedding its layers one by one, in the most unlikely way, each discarded layer revealing a different core, a different face. Which was the most dangerous one, the one they should concentrate all attention on?

"And we believe," interjected Anjie, "he is Becca's link to the outside world."

"To Meme, to be exact," added Matt, explaining further.

"We've found a way to remove the tags," he continued, pointing to the instruments on the table. "We can now go ahead and remove them from Jenny and Kate, but we'll have to inject them into new hosts to buy us time."

"What do you have in mind?" croaked Myra.

"They have two pets," answered Matt, "a cat and a dog. The plan is to use them as the new hosts and lock them away securely until all this is over."

Guidrius locked eyes with him and Matt knew this was breaking new ground.

"Just make sure these animals don't escape, Matt," he offered for all to hear. He didn't need to elaborate; imaginations were already working overtime.

"There's only one other thing," continued Matt. "I believe there is a breakout planned for midnight, through the concealed tunnel, to Brierly. I plan to be there," he added strongly.

"You'll need to be," said Myra. "Everyone on Greenway is tagged. You'll have to work fast."

"I'm with you," offered Carney.

"Me too," said Tullie suddenly to everyone's surprise, especially Matt's, and a faint flush rose up his face.

Guidrius nodded. It was risky, but right.

"Matt's missed one small detail," interjected Rick from the back. "BB's wife may be on that island, alive and well."

"Myra?" demanded Anjie, turning to her fully for the first time, all sympathy evaporating again instantly. Damn the woman! She was infuriating!

She gulped. She had left out this one because she genuinely didn't know what had happened to her, just that she had volunteered one day in the Diner before Myra could stop her when she overheard them talking. Once she had spoken, she would be disappeared anyway, she knew, but she was past caring. Each day was a trial beyond belief but she hid it as well as she could from BB. She was determined to enjoy every second she had left even if it took all her strength and willpower. The last Myra had seen of her was a shadow of a face waving a shadow of a hand through the back window of the caddy. She had played her part; identifying a body that wasn't Myra's under duress but BB knew; somehow he knew! Then Rosa's started delivering food to Greenway and Brierly; he was caught in its web as surely as she had been. He would never let Greenway go up with Maggie in it!

Her voice trailed away and suddenly eyes were avoiding her now, and she felt more like an outcast than she had in all the years she was tagged. But Anjie hadn't looked away, she saw. He was regarding her with distaste.

"Is there anything else you would like to share with us at this juncture?" he asked sarcastically. "Or would you prefer

383

to wait until we are all dead or dying," he finished forcefully.

"Good Lord, woman!" he roared, "Don't you have any idea how vital this information is!"

"I've found the way in," interrupted Guidrius calmly, sparing Myra the need to comment further. "I'll bring them both out safely," he said, as he turned towards the door.

"Keep your men back up top," he added. "I'll find the way through for them," then he was gone. Tullie felt him go and Anjie reached out to her and put a protective arm around her. Then the questions started for real and the discussion flowed backwards and forwards for several tense minutes until all felt they had a handle on what was about to go down.

*****

The sub picked up Mahler's position perfectly, surfacing briefly to retrieve their boss. He clawed his way into its belly, finding solace in the presence of old friends.

"I see you've been swimming against the tide again," mumbled Friday as he drove the syringe into Mahler's butt with impunity.

A grunt was all the reply he got.

"That should take effect in a few seconds," he grinned, punching his friend playfully on the shoulder as his head dipped deep into the soft pillow. "So, the party was a bit rough?" he queried, settling down on the next bed, arms behind his head, waiting for the denouement.

"You could say that," grunted Mahler. "Lots and lots of courses!" and he went over the events sketchily. Friday whistled!

"Well, you certainly raked over that hornet's nest good and proper," he concluded. "They tag you?" he continued.

384

Mahler nodded. There was a moment he wasn't sure they'd let him get away but when by the time he had got to fifty, then sixty, all the way up to a hundred, he knew the game was on. OB had swallowed the bait. He just had to reel him in now by letting him believe the reeling was the other way around.

"Well, you'll be pleased to know we've got a new bit of intel while you were away on holiday," said Friday, softly, and now it was Mahler's turn to whistle! Oswald didn't know!

"We still have enough antidote on board?" he asked, softly.

"What do you think?" replied Friday, his wide smile creasing his eyes into mean slits.

CHAPTER 58

"You want to live, you tell me what you've done with these," hissed Ken, as Jed disappeared out of view up the tunnel.

"As if!"growled Jake, glaring intently into the dead eyes above him.

"Well, let's say you'll at least have the pleasure of watching the fireworks firsthand," smirked Ken, a real generous gesture on his part. "Now, do you want to deal with me or your son?" he added silkily, and Jake decided he had better options with psycho Ken; at least, until he had repaired the detonators for them. Ken was predictable; Jed was not. He could work a second chance with Ken, he was sure, but Jed had shown his hand. It was just a matter of time, with him, he reasoned sadly. His eyes searched the shadows above him for BB but he found no sign of him. Now would be a perfect time for that ambush, he pleaded silently, but no help came. Instead the noise and debris from the explosion blasted around the cave throwing Ken off his feet but it was of no use to Jake; he couldn't move if he wanted to, his useless leg pinned him to the ground as if he had been tethered there with chains. He writhed in agony as small rocks peppered where he lay and he could feel himself fade from consciousness.

"No, you don't!" growled a frustrated Ken and he jabbed an epi-pen viscously into Jake's good thigh. "You're not going to bloody-well die on my watch!"

The rush was incredible and Jake shot alert in an instant his heart palpitating loudly in his chest. It intensified the pain a thousand-fold; it was excruciating but he ground his teeth together with a superhuman effort. He glared into Ken's gritty face a millimetre from his own and spat. The blow was swift in coming and he welcomed the pain balance despite his broken nose. More blood pumped out of him, the new patch on his shirt front complimenting the pool by his leg. He sucked in air through his teeth and turned his gaze back on Ken. He saw rather than heard the words coming from his mouth through the ringing in his ears but was unable to respond in time. The second blow caught him on the side of the head and his neck snapped sideways throwing him to the ground. Ken grabbed him roughly and hauled him to an upright position, shouting the same question at him time and again as he continued to beat him about the head with his fist.

"What did you do to the detonators?" he repeated, coldly, each time.

Jake knew he was not going to live through this. Ken was in the groove and he would milk the situation to his advantage while inflicting the optimum amount of pain possible then he would look into his eyes as he administered the final blow. He felt him move to his ribs and despite the din in his ears he could hear the snap as the first one went. He waited for the pain but he was beyond that now which worried him somewhere in the back of his mind. He began to slip again. Where was he anywhere? And why was Jed here?

From his vantage point BB watched the beating, his mouth dry and his hands clammy. Ken wouldn't kill Jake just yet, would he? He'd stop in time to get the info he wanted then deliver the kill blow. But Jake looked done-in and Ken was in no mood to stop. It was just a matter of time; a short time, he reasoned, the usual sickness rising in his chest. The dust clearing, he pressed himself against the rocks, Ken clear in his sights, his finger pressing gently on the trigger. One sharp thunk and Ken crumbled across Jake's bloody form on the ground, a neat hole in his left temple. But there was no time to rejoice as BB felt the cold steel of Jed's gun press against his temple. 'Drop it!' was the only command given but it was enough. Letting the gun fall, BB raised his hands slowly and visibly in the air and stepped cautiously from hiding, Jed bringing up the rear. He hadn't heard him coming! He'd been found wanting. He'd even failed his oldest friend! Hands now on his head, with sinking heart, he moved towards the bodies on the ground. Moving around in front of BB now, Jed checked his fallen comrade and a red anger filled his vision. They had come so far! This far! And then to be taken out by BB! He had underestimated the man but never again! He raised his gun slowly letting it come to rest on the centre of BB's forehead. The two men looked at each other coldly. BB's eyes flicked sideways and Jed's followed instinctively but it was too late. Jake kicked him behind the knees with all his might as BB parried, snatching at the gun and the two men crashed to the floor on top of Jake and Ken, scratching and clawing to stay alive, rolling off the two towards the cave wall. The shot, when it finally came, was muffled and the two lay still. Tears streaking his bloody face Jake stretched to see what had happened. Ignoring the searing pain from his broken and crushed body he shoved Ken off him and pulled himself along the ground to where the two lay, the gun hidden underneath them both.

"BB?" he called anxiously. "You ok man?" and to his relief his friend lifted his head wearily and he could see the intense pain in his eyes.

"I've killed your son, Jake!" he sobbed, struggling free slowly, trailing a bloody hand and an even bloodier gun. "I've killed Jed!" Tiredly, he waved the gun about as he spoke and Jake had to dive as it went off randomly.

"BB!" shouted Jake. "Put the gun down! If you didn't kill him he would have killed us both! Bring it over here! Give it to me!" and he held out his hand for Jed's gun. BB did as he was told, auto-pilot kicking in, and sank to the floor gratefully beside Jake, scanning him wordlessly.

"You'll live," he grunted eventually. "Maybe even more handsome for it all."

Jake's grin came out as a lopsided grimace.

"Close call," he said, spitting blood, and laying back wearily on the ground.

To the side, Jed moved and BB was on him in a flash.

"Jake!" he shouted, triumphantly. "He's alive! I missed! Hit his bloody shoulder, is all!" and he crouched beside him on the floor. Jed's head was rolled back and his face was ashen. His breathing came in bursts and with each breath a fresh spout of blood erupted through the hole in his shoulder. Tearing some fabric from his shirt, BB reached over to staunch the flow. Grabbing the moment, Jed lunged and thrust his knife deep into BB's heart but his instinct was off and the knife hit a rib, jarring it out of his hand. BB pulled back sharply, holding the knife in his side, blood spurting along its handle. Jake watched helplessly. He couldn't reach his friend to help him but he did have the gun. As Jed regrouped, Jake strained upright and levelled the gun on him.

"Be my guest," he growled through clenched teeth and Jed stopped instantly. He had been too engrossed to keep track of how many bullets were fired; he didn't know for sure how many remained in the chamber. One look at Jake's face was enough. The son-of-a-bitch would fire, for sure.

"BB!" he shouted, never taking his eyes off Jed for a second. "Look at the blade, man! It's only a shallow wound! You're going to be ok! Pull it out, man, and staunch the flow! Quickly!"

BB looked from his bloody hand on the knife to his oldest friend. Jake was in control but for how long? Pushing his attention back to the crouching Jed, he yanked the knife free.

*****

In Greenway, a small group of special ops were gathered around a terminal, listening to the sounds again.

"That's not far from here," one said, indicating the area on the map before them. "Three clicks as the crow flies; but about fifteen down from the top of the mountain."

"Underground?" asked a second.

"No question about it!" was the measured reply.

"What do we have on the terrain?" asked their Commander, pushing into the room.

"Not much," replied a techie, bringing up some old maps. "It's a ways off our directive although the old backup generators are housed in that area."

"Under Traveller's Mountain?" she gasped. "The explosion was under the Mountain, right here?" she asked again, pointing to the exact area where the generators were housed.

"How did you know?" he asked back.

"I know that area," she said. "There are small entrances here and there," she indicated on the screen, "likely to be some underwater as well."

"The explosion wasn't under water, Ma'am," interrupted another. "We have some indication it came from up here."

Following the trail upwards, she spent several tense seconds aligning angles while they watched uneasily. Pushing the techie aside, she punched in co-ordinates from memory and the image tilted to display hillside contours. Panning 360 she settled for a section above Bear's Lake and moved in deeper. Frustrated, not finding what she expected, she flung north to the tree line and stopped. Was it possible, she mused? Could someone have come so far? She was distracted by the techie pulling up underwater surveys on an adjacent terminal.

"What is it?" she glared at him, and he was glad he did have something worthwhile to share.

"Look!" he said, in a rush. "The channel splits here and here. It is possible that there is a line underneath the island."

"What do you mean 'underneath the island'?" she growled, pulling him off that terminal and taking charge.

She threw image after image on the big screen for them to manipulate and sort. Pushing back to the other terminal she added the images from the Mountain. There wasn't a sound in the room as they looked in shock at the links they revealed. All around the island were channels and passages that led directly or indirectly to Greenway. Not waiting for anyone she superimposed the facility layout on the screen, morphing it this way and that into the position above the explosion. Throwing up the security grid did nothing to relieve their uneasiness.

"We're compromised," she mouthed, stunned, furious at herself for not remembering the bell shaft.

"Get a detail down there immediately!" she barked, in command again. "Be prepared for hostiles! Bring every single one of them back! Dead or alive! Then bury the area. I want it gone! Obliterated! Well, what are you waiting for?" she roared as she reached for her phone.

*****

Standing on the lake side, Guidrius searched his memory, reaching out to the water inhabitants for advice. They came instantly, bursting into the shallows in excitement.

"Is there a way in for me?" he asked, without delay, and the water churned with their posturing and settled into a lead south of Greenway. Not hesitating he pawed his way into the maelstrom left in their wake and encasing himself in an air bubble, disappeared under water in their flow.

The lead was swift and sure, and he was in darkness before long following with his mind where his eyes could not discern. In the back of his mind he could feel Jake's presence get stronger the more he swam but weaker the nearer he got. His friend was in trouble. Reaching out to him he tried to communicate how to make a survival bubble but he wasn't sure if he was getting through. He didn't know if Jake even understood the process but he had to try.

"How much further?" he asked but his guides just kept going. They could only deal with one instruction at a time, he realised, cursing. He was getting desperate. His air was running out and he knew he was close to losing his first Keeper. Focusing intently, he sent out a signal to Tullie. The further he went the more he needed her help.

"Tullie?" he called. "Tullie, can you hear me?"

In the crowded kitchen Tullie dropped her coffee mug with a loud crash, and pushed her hands against her ears. To her left, Matt was doing the same while Bucks simple folded at the knees and crashed to the floor.

"We hear you," railed back Matt. "Tone it down! We're in agony here!"

"Matt?" asked Guidrius, more softly now. "So am I!" he coughed. "I need air! Ask Tullie to magnify," and he trailed off.

"Dad," whispered Tullie aloud and all eyes turned to her.

"Do it now!" instructed Guidrius. "Picture my air bubble and magnify! Use your sama!"

Tullie looked around helplessly.

"I don't know what to do," she whispered to Matt.

"Tell me," said Matt to Guidrius and some tangled images flashed across his mind, enough for him to get started. Rushing to Tullie he grabbed her right wrist and pushed it up against her left. Immediately she made the connection and while the room looked on, her left arm glowed and they could feel a whisper of a breeze pulse around the room, then a soft whoosh and it was gone. In her mind she heard Guidrius gulp the much needed air and felt his thanks. It was only then she realised that Matt was still holding her wrist; that he had, in fact, provided the conduit for the transfer of energy she couldn't yet gauge.

"Is everything ok?" asked Anjie anxiously. It had all happened so quickly nobody had time to intervene which was just as well.

"Guidrius just needed a bit of help," explained Matt, moving away from Tullie and helping a groggy Bucks to his feet.

"Don't ask," Meryck whispered to an intrigued and excited Jo, "at least not yet."

"But I felt it, Vince," she said trembling. "Whatever it was, I felt it!" and she slowly moved closer to Tullie.

"You ok?" she asked her gently, and watched, fascinated, as Tullie released her arm-shield.

"Sama" Tullie heard Guidrius correct.

"Sama" she repeated out loud, still looking at her arm in wonder.

"Sama?" queried Jo, and when Tullie turned her full gaze upon her, she felt a shiver trip up and down her spine as Tullie delved her depths unhindered.

"Tullie!" Matt called urgently, and the link was broken as she turned back to him.

CHAPTER 59

"We go now," Anjie began, while Matt pulled a confused Tullie away from the centre of the room to a quiet spot at the rear.

"Where am I?" she asked confused, shaking her head to clear the memories that were flooding through her system. "I can see everywhere and anywhere," she added, "and I don't know which is real!" The more she tried to clear her mind the higher her agitation levels became and her sama began to glow eerily, light pulsing up and down her arm in ever increasing ellipses.

"Tullie!" called Matt again, grabbing her by the shoulders and peering into her eyes. "You have to stop this! You need to let go! Do you know how to do that?" Her wild eyes looked unseeingly back at him.

She heard him loud and clear through the sensory overload and instinctively she rubbed her right wrist against the sama and the world went grey. The clamouring stopped instantly, and she stared past Matt at the people calmly leaving the room.

"It's stopped," she whispered dully to him, and he risked pulling her towards him to embrace her. She went willingly, fitting into his shoulder perfectly. By the heaving of her shoulders, he knew she was struggling to hold back the tears and he just held her, giving her the space to regain control again. Guidrius was silent now, for both of them.

"Guidrius is ok now," whispered Matt, patting her hair away from tickling his nose, and he felt her nod. She was coming around. He held her now because he wanted to not because she needed it yet she didn't pull back but he felt she knew nonetheless. It felt good; it felt right, and deep inside he hoped she was as happy with it as he was.

"We're bringing the plan forward," Anjie said quietly coming across to them through the now near-empty kitchen.

"You ok, Tullie?" he asked softly reaching out to touch her arm. Her sama glowed briefly then faded but not before Anjie could feel the energy that flowed through it. Images of faraway places buzzed through his mind and the face of a beautiful woman filled his vision briefly before she abruptly disappeared. She was angry and protective all at once; he knew instinctively that in a different context she would kill anyone who touched Tullie so lightly.

Tullie remained silent, tensing up again, locked in a world he could not engage with. He looked at Matt but he just shook his head slightly.

"Matt, we need to go," said Anjie reluctantly.

"She comes with me," said Matt, and Anjie nodded. It was best this way. He'd add Meryck and Jo to their group; have them travel behind them, for emergency backup. But backup from what, was the question he couldn't quite explain to himself as he turned away. Demonstrations like the one Tullie had just pulled off unsettled him. He liked to know where he stood, and this was shifting sands big time! He could tell Jo had misgivings too. She was rattled, and it took something to rattle her!

*****

Kate shot fully awake with the ring of the doorbell. The sky had turned to deep velvet shades; it was late already, she realised. Switching off the television, she walked slowly towards the front door wondering who could be calling at such a late hour.

Hi Kate," said a buoyant Jane to the slightly dishevelled

396

woman who opened the door.

"Jane!" replied Kate, delightedly, hugging her friend. "What brings you here at this late hour?"

"Come in! Come in!" she continued without waiting for an answer, and held the door wide open.

"I've brought company, if you don't mind?" asked Jane, pausing briefly as Tullie and Matt came into view, followed by Carney and Johnson.

"Tullie!" shouted Kate, excitedly, grabbing her in a warm embrace. "I'm so happy to see you! Are you ok?" she continued, holding onto her and leading them all inside.

"I'm great, thanks, Mrs Mallin," answered Tullie. "Just a bit jaded and surprised by it all."

"Bet you are, love!" sighed Kate back. "Should you be up and about at all? Here, set yourself down here and I'll go get Jenny," and she made towards the stairs. "Bit dark in here," she mumbled, reaching for the light switch but Jane stopped her.

"Kate," she said quietly, "we need you to sit down, please. This light is fine, for now," she added.

Turning, Kate realised she'd missed something big; something real important. She sank into the nearest chair, looking worriedly at them all for the first time.

"Who are these guys?" she whispered fearfully to Jane.

"Friends, Kate," said Jane quietly.

"What kind of friends?" began Kate, then her hands flew to her mouth. "It's Ben, isn't it? Something's happened?"

"No, nothing like that," Jane assured her, sitting beside her on the chair and putting a protective arm around her.

"In fact, it's the exact opposite!" she continued, smiling. "We're here to get you all out tonight."

Kate's eyes grew wide, the whites increasingly visible in the shadows in the room.

"Out?" she whispered. "What do you mean out?"

Before Jane could begin, Johnson interrupted.

"Hi, Mrs Mallin," he said stepping forward, holding out his hand, "I'm Detective Johnson. Your daughter, Jenny, helped us with our inquiries into Tullie's accident. Is she here? She should be present for this too?"

"Oh, you're the nice policeman she was talking about," said Kate, grinning warmly as she shook his hand robustly, and he was glad the room was dark as the warm colour spread up his face. "Hang on, I'll go get her," she continued, rising. "She went to bed early. Headache, or something," and she skipped up the stairs to knock gently on the first bedroom door on the right.

"Jenny," she called, "that nice Detective Johnson is here. He wants you to come down, please," and she continued to knock.

Johnson watched carefully, his sixth sense kicking in. There should have been some reply from inside by now! Drawing his gun, he dashed up the stairs, two at a time, holding a finger over his mouth, and pointing with intent at the door, motioning Mrs Miller to the side. When she was safe, he gingerly reached for the door knob, turning it slowly. The door gave without resistance and swung inwards silently. In a flash, he was inside, searching the room methodically but there was no sign of Jenny.

"All clear!" he called back, and reached for the light switch. Jenny was gone!

"Matt," he called, "see if her car is outside!"

"Mrs Miller," he said, turning back into the room, "what car does she drive? Mrs Miller!"

"There's no car here," shouted Matt up the stairs.

That got her attention.

"No car?" she called down, rushing downstairs.

"My car!" she cried, looking at the empty driveway. "It's gone! Jenny must have taken it! Hers is in for a service."

"The keys," called Jane, "where do you keep the keys?" The keys were gone too. While Kate gave a description of the car to Johnson, Jane was reporting in to Anjie.

"Is there anywhere she'd go, this late?" called Jane.

Kate was silent for several moments, and then turned reluctantly to face Tullie.

"I think she may have gone to Jed's place in Tinakilly," she whispered.

"Grant's Cottage?" asked Tullie back, astonished. "What would she do that for?"

While Kate tried to explain to a dumbfounded Tullie, Jane passed the information along. Within seconds, members of the mountain assault team were on their way down.

"It's time, Kate," said Jane firmly, as Matt withdrew the kit from his pocket and Carney prepped for the procedure. "Sit down. This won't take long. We need to get Jenny asap. She's heading into danger. We can talk in the car. We'll pick up Ben later. I'll explain as we go along. Ok?"

*****

Man-x was twitchy. It was taking all his energy to remain calm and neutral with Guidrius so close. Damn! He could feel him right under his feet this time! It was like a bad

399

itch he couldn't scratch and his temper was beginning to fray. Breathe in, and out! In and out! In and out! He dug his fingers into the ground until he could feel the crack as some small bones split and the pain helped him focus. Focus: in and out; in and out! Where the hell was he!

"In! Out!" grated a voice in his head that he recognised instantly. The old geezer was getting through his defences! He had to get a grip!

"In! Out!" laughed the voice again, and he felt himself snap!

In the Control Room, Ben watched the awesome display of abandonment with fear in the pit of his stomach. This was the beast they were to take with them later. How could he let that happen? Man-x was in a frenzy punching the walls systematically, then the floor, leaving a trail of blood from his mangled hands but still he continued, on and on. From the safety of his eerie, Ben began to see a pattern. His actions weren't random at all; he was focussing on something. He had to tell Ella, and fast! As he reached for the door, it opened before him.

"Going somewhere?" she asked smoothly, slipping past him to the monitors poised over Man-x.

"He's a bit unsettled, I'd say?" she ventured, eyebrows rising to her hairline.

"Yes, Ma'am," he replied silkily.

"Been at this long?" she asked.

"No, Ma'am," he answered truthfully.

"And you were going to call the alert, when?" she was standing nearby now, he could see the edge of her makeup on her jaw line.

"Just about to do that, Ma'am," he replied, his outward

calm belying the chill he always felt to his core when he met her. He reached past her and pushed the button. Instantly, alarm bells pulsed through the facility but rather than instil some semblance of order into Man-x's demeanour, it infuriated him more. They watched silently as he increased his attacks, moving now towards the rear of the tunnel, towards the abandoned generator shaft, she saw.

"The gas?" she reminded him, evenly, and he set the lever at 5.

"Increase it," she ordered coldly.

He pushed the lever to 7.

"All the way," she added, calmly.

"All the way?" he gasped, looking her full in the face. "That'll kill him, Maggie," he said solemnly.

"Maggie?" she drawled frostily, and he backed away quickly, holding his hands placatingly in front of him.

"Please, Maggie," he begged now. "They'll kill me if I do that! They want him alive!"

She eyed him menacingly for several seconds, the tension reaching for the roof now, and then she shrugged, stepped past him and pushed the lever to 10.

"New orders, Ben," she said. "What do I care?" and she made to leave but changed her mind and approached him again.

"Maggie's gone, Ben!" she whispered, her vulnerability sneaking through briefly. "Gone! You understand! We'll have no more 'Maggie' ever! Is that clear?"

"Yes, Ma'am," he nodded slowly, his eyes never leaving her face. He thought he saw it crumble briefly as she turned away. She was his best ally and worst enemy in this place, he knew. What she had sacrificed, he could only guess. Instinctively, he thumbed his phone looking for Kate and Jenny. What he found was no salve to his nerves. One was at home, and one close by. What in the world was going on!

The increasing quiet interrupted his reverie and he turned back to the screen, his heart skipping a beat. The gas was doing its job. Outside the door, the security waited to secure the area, unaware of the drama unfolding only feet from their position. Man-x was standing still now, his hands drooping by his sides, his chest heaving. This was different, he realised suddenly, slowing down his metabolism as quickly as he could.

"In! Out!" he could still hear the old geezer intone, as he slid down the nearest wall to a sitting position, bracing himself with his elbows. Down here the gas wasn't as strong but an inner sense added 'yet!' What was he to do? For the first time he registered his frailty at the hands of these humans. For the first time, he knew he could die in this place and he would never get to accomplish his mission. He could feel the lethargy begin to take over his body and he had no way to combat it this time. His battle over, his inner senses were clear. The old geezer was puzzled, then worried. Guidrius was puzzled too. Something wasn't right for him either. But the one person he wanted to meet most in the world had gone dark again. Sha-ma Endora, he called, but no answer came. Ben watched the numbers on the monitor increase; he shouldn't be even breathing now, he marvelled, but Man-x's chest still rose and fell, rose and fell, quietly and systematically.

*****

"Stop the car!" Tullie cried. "Stop the car now!" she tried again, louder this time, to be heard above Kate's sobs.

"What is it, Tullie?" asked Johnson, grinding the car to a halt on the outskirts of Tinakilly.

"Something's not right," she stated, bounding out of the car and leaning weakly against the bonnet, Matt following instantly from the front seat.

Bucks screeched to a halt behind the sedan, jumping to help.

"What's up, Tullie?" demanded Matt, gripping her firmly to stop her shaking.

"I don't know," she cried, tears flowing unhindered down her pale face.

"Go on without us," called Matt, pulling Tullie away from the front, supporting her with both arms now while Bucks hovered, ready to help. "Carney can work the equipment just as well as me! Bucks will stay with us," he instructed, leading Tullie back to the sedan.

Neither Johnson nor Jane was happy with this but they knew the benefit of speed. Pulling away, Jane dialled Anjie with the latest development. He wasn't happy either but he knew that Bucks had backup no one knew about so he approved their choice and turned to check the status of the team on the mountain. You're good to go, he told them. Johnson would connect with them there.

Tullie stopped at the car door, refusing to enter.

"No! I need air, Matt!" she choked, doubling up. "I cannot breathe!"

He could see she was deeply distressed but didn't know what to do. Instinctively, he knew she was right. She needed open spaces.

"Cover us," he called to Bucks, and led her off the road and into the trees as Meryck and Jo's car slid into view.

"Guidrius!" he called. "I need help, man! Something's up with Tullie."

"I know!" he heard back. "It's Man-x! They've decided to eliminate him. They're gassing him. He's only got a short while left. Somehow Tullie is caught up in this. She needs to use her sama to help him. I fear if he dies, she will. I don't have the time to work it out with her! You've got to take her through this, Matt; like you did for me. She must give him air! Now, Matt!"

Tullie was crumbling now, her back against a tree trunk, her breath coming in short gasps.

"Tullie, can you hear me?" asked Matt worriedly, and she weakly waved her hand at him.

"Tullie, we have to create an air bubble for Man-x," he told her simply, "like you did for Guidrius. You have to use your sama again. Do you understand?"

All he got was a bare nod.

"I'll make the link when you activate your sama," he promised.

"Tullie, do it now!" he instructed forcefully.

She was weak, fading fast. As he watched, she began to topple forward.

"Tullie!" he roared, and caught her in his arms. They fell on the ground together and he pulled her roughly over, hauling her onto his lap as he braced himself against the tree trunk. Reaching his arms around her, he placed her right wrist over her left arm, activating the sama. It came alive instantly. He felt the jolt of energy rattle through her body and his, and she gulped in air gratefully.

With his dying breath he found her again. "Sha-ma," he called faintly, and the horror of his life hit her full in the gut.

"Rak-na," she called back, and she felt the impact of his true identity claw feverishly at the persona that was now

404

Man-x. Reaching out with her mind, she placed him in a clear bubble of air and the constriction in her own chest lessened. Feeling him safe, she let go.

*****

Man-x lay still on the floor of the tunnel locked in the world of his mind, far away, where the youth that was Rak-na, was honed for service. No deed was too much to honour his Queen. He had thought Rak-na long dead but she had resurrected him, and with him came the final piece of the puzzle. She had healed his pathways. He knew who he was again. Watching, Ben was sure he had just witnessed Man-x's final moments and his heart sank. He hit the release button and the gas began to disperse. It would take some time, he knew, for the area to be declared safe for use again; some time before they could confirm his suspicions. The old geezer had gone silent. Ben could sense reproach but nothing mattered now. He was a man on borrowed time despite Maggie's new orders. Burrowing deep in the code, he erased the gas commands forever. Then he pushed all the vents to open. Turning to the electrics, he set the thermos to overload. He had thirty minutes tops. Would Ella be ready in time, he wondered, as he reset the entrance code to the control room as he left. Greenway was his now!

CHAPTER 60

The noise from the tunnel drew BB's attention as he secured Jed to the submersible before hurrying to Jake's side. Blood dripped freely from the wound in his side but it was beginning to slow. He hadn't lost much; he would recover quickly. Pausing briefly to wash the stickiness from his hands he was surprised to see fish of all sizes pour into the pool and shoal about languidly. Quickly he pulled his hands free afraid that the blood had attracted some primeval species that lurked under the mountain. He slid back on his backside wiping his hands on his trousers as he got his fear under control. He'd be very happy never to see this place again!

"What is it?" called Jake faintly.

"Fish," answered BB truthfully. "Loads of bloody fish!""

"Keep back," whispered Jake, and he rested his head on the floor.

"Jake!" shouted BB and dashed towards his friend but froze in place at the sight of the giant dog that crouched over his friend, water dripping from his shaggy coat. He was weaponless and defenceless. The large dog ignored him and a strange light began to surround them both. Jed's eyes were on stalks, and he thrashed feverishly trying to get away from this unknown threat. Jake was the only one unconcerned.

"Jake!" shouted BB again, finding his voice and he grabbed a bundle of cables to chase the dog away.

"It's ok," called Jake, never opening his eyes. He looked at ease with the animal, and as BB moved cautiously closer he could see that his old friend was somehow better.

"Stop where you are!" came the command from the bottom of the tunnel and BB could see from Jed's demeanour that their time was up; they had been discovered. He slowly raised his hands in the air while the dog snuggled close to Jake, lowering his large head onto the ground in submission. Within seconds they were surrounded by troops and securely handcuffed. The large dog just lay patiently, tongue lolling out its mouth, its thin sides rising and falling with every breath. The pond was serene again. It was as if BB had somehow imagined it all and that the dog had been with them from the start. But glancing at Jed, BB was jolted back into reality. How long more did he have, he wondered? The answer wasn't long in coming.

"Take him," the leader instructed, putting his phone back in his pocket, and BB was separated from the other two and disappeared up the tunnel.

"Maggie's alive up there somewhere," muttered Guidrius for Jake's ears alone.

"What!" Jake exclaimed.

"She's alive, Jake," continued Guidrius whilst never taking his eyes off Jed for one second. "BB is caught up in this somehow."

Guidrius felt Jake's confusion keenly, and his pain for BB, and he passed on as much information as he could. Jake was still poorly but he had healed his broken ribs before being interrupted. At least, this way, he had a fighting chance. And the rest of his injuries would provide authenticity.

"What do we do with the dog?" asked one of them.

"Bring them all, she said, so he comes too," was the short reply. "He looks strong enough to make it up on his own."

They watched as the crew searched the submersible in fine detail then let it slip back into the water.

"The detonators are worthless, Sir," reported one, whistling. "Very clever job! Somebody knows their onions! But the cable and explosives are ok. We can use these. No need to bring down some of our own."

"Ok! Do it!" was the reply. "Move out!"

They moved Jake and Jed towards the tunnel, and Guidrius trotted alongside Jake submissively.

"Up!" they were instructed and Guidrius bounced into the space excitedly, pushing energy back to help Jake climb. The going was tough. The pain in Jake's leg was intense while Jed struggled with every other handhold. But the ropes they had looped through their handcuffs provided the extra grip. Jake was impressed that BB made this on his own! The light ahead beckoned and as they drew close muffled voices called out instructions.

The tunnel opened into a much smaller space than Jake expected and the smell of wet dog was overpowering. Guidrius was cowering in the smallest corner he could find, his head lowered, looking absolutely dejected. His tail swung excitedly at the sight of Jake.

"This your dog?" asked a burly guard, pointing his semi from one to the other.

Jake nodded, breathing deeply.

"He's my eyes," gulped Jake reaching out to feel his way forward.

"Your eyes?" growled the incredulous guard.

Jake nodded again.

"Been blind two years now," he confessed. "Bad fall.

Where is he? I need to touch him for him to guide me in unfamiliar places," he pleaded quietly.

Bringing up the rear, Jed sneered, but said nothing. Any ploy was a good ploy when you're in a squeeze, he thought, playing along.

"Is this true?" the guard shot at Jed, and Jake froze.

Jed shrugged.

"Never seen the man in my life before," he offered, calmly.

"We'll see about that soon enough," the guard offered testily. "Take them!" he ordered.

*****

With Bill Boyd at the wheel, an empty Golden Belle bobbed lightly out of port into the path of the setting sun. This was a job he had to do alone; the crew had been given the night off. Every scent, every movement was glorious. He loved this girl! And after tonight, she would be his no longer. But he had been paid well, twice! And these days, that was what mattered. The money from Grant's Cottage was already gone; gambled away in the late hours. The only place he felt alive now was on the Belle. Somewhere deep inside, he knew this was his last trip – ever, and memories of his earlier life came back to haunt him. But shaking his head, he battered them down. What was done was done! Sometimes the past cannot be redeemed. And sometimes the future was certain!

"You there, Bill?" said a grumpy voice as the radio cracked into life.

"Yup," replied Bill airily. "Welcome Point coming up! On schedule!"

"You enjoying the peace and quiet?" was the next

question.

"Yup!" he replied again, keeping his enthusiasm even. "All silent on board!"

"Maintain, course," Oswald instructed, and the radio fell dead.

Bill felt the movement of the boat change as he rounded the headland and met the full blast of the wind for the first time. It rose and fell harder now on this choppy patch and he relished the roil and rumble in his stomach. It was as close to feeling alive he got these days! The cargo lane spread out to left and right, huge ships disappearing as dots on the horizon. He didn't know how far out they wanted him to go; as the motion of the boat settled, he pushed the throttle a little further and the land began to fall away behind him.

"Is he following course?" Mahler asked Friday.

Friday nodded. They had Boyd where they wanted him. He'd do as he was told.

"How long to rendezvous?" he asked.

"Forty-eight minutes," smiled Friday.

It was going to be a great night, grinned Mahler, as he absent-mindedly scratched at his left arm. This damn bug was getting to him!

"Antidote?" asked Friday, but he shook his head.

"Too soon," he replied, calmly. "But have it ready. I don't want to have this thing in me for a second longer than necessary!"

CHAPTER 61

For the last hour Oswald hadn't moved a muscle. The crew circled about him on deck, giving him the space he demanded but remaining within earshot should he call. Staring into the distance, he ignored them completely, a survival trick he had learned well during his long holiday in Albania. Inside his head he was viciously alive, replaying the unfolding scenario time and again. Something didn't match up! He was sure of it now. His instincts had never let him down. There was trouble ahead. Turning abruptly, he went below.

"Mahler still on screen?" he demanded

"Yes, Sir," was the breathless reply.

"Same heading?" he asked, more calmly now.

"Same heading, Sir!" shouted the man.

"And the Golden Belle?" he asked next.

"Heading straight for Mahler's position, Sir!" was the response.

Oswald grunted and turned for the kitchen. He needed something to eat. It'd be a long night.

"Call me when the Belle enters the lane," he instructed as he left.

*****

Carla watched Oswald go below with relief. It was difficult to keep up the indifferent front for such a prolonged time. Beside her, Bowen sighed deeply with relief.

"Hang in there," she whispered, glancing furtively to where Boris slumbered easily in his soft chair against the railing. "We're nearly home. I won't let anything happen to you! This is my funeral!"

"Don't use that word, darling," he groaned, grasping her hand tightly. "I don't know what I'd do if I lost you!"

Carla looked at him intently. He really didn't get it, did he? It was all about him, wasn't it? Maybe her father was right! He really was just a pretty face. Well, not just, she grinned. He was good in bed too! A stud really! And as always, he read her thoughts perfectly, and she could see his erection through his cotton shorts.

"Pleased to see me, are you?" she teased, but he didn't do teasing. His warm eyes burned into hers, and the pressure on her hand increased, then lessened as he began to caress her palm with his thumb. She could fell her body respond, her nipples perking through her own light cotton shirt. She moved close to him and they kissed passionately.

"Get a room!" grumbled Boris without moving an inch, and they drew apart reluctantly.

Carla could see from the telltale signs on Bowen's cheeks that he was getting angry; might as well let this play out, she thought, calmly.

"Mind your own fucking business," growled Bowen, his fists balling now, his aggression beginning to peak.

What a Neanderthal, she wondered. It did have its benefits, she laughed.

"What's so funny?" he growled at her now, and at the corner of her eye she saw Boris shift slightly. Bowen hadn't seen it. He was glaring at her full in the face. He didn't like it when he had to call a halt on his erection. He had to channel his energy elsewhere.

412

"You're such a stud," she purred, reaching out to rub his arm, but he pulled away abruptly.

"You're my stud," she began again, stretching out a leg provocatively, letting her wrap slip up. His eyes followed.

"Oh for God's sake!" sighed Boris loudly uncoiling himself from the chair. "Take her where she is or I'll do it myself for you! Can't you see she's gagging for it!"

Before Boris had even finished, Bowen had lunged for him while Carla pushed back her head to reveal a long and delicious throat, and laughed.

"Boys!" she called delightedly, as they thrashed about the deck, taking out their full frustration on each other. She loved being fought over! She was happy to share the spoils. Boris looked fit for a forty-something, she mused, feeling her arousal even more intensely now. She licked her lips in anticipation. She wondered absently if he was a long or short before man, and decided, definitely short. He'd expect his woman to be ready and waiting. Well, she might have a shot at changing that, she mused, rising to the challenge.

The noise drew the attention of Oswald's staff but they did nothing to stop the fight. Instead, they stood around in a circle, hemming the two in. The woman was there too, Carla noticed, and she spoke rapidly on her phone. Her eyes were hard as she watched the battle, and suddenly Carla realised it was to the death! Catching her breath sharply, she rose abruptly from her seat. Bowen noticed her instantly and realised something was bothering her. Boris seized the moment and bashed Bowen's head against the floor. The crack was audible across the waves as his skull caved in, and his body followed rapidly. The fight was over. Blood pooled slowly around Bowen's head and Carla was horrified, rushing to his side and pummelling his chest urgently while keeping daintily clear of the blood.

"Get up!" she called urgently. "Bowen, get up! Oh my

God! Bowen! Bowen!"

Boris reached down roughly and pulled her to her feet. She flailed against him but he held her at arm's length, unconcerned by her outburst, waiting for it to burn out.

"To the victor the spoils then," he laughed, and pulled her close to kiss her passionately.

"Who needs a room now?" he gloated, pushing his hands up inside her shirt to grasp an unfettered breast.

"Enough," roared Oswald, thumping on deck, breaking the spell.

Quickly, Boris pushed a dishevelled Carla behind him, and faced his captor silently. They faced off in silence, animosity sparkling between them.

"Get rid of the body," instructed Oswald through clenched teeth, never once taking his eyes off Boris. Bowen was dead weight anyway, a toy boy along for the ride with more money than sense, his brain between his legs! His death only simplified things. He should be grateful to Boris. He had confirmed two things for him: Carla was a cold-hearted bitch who would stop at nothing to get her hands on the antidote and Boris would obviously kill for it. They were welcome to each other! But he needed them alive, for now. He had to have their contacts, their distribution lines.

"Lock them below!" he bellowed. "Together! And throw away the bloody key!"

"You can't do this!" squeaked Carla, incensed. "You can't lock me up with this monster!" and she struggled against her captors. Boris just grinned lasciviously which increased her discomfort. How could she have ever thought him exciting! He was a brute!

"Help!" she cried, but her pleas fell on deaf ears.

Oswald watched it all with a thoughtful look on his face, and the remaining crew on deck found urgent reasons to melt away.

*****

Jenny moved slowly around the Cottage, her feelings threatening to choke her. Jed's truck was parked outside, the doors unlocked, his useless phone in bits on the passenger seat. There was no one home, the door unlocked, the lights left on. The silence beat against her, hard, and she shivered. It was as if the Rapture had happened and she was the only one on the surface of the earth found wanting; the only one left to bear the memories of the many, the sins of the world. She moved from room to room downstairs, calling to Jed but there was no reply. She climbed the stairs laboriously, her feet dragging at every step, the silence clinging to her like a thick fog. She sank into the soft bed they had shared such a short time ago; it even still smelled of their love. And the tears came again. She let them flow as the darkness gathered around her. She hadn't bothered to turn on the lights up here, preferring to leave it as he had; a mausoleum to Jed, her incredible lover. Where was he, she wondered for the umpteenth time. And why has he blown her off so cruelly?

A slight noise from outside drew her attention and she lunged for the window, her heart somersaulting. He was back! But in the darkness below, she could see nothing, except her tear stained face peering back at her accusingly from the window. Pulling back abruptly, she came to her senses. She had cried enough. Pounding her way to the bathroom, she threw cold water unceremoniously on her swollen face, tidied her wayward hair and prepared for battle. She'd have it out with him, if it was the last thing she'd do! He had to be in that barn somewhere!

*****

"She's here, Sir," whispered a voice in the darkness,

"middle window, two o'clock."

"Copy that," was the short reply. "Going in now."

"Wait, incoming," was the reply back. "Hold! Watch and wait! I repeat, watch and wait!"

"Copy," replied the unseen contact. "Watch and wait it is."

*****

Jenny powered down the stairs, a new resolve filling her with energy. Passing the phone in the kitchen, she thought about calling her mother and letting her know where she was but she didn't know what to say, just yet. Later, when she'd met Jed and had it out with him, she resolved, her conscience settling a bit with this decision. She'd probably be asleep by now anyway, she reasoned, as she pushed against the patio door and let herself out into the darkness waiting for the sensor light to come on.

"What the hell!" she fumed aloud when nothing happened and let herself back in to search for a torch. To the side a young soldier grinned, relieved. He'd got the light just in time!

From inside came the unmistakeable sound of drawers being dragged open and slammed shut again as Jenny searched for a torch to no avail. Cursing, she marched outside, slowly making her way around to the side where Jed's truck was parked. The interior light from the boot shone a pathway back to her car which was parked outside the gate. As she expected, there was a torch in the side pocket. Hefting it in her slight hand, she slammed the door shut and powered it up. The beam was intense, cutting a white swathe across the garden, forcing into stark contrast the light and the shadow. Amazed by its brightness, she shone it straight up, convinced it would even reveal details on the surface of the moon! Then, its capabilities plumbed,

416

she made a beeline for the barn.

The barn door was ajar and she tentatively pushed against it.

"Jed," she called, clearly. "Jed, it's me Jenny. Are you in here?"

But there was no reply, the door just swung silently open to reveal an empty barn. Slowly, she began to make her way in.

*****

"Sir, she's going inside," came through the headset. "Shall I intercept?"

"Negative," said a disembodied voice. "Hold your position. I repeat, hold your position."

"Copy that," said the first voice calmly.

*****

The air inside was a musty sweet, and she wrinkled her nose in disgust, panning the light around the interior to get a better view. Spotting the switches, she tiptoed across the rough ground, noticing the tyre tracks on the dusty floor, and flicked the light switch. The inside of the barn glowed into life and in the rafters some creatures scurried balefully for the safety of darkness. She shuddered. She wasn't an outdoors person; she hated wildlife, and switching off the torch, she brushed agitatedly at imaginary bugs, waiting for the moths to appear. She hated moths too! But the light also illuminated in stark contrast the grooves from Jed's truck, and she traced the dark parallel lines outwards to where he had last parked and inwards towards where her feet were, right between the two lines. Turning her back to the door, she followed those inwards, and began to walk forward towards the rear of the barn, head down, one tiny step at a time. The tyre marks went right up to the end, and she stood there, puzzled, for several seconds, her face millimetres from the back wall. Then lifting the torch, she tapped at the obstruction in front of her. She wasn't surprised to hear the hollow sound that echoed both inside and outside the barn, and she remembered the night she had spent with Jed, when he was gone for some time, and she had stood outside the barn, looking inside, before creeping back to bed. There was a space behind this door, she was sure of it now. Turning on the torch again, to fortify the light in the barn, she began to look for a switch.

*****

In the darkness outside, a quiet discussion was taking place.

"Sir, she's found something," said the same disembodied voice again.

"Where?" questioned his superior officer.

"Back of the barn, Sir," was the reply. "We could hear the sound from here."

"The sound?" said the second voice again

"When she tapped on the back wall, Sir," came the answer, "we heard the empty sound. That wall hides another space, Sir. She's looking for the switch now, Sir, to open the door."

"Stand by," came the instruction, and the soldier could hear another conversation going on in the background.

"Wait and see," came back the instructions. "Wait and see. You copy?"

"Copy that, Sir," came back the reply.

"Intercept party three minutes out," was the follow up. "Copy?

"Copy that," replied the young man.

"Prepare for takedown," came the additional instruction, "two minutes forty."

*****

As the car topped Willow Hill for the ride down to Grant's Cottage, the occupants became silent, straining their eyes for the first glimpse of the building. Johnson had cut the lights at the beginning of the climb and they were travelling at a crawl now, the trees on either side hemming them in, the darkness to either side complete. Only ahead, and up, was there light. It wasn't yet completely dark; facing west they could see the last pink hue from the setting sun peeking around Traveller's Mountain but even that disappeared as they descended. Tipping down was an anti-climax. The road ahead was straight, and eerily reflective. Kate wasn't the only one in the car to feel the sweet tendrils of disassociation wind their way into their core. The atmosphere became more and more otherworldly, the only sounds being the slight noise from the tyres on the road surface and their increased breathing rate. If a headless horseman had ridden out from the trees and held them up at pistol point, they would have acquiesced immediately so strong was their illusion of timelessness. Then, the phone rang, and the spell was broken. Though jarring the senses, it brought them back to reality, and just in time too. The light from the barn threw a ghostly shadow against the side of the Cottage. Johnson cut the engine and coasted to the side, a little ways back from Kate's car, while Jane answered the phone.

"You ok?" asked a concerned Anjie. "Where are you?"

"Just at the Cottage," replied Jane, clearing her throat. "The barn light is on. What's up?" Before he could answer her there was a light tap at the window. She jumped, as did everyone present except Johnson.

As Anjie filled her in from his side, the heavily camouflaged soldier gestured for them to follow him. Stalling the occupants, Johnson disabled the inside lights, then signalled for them to open the doors slowly and leave them ajar. It was like following a shadow but they managed it, tiptoeing lightly back up the road to rendezvous in a small clearing.

Carney was seriously jumpy, and Kate was jittery; it took all her resolve to keep her teeth from chattering! Back on familiar territory, both Johnson and Jane were on track again. More shadows appeared from the tree line and Jane reached out to instinctively to grab Kate's arm to keep her from calling out. Despite his best efforts, Carney swore loudly and the group froze.

"Where's my daughter?" whispered an anguished Kate to the Shadow pushing forward to meet them.

"She's safe, Ma'am," he replied evenly and his calm tone had a soothing effect on them all.

"She's in the barn, looking for the switch for the back wall," he added quietly. "How do you want to play this?" he asked Johnson.

"I knew there was something odd about that back wall!" affirmed Johnson. "Do you think it might be booby-trapped?" he asked in a whisper, drawing the guy away from the rest. No need to bother them with that just now, he thought.

"It's possible," was the reply. "We didn't have time to check it out before she got here. I'm keen to take her out of the picture as soon as possible so we can go in and check. What's with this tagging bug anyway? How will it affect our mission here?"

"We're threading water with this one as much as you," replied Johnson, turning back to search the group.

"He'll be able to disable it," he added, pointing to where Carney stood slightly apart from the others, "but once we do, Greenway will be aware. You'll have to be quick. How are you going to open that thing if she doesn't find the switch?"

"Laser," he replied.

"Ok," said Johnson, putting the pieces together. "Let us take the girl. Keep out of sight until then. And Captain," he said purposefully, "there's a few crates in there that need to be kept intact. Or at least, the contents were in crates the last time I saw them."

"Scale of importance?" asked the Captain.

"On a scale of 1 to 10, 1000," answered Johnson, and they understood each other perfectly.

CHAPTER 62

BB could hardly breathe as he waited. The pain in his side from the knife wound was exquisite but he couldn't relieve the pressure in any way. But it wasn't the physical wound that was causing him to sweat profusely. A dreadful excitement coursed through his veins. He was on her territory now. Was she really alive still? His heart skipped at the hope of a possible reunion after all this time! He had never stopped loving her. But, had she stopped loving him? Why had she not been in touch all these years? And how could he explain all this to Jake? The questions didn't stop there. On and on they came as he sat slumped in the half shadow, the silence pouring into his soul, freezing the life out of him.

"Uncuff him," she said brusquely, and he shook himself awake instantly.

"Maggie?" he whispered wonderingly as his wife stepped into the pool of light in front of him.

She looked amazing but different. He would still recognise her anywhere but the softness had gone. It was replaced with steel, and when he lifted his gaze to look her fully in the eyes he realised that all was not well. She gazed back unblinking, her amethyst eyes pinning him to the chair more effectively than the cuffs ever did.

"BB," she said crisply. "To what do I owe the honour of this visit?"

She hadn't moved but he was compelled to answer her instantly. His mouth moved before his brain could get in gear!

"We followed Jed through the mountain," he wheezed in one quick breath, and he saw her eyes narrow.

"Jed?" she queried coldly, and he cursed himself inwardly for divulging even that.

Forcing his mouth closed, he nodded slowly playing for time.   Maggie didn't push the issue; she'd know soon anyway. Stepping back out of the light she peered at him closely. He'd aged a lot since they last met; his hair was whiter and the lines around his mouth had deepened. His hands, lying calmly on his knees as he regarded her back, were the same though. She vaguely remembered their tenderness, and their strength. Impulsively, she pushed at a strand of hair that was perfectly in place.   The vein in his neck beat faster, she saw, and she suddenly realised he was afraid of her, and this bothered her, and she was puzzled at her response. Everybody was afraid of her these days and she relished their fear; she drew deeply on it to get her through another day. It added vibrancy to her dull life. Why now should she be bothered that this man would fear her? In her mind, she let go of a tiny part of her fortress wall, and the effect was unsettling. Long forgotten longings shoved against the weakened barrier and threatened to overwhelm her.

Flecks of light played in her eyes as BB watched her regard him from the shadows. It was deeply unsettling but he kept his gaze direct and focussed. She seemed to have come to some decision.

"I see you're injured," she said matter-of-factly, removing a glove, stepping close to him now to inspect the blood stain on his shirt. Her fingers were like iron as they prodded his side and he winced. She drew back instantly bringing her hand to her face to inspect the blood on her fingertips. It was the first time he had seen her up close in over ten years but nothing had prepared him for the revulsion that flowed through him at the sight of her hand. It was angular and smooth, in perfect proportion, but covered in a strange metal that glowed in the dim light. Or was it completely metal?

"Take this man to hospital immediately," she barked, moving away from him to the door. Looking back at him briefly, he thought he saw a fleeting moment of recognition on her face, and them she was gone.

*****

"Jenny?" called Kate, rushing around Jed's truck towards the barn. "Jenny? You there, love?"

"Mum?" called Jenny, and she turned away from her search of the far left corner to intercept her mother at the door. "What are you doing here?"

"Oh Jenny!" cried Kate, hugging her daughter to her forcefully. "What am I doing here? I was afraid I'd lost you!"

"Lost me?" gasped Jenny. "What are you talking about, mum?" she added, pushing her mother away to hold her at arm's length. "I'm not a child anymore!"

Kate's tears rolled silently down her face as she regarded her daughter's own swollen face.

"Jenny," she gulped, "I have something I need to tell you. Come into the house, love. There are some people I want to introduce you too," and she turned away, still holding onto her daughter.

"Mum!" said Jenny sharply, grasping her mother's arm to look at the bloody bandage. "Mum, what's happened? What's wrong? Are you ok?"

Kate stopped to hug her again.

"Oh Jenny," she said breathlessly, shaking her bandaged arm about, "it's about what's finally right! After all these years! Come on, girl! Your dad and I need you with us tonight!"

Jenny sat in the kitchen, her eyes on stalks, as Kate, then Jane, explained the situation in more detail to her; enough at present to get the job done, blocking her line-of-sight to the barn. Carney fussed about at the edge of the room, keen to get the job done, yet increasingly anxious as Kate's arm continued bleeding. The waiting was grating on everyone, but with no host for Jenny's bug, they had to time their extraction finely.

"So you're saying I'm carrying a bug around in my arm?" asked Jenny falteringly, her courage finally failing her.

"Take it out!" she screamed, suddenly. "I hate bugs! Take it out now! What are you waiting for!" she roared at Carney pushing her arm into his face as he retreated before her at this outburst. He looked at the others beseechingly but no one came to his aid.

"Jenny," he said calmly, grasping her outstretched arm firmly and examining it above the elbow, "the removal only takes seconds. I know exactly where it is but I have to wait for orders. It's critical to you and your Dad. Do you understand?" he looked at her directly, still holding onto her arm gently. He watched her carefully, smiled at her calmly, and though it seemed forever, and everybody was holding their breath, the wildness began to go out of her eyes, and she finally nodded slowly.

"Good!" he continued. "Now, I want you to sit down and relax. You have to stay close. I want you to be ready the moment I get the go ahead. Understand?" and he led her to the far corner where two soft chairs stood side by side. Settling her into one, he folded himself comfortably into the other and the wait began.

*****

Jake slumped back onto the blue hospital pillows,

relieved for treatment and the meds for his pain-wracked body. Guidrius had begun the process and now the doctors on Greenway would complete it. Gingerly he rubbed at his left elbow and noticed wryly that Jed, in the next bed, was doing the same. Even here, in this antiseptic environment, the smell of wet dog overwhelmed the senses as Guidrius draped himself on the floor underneath Jake's bed, within full view of Jed. The medics couldn't wait to get away from the smell, the door slapping shut as they left their charges alone. But they weren't alone for long. The door whished open and BB was routinely tossed onto the remaining bed and shackled like the other occupants to the side rail. They looked at each other silently knowing that they were being monitored, possibly visually, but definitely aurally. Beneath Jake's bed, Guidrius began to growl softly.

Several metres above the pond, they experienced the explosion only lightly. Jed swore volubly, tugging at the bands that held him in place as the slight rattle quickly subsided. Jake risked a quick glance at BB; the life seemed to have gone out of the man!

"We've seen enough," she said. "Separate them. I want answers. And quickly!"

Within seconds, Jed was hauled out of bed and manhandled away, his curses following him down the corridor. The door opened again and Jake forced himself to keep his eyes averted but he reached a hand out to Guidrius.

"Hello, Jake," said a cold voice, and he looked up to peer into Maggie's stark face.

"Hello, Maggie," he said calmly, noticing her eyes. "I thought you were dead. You had a lovely funeral."

She said nothing in reply, looking from one to the other, wrinkling her nose at the smell.

"It's ok. You can reveal yourself now," she said evenly, looking at Guidrius.

"What are you planning to do?" she laughed, mirthlessly. "Kill us by smell?"

BB's eyes bulged as Guidrius reformed and stood glaring at Maggie, amethyst eyes blazing into green eyes, the air crackling with energy.

'So, BB didn't know,' she thought.

'But I did,' mocked Jake, and was gratified to see her eyes widen.

'You have one choice, Maggie,' began Guidrius calmly, and time faltered in its step.

*****

Leading the way, Johnson moved swiftly into the barn towards the last spot Jenny was examining, two soldiers following him inside while the others secured the perimeter. Fanning out, they covered the area in quick time but the outcome was negative. Pulling back, they regrouped outside, readying the laser equipment. Time was running out. They had to work fast. The sound of laser against the reinforced metal Jed had installed echoed through the kitchen.

"What's going on out there?" asked Jenny. "Mum, what are these troops doing here? What haven't you told me?" she asked angrily, walking towards the window to see for herself.

The blast from the explosion shattered the window in front of her, shards blasting inwards to pepper the room, and its occupants, liberally.

"Is everyone ok?" roared Jane, wiping blood from her face. "Carney? Kate? Jenny? Answer me!" and she rushed

427

towards their prone bodies, the whole scene flickering wildly in the light from the fire. She could hear the groans from outside as casualties lay where they were thrown on the lawn.

"Johnson!" she called. "Johnson! You ok? Is everyone ok out there?"

Nearby sounds drew her attention back into the kitchen. Carney was up and checking Kate and Jenny. His shirt was ripped in several places, his body scratched by the flying debris, but he was otherwise ok.

"You ok?" he asked Jane as he came closer, looking intently at her face.

"Grazes," she confirmed. "Are they ok?" she asked, indicating the women, and he nodded, hurrying past her to the wounded outside.

Johnson dragged himself upright, his ears ringing. He couldn't hear anything but he could see the disaster strewn around him. Then Carney was there, checking him and pointing to where others clawed their way upright.

"You take those three," he thought he heard Carney say, and turned to assist.

Looking back, he could see Carney make his way from one form to the other, moving fast, then slowing as he approached the barn door, or what was left of it. Dark smoke was now rising in vicious tendrils from the charred frame of the barn as the water from the pond found release. Inside, the floor was a gushing river bursting around a jagged hole in the back wall where they had been working only seconds earlier. Johnson looked from him to those he had checked and back. Carney shook his head. Then Jane was there with her phone, pushing it at him relentlessly and he heard Anjie's voice from down a tunnel.

Carney had had enough! Wading from the hissing

building, he pushed back into the kitchen, grabbed Jenny roughly, and sucked the bug from her arm in one swift action. It clawed the air, and they watched it writhe and twist in horrified fascination. Then Johnson was there, grabbing the thing from Carney and crushing it under his foot violently. Hell couldn't stand against him tonight, he was so angry! Mustering the walking wounded, he dived through the new gaping hole in the back wall of the shed, the smoke and dust obscuring him from sight instantly. Jenny's heart-felt sobs filled the acrid air.

"Come on," said Jane, ushering Kate and Jenny urgently towards the car. "We've got someplace else to be."

CHAPTER 63

Carla watched Boris anxiously from across the room. She had put as much space as she could between them but still the room seemed too small. Boris ignored her. He was at the window trying to get his bearings. They had turned, he was sure now, probably while he and Bowen were fighting. He was sorry he had to take him out like that; he deserved better but he could think of no other way to get Carla by herself. Turning slowly, he watched her bravado quietly. She was brave, he'd give her that; but she was foolish too. Paulo was right to be worried about his daughter but at nineteen she had already made decisions most could never bring themselves to in a lifetime. Mancini blood ran thick and strong through her veins. He hoped her father could rein her in. He hoped he could rein her in, for both their sakes.

"We don't have much time," he began, moving towards her.

"Stay where you are," she warned in a low growl, holding her stiletto in front of her as a weapon.

He didn't pay her any attention but increased his pace to cover the distance between them in a heartbeat, slapping the shoe out of her hand and pinning her against the wall. She squirmed and writhed, pushing against his brawny frame, scratching wherever she could make contact, using her teeth to bite savagely into his arm.

"Bitch!" he yelled, releasing her slightly. Taking advantage of the moment, she raised a knee and connected hard with his groin. He collapsed on the floor in agony. Carla raced to the door, banging for all her might, screaming for help. He lay, sweating, on the floor, watching her. Grimacing, he realised it couldn't have played out better, from a subterfuge point of view, at least, he reminded himself grimly as he staggered up slowly. Turning around, she saw him begin to approach and grabbed a lamp and lashed out at him anew. He batted it past easily and it smashed against the hull harmlessly. The sound of laughter from outside the door penetrated into the room and it spurred her onto even more destruction. Anything that wasn't nailed down flew airborne in his direction. The ducking and weaving gave him time to recover but he was going to be sore for a long time. Feigning incapacity he moaned and let a few small items glance on his bent-over back. She was running out of steam at the same time as she was running out of projectiles. He was ready for her. Like a cat playing with a mouse he let her come closer and retreat without making a move several times, and then he pounced pinning her across the bed in a sideways movement. But he was wrong. She might be out of projectiles but she wasn't out of steam. His nearness incensed her; the memory of his hand on her breast etched angrily on her memory, and she fought with every ounce of strength she possessed, but he was stronger by far and finally he had her pinned underneath him and the room went quiet. Baleful tawny eyes glared up at cold grey ones.

"Carla," he said quietly, stressing each word carefully, so they'd be no mistake, "I'm here because Paulo sent me to look out for you. You know what he thought of Bowen."

In reply, she spat at him and tried to wriggle free yet again.

"You're lying!" she hissed at him through clenched teeth. "My father would never send a thug like you," but even as she said it he could see the realisation dawn on her. He was exactly whom he'd send; a thug. Shrugging, he released her slowly, backing off her to stand in front of the door. He could hear them outside, listening and taking bets. Looking back at her, he motioned her to be quiet, not to say anymore.

He didn't know if the room was bugged but he suspected it might be. Looking around casually, giving her time to compose herself, he saw there wasn't much left of the sophistication that was Randell's retreat. 'The Carla effect,' he grinned.

"What's so funny?" she asked, rearranging her clothes to regain some semblance of composure much to his distaste. He preferred her dishevelled and half-naked though there was nothing much he could do about that in the short time.

"Paulo calls this 'the Carla effect'," he grinned at her, and she knew then he was who he said he was for certain. This was their catchphrase, only used in private, or so she thought, until now. Now she had another reason to hate Paulo; another lie exposed. Boris watched as the veil came down, as Carla retreated behind her wall of ice, and he didn't interfere. She'd need all the ice she could muster before they were safely home again.

*****

Powering back the Belle, Bill turned her to land once more, and switched off the lights ready for the rendezvous. The ocean was so still, the whole world seemed caught in a timewarp where this moment existed forever. He revelled in its transcendence, losing himself in eternity in a moment, leaning back his head to peer at the indigo sky playing chase with the dying rays of the sun, banishing it over the edge of the world. Then from the depths of Hades, bubbling and frothing came the sub, and the moment vanished forever. But their movements were slick and silent, and within minutes they were on their way to Greenway, a hiss of water covering the spot where the sub slid back under the waves. Mahler took his men below, and Bill was left alone again as the silence returned. There was no need for conversation; that had taken place in another place and time. Looking around at the calm water, Bill was unsure which reality he now inhabited.

"Sir, they've turned for Greenway," Oswald heard as he answered the call.

"How long?" he barked into the mouthpiece.

"At current speed, they'll reach Welcome Point in thirty," he was told.

"Bring us straight into Greenway in twenty five!" growled Oswald "I want us in place before the bastard turns up!"

Adrenalin coursing through his body, he dumped his half eaten sandwich in the bin and made his way downstairs. He hoped Carla hadn't spent all her energy!

"Bring her," he instructed his assistant. "Bring them both," he chuckled to her departing back.

*****

"Let's go over it one more time," said Mahler, and Friday nodded.

"We dock here," he began, pointing to the space on the map in front of them.

"Then we infiltrate here, here and here," added the man to his left, sweeping his arm to indicate the remaining two and himself.

"We enter here," said Friday, meeting Mahler's gaze.

"We take out the guards and set the explosives here before we met up here," added the other, circling the targets this time.

There were no questions. The cabin was silent.

"And the main target?" prompted Mahler, and Friday looked at him guardedly, and nodded.

Turning to the men, he explained.

"We will be taking on board a number of patients, plus their doctor," he pointed to the hospital ward. "This is a minimum security area; present intel tells us there are ten, maybe twelve patients, in care there now. We will need to hit this area too, for the meds," he added, pointing to the lab that ran parallel to the hospital ward across the corridor. "The main security is focussed here and here, as we already discussed, in the transgenics area. This is the area Oswald is going for. That, and one other," he explained, pointing to Ostenwalder's room. "A debt to be paid there," he continued. "I wouldn't want to be the old man when Oswald catches up with him!"

A grunt from Mahler brought them back to the present.

"We have twenty minutes tops," he said calmly.

"Fifteen to move the patients and five for us," he emphasised, looking each in the eye, "then back here, and we rendezvous back at the same point."

"And the Belle?" ventured one, looking around him appreciatively. "She's a nice vessel!"

Friday looked at him.

"Friday," Mahler said, interrupting the staring match, "it's time."

As the three watched, Friday dug deeply into Mahler's left elbow and withdrew a squelchy, wriggling bug. They drew back instinctively. They all knew what it was. Up top, Bill wondered what the tramping was about but knew better that to call down and ask. Sometimes, what you don't know is better for your health, he shrugged.

'I'm so sorry, Jane,' he cried silently to the night's sky. 'I'm so sorry. Please forgive me!

*****

The tunnel was awash but they waded purposefully after Johnson. In here, the smoke was lighter, and the beam from their powerful lights cut sharply through the darkness. Without warning, Johnson slipped and disappeared, the ground curving downwards towards the natural pond at the bottom, whose pathways had been so abruptly altered. Those bringing up the rear backed up onto firmer ground, watching the water anxiously for their young leader. Then his light beamed back at them, rising fast, and his head burst through water, his mouth sprouting out a fountain of dirty water as he swam towards them.

"Hope all your shots are up to date," grinned a relieved soldier as he wrenched Johnson bodily out of the new-born lake.

"Thanks, owe you one," gulped Johnson. "Took me by surprise, that did," and he grinned back.

"Well, maybe if you let us experts lead the way, then you'd be ok," grinned their commander, coming up and slapping him on the shoulder. "What did you see down there?"

"Not much," hiccupped Johnson. "It all happened so fast!"

"No problem," was the reply as the guy hunkered down in front of him. "By the way," he asked casually, "did the water fill all the cavern, in there?"

Johnson grinned. He knew exactly what the guy was up to, and it worked.

"No, Sir," he replied, jovially. "The ceiling of the cave is high, very high. Lots of ledges – well, shadows, really, so I'm supposing ledges. And a few stalactites! Bloody high, that thing is! Plenty of room up there for a package!"

"That's all I need to know," said the soldier, gesturing to his remaining men. "Hang tight! We'll find your Pandora's Box for you," and he strode off to join his men.

"Get out of those wet clothes," he called back. "Must be something you can change into in there," he added, pointing to the Cottage.

CHAPTER 64

Time passed in a blur of emotions as Matt held Tullie until she was able to breathe normally again. Her sama glowed light blue in the deepening light, enveloping them both in a soft glow. He breathed with her, their breaths as one, while Bucks stood a little ways off, providing the safe space they both desperately needed. It was cosy in this shared space; he felt safe in here with her.

Tullie relaxed against Matt gratefully feeling his heart beat pace with hers. He had saved her as sure as she had saved Man-x. Enwrapped as they were together, she had never felt safer, and wondered about the nature of the relationship that was surely developing between them. They both wondered, she suddenly realised, but she didn't push the intrusion away. It was nice to hear him in her head. He had a lovely voice and a strong body, she thought, and she felt him grin. Likewise, she heard him say, and now it was her turn to smile. In that precious moment it felt like they alone inhabited the earth and as if to seal this illusion the full moon slid serenely from behind its cloud cover briefly playing peek-a-boo with their senses. She reached out a slender hand, encased to the wrist in a glowing sama, towards the playful moon and suddenly she saw two moons, closing together irrevocably, one a creamy white, the other more silvery. Matt had seen it too, she realised. They rose together, she still holding her arm skywards, and watched as silvery threads spun from her sama to coalesce in a silver globe, a smaller replica of earth, Silvamon, tethered before their eyes to Traveller's Mountain. They were at once outside it and inside it, looking through it to the twin moons as they hung lightly in the air. A vague commotion impinged on their senses and at first they couldn't tell from which world it came. Then Matt turned towards Bucks in the same instant as Tullie let go her sama to find him preventing Meryck and Jo from joining them.

"It's ok, Bucks, thanks," called Matt. "We're coming. Tullie's fine."

Tullie searched Matt's face for a long time before moving, her confusion and vulnerability clear in her eyes.

"It's ok, Tullie," he said softly, reaching out to touch her face tenderly. "I'll never leave you. I seem to belong in both worlds too. It'll be ok, I promise," and he reached for her, drawing her gently into his arms where she met his kiss fully. The moon chose this moment to reveal itself fully, bathing the young couple in light.

"I like happy endings," muttered Meryck for Jo's ears only. She squeezed his hand in response.

Bucks looked embarrassed.

"Time to go," he called to the two, and they slowly unfolded from their passionate embrace and climbed back up the incline hand in hand.

"Are you ok, Tullie?" asked Jo, stepping forward.

'You should have told him, Jo,' she heard Tullie say in her head, and was glad of the darkness that hid her white face.

'Keep out of my head,' raged Jo.

'Why?' asked Tullie, standing face on to Jo now. 'You want to get in mine, don't you?'

"I'm fine, Jo, thanks," she answered out loud, moving past her to the car, and Matt was relieved.

So was Bucks. They had to get to Brierly Hall fast. Time was running out.

*****

The Hall was in darkness, Matt saw, as they drove slowly through the open gates. A few metres up the drive they were waved to a stop.

"You took your sweet time," growled Anjie. "We thought we'd have to go without you. I even brought her along in case," he said tersely, pointing towards where Myra sat in the front seat of his truck.

"Where do you want us?" asked Matt, taking the lead now, Meryck noted.

"They're expecting you, Matt," he said, "but I'd like to come with you, if I may."

"Me too," offered Rick, and as the three of them crunched their way up to the front door, Matt had a strong vision of the Three Musketeers in his mind.

"One for all then . . ," he whispered, trying to choke back a laugh, then the door opened and the laugh died on his lips. Miller was there, clutching at his chest, and gesturing wildly towards the basement.

"Miller! Miller!" called Matt cradling his frail old body as he laid him gently on the ground, while Meryck gestured back to Anjie. "What's up, Man? Are you ok?" but all he got was a rasping sound. Miller had been stabbed, he realised, his lungs gasping for air.

"Tullie! Tullie!" called Matt, anxiously, and then she was there, wrapping Miller in healing, her sama coming at will now, and Matt could feel the old man cease to struggle as his airways knitted together again.

"Meme?" asked Matt fearfully, and again Miller pointed downwards.

"Go!" said Tullie, "I've got him!" and he raced for the stairs, Bucks at his heels.

Tullie watched him go, noticing he too had a Protector. The bond between them was strong, she mused, grateful that he had backup. Then Jo hunkered down beside her, and she knew this woman would be part of her life for a long time to come. Together, they half-lifted, half-dragged Miller to the kitchen, settling him gently into his battered old soft chair; sleep would do the rest now.

Matt burst into the lab, Meryck and Rick close at his heels, Bucks bringing up the rear, followed by Anjie and his men. There was no sign of Meme but the entrance to the tunnel lay wide open, the guiding lights glimmering softly in the darkness. Pushing Matt to the side, Meryck drew his gun, nodding back to Anjie.

"Matt, we take it from here," he said urgently, including Bucks in his look. "You need to stay here and look out for Tullie and Jo."

"You three," gestured Anjie, "you're with Bucks," and they stepped into the semi-darkness gingerly, weapons at the ready.

"Come on, Matt!" said Bucks. "Let's go!" and Matt hesitated briefly before delving into his pocket and throwing the key to Meryck.

He trudged upstairs, Bucks leading and the three at his back, his mind in overdrive. Someone from inside the house had done this, he realised. The perimeter was sealed; had been sealed since nightfall. Possibly the same person who had cut their cables? Miller had been agitated because they'd stayed too long, hadn't he? Who could that be? Who might Miller and Meme be harbouring or protecting? Who would want them dead? He shook his head. He wasn't getting anywhere! He was asking the wrong questions! Or maybe he was asking of the wrong one!

"How's he doing?" he asked Tullie, coming into the kitchen loudly, Miller starting awake at the sound.

440

"I tried to stop her," he whimpered, reaching out to Matt, "but she wouldn't stop. She's gone for the boss," he sobbed.

"What's she going to do?" Matt asked urgently, holding his gnarled old hand gently, and Miller's eyes flew upwards, towards the ceiling.

Bucks was on it in a flash. Throwing a gun to Jo, he took the steps three at a time, two of the squad on his heels. He found the adults cowering in the back room; six patients and a doctor, their eyes wide with fear as they crashed into the room. He read them perfectly, at least the patients, and they responded gratefully.

"It's ok," he said. "You're safe with me. I'm going to leave these two guys to look after you."

Their relief was palpable but the doctor just stared at them strangely.

"Keep an eye on that one," he instructed them quietly, as he left. "The six are ok. They're on the same wavelength as me."

*****

"She's already brought out six," Bucks reported, "and a doctor."

"The transgenics," muttered Miller. "She went for them first. Your grandad's life work realised," he opened up. "They're not fully, what do you call it," and he searched around for the right word.

"Ripe," Tullie filled in, and all eyes turned to her.

"They're not fully ripe," she answered in full, "like foetal growth. They're not fully birthed yet. But soon," she finished.

"What!" said an astounded Bucks. "You mean those

441

'patients' upstairs are babies?"

"No, not babies fully yet," she said slowly, eyeing him closely.

"But . . ," he began, confused.

'But, you spoke with them already, didn't you?' he heard Matt say.

'You spoke with them?' asked Tullie, incredulous now.

'So. . .,' he said back belligerently.

'Well, in my culture, that makes you a daddy,' grinned Tullie, and Matt laughed out loud.

"Care to fill us all in on the joke?" asked Jo acerbically, looking at Bucks who was shaking his head violently, his eyes on stalks.

"Looks like Bucks found some friends upstairs, Ma'am," answered Matt solemnly.

"Miller," said Matt, softly, "are these transgenics offshoots of Man-x by any chance?"

"Who else?" grumbled the old man, nodding comfortably now that he was sure he was going to make it.

Matt looked at Tullie and she shook her head wonderingly. She could feel no malice in them; just the opposite. They were healers; their life's work to heal in body, mind and spirit.

"He always believed in the good of it," mumbled Miller, then the sound of gentle snoring filled the kitchen.

"Well, I'll be dammed," said Matt, to no one in particular.

"Bucks, watch that doctor in case he does something foolish," he told his friend. After a dark glance in his direction, Bucks slowly made his way back up the stairs.

Looking at Jo, Tullie let her have something, and watched as her expression changed from curiosity to incredulity.

'They can't be!' she stuttered.

'They are!' replied Tullie firmly.

"Matt," called Tullie softly, "let's get Myra in here. I bet your grandad will want to catch up with her as soon as possible."

CHAPTER 65

Oswald prowled the bedroom waiting for his guests, tapping the printouts against his thigh.

"Welcome, my dear," he purred at Carla as they thrust her through the door.

"Please make yourself comfortable," he grinned, pointing to the bed, watching Boris while they secured him to the chair. "I'll be with you in a second!"

She stood defiantly by the dressing table. Boris steadied himself for the 'Carla effect' but Oswald was talking again.

"You'll want to see these, my dear," he gestured towards her. Then strode forward and shoved the pictures under her nose.

"One Boris Polanski," he said silkily, then pulled them back to compare them overtly with the man sitting in front of him.

"Funny," he said quietly, his voice devoid of emotion, "you don't look a bit like him! Why's that, I wonder?"

"Carla, my dear," he added, turning to give her his full attention, "do you know the answer?"

"Hmm, I thought not," he replied, backhanding Boris across the mouth, and blood trickled down his chin and onto his shirt.

Holding the pictures close again, he regarded Boris evenly.

"No, they still don't match," he said. "Maybe a nose

adjustment will help," and he thumped him full in the face, knocking him backwards onto the floor. The lackeys rushed to right him again.

"Hmm, no improvement yet," mused Oswald innocently, punching him in the ribs, doubling him over sideways.

"Well, that's a little better," he surmised.

"What do you think, dear?" he asked smoothly.

Carla said nothing, her eyes betraying her inner turmoil. He laughed indulgently.

"What would you suggest, my dear?" he asked again, brushing a stray strand of hair from her face. She didn't move. Time for 'the Carla effect' now, Boris begged silently, but she was working her own angle. Inwardly he groaned. She didn't have a chance with Oswald.

"Hmmm," he commented again, letting his hand drop, and adopted another angle. Without warning, he drew his gun and pointed it straight at Boris's forehead. This time, he was pleased to see her eyes widen involuntarily. He had her!

"One shot, Carla, and it's all over," he said coldly.

"Now, tell me who he is?" he demanded.

"I don't know," she whispered, grabbing at the dressing table for support.

"No!" she shouted in anguish as Oswald's finger closed on the trigger. "I don't know! My father sent him!"

"Ah, is that so?" said Oswald, looking Boris in the eye. "Now who told you that, my dear?"

"He did," she answered weakly.

"Mmm, I see," said Oswald, who clearly didn't see at all.

"But who is he, Carla?" he asked. "He's not Boris Polanski for sure," thrusting the pictures in front of her face, tiring of the game quickly.

Carla looked from the pictures to Boris, her face a study in confusion.

Without warning, Oswald grabbed her, pinning her arms behind her back in one swift move and turning her before him to face Boris. She screamed in fright and he hit her hard in the side, doubling her over in pain. Grabbing her at the waist, he flung her onto the bed.

"Out," he shouted, and the room emptied quickly.

"Now let's see what daddy's little girl is good for," he grinned maliciously, loosening his belt.

Carla groaned on the bed unable to move, her eyes beseeching Boris to save her.

"Stop!" he called, buying time desperately. "I'll tell you everything."

"So you will," replied Oswald silkily, letting his trousers fall to the floor and sitting heavily on the bed beside her, his hand caressing her thigh.

"I'm not Boris Polanski," he said slowly, following Oswald's hand.

"That I know already," replied Oswald, letting his hand wander further up. Carla cringed and rolled up into a ball. "Tell me something I don't know, and fast," he warned, digging his fingers into the tender skin.

"My real name is Angelo," began Boris, "and. . ." A loud commotion started outside the door drowning out his words. Oswald swore magnificently! Then the door burst open, saving him further disclosure.

446

"Sir! Sir!" breathed the technician. "Mahler's gone, Sir! We've lost him!"

Oswald was already at the door, buckling up his belt as he went.

"Watch them!" he shouted.

"I'll be right back, love! Don't go anywhere," he flung back at Carla before the door slammed shut with a bang.

Boris watched the guard impassively, and the look was returned. Leaning over, he spat. Blood from his battered mouth flew towards the guard who looked back with distaste. Carla sobbed uncontrollably on the bed. Boris spat again, this time catching the guard's shoe. It worked a treat! He moved towards Boris, fist raised to hit him in the face, and Boris lunged forward to meet him, his head connecting powerfully with his sternum. He heard the crack, as did Carla. She was on him in a second, banging his head on the ground the way she had seen Boris dismiss Bowen earlier.

"Untie me!" called Boris. "Leave him! He's done for!"

"Why should I untie you?" she asked wildly. "I don't know who you are!"

"I'm you're only way out of here!" he replied tersely. They only had seconds. He had to get through to her instantly.

"Untie me!" he roared, and this time she jumped, obeying instantly.

Glancing around the room, he spotted the thumb drive Oswald had left behind. Grabbing it swiftly, he pushed ahead of her out the door dragging her behind him. Luck was with them; they saw no one. Reaching the railings, he climbed across and held out his hand to her.

"Come on, Carla!" he called. "This is the only way!"

Then as she stood stock still, fear etched across her face, they were spotted. Grabbing her unceremoniously as bullets whistled in their direction, he hauled her over the side and they plunged awkwardly into the ocean.

Oswald pulled himself away from the search for Mahler and dashed below. It took only a millisecond to recognise that the drive was gone! The groaning form of the guard caught his attention. Drawing his gun, he poured its contents into the man.

"Track the other two," he ordered coldly, returning to the Control Room. He'd lost Mahler but he'd play the hand he had for the moment. Twirling the knobs brought the two blips on screen, moving behind them fast. He had time for a quick decision only.

"Keep them on screen!" he roared. "Increase speed for Greenway. Douse the lights. We go in blind. Lock it down!"

Within seconds, the ship was on silent protocol, only the faint lights from Boris's and Carla's blips visible in the darkness.

"Sir," whispered the operator, excitedly. "We have another echo! Coming up quickly on the two!"

"Explain," growled Oswald from the darkness.

"I think it's a sub, Sir," he replied, cautiously now, "and it's surfacing."

They watched the scene play out on radar. The dots that were Boris and Carla came together and then instantly disappeared as the sub dived for deeper waters.

"I've lost them, Sir," reported the operator unnecessarily. No one dared breathe.

"Five minutes out, Sir," he continued uncertainly.

"Battle stations!" roared Oswald, and the darkness shimmered with silent motion.

*****

"Well, what's it to be, Maggie?" asked Jake, out loud for all to hear.

"For God's sake, Maggie," burst in BB. "Help us out here!"

"What do you want that is any different from the others?" she asked coldly, ignoring BB and Jake, focusing solely on Guidrius.

"What you're doing here won't save humanity, Maggie," he replied quietly, as if they had all the time in the world. "It'll only complicate things; prolong things. It's not everything."

"What others?" interrupted BB again but Maggie was looking for answers in Guidrius and wouldn't be deterred.

"I'm past help," she told him. "Why should I care?"

"Maggie, please!" begged BB.

Guidrius looked at her intently.

"There's damage, for sure," he acknowledged, "but beyond help, no; not if you want it."

He felt no uncertainty in her, only logic, and he was puzzled. Yet he waited patiently and she was grateful to him for that. Mahler wanted the patients. They had all the processes and antibodies he required, not to mention ransom opportunities. Oswald wanted the bludgeoning transgenics to loose an army of Man-x's on the world. What did she want? She'd never asked the question before since it seemed irrelevant. She'd never had an alternative to living in this place. She wasn't human anymore. Ostenwalder had seen to that before they locked him up. What had he wanted, she wondered? Ah yes, to live forever! Well, he'd got that but maybe not the way he really wanted, she thought.

"What do you want?" Guidrius interrupted her.

"I don't know!" she answered truthfully.

"May I make a suggestion," he offered gently, coercing her slowly, while Jake and BB watched anxiously. She was a broken soul, in a broken body.

She nodded, waiting.

"Come with us," he encouraged, holding out his hand to her. "See the outside once again. And take the time to find out what you want away from this place. I promise you, I will help you every step of the way."

His sincerity burned through her defences and a small sliver of the old hopeful Maggie found its way to the fore. Reaching to the console above the bed, she pushed the alert and the facility burst into frenzied activity.

"We have to hurry," she said. "It's almost time."

CHAPTER 66

Ben walked with purpose in his step through the white corridors towards the kitchen, and Becca. All at once there seemed to be extra activity everywhere and he wondered if he'd been rumbled but people passed him by as if he just didn't exist! Well, keeping to himself all those years had to have some benefit, he thought grimly, avoiding eye contact.

"Becca," he called quietly as he pushed the door open but there was no one inside. Glancing around, he could see that her laptop was on her desk, open, so she had to be somewhere close. The kitchen was in a bit of a mess, unfinished meals strewn around the tables and chairs hurriedly pushed back.

"Becca," he called again, but still no answer.

Backing out into the now-deserted corridor, he wondered where she might be. Had she gone ahead without him thinking their plan was dead now that Man-x was out of the picture? He had to be sure. Six minutes had gone already! Acting nonchalantly, he headed for the elevators, and got his first inkling of trouble. They weren't working! The alarm ran, directing all non-essential personnel to the East Wing. So that's where everybody was rushing to, he thought! And that's where I'm headed too, he realised! Pushing through to the stairwell, he began his ascent.

Man-x stopped dead on the floor below. Someone else had entered the stairwell! But he relaxed as the steps led upwards, and he followed at a safe distance. Ostenwalder rattled around in his head, excited about something but Man-x couldn't tell what. At one stage, the steps ahead faltered and he thought he'd have to deal with the man but then they restarted, to stop again at the Exit door to the Second Floor, the same one he wanted to access. He smelt fear for the first time and quickly realised that whoever this was, he was on a mission as well, and a covert one at that. He waited in silence.

Ben stopped to gather his senses at the door to Ostenwalder's ward. For several seconds now he had felt a presence behind him and fear gave his feet wings. But now he was at the door, he was out of breath. Twenty minutes to go! The corridor ahead was deserted. Then he saw her! Becca! She was talking animatedly to a frail old lady he'd never seen before. Taking a deep breath, he walked forward, letting the door slide shut behind him.

"Becca," he called, urgently. "We've got to go! This place will fall apart in twenty!"

They turned to look at him, horror registering in their eyes, and he shrugged.

"What?" he asked aggrieved, walking briskly towards them. "I only did what we decided. Come on! Let's go! Who's this?"

But they remained rooted to the spot.

"What?" he asked, angrily this time, and Becca pointed behind him and suddenly he was afraid to look back. He slid to a stop, feet away from them, realising for the first time that several doors were open and their occupants missing. But that was not where their attention was focussed. Slowly, his heart in his mouth, he turned to face the awesome presence of Man-x up close, and, very much alive.

The man-creature filled the corridor entirely, his head brushing the ceiling while his swarthy legs brushed the side walls. His brush with death had unsettled him; his amethyst eyes shone feverishly but it was his body that held their gaze. From foot to forehead, swirls of silver and purple meshed and spun, twisted and wheeled, while on both wrists bands of blue-white glowed serenely in the midst of it all. His huge hands dripped blood from their encounters with the walls, and his voice, when he spoke, seemed to come from the bottom of a deep, deep barrel.

"Move," he intoned, and they flattened themselves against the walls but still they felt the brush of his cold body as he passed.

"You're alive!" Ben called out to his departing back, despite his fear. He was really, really glad that he hadn't been the cause of this creature's demise after all. Man-x looked back enigmatically. These were no threat to him. Ignoring them, he stepped past them to Ostenwalder's room.

"Well, come on then," croaked the old man, shoving his skinny head out the door. "What the hell are you hanging about there for, gawking at each other? Let's go!"

"We have to move all of them," the old woman began, and Man-x stopped in his tracks and turned to look deeply into her eyes. Something about her reminded him of another place, another old woman, but it wasn't her.

"Go on," continued Meme. "I'll get them!"

"You don't have time!" Ben called to her fast retreating back. He was astonished at how light she was on her feet; how fast she moved over the ground. He heard Ostenwalder guffaw with laughter at his innocence.

"What you think we've been doing here, boy?" he gloated. "Making clothes pegs?" and guffawed again.

"We got to stop this once and for all, Ben!" called Becca, hastening after Meme, leaving Ben in the corridor with Ostenwalder and Man-x. As he pondered this odd predicament, they too turned and hastened away.

"Wait!" he called after them, but it was too late. He had five minutes left. He'd never make it to his consul but he should be able to access the mainframe from any terminal. Turning, he dashed back the way he had come, straight into the path of Anjie and his men.

"Stop!" yelled Anjie, and Ben froze instantly.

"I gotta get in there!" he roared, despite the gun levelled at his chest.

"Why?" asked Anjie, his eyes closing to slits.

"That's Ben Smith," called Meryck, rushing forward and pushing Anjie's gun aside.

"What's wrong, Ben?" he asked calmly. "What's so urgent?"

"The building," fumbled Ben, pointing incoherently at his watch. "We've less than four minutes!" he gasped.

"What do you need?" asked Meryck, grabbing hold of his arm.

"Ben! Ben!" he shook him firmly. "What do you need, man?" nodding Anjie and the others ahead.

"Access," fumbled Ben again, then more clearly. "I need terminal access! In there! In that lab! The electrics are set to overload in four minutes but if I can get through I can overwrite the instructions!"

"Go!" shouted Meryck.

"Paul? Where's Paul?" he roared. "Get in there with Ben and see what you can do!"

"Ben!" he called suddenly. "Where's Becca?" and Ben pointed ahead.

Running at full pelt, Meryck set off to join the others.

*****

"Where do we start?" asked Paul grabbing a terminal, but Ben was already up and running.

"Code?" he called and Ben responded with BE-CcA.

"Nice!" he muttered as the server booted and they were in.

"Multi fronts," called Ben, working furiously. "You move the elevators; they're our best exit. Right now we need them to move the patients. Just Elevator 2 and 4 will do," he added.

"Done!" Paul called back. "What's next?"

"The force field," muttered Ben, beginning to sweat as the indicator dials continued to climb. It was taking too long! Something wasn't right!

"What about the bloody force field, Ben?" shouted Paul now, and Ben reeled off the disable algorithm. But it was already down! But noting Ben's accelerated anxiety, Paul didn't mention it as he joined him.

"What's this?" he asked. "The bad boy?"

"Central boiler," Ben nodded. "It should be cooling down by now," he added pointing to the dials.

Paul whistled.

"What are you using?" he asked, ideas spiking through his brain.

One by one they called out possibilities to each other but discarded them as soon as they hit the ether. The time clicked down to sixty seconds.

"We're not going to make this, man," said Ben. "Get out now. I'll keep working! It's all my fault anyhow."

455

Ignoring him, Paul walked back to his own terminal and began to run simulation after simulation while Ben worked at the interface.

"Try this," called out Paul excitedly. "It should buy us some time!"

Tapping in the digits as fast as he could, Ben was chronically aware of the ticking clock. Hitting the enter button, he stepped back and waited. They had done all they could. Sweat poured down both their faces. Ten seconds and still the temperature rose. Nine, eight, seven, and they prepared for the end. Then on five seconds there was a slight dip, then more. With two seconds left the needle had exited the Red Zone. They were saved by a whisker! They'd done it! Greenway was safe! Before them the needle kept dipping, down and down, until finally it entered the Safe Zone and they drew deep breaths to steady themselves.

"That was a nifty piece of programming, Paul," offered Ben.

"Not bad yourself," answered Paul holding out his hand "Whew! That was the fastest bit of work I've seen anyone do! Been an honour working with you! You even got the force field down before I could!"

Ben stood stock still; he didn't do mistakes.

"What do you mean?" he asked Paul.

"What?" said Paul.

"About the force field," prompted Ben, "it being down already?"

"Yeah," said Paul, picking up his ears. Something wasn't right. He could see it on Ben's face.

"It came down before I finished entering the algorithm," he explained. "I thought you did it, on auto-pilot, you know.

456

That was one long string of characters!"

But Ben was shaking his head, his mind whirring. He had to go back to the Control Room. Someone else was here and he wanted to know who!

"I gotta go," he shouted, suddenly and rushed for the door.

"Hey! Wait up!" called Paul. "I'm coming with you, man!"

"Whatever," Ben flung back at him, running full pelt for the elevators.

*****

Guidrius and Maggie waited patiently on the stairs for Jake and BB to catch up. The elevators had been disabled; the facility under lockdown, the guards posted to the perimeter. She was in no hurry. She knew where they were headed. One more level to go and they'd access the old labs. She didn't know what they'd find there. This level hadn't been used in years. Passing the Exit door to the Control Area she paused briefly as she saw Ben rush headlong down the corridor, followed by someone she didn't recognise. He wasn't supposed to be here; she had evacuated everyone half an hour ago!

"Wait," she called, stepping out after the two. But Guidrius followed her out, motioning to Jake and BB to continue downwards.

Stepping lightly, she flattened herself against the wall, to peer through the glass. Ben was in a major flap; she had to get to him before he broadcast the news. He seemed to have found a helper too, she noted.

"What's the matter," said Guidrius, and she jumped. She hadn't heard him follow her.

"It's Ben," she explained. "I'm afraid he's up to no good.

He should have left along with the others."

"The others?" queried Guidrius mildly.

"Mmm," she said absently, and he could see she was distracted.

"Where did they go?" he pushed.

"East Wing," she replied absently, stepping forward and drawing her gun. "They can take boats from there to the mainland without being observed."

"What you going to do?" he asked her, fearing the worst.

"Stop Ben," she replied calmly, looking back at him emotionlessly.

"Let's see what he's up to first," he suggested, and she agreed as he knew she would.

*****

"Gotta back this up, man," called Paul urgently.

"Do what you have to," replied Ben, punching at the keys like a madman.

"There! Look!" he shouted.

"What? Where?" answered Paul, squinting at his screen. "I don't see anything! It's dark out there!"

"Exactly!" roared Ben now, throwing the image up on the big screen where he began to pan in and about furiously. "It's dark and it shouldn't be!"

"Look! There!" called Paul, and they saw the shadow of the Glory Rising sneak around the east side of the island.

"So, that's who took down the force field," sighed Ben.

"Who is that?" asked Paul.

"Oswald," replied Ben dully. "He's come for his products. We gotta get out of here!"

"Hang on, Ben," continued Paul evenly. "You say, he's come for his products. What products?"

In answer, Ben flicked a switch and the transgenics ward flickered on screen.

"Something's wrong!" he said. "It's too quiet!" Then from behind a bed, they could see the body on the floor.

"We really must go! Now!" said Ben again, starting for the door.

"No!" said Paul. "We must stay and help the others! We've got eyes everywhere here! I need your help, man. This is your system!"

"Stop right where you are," said Maggie from the doorway. "It's over, Ben," and she levelled the gun at him.

"No, it's not!" shouted Paul, and he pushed Ben out of the way as Maggie fired, letting off several rounds in her direction as he fell.

"She's gone," said Guidrius calmly, stepping over her body into the room. "You guys ok? Have you got them on camera?" he asked an astounded duo.

"Who?" said Paul guardedly, training his gun on Guidrius.

"Anjie needs this info," he replied. "Now, Paul!"

"Ben," he continued, without taking his eyes off the screen. "Kate and Jenny are fine; they're waiting for you in Jake's place, Traveller's Mountain. Paul's right. We do need your help. How can we broadcast to the guys without letting everybody know?"

Straggling up, stupefied and delighted by the events of the last few moments, he pointed to where Paul could manage the system.

"We've got company," said Guidrius, watching the screen carefully.

"We know," they replied in unison. "The Glory Rising just docked, east."

"Then, what's this on Skyway's side?" he asked, pointing to a slow moving blackness on the screen, his keen vision making the mark before they did.

"Paul, tell Anjie he's got company on both sides," he said, rushing from the room. "He's got to get out of here now! This whole place is going to go up!"

CHAPTER 67

"Track her in on these exact co-ordinates," said Mahler, handing the paper to Bill.

"We'll hit the force field full-on," whispered Bill, reading the figures.

"No, we won't!" replied Mahler confidently. "The Glory docked the other side of the island five minutes ago. We're clear to go; silently, now!"

As Bill manoeuvred the Belle into position he could hear scuffling as the men came up top, lugging their gear. Cutting the engines, he could hear the slight splash as the first three slipped overboard. He saw Mahler fix his watch, co-ordinating time with Friday. Then Friday went below for a short time, giving Mahler a thumbs-up when he returned. Minutes passed slowly as they waited for the signal from the Island.

"Keep this exact position if you know what's good for you," growled Mahler and then they too were gone, slipping over the side into the dark water.

*****

Cruising into Bear's Lake, the Glory hugged Greenway's coastline, downing the force field seconds before access. Her deck was black with combat troops prepared for battle. This was a take-and-destroy mission. The only thing he needed was his six protégées. The rest was collateral damage. Time to start anew, he smiled. He wondered if Maggie had carried out his instructions to the letter?

"Anything?" he asked the radar operator.

"Not so far, Sir," was the reply.

"Keep your eyes open," he instructed, needlessly. Everyone kept their eyes open around him.

"Bring up the doors," he called, and on the Island, a set of massive steel doors drew back noiselessly and the Glory snuggled inside. Instantly, the lights came up and he could see she had indeed followed his instructions. Lines of ancillary staff waited for salvation, and he didn't disappoint them.

"Fire at will," he called, and the sound of gunfire rattled around the sealed cove.

*****

"They're here!" called Anjie, as the distant sound of gunfire echoed through the eerily empty facility. "Move!"

Eleven wheelchairs rattled along the corridor towards the elevators pushed by the medics that had stayed behind to look after them, and they manfully held IVs aloft, or carried cartons of medicines; anything they could bring along that would continue the treatment they had started.

"We need more elevators now!" Anjie swore at the cameras, and Paul and Ben worked feverishly to get 1 and 3 working. As they pushed the keys for descent, Paul noticed it first.

"Ben!" he called urgently. "The patch! It's not holding!" The temperature dial had begun to rise again.

"Anjie!" he roared. "We've got more trouble! It's going to blow from inside! I can give you two minutes tops!"

"Copy that!" replied Anjie, going back to hustling the people along. They weren't going to make it. It was too tight!

"Paul," he called, "can you get me one more?"

"Not sure, man," replied a frustrated Paul.

"If we cut life support on the bottom levels to minimum we may buy another few seconds," shouted Ben.

"Hang on," replied Paul.

"Anjie," Paul called into his mouthpiece, "is there a safety door on the mainland side? Can you get your air supply from there if we cut you off here?"

There was a hurried discussion.

"Yes! Do it!" called Anjie, and Paul nodded to Ben.

"Rick! Meryck!" Get your arses down here immediately! We've got two to go!" spat Anjie into the com.

"Paul! Ben! You copy?" he asked.

"Copy that!" replied Paul. "We're outta here!"

"Ben!" he called. "Let's go!"

But Ben was searching the screens frantically.

"Who you looking for, man?" asked Paul, beginning to sweat. They'd just make it if they went now!

"Becca!" replied Ben. "I can't see Becca!"

"Have you tried the kitchen?" asked Paul, and Ben looked at him loftily.

"Well, she did work there," said Paul, sarcastically.

"Come on, man! Get a move!" and he pushed Ben aside and keyed in the kitchen.

Sure enough, Becca was there, but she wasn't alone. Three figures silently pushed through the dining area heading to where she hid, grasping her laptop, behind the serving counter.

"Shit!" roared Ben, rushing for the door.

"What do you think you can do?" roared Paul, grabbing his shoulder and spinning him around.

"We do this together! Understand!" said Paul evenly now, drawing his weapon.

"Anjie, man!" he said into his mouthpiece. "We're heading to the kitchen. Becca's in there; three hostiles heading her way."

"Copy!" said Anjie. "Good luck!"

"Copy!" said Rick. "I'm on my way!"

"Me too!" said Meryck. "Don't bolt the backdoor just yet!"

*****

The lower levels on the west side were empty, the ground dusty, the air stale but the generators still hummed gently as they set the explosives. They didn't worry about leaving evidence behind; nobody would ever see it. Their job done, they headed back to rendezvous with Mahler and Friday.

The noise in the kitchen drew their attention and they swept in to sweep the area.

"Sweeping the kitchen," they reported in.

"We don't have time for food," roared Mahler. "Get up to the next level asap!"

"Copy," said the leader, pulling up only feet away from Becca and signalling the other two outside and up.

Becca watched nervously as the last of the transfer reached its destination. They were at the door when the silence was broken by 'Upload Complete!' Swirling, they targeted her area immediately. Without weapons, she was completely vulnerable. Rising slowly, she raised her hands in the air.

"Don't shoot! Don't shoot!" she called. "I'm just the chef!"

"We got a live one," radioed the leader.

"What the fuck you telling me that for," roared Mahler. "We take no prisoners on this one!"

Becca watched as his finger tightened on the trigger, then she dived for cover. The space around her was spattered with bullets before another sound caught her ears; the sound of bodies falling!

"Becca!" called Meryck. "You ok, Becca?"

"Becca!" called Rick, as Paul and Ben burst through the door.

"I'm ok," she called faintly, struggling to her feet. Rick was there in an instant, grabbing her in his arms, and holding her like he'd never let her go!

"Hi, Petal," said Meryck, tapping her on the shoulder. "We got to go! Now!" and he wiped his eyes on his sleeve as he turned away.

"Daddy! I'm so sorry," she grabbed at his departing form, and he caught her to him and pushed her ahead of him roughly towards the door.

"Go!" he roared, rushing after her. "They'll be plenty of time for that!"

"Well, what are you two doing hanging around?" rasped

Rick, as Paul went to grab the laptop.

"Leave it! We don't have time!" he shouted, grabbing them both and hauling then towards the door. Behind them, the heard Mahler's voice loud and clear calling to his men. Ben checked his watch as they fled.

"The stairs!" he called out. "We must take the stairs! There's not enough power left for the lifts!"

*****

"Damn! These bloody lifts aren't working," Oswald swore, before turning for the stairs, taking them two at a time. He expected no resistance but he took no chances.

"You and you, that way," he said, and he waited for his henchmen to get in place. The quiet of the Second Floor was broken by gunfire below them.

"Check that out!" he ordered, striding forward, the Transgenic Lab right in front of him now. His excitement rising, he palms felt sweaty, and he brushed his forehead absent-mindedly. It was hot in here!

The explosion caught him straight in the face as the lab exploded before him, taking him and his men with it. All at once, big and small bangs could be heard around the facility as the systems overloaded. On the bottom level, the doors to the cells crashed open but there was only one prisoner that it benefited. Jed struggled out through the dust and the grime, gasping for breath. The only way out was up, and he staggered towards the elevator but it wasn't working. The building shook as the generators exploded, going off in sequence. Then the emergency lights failed and he was in darkness. But he'd been in worst places before, he consoled himself, methodically searching for the stairs. Climbing slowly, he searched out sounds above him; there were others making their way up too. A lifetime of stealth and cunning came to his rescue, and he went on auto-pilot.

466

Then the shooting started and he retreated a little but it was no use. The air was dwindling. He had to get out. Fleeing downstairs, Meryck and Becca had come face to face with Mahler and Friday.

"It's going to blow, Mahler," shouted Meryck. "There's no way out! Give up now!"

"Or else what?" cooed back a complacent Mahler, and he and Friday retreated downwards a little.

"They want to come down," whispered Mahler, "but why?"

"Don't know," replied Friday.

"Go see what's down there, while I hold then off," ordered Mahler, and then Friday was coming right at Jed, at the run. Moving from pure instinct in the dark, Jed lashed out as he passed within an inch of him on the landing, catching him in the neck. Checking he was dead, he laid him down quietly and checked for his gun.

"Anything?" whispered Mahler hoarsely, and Jed raced up the stairs.

"Just this," he called loudly, and as he emptied the gun into Mahler's chest he felt he could hear the hur-rah from the other side and feel them slapping his back. It didn't work out the way he'd planned but he'd got the job done. Bending down, he slipped the bracelet onto Mahler's limp wrist. But vengeance wasn't the sweet trip he'd expected. Instead, there was emptiness, a nothingness like he'd never felt before. Now, he was truly on his own.

"Jed?" called Meryck incredulously, above the sound of the next explosion. Debris plummeted down the steps covering them with dust.

"It's safe!" called Jed, throwing down the gun.

Then Rick was there, pushing Jed ahead of him.

"This way! Quickly now!" he called, and they followed doubled-over in his wake.

*****

"You must close the doors now, Anjie," Meme called, as light from the explosions flashed back up the tunnel.

"Ten seconds," replied Anjie tersely, "ten seconds more!"

The seconds ticked away far too quickly, punctured by louder and more ferocious blasts as Greenway collapsed in on itself but still there was no sound or sight of them.

"The button!" she cried. "Anjie, you've got to hit it or we're all dead!"

Looking around their serious faces, he pushed. The doors shuddered initially, and then silently crept towards each other. A huge explosion wracked the island and the doors stopped moving briefly. He turned away, his heart in his boots. Suddenly, there was a thumping sound as the closing doors hit an object in their path and turning back he saw the bent half of a crutch sticking through the slight space.

"Get the doors open," he roared. "They made it!"

*****

In the dim light, Jake staggered along the tunnel, stopping regularly to catch his breath. Meryck, Rick and Becca followed; Ben and Paul in the lead. Then a helping hand reached for Jake, and young strength supported him. Meryck let him go. Who was he to say what happens between a father and his child.

CHAPTER 68

In Brierly, the kitchen shook as each new explosion wracked Greenway. Bits of plaster slid off the old walls and fell unheeded onto the floor. Miller slept on peacefully. Matt and Tullie looked at each other nervously. Now that the moment was here, neither was ready to see what fate had to offer. In the face of so much destruction, they felt they were the babies, not those waiting above. Jo and Myra only gave them a passing glance as they left the room. A shadow surprised them, but it was only Guidrius and they followed him quietly to the back of the house.

"It's done," he told them, the light from Greenway playing across his face. "They're all safe."

"All?" asked Tullie tremulously, and he knew whom she meant. In the semi- darkness, she saw him nod.

"Something's different about him, Tullie," he said.

"I know," she said, "I felt it when we met. His name is Rak-na" she continued, and Guidrius drew a deep breath. In that instant, she knew he knew, had always known. Why hadn't he told her? What was he waiting for?

"We saw Silvamon," Matt interrupted the awkward moment.

"You saw Silvamon!" Guidrius said with a sharp intake of breath but before Matt could reply a large shadow detached itself from the trees and Tullie's sama glowed. They stared at each other in the light from the fire, neither party moving, each taking in the measure of the other. Then Greenway exploded, tossing them to the ground in its fury. When Tullie looked up again, Man-x was gone.

Then a skinny figure cart-wheeled towards them, cackling madly, and as Tullie drew back, Matt stood in front of her to protect her.

"So this is the Queen bee!" screeched Ostenwalder.

"Grandad!" squawked a surprised Matt.

"Ah! Matt, me boy! Good to see you again! Hmm, how you've grown. Not as big as I expected, though! Handsome enough! You'll do!" spluttered Ostenwalder, jumping around erratically. "Now, gotta go! Work to do, you know! Where's that Myra?" and from inside they could hear the squeals from the women as he bounced into the kitchen.

"Well, I'll be dammed," said Matt, for the second time that night.

"Where's he gone?" Tullie whispered. "I can't feel him!" and Matt knew it wasn't Ostenwalder she was talking about.

"Let's stay out of this a while," he said, nodding towards the sheds.

Guidrius watched them go, puzzled. He couldn't feel Man-x either. Something wasn't right!

Then the first sound of police sirens wailing reached their ears, pounding past the Hall, destination Greenway. Overhead, the sound of rotor blades hurried their steps.

CHAPTER 69

Johnson waited patiently beside the broken window, watching the glow from Greenway light up the night sky. His mind was elsewhere though, pacing back and forth over the events of the last few days, ordering everything into line, and noting what was still popping up; out of place; unsolved and unaccounted for. The line wouldn't form properly; there were just too many variables, too many twists and turns. But one thing he did know: Tullie was the fulcrum, the centrepiece. And the seals were the keys. He didn't hear them coming and he chided himself roundly for losing concentration.

"Found your Pandora's box, Sir," the commander said, shrugging a small crate off his shoulder onto the floor in front of Johnson, and stepping back and ushering in the others. "We found seven in all. Is that the lot?"

Johnson didn't reply immediately. He watched impassively while they surrounded his position with crates of equal dimension. It was impossible to know for sure.

"I'll need to check," he replied, and waited.

"Oh! Right, Sir," replied the commander. "We'll be back there if you need anything."

"How about a crowbar?" called Johnson as they departed.

"Hey," he called after them loudly. "You checked that these things are safe?"

Waves and grins told him all he wanted to know. Closing curtains across the bare window, he switched on the overhead lights and looked closely at what he got. Pulling his phone from his pocket, he called Meryck and got no reply but Rick answered on the second ring.

"I'm about to open these crates, man. Can you get Tullie to give me the thumbs up before we close shop?"

Guidrius watched them enter the barn, his face a mixture of consternation and fascination. Matt's progress was moving way too fast. What this meant for Silvamon was uncertain. What was not uncertain was that he had to find a way to separate her from him, and fast! He needed time alone to mould her to her role. And time was something neither of them had too much to spare. But first, there was Man-x to deal with.

*****

"Is this everything, Tullie?" asked Johnson, and she took her time before answering him.

"That's all the main pieces. What I don't see is the small pile of fragments I haven't been able to place yet," she replied thoughtfully.

"Do we need them?" asked Rick.

"Maybe; maybe not," she said, looking at him, and he could see the first flecks of amethyst in her powerful green gaze. Matt had noticed them for the first time too, and he looked shocked.

"Tullie," she heard him say, "use your sama and see behind the obvious."

Intrigued that he had seen a way forward she hadn't, she did as he suggested. The small room lit up with a silver glow while Johnson's images flashed and glowed before finally settling into new forms. They could see where the colour joints were out of place and where they really belonged. Tullie pulled the images forward into the air around them and while they watched, she reorganised them to her satisfaction before sealing them into a shape the size of a golf ball which she then plucked from the air and tucked smartly into her pocket letting the sama fade.

"We're good," she said aloud, and Johnson visibly relaxed on the other side of the screen, rubbing his tired eyes and yawning to stay awake. "I've got them! But we still need to keep these safe. They mustn't fall into the wrong hands before I get to use them or I cannot assure you of the outcome."

"Traveller's Mountain?" nodded Johnson to Rick.

"No, here!" interrupted Jake from the doorway. "I want them here when we interrogate Jed. I want to know what he knows!"

"Now Matt," he continued, "can we do that bug removal now? I've got a whole lot of tagged people out there, including me!"

Matt looked at him dumbfounded. He'd forgotten all about the tags! Reaching into his back pocket, he realised with horror that Carney had the instruments in Travellers Mountain. He'd never get through the cordon outside to retrieve them!

"What's the matter?" asked Anjie joining them and seeing the consternation on Matt's face.

"The tag remover," spluttered Matt, "Carney's got it!"

Anjie looked thoughtful, and reaching for his phone he left the room but stuck his head back in immediately.

"Anyone seen BB?" he asked.

CHAPTER 70

Myra didn't know whether to laugh or cry when Ostenwalder bounded into the kitchen and grabbed her unceremoniously, kissing her full on the lips before Anjie pulled him off her to throw him against the wall.

"Hah!" he chuckled gleefully. "Got yourself a boyfriend then Myra! 'Bout time too! You're no spring chicken anymore but I can fix that if you'd like!"

Myra and Anjie looked thunderous but Ostenwalder was unrepentant. Why change the habit of a lifetime, thought Myra viscously.

"Nobody's fixing nothing," said Meme quietly coming to their rescue. "It's not all it's cracked up to be, you know!"

"Maybe it's time for some more, Meme," said Ostenwalder, kindly now, his eyes gentling as he looked at the frail old woman.

She shook her head.

"When you meddle with nature, you don't know how things will turn out," she whispered, her eyes involuntarily moving upwards.

"Ah! That's where they are!" he cackled and despite Anjie's firm grasp, he slithered away upstairs and now it was Bucks's turn to roar. Then they heard Matt's voice and some semblance of normality returned.

"Anjie," called Tullie from the doorway and he hurried over.

"I think I can help with the tags," she whispered, "but I'll need to talk to Ostenwalder beforehand."

"That would be great, Tullie, but I'm not keen to expose you to that madman just yet."

"But won't that put people in danger?"

"Maybe," he said, "for a short while, at least. I've sent for Carney."

"Ah!" she said knowingly, and he smiled. He didn't mind her in his head; well, part of it, at least. "Let me know if anything changes."

From the shadows, Guidrius overheard the exchange without being observed. Changing into his dog form, he curled up under the stairs and nodded off. He needed all the rest he could get to execute the next part of his plan.

*****

Carney checked behind the fridge and the door swung open silently. Adam grunted with surprise but Carney was already dashing down the stairs, two at a time.

"You know how to work this thing?" he asked, pausing by the dingy, and Adam grinned. He'd give this guy a run for his money for sure!

"Water's a bit low," said Adam, "or else we're missing a step," and Carney noticed the two foot drop to the boat for the first time. By then Adam was down, holding out a hand to Carney.

"This way," said Carney, passing his phone to Adam, who just took one look and started the motor. It hissed into life ever so quietly: pimped, though Adam with satisfaction. These guys had thought of everything!

"Better hang low," he called back to Carney. "It gets a bit tight in places!"

Tight didn't quite describe it, thought Carney on several occasions as the dingy buckled and squelched through apertures he initially thought inaccessible. Adam kept the light focussed downwards; at times, it was only the deeper shadows that revealed the overhangs. Not once did they have to break cover, he marvelled. Then Adam was manoeuvring into a small lit alcove: they were there! And in record time, noted Carney! The welcoming committee of one had nothing to say; he motioned for them to follow and keep alert, and they were off. It took nearly as long as the boat ride to enter the cellar; and the scene that greeted them was grim. It looked everything like a war zone but where were the victims, thought Adam.

"Up," said their guide, and Carney noticed the stairs for the first time.

"Not you," he said to Adam, putting out a swarthy arm to block his way.

Anjie was waiting for him.

"Good man!" he said, and led him into the kitchen.

He started towards Miller but the old guy was too restless so he removed Meme's tag first. Then Jake was there, proffering his arm, and he forgot all about Miller in the line that followed. Tullie moved in his wake, healing the wounds instantly and giving each patient a little more energy to deal with the trauma. Myra watched anxiously, keeping a safe distance should anything go wrong but Carney had it covered, especially with the unusual help he had.

"Just one more," said Jake, leading Carney along the corridor towards a guarded room at the end. Absorbed in her work, Tullie followed calmly, noticing the slumbering Guidrius as she passed. Handcuffed to the bed frame, Jed didn't look up as they entered. Jake stopped Carney from rushing to remove the tag. He needed to be sure Jed wouldn't harm him. But Tullie flew past them both to his side.

"Jed!" she called softly, reaching out to touch him. "Jed! Are you ok? It's me, Tullie!"

But Jed was unresponsive. A dam had been breached with Mahler's death and the freedom he'd so ardently sought had proved an illusion; fool's gold. Instead despair rushed in and cradled him deep in its embrace, and with his energy spent there was no way of fighting back. It was over; all over.

"Get the tag out of him," instructed Jake, while Tullie sobbed quietly by his side. She was intensely distressed by what she found. His life was laid out before her like a road map to hell, and he had shut the door behind him!

"I can't heal him," she cried. "He won't let me in!" and the blood from his new wound dripped slowly down his arm and onto the floor.

"I'll be back," shouted Carney and he dashed for the door leaving Jake and Tullie alone with Jed.

"Sometimes people don't want to be healed," said Jake softly, his voice threatening to break. "It's too painful; too hard to return. I miss him, you know," he gulped. "It's my entire fault! If I'd been there for him, this would never have happened!"

"You can't blame yourself, grandad," she whispered. "He had a choice too! We all do!"

And then she saw it: the choices he had made to keep her safe had kept him apart from Jed and she was mortified!

"But you could have had both of us," she cried, beating at his chest.

"That was never possible, Tullie. You don't know Jed like

I do," he replied sadly, looking into her eyes.

He was completely taken off guard with her next question. "Do you have the other ring with you?"

He nodded.

"Well, let me have it!" she said, taking control, and holding out her hand.

Behind her, Jed stirred. Something was drawing him back and he fought it with every ounce of his remaining strength. Carney burst into the room with the bandages and rushing past the two, he bound Jed's wound tightly. But then Tullie was pushing him aside and reaching for Jed's left hand, she slid Jake's second ring onto his finger. It fitted perfectly! Time stood still in the room and the three eyed each other curiously while they waited for something to happen. Tullie felt it before the others could observe it: the tiniest bit of energy was seeping from the ring into Jed's body, and he began to mumble. Deep in his mind, he was being drawn back and forwards at the same time but it was a short battle. Something had changed. He had to go back! Gritting his teeth, he let the pain back in.

CHAPTER 71

The noise in the barn roused Rak-na. People were talking calmly but the energy was intense.

"Why did you do it, Becca?" asked a male voice.

"Now's not the time, Rick," she answered coldly.

"If not now, when?" he said roughly, and Rak-na knew he was at breaking point.

He felt her shrug. He didn't know what to do. He felt he was intruding but it was they who had come into his space.

"Did you think I wasn't hurting too!" he flung at her. "He was my son too," he sobbed, walking away from where she stood, rooted to the spot.

"I don't want to talk about him!" she whispered fiercely.

"Why not," demanded Rick, angry now, "because you abandoned us both?"

"I didn't abandon you both!" she screamed at him now.

"But you did abandon me," he replied, ever so softly, "and your parents."

"I had a job to do," she answered flatly, turning to go.

"Running away again?" he asked sarcastically, but Rak-na could feel his burning pain in his own chest.

She looked at him for what seemed an eternity then turned and walked out. There was silence for a millisecond then heartbreaking sobs rented the air. Rak-na became alarmed. He didn't know this expression and it filled him with dread. He was ready when he heard the click of the safety being removed. This man deserved better!

*****

Relieved, Johnson began to close the crates. He wouldn't have to send the troops in again. A quiet voice outside the door interrupted him.

"We got a problem, Sir," said the commander. "You might want to douse those lights," and he quickly entered the dark room. "The lookout has informed us that several cars are heading this way."

"Ok," said Johnson, thinking furiously. "Close the backdoor; permanently. And get me two of your best drivers. How long do we have?"

"Five, max," he said, unhurriedly, and Johnson was grateful for his expertise. A minute planning is worth four panicking.

"Which way they coming?" he asked.

"Both sides," was the reply.

"Decoy then," said Johnson, his plan formulated.

"Decoy," agreed the commander calmly, and set off to put his side of the plan into action.

Johnson worked furiously and with a minute to spare they were off; two heading back to Tinakilly and one away. The ground shook once as Johnson spun Jed's truck out of the driveway, in the opposite direction from his pimped ride and Kate's car. With mere seconds to spare he swung into the abandoned quarry. The two police cars screamed by, lights flashing, but it was third vehicle that caught his attention. Inspector A. Gross was in the driver's seat, her red talons gripping the wheel lightly; her eyes feverishly lunging ahead. Rolling down the window, he listened to the noise. They spun past Grant's Cottage and then the noise stopped. He palmed the steering wheel bringing the truck around full circle and drove for Skyway, the devil at his heels.

CHAPTER 72

Bucks was having a hard time staying awake. The room was warm and humid, and the even sound of their breathing filled the air. He could feel Matt close by and he knew he was with Tullie so he didn't interrupt. Getting up from his hard chair he wandered the room quietly using his time to observe the transgenics more closely. They looked human as they slept peacefully, apart from their large size. The sacs surrounding them seemed empty but moved slightly as they breathed. Looking up, he couldn't see where they were attached to: they looked like giant teardrops floating about a foot off the floor. But there was no mucus; no dripping foul essences, like you see in the movies, thankfully. It was all clean, contained and very clever, he decided, even the markings. At first he thought they were all the same but moving closer he could see differences in colour and design. The ones on their backs all seemed the same; it was just their face and upper arms that differed, and then very slightly. He wondered if this would continue to be the case as they matured. Slipping out his phone, he took pictures of each, back and front. They didn't move, just slept on, but in the corner the doctor opened one eyelid slightly before returning to his rest. Bucks didn't notice so absorbed was he in his new family.

"Ah! My babies!" cackled Ostenwalder, bursting into the room. The doctor responded instantly, flying at Ostenwalder, putting himself between him and the transgenics. Then all hell broke loose! As they two grappled awkwardly on the dusty carpet, Jed's screams curdled the air and the transgenics awoke instantly and howled in response. Grabbing his head, Bucks squirmed on the floor in agony, vaguely aware that the two were following suit. It felt like a cold breeze had pushed open the door, and then

Matt was there, and the noise abated as suddenly as it had started.

"Out!" he roared, and as the two were frogmarched away, Ostenwalder glanced back, deep twinkles in his eyes. His grandson was proving to be a lot more than he had ever hoped for! Helping Bucks to his feet, he turned to his siblings. They were quiet now, peaceful again; but watchful, their dark eyes following his every move. A sense of expectation filled the air and Matt felt the trickle of apprehension that passed down Bucks's spine.

"Is it time?" Bucks whispered, his voice tremulous. He wasn't at all sure he wanted to be present for this.

"Nearly," said a voice from behind them, and they turned to see Rak-na stooped in the doorway. A flow of energy oozed about the room and, for an instant, Bucks thought the walls were going to cave in. He felt faint, lightheaded, as though the air no longer had the elements he needed to fill his lungs. Matt grabbed him as he collapsed and laid him gently on the floor. Rak-na was taken aback.

"I'm not like him," said Matt.

"I can see that," droned Rak-na.

"I'd like to stay."

"Why?"

"These are yours, right?" asked Matt, gently stroking one sac. Rak-na didn't reply. The transgenic moved against Matt's hand, caressing it from the inside, and Rak-na was again transported to another time, another place where he had done a similar thing.

"And who else?" asked Matt, and this time Rak-na's eyes widened. Matt was talking in his head! This wasn't possible. Only Silvites had this ability. Moving with a swiftness that was totally incongruent with his bulk, he grabbed Matt's arm and delved. Matt felt the intrusion forcefully, and he fought back valiantly, but the struggle was short-lived. Rakna had the information he wanted. Matt was his son, as sure as these fledgling transgenics. The woman with her hand on the glass had done him the highest honour; she'd carried his son, the ancient earth way. His mind spun back through the ages to find when such a noble deed had been done before and he couldn't find any in Silvite history, only in the tales of old. His son stood before him, an Original, but before he could respond suitably the sacs began to stretch and he turned, and methodically began to birth his other children. Matt watched in wonderment. The process was simple and the moment of first intimacy delicate and beautiful. Rakna created the first tear in the sac, near the middle, and the adult child inside moved the membrane aside instantly, reaching for its parent. A delicate flush of pale amethyst energy surrounded the two as they touched forehead to forehead, and it seemed the air was sweeter, lighter. Then the two turned expectantly to Matt and he walked forward to his destiny.

In Bucks's dream, the whole world was bathed in gold.

Beneath the stairs, Guidrius's growl was low and ominous.

CHAPTER 73

"Maggie?" called BB frantically. "You there, Maggie?" but all he could hear back was the noise of the building collapsing around him. Despite what she had become he couldn't leave her in this hell-hole. He wouldn't leave her. He'd never be without her again, ever! Coughing violently in the dust-laden air, he grabbled at the nearest wall for support but it collapsed away from him and he fell headlong down to the next floor, debris trailing in his wake. Winded, he lay still, bracing for the bigger falling masonry to be his coffin but it never came. Twisting around cautiously he could see where it teetered at the brim above him. It wouldn't take much; another minor shake. He could feel the panic rise up in his chest but he battled it down. He'd been in tighter spots! Forcing his breathing to still, he looked around for an escape path.

The first bullet hit deep in her chest and Maggie was thrown backwards, the bullet from her own gun missing Paul by a mere finger. Her circuits went haywire, flat-lining her instantly, then the backup kicked in and she convulsed violently but there was nobody there to help. They were gone. She'd lost blood; a whole lot of it, but more worriedly, she'd lost her vision pathway. She had no way of knowing how badly damaged her surroundings were. All she could feel around her was rubble. But her memory was intact and she replayed the last moments before her accident. So, she was in the Control Room, or what was left of it. The sound of destruction happening around her was frightening. She knew she was being buried alive, and she realised suddenly that she was all alone. Pinned under console debris, in the dark, she let herself remember the other Maggie, and she played make-believe, and let the memories come. They brought with them the tears she'd held back for years.

A cracking sound from underneath him this time forced BB's hand. He swung his body to the left as the floor beneath him gave way and a deep chasm opened clear to the water below. He couldn't see it but he could hear the hissing sound of rushing water when hot debris hit it. Clinging desperately to a side wall, he contemplated failure for the first time. He was too deep in the building to escape, he knew that. But while there was life, there was hope, and reenergised he swung his legs up, levering himself out of the hole he'd fallen into.

Maggie felt the room wobble around her with the last big collapse and she held her breath, waiting for the end, willing it to come. It was her only escape. A blissful crushing moment, then she'd be gone, like she was meant to years ago. She turned her thoughts to the greatest love of her life; she willed her last moments to be happy ones, far away from Greenway. Then the floor collapsed and she was falling, screaming towards the sound of water.

He cleared the hole just in time! The whole upper section collapsed, plunging jaggedly into the depths. More dust and debris clogged the air around him but he thought he could see light through the new space above him. He might have his way out after all! The place gave him the jitters. It was as if it was alive, screaming in anger at its own destruction.

"Maggie?" he called again, but there was no heat in his voice any more. He was done in! Defeated! 'Maggie! Maggie! Maggie!' echoed the building back at him derisorily. Above him, the dust and smoke cleared, the fire had done its worst, and he could see the pink shades of dawn trace its way in the sky. The aperture looked small from where he was but it was freedom. Half-coughing, half-crying, his breath rasped in his chest.

"God damn it, Maggie!" he roared above the noise. "Where the hell are you!"

He let the echo pass before beginning his ascent. He was

concentrating so heavily he almost missed it.

'BB! BB! BB!' whispered the building, and he knew he'd found the love of his life once more.

*****

Bill Boyd heard the first explosion up close and his heart skipped a beat. Before he had time to recover, they were going off everywhere and the Golden Belle bobbed uncertainly on the water. He wasn't sure if this was what they had planned to do so he waited, his stomach roiling at the destruction he could only guess at.

"Time to go," said a low voice, and he jumped. There was a last man on board!

"Go?" he said shakily.

"Right now," was the cold reply.

"But I was told . . .," he began but the feel of cold steel in his side stopped his mouth.

"New orders!"

"But . . .," he started again, fearing those he knew on the island more than his current guest.

The shot echoed across the turbulent water and Bill fell to the deck, grasping his bloody foot.

"Now, if you please, unless you want me to even things up for you."

Bill had one chance. Like lightening, he lunged for the flare gun he had ready and waiting. He caught his attacker straight on but not before he felt the pain in his side. Standing over the body, he could feel the wetness spread beneath his jumper. He had one chance to live. Grabbing the first-aid kit, he manoeuvred the Belle to sea, while he

487

packed the bandages to his wound. No matter how hard he tried, his hands were too slippery to load the second flare. Switching on the radio, he called for help. Whatever the outcome, he wanted to live, desperately.

CHAPTER 74

Miller prowled the house but no one paid him any attention. Jed's screams had been a wake-up call. From a discrete distance, Meme followed, her eyes betraying her deep concern. He was a man on a mission, and she knew exactly where he was going. Beads of sweat dribbled unheeded down her back, and she clutched the hypodermic tightly in her hand as she sped along the corridors. She was too late to stop Maggie; their interference had thwarted her plans, but no more. Tonight, it was over!

There were no guards at the door when she arrived and silently she turned the doorknob and peeked in. Feelings of deep peace drifted uncontained from the room where Matt sat with Rak-na surrounded by their new family. Calm, intelligent gazes flickered her way then they turned to resume their conversation unhurriedly. To the left, Bucks slumped against the wall, his head resting on his chest which rose and fell slowly. Gathering strength from the miracle of birth, she quietly closed the door and walked on.

"What you doing here, woman?" he ground out, reaching against the wall to steady himself.

"Waiting," Meme replied.

"This is no place for you! Get downstairs where you belong with that filth!" he hissed.

"I'll not let you do it," she answered.

"You think you can stop me?" he roared, and she stood before him, hypodermic at the ready.

He laughed, inching forward with each shuffle until he

was just outside her reach.

"So, you going to finish it then? With that?" he chuckled.

Meme watched his eyes narrow and knew the moment was coming.

"This is not just about Maggie any more, Miller," she whispered, taking her stance. "It's about Matt! Our Matt! You almost had him killed! Why did you have to cut the brakes? Why, Miller? He's all the family we have!"

"Family?" spat Miller, sidling closer still. "He's no family of mine! Spawn of the devil, he is! And I'll see him dead! I'll see them all dead! You too!" and he lunged but she was ready. Maggie's control had lessened somehow; his movements were awkward and uncoordinated, and she parried easily, driving the needle deep into his spine before standing aside. He stumbled and hung in the air for what seemed an eternity before crumbling like an empty sack onto the floor, the semi bouncing from his hand, through the banisters and onto the floor below. They heard shouting, then footsteps pounding up the stairs. But he was not done. While she was distracted he lunged for her ankle and she fell hard against the wall, cracking her head badly. They lay opposite each other on the empty corridor, looking deeply into each other eyes as the lights went out.

'Got you, you ugly bitch,' he ground out, Maggie's vitriol pouring out to the end.

"I'm so sorry, my love," she whispered.

*****

Rick was the first on the scene and stood rooted to the spot, his heart pounding fiercely at the tragedy before him. A lifetime, and more, of love and it comes to this! He shouldn't be surprised but he was. Despite all that had happened between himself and Becca he still believed in happy-ever-after. Maybe even for them both still. The guards rushed past him, checking their vitals.

"They're gone, Sir."

Rick nodded. He didn't trust himself to speak. He watched while they straightened out their bent bodies; watched while they checked their possessions; watched while they bagged the evidence. And all the while, there was only one question on his mind – why? And as they wheeled the gurneys away, a wisp of paper fell from her clenched fist. It contained one shaky word only. MAGGIE

CHAPTER 75

"I'm worried, Jo," Meryck said quietly.

"Me too," she whispered back, trailing Becca with her eyes.

"Doesn't look too good," he said. "You talk to her, love. She always listens to you."

"Not sure now's the right time, Vince. She's awfully upset about something."

"Wouldn't you be?" he replied.

Becca strode across the room purposefully to where Anjie sat resting, and plonked herself down beside him.

"I need access to the patients," she said.

"Why, Becca?"

"Need to know, Anjie."

"Not enough. Not now. Give me a reason?"

"And you'll let me?"

"Maybe."

"How about Oswald Balmier, the Fourth?"

The noise from Anjie's mug shattering on the hard floor tiles drew everyone's attention. In the dawn light, his face looked grey. Becca looked grim. Ignoring the debris, he shoved his face into hers.

"Why?"

"He killed my son!" she whispered, fiercely. "You know that!"

"I can't let you do this," he said quietly. "It's not the way. Revenge isn't all it's cracked up to be, you know!"

"Don't patronise me," she ground out. "Just give me five minutes alone with him! Please!" she begged.

"Five minutes alone with whom?" asked Meryck, and the tête á tête was broken.

"Stay out of this, dad," she warned.

"Why?" asked Jo, making up the foursome.

"'Cause it's none of your bloody business!" she hissed back.

"That's no way to talk to your mother, Becca," growled Meryck. "Don't you think we've been through enough of this shit for one life!"

"First Rick! And now you two!" she roared. "Cut me some slack here! I've got a job to do!"

"We all do, love," said Jo, but Becca wasn't having any of it.

"So, no secrets then," she fired back and was rewarded with Jo's sudden intake of breath.

"That's not what I mean, and you know it," Jo rounded on her, her hands shaking. "We all have our secrets, but murder is another thing altogether."

"Who said I wanted to murder him?" purred Becca, and Anjie nodded.

"Murder is too good for the likes of him!" he said flatly.

"Exactly!" she agreed softly.

"It's not happening, you hear!" interjected Meryck. "Not on my patch!"

"The 'you'll have to go through me' routine, dad," she said sarcastically.

"What's happened to you, love?" whispered Jo.

"Life, mum! Life is what happened," she replied shortly, and spun away from them without a backward glance.

"They'd better be secure, Anjie," growled Meryck.

With a knowing glance at Meryck, Anjie followed Becca from the room.

*****

Carney and Rick stood together in the storeroom with the bodies of Meme and Miller.

"What's in that thing?" asked Rick, tiredly, pointing to the hypodermic.

"Cyanide, possibly," was the terse reply. "I won't know for sure 'til I run some tests." He was exhausted, both physically and mentally, and he needed all his concentration not to stab himself with something he'd regret or worse. He moved with caution around the bodies, checking each thoroughly. Something was gnawing away at the back of his mind, pushing at his temples, leading him against his normal line of observation. Examining Meme's arm, it hit him!

"I never removed Miller's tag," he announced, standing stock still.

"Excuse me?" asked Rick.

"His tag," he answered, "he was too agitated when I went to remove his tag so I left him, promising to come back later when he was calmer."

494

"Was he agitated before you approached him?" prompted Rick, fully alert now. "Think, man! Think! It's important!"

"Every bloody thing is important to you people, isn't it?" pushed back Carney, irritated as much with himself as Rick.

"Then think! What is it? Yes or No?"

"I don't think he was but I can't be sure.",

"And the others?" pressed Rick. "Were any of the others agitated?"

Carney shook his head slowly.

"Right! Let's see what this one looks like," said Rick. "Well, go on then! What's keeping you? Let's have it!"

But there was no tag in his arm. Nothing! Not even the tiniest scratch to suggest it might have been there once. They looked at each other, puzzled.

"Scars," they both said together but the well preserved body yielded no results.

"Let's turn him over," insisted Rick. He was light to lift. Another puzzle, they agreed wordlessly.

"Try his scalp," instructed Rick.

Under the back of his skull they got the first beep.

"Brain stem," said Carney, and Rick nodded. It made perfect sense in this context. She'd gone back to the beginning of time, plugging into his ancient channels. Spock couldn't have done better. She had achieved the perfect mind meld, if you believe in such things. Miller may have lived in Brierly but only Maggie was at home.

"Something doesn't add up," said Carney. "The beeps are different," and before he had finished talking Rick had muscled him to the corner of the room.

"We're in dangerous waters here, Carney. Better to be safe than sorry. Go get Guidrius. Hurry! I'll hold the fort."

"We need to talk, Anjie," he said quietly into his phone when Carney had left. "Any ETA on Johnson?"

CHAPTER 76

Jake woke with a start as the door opened.

'Outside,' nodded Anjie, and Jake gently lifted Tullie's head from his shoulder.

"How's he doing?" he asked. "We need to find out his side of the story, and quick."

Jake scratched at the stubble on his chin as he figured out how to answer.

"We need to wake him up now!" insisted Anjie.

"What's up?" asked Jake, resting his hand on his friend's shoulder.

"What's not up, you might well ask," he answered in exasperation.

"Ok," said Jake. "Johnson?"

"Will be here by midday; latest."

"The . . .," stumbled Jake.

"All six up and walking!"

Jake whistled softly. "So soon!"

Anjie nodded.

"Got some news," he said. "Brace yourself!"

"That kind of news?"

"Yep!"

"Here?"

"Yep!"

"Guidrius involved?" asked Jake tersely.

"Nope! That would be too easy," was the answer he got.

"Then out with it, man!"

"How about one Oswald Balmier, the Fourth then?" smirked Anjie.

"Where?" demanded Jake.

"Right here! Downstairs!"

"One of the patients?" queried Jake, incredulously, and Anjie nodded.

"Did Balmier know?"

"Must have," replied Anjie.

"But he was only after the transgenics," said Jake, stunned.

They stood in silence for several minutes, each working out their best angles.

"There's something else, Jake. It's very delicate."

"What?"

"Becca knows it's him. I've had to up security. She's gunning for him. I'm not sure I can prevent her."

"Course you can, Anjie," replied Jake. "The real question is, do you want to? I'm not sure I would, if that helps. Looking over your shoulder all the time wears one down."

They understood each other perfectly.

"Get Jed up, Jake. See how he's doing," said Anjie as he turned to go. "Let's set the meeting for ten."

"Anjie," called Jake softly to his departing back. "Find out what he knows first."

"Oh, by the way," nodded Anjie. "BB's missing."

*****

BB listened intensely then he heard it again. 'BB! BB! BB!' echoed up from below, way below, 'I'm here! I'm here! I'm here!'

"I'm coming, Maggie," he roared back. "Hang on!"

The echo mocked him, distorting direction and confusing his senses. He had to go down blind. There was no other way.

"Keep calling," he shouted. "I need to find you."

'Find you! Find you! Find you!' sang the depths.

"Call every thirty seconds," he told her, and waited. The first set of 'BBs!' sounded almost immediately and he waited. Thirty seconds later he heard the second set. She'd understood. He waited for four more before moving, stretching his hearing to pinpoint the first echo. She'd be near there; within feet, he reckoned. It was a long way down. He didn't think of what he'd find when he got there.

CHAPTER 77

"Jed," called Tullie softly. "Jed. Wake up. It's morning."

Standing to the side, Jake watched her. She was so gentle with him. It broke his heart to see how much she really cared for him. He couldn't let her be present for the interrogation. It was unlikely he'd give up details easily; especially now as he had no bargaining card left. He flicked through the documents on his laptop, ready to intervene if he proved a threat to her. But he had no need to worry. The Jed that woke up was nothing like the Jed from the encounter by the pond.

"Tullie," Jed smiled. "What are you doing here?"

"Looking after you, of course," she smiled back. "Can you remember what happened?"

As he struggled to sit up, he realised he was handcuffed to the bed and pieces began floating back to him.

"The Seals, Tullie?" he asked urgently.

"They're safe, Jed. It's ok," and he flopped back down, relieved.

Jake walked into view. "We need to talk, Jed."

Jed looked at him openly. "I guess we do, and some," he answered evenly to Jake's surprise.

"Come on, Tullie," said Jake, taking her arm and moving her towards the door.

"Get cleaned up," he said back. "We'll have that talk in an hour from now."

Guidrius stretched and yawned widely. The rest had done him good. All around him the day sprung into life but he could feel the tensions under the surface. It was all far from over! In fact, it had just begun! He could feel Matt upstairs with Rak-na and their six new baby-adults; it would keep him busy and out of his way. Tullie was in the kitchen, tucking into breakfast, and he let her be. It could be some time before she'd eat that way again. Jake had closed up again! That man had more tricks up his sleeve than he had ever imagined. But then, wasn't that what the stories told? Originals were complex; they surprised you more often than not. But they were predictably unpredictable once you got to know them, he smiled. Jake had trouble written all over his mind. And the more he had to deal with, the less time he'd have for me, Guidrius knew.

Padding out of hiding, and keeping his eyes down, he sniffed around the house. Only a few knew his true identity and they were in the kitchen. He poked around the lower levels first. He wanted to see the patients first hand but the door was guarded and he had to make do with what he could sense. The guards welcomed him at first until the smell became too much and he had to move on. But he was ok with that; he'd found what he'd been looking for. They posed no threat to his plans despite their treatments. The effects would wear off in time. He could safely leave them be.

He moved upwards, past Matt's door, to the other group. Security was lax here and initially he was puzzled. Then he read their minds and understood. Eleven empty shells echoed back at him. These were the clones; the initial living experiments; the ones that didn't work on their own. They would be put out of their misery on Silvamon, he knew. As he turned to leave, a faint trickle of energy caught his attention and he stopped still. They were linked. How on earth did that happen, he wondered, astonished. They had never been able to perfect that on home soil. And he couldn't identify the link, but it was close, in the very same building. Cautiously, he followed the trace. He didn't have far to go. Turning a corner, Rak-na stood in his path.

"You will not interfere," he directed calmly.

"No," replied Guidrius. "They're still your children. Not every day a man finds out he has eighteen children!"

Rak-na's intake of breath warned Guidrius.

"We will have none of your meddling," warned Rak-na.

"I don't know what you mean," replied Guidrius, assuming his full form. Inside, he was annoyed at Tullie for setting this Halfer free! Now he had her, he didn't need these people any more. They were welcome to each other!

"I know you," warned Rak-na.

"Next time you won't be so lucky," Guidrius whispered as he pushed past.

"Ah! I am free now to make my own luck," Rak-na flung at his unguarded back.

That was a truly disturbing thought, Guidrius decided, as he went to find Tullie. Their time here was over!

*****

Matt listened in on the exchange, horrified. This was a side to Guidrius he hadn't seen; none of them had seen, and it took Rak-na to expose him!

'Tullie!' he called. 'Tullie!' but she was focused on Jed and didn't hear him. And he couldn't leave his siblings. One of them had to stay with them at all times.

'Rak-na!' he called but got no reply.

Rak-na was working on another agenda now that his babies were safe with Matt.

"Bucks!" roared a demented Matt now, and the newborns shifted in their slumber anxiously.

'Bucks!' he whispered desperately inside his head but Bucks just slept on.

Grabbing Bucks's phone, he rang Myra. She answered on the first ring.

CHAPTER 78

Jake was glad to see Guidrius and he motioned him over, pulling out a chair for him for breakfast. Tullie smiled her 'Hello' from across the table where she was deep in conversation with Jo. Becca and Meryck sat with Anjie who was on the phone. Around the crowded room, the conversation was all about the night's work. Jake, however, was silent.

"I need a favour, Guidrius," he whispered.

"Anything," was the reply.

"I need you to look after Tullie for a bit," he said. "I want her out of the way while we conduct the interrogations."

Guidrius nodded, unwilling to trust his voice. This man had done it again! He was going to miss him. He made his life so much easier.

Bit by bit the room emptied until only Tullie and Guidrius remained. She walked over to him and he wrapped his arms around her. It all happened instantly, without warning.

Seconds later, Myra and Anjie came crashing back into the room but it was empty. There was no sign of Tullie or Guidrius.

"They're gone," said Rak-na, unfurling himself from the corner.

"What do you mean 'gone'?" roared Anjie, grabbing him by the arm.

"He's taken her back," replied Rak-na calmly.

"But how could he do that without the seals?" gasped Myra.

"Back where?" demanded Anjie.

Then Jake burst in.

"Where is she?" he called anxiously. "Tullie! Tullie! Where are you? Tullie!"

"It's no use, Jake," sighed Anjie. "She's gone. Really gone!"

"But they don't have the Seals!" reiterated Myra, pedantically.

"I'm not so sure," replied Johnson from the doorway. He looked shattered. Behind him came a line of soldiers carrying the small crates.

"Tullie has a globe of these," explained Rick, pushing out from behind Johnson. "I think they may be enough."

"I'm sure of it," said Rak-na softly, and all eyes turned to him.

"Why the hell didn't you stop them?" roared Jake, and Myra put a halting hand on his arm.

"You couldn't," she said quietly, "could you?"

"No," he replied, downcast. "If I interfered, Tullie might be harmed. She doesn't know our ways yet. The more you fight, the more danger you're in."

"But we still have the Seals, Sir," interrupted a jaded Johnson. Jake looked at him gratefully. He had a way of cutting through the chaff. And he had brought them their only hope of ever finding Tullie again.

"Back to square one again then," he said solemnly to the circle of worried faces.

"Not quite!" cut in Rak-na. "I'd like to help."

Pulling Jake aside, Anjie asked, "Can we trust this man?"

"Who am I to say," Jake whispered back. "I handed her to that dog bastard on a bloody plate! This is all my fault! I should have seen it coming!"

"Your mind was too busy," Rak-na said.

"What do you bloody-well know about my mind," Jake hurled at him, but already, inside, he recognised the truth of it. Guidrius had used the situation against him!

"I apologise, Rak-na. You are absolutely right," added Jake slowly, nodding twice.

Rak-na was utterly taken aback; he didn't know how to respond. No one had ever apologised to him before. But Johnson saved the day again.

"What do we start with first, Sir?" he asked, ready for action despite his weariness.

"And how did he do it?" asked Myra, when she got the chance.

"I know why," said Jake to no one in particular, "but I'm stumped as to how!"

"I think I can help you there," Rak-na began to be interrupted by Adam staggering through the door, blood dripping down his face.

"She's gone, Anjie," he called, urgently.

"We know," said Anjie calmly, guiding him to a chair. Adam was looking at him in shock.

"How could you know?" he asked. "It's only just happened!" then his face sagged.

"Didn't know you had cameras down there as well," he said sheepishly.

Anjie spun around instantly.

"Cameras?" he demanded sharply. "What cameras?"

"Who's gone, did you say?"

"That woman from Greenway. The one in the chef's gear," he answered. "Held me up at gunpoint, she did. Her and that other guy . . .," but before he'd finished, Anjie was off at a run for the basement.

"Let's get Meryck and Jo," Jake said to Myra, "and Carney."

"Hang in there, Adam," he said, grabbing the man's shoulder as he waved about on the chair. "Help will be here soon."

"Jake! Jake!" called Anjie, urgently, drawing him away from the others.

"It's Jed," he hissed angrily. "He's gone too!"

EPILOGUE: RANDELL KANE
DEAD ON GREENWAY

Late last night, a spectacular series of explosions tore through the Kane Foundation Research Laboratory on Greenway Island, killing several people and seriously wounding dozens more. The owner of the facility, the entrepreneur and billionaire, Randell Marcus Kane, is suspected to be among the casualties. His boat, the Glory Rising, was destroyed by fire but miraculously the fuel tanks remained intact. Concerns for the safety of Carla Mancini, the only daughter of Paulo Mancini, the South American tycoon, who had been on board with Kane, celebrating her nineteenth birthday, were laid to rest this morning when Ms Mancini turned up safe and sound having left the boat to go shopping.

Two unnamed suspects were apprehended aboard the Golden Belle as the boat was boarded west of Skyways port after a distress call. Explosives and ammunition were said to be found on board. The owner is in a critical condition in Matheson General Hospital having been shot twice. A full police investigation is underway as to ascertain their involvement, if any, in the destruction on Greenway Island. The Island, and its environs, remains closed to the public as the investigation continues.

Local farmers and fishermen poured onto the streets of Matheson today concerned over the possibility of pollution from the science facility, and a spokesperson for the local police, a Ms Amelia Gross, said it was too early to tell what impact the fallout from the explosion might have on the local community, and advised concerned citizens to get in touch directly with her office should they discover anything unusual. Geologists are already investigating the new river spewing out of the mountains beside Grant's Cottage, west of Tinakilly. This area remains cordoned off until further notice. Owner, Jed Bell was unavailable for comment. He is said to be helping police with their enquiries. Ms Gross, speaking from the scene, said that everything was under control.

The Tinakilly Post

ABOUT THE AUTHOR

Geraldine Donnellan is CEO of Gallan & Amral Enterprises Ltd. While she has written many articles on life coaching and alternative health, as well as IT manuals, The Greenway Conspiracy, Book 1, A Symphony of Time Novel, is her first full-length book. In the pipeline are: Silvamon, Book 2, in the Symphony of Time Series; and a gritty non-fiction book on expatriate living.

Geraldine is married to Martin, her lifelong partner, of thirty five years. Together they have lived, and worked, in Dublin, Ireland; London, UK: Tokyo, Japan; Prague, Czech Republic; Lagos, Nigeria; and Shanghai, PR China, where they currently live.

Visit her online at www.gallanamral.com